This is Catherine Fatica Compher's second novel. A lover of travel, good books, and family, she has lived all over the country and been fortunate enough to meet very interesting people along the way. Originally from Cleveland, Ohio, but raised in North Carolina, she loves a great southern story and finds her inspiration from so many she's picked up along the way. She is a proud graduate of North Carolina State University. Go Pack! She lives in Chicago with her husband, Jeff.

To my family

Catherine Fatica Compher

COTTONMOUTH DROPPINGS

AUSTIN MACAULEY PUBLISHERS™

LONDON • CAMBRIDGE • NEW YORK • SHARJAH

Ordering Information
Quantity sales: Special discounts are available on quantity purchases by corporations, associations, and others. For details, contact the publisher at the address below.

Publisher's Cataloging-in-Publication data
Compher, Catherine Fatica
Cottonmouth Droppings

ISBN 9781638297062 (Paperback)
ISBN 9781638297079 (Hardback)
ISBN 9781638297086 (ePub e-book)

Library of Congress Control Number: 2023901610

www.austinmacauley.com/us

First Published 2023
Austin Macauley Publishers LLC
40 Wall Street, 33rd Floor, Suite 3302
New York, NY 10005
USA

mailto:mail-usa@austinmacauley.com
+1 (646) 5125767

I have spent the greater part of my life as the wife of a college athletics administrator and the ups and downs of wins and losses. There have been days watching teams win championships and others watching teams fall in defeat. But the greatest joy I have taken away from all of it is to see the student athletes compete at the highest level and when they are finished on the field, they continue to do the same thing in the classroom. So many times, we hear all the negative but when it comes to the student athlete, they are rare and wonderful and beautiful and some of the hardest working men and women I have ever met. I have carried great respect for them for over thirty years. And I thank them from the bottom of my heart. I have been very blessed to be a part of such a wonderful season. And truly respect the position the athlete is put in through their years of competition, even when they see the adults around them behaving so poorly. The tragedy is always set in the example they have before them from both the administration and the fan base. Yet they rise above all that to be the best they can be.

I would like to thank my publisher, Austin Macauley, who has once again stood behind me and supported me as a novelist. And for my family for reading and rereading the manuscript. It was an extremely difficult write and a challenging read. To my husband who gave me critical feedback when I often times didn't want to listen. To my sons and their spouses who spent years playing sports and competing at the college and AAU level and gave me brilliant insight in to their world. To my mom and sister who spend hours on the phone listening to me complain, cry and even curse at the injustice in the industry. To my dear friends who read the original manuscript and gave me critical feedback. You know who you are and the hollows from which my words came.

To Rene, a brilliant sculptor and entrepreneur. Your work was my inspiration to build a character around and your insight gave life to my beloved Helen. To Dr. Paul Barry who shared so much about the medical field of which I know nothing about. I thank you for your years of service and your time you so graciously give.

Thanks to my mentor and dear friend Patsy. You are my Helen, Patsy, and Rita Faye all in one and the beauty that springs from all of those women.

And finally, to my husband of thirty-plus years. We have ridden this wild ride together and it sure isn't over yet, it's only just begun. Cheers to the second half.

Table of Contents

Chapter 1

A bluish-green stream of light scattered across the kitchen and puddled onto the white linoleum, casting a dark red shadow across the floor.

"Jackson, there certainly will be a storm this evening." Sarah wiped her hands on her well-worn apron, looked fixedly out the kitchen window, and watched the old wooden swing sway from the branch of the ancient oak.

"Mama, call me JB like daddy does." He hated Jackson. Jackson Bedford Taylor, his strained adolescent face dotted with pimples, looked up from his book as he sat in the corner chair of the cozy keeping room in the kitchen.

"Daddy calls you JB because your given name is so long." She turned. JB's daddy, Nathan, took pride in his Southern history. When JB was born, Nathan Taylor insisted he be named after the great grand wizard of the KKK, Nathan Bedford Forrest. But Sarah would have no parts of that. She relinquished to the second choice, Stonewall Jackson Taylor.

"It's a handsome name," she said that first week JB was home. "Just like my daddy."

Nathan declared when he had a son, he would name him Jackson Bedford Stonewall Taylor. "Some of the greatest names in confederate history." JB's mama lost the names she loved along the way, along with several children from her sickly uterus, that it was such a victory when Jackson was born, she let go of her father's beloved name.

"Next year, in high school, I'm going by JB." He snapped his book shut. "I'm tired. Do I have to wait up for daddy?"

Sarah walked over to her lanky son and gave him a peck on the cheek. "Get some rest."

It had been a day of picnicking at Middleton's Lake, right in between Sweetgum and Oak Grove. The Sweetgum Burrs were the arch rival of the Oak Grove Knights, but the towns were so close no one knew where one started and the other ended. Only on one fall Friday night, when the two high school football teams met, would there be a clear line of separation. JB was raised in Sweetgum, where many of the mill and country children went to school. It was always a treat to go to Middleton Lake. Tucked back off the main road low and quiet were kayaks, small boats, and a large pavilion nestled right next to Middle Carolina University.

Crickets chirped in the evening while water striders pretended to be mosquitos and picnickers said their final goodbyes. Dragonflies danced across the glassy sluice and reminded the local swimmers to seize the moment. But on that day, Middleton Lake was just like the dragonflies that lighted. A range of reactions had flooded the picnic, from joy to woe in just a few short hours.

Right after lunch, the moms held everyone out of the water just long enough to let their food digest. Hot and sweaty and spent, the kids rushed back in to cool off, waiting for the next meal to be served. The men fired up the charcoal while the kids swam. The parents had decided this particular day to grill a little later. Usually, they all went home in the early afternoon because of the fervent summer sun in the South. It was the children who wanted to extend the day and thought a late afternoon cook-out would be great capped off by s'mores and ghost stories. They begged to hear old tales of haunted houses and strange lights while their imagination ran wild, wondering if the eerie sounds in the far-off distance could possibly be one of the haunts.

The cool water provided an ideal respite from the suffering southern sun. With the kids back in the water, the dads gathered around the grill while the moms set the tables. JB and a few other boys were out in the lake throwing a football. Mary Claire Barnes, a small girl for her age, swam out to the group and begged to join. She would do anything to be close to JB, embarrassing him at lunch when she sidled right next to him while he ate his chips and sandwich.

Her older sister, chatting with senior boys from Oak Grove on the lake's edge, watched Mary Claire swim out to the boys. The kids lighted all over the lake with kayaks, small boats, and tubes splashing around. The grill cooked the last of the meat and the dads called the flock in to fill their empty stomachs. You could smell the hamburgers and hot dogs all the way out in the water. Water logged and tired, the kids streamed in. Everyone came except for Mary Claire.

JB followed the last of the boys and settled his plate, chewing and chatting. It was Mary Claire's mom that asked, "Hey, has anyone seen Mary Claire?" She glanced in JB's direction, having noted that he was one of the last to come in. Between bites there was a universal "No." It took more than several minutes for the families to notice she was not with any of the groups and when they did, panic ensued.

Her mom checked the bathrooms and a few others walked to the nearby park and picnic area, but she was nowhere to be found. Uncertainty shadowed the day when Mary Claire's big sister said she last saw her swimming near the boys throwing the football. Screaming, rapid running into the water, and panic ripped through the families as the men jumped in to scour the water. Mary Claire's mom screamed while her dad, Dr. Barnes, called 911. The men stirred in the lake, diving and dodging, hoping to find life in the water.

Mrs. Barnes, carried away by the other mothers while the children followed closely like baby ducklings, hurried them into their cars for fear of a similar fate. Sirens blared and the sound of police radios and dogs filled the air. A brand-new young cop named Whit Cain pulled up and began to question the men. Whit had just graduated from the police academy and was not much older than half the kids and as green as the jacket he wore. Along with that came rookie pressure. JB's daddy, taking control, stood at the head of the group and shouted orders. He knew a thing or two about water. Hog farms were notorious for their drainage issues.

Hours later, after the kids were put to bed, phones began to ring.

It was late into the evening when JB's daddy walked through the door. Sarah sat holding her bible with hope in her hands, realizing the worst from the look on Nathan's face. Getting up from her chair and setting the good book on the table, she raced to her husband as he wrapped his arms around her. He smelled like sweat and water and death.

She knew what all those dragonflies meant, knowing the dead one she had picked off the picnic table earlier that day was more than just a coincidence. She knew then and there that the death of Mary Claire Barnes would always be a defining moment for the community. Sarah held tight as she buried her face in her husband's sturdy chest. The young girl's body had been found, naked, just beneath the water's edge. The look of shame cast on her face.

The investigation, though short, deemed the death a drowning. The mystery of how and why ended before it began. But, despite the permanent closing of the lake, that didn't stop questions from washing over the town of what really happened to Mary Claire.

After Nathan consoled his wife, he walked into his son's bedroom and shook him awake. His large hand heavy on his son's arm. "I heard your name mentioned. When did you see her last?" JB turned over, willing his sticky sleepy eyes open with a knowing struggle to sit up in his tangle of covers.

"Answer me. Your mama has gone to bed."

"I have no idea, Daddy."

"What the hell did you do? Why was that little girl naked?" Nathan would never forget the layer of tinted green water washing over her glassy blue eyes, staring right though them. "I will deal with you in the morning."

The next day, JB heard his mother crying into the phone. "I can't believe the child is gone," he heard her whimper.

His door creaked open and Nathan's huge form filled the frame. JB shivered awake to his father's dark stare.

"What happened?" His words resolute. "I need to hear it before Officer Cain comes around asking. You hear me, boy? You better have a solid story. I know how fast facts can change."

"Why would I hurt her, Daddy?"

"Because I heard you talking about her to your friends earlier. You said you were embarrassed when she sat by you at lunch. Did you like her?"

JB dropped his head. "I did," he whispered to his gripped covers.

"Well, what happened?"

"One minute she was there," he mumbled. "Then she was gone."

Nathan puffed, "Gone, what does that mean?"

"I was teaching her to swim." He changed his story. "The girls were leaving her out," JB muttered his varying versions.

"Which is it, were you helping her or were the girls leaving her out?"

"They were jealous," he whispered.

"Why the hell were they jealous of a little teenage girl?"

"Because all of us boys liked her swimsuit." JB stopped, chewed his dry, crusty bottom lip. "We could see through it and we liked looking at her."

JB's dad shoved him. "You are to never breathe this to anyone, you hear me. That young girl was naked."

"Yes sir." His words fell back with him against the pillows as dry tears bubbled.

"I never want to hear another word about this again."

Whit Cain's scribbled unassuming words stood in the report. It was an accidental drowning. There was never a mention of the unclothed body. She was laid to rest in a simple white coffin, in a pretty pink dress.

Months after the funeral, the Barnes family struggled to the surface. Flowers lined the locked entrance of the lake while the community continued to carry covered dishes to their house. It would all go to waste.

But it was the huge arch that loomed over the road out at the main entrance of Oak Grove that gave life to the lifeless child. The arch, adorned with dragonflies, was a constant reminder of the unwelcome tragedy that had come to the community. Many locals protested its construction, saying it would be an eyesore. But the family proceeded from the support of the county board and welcomed the ornate structure, saying it was a symbol of strength and freedom and joy, just like their daughter.

Dr. Barnes, along with the help of Helen Abernathy, the local famed artist and wife of the town pharmacist, designed the arch. A dedication stone was placed below the large cauldron that held the eternal flame with the inscription, Mary Claire Barnes lived her life like the dragonflies. Lighting everyone's life with her touch. They refused to put dates on the stone, as this signified her end. Below the loving words from author Nicholas Evans, *Listen for my footfall in your heart. I am not gone but merely walk within you.*

It was too much for Dr. Barnes to keep what was left of his family in Oak Grove, so they packed their personal belongings and left their memories along with their grand home behind as a generous gift to the university.

The house held unresolved mysteries that many locals spun tales of ghost stories and myths around. Maybe it's the heat, but a ghost story of the south comes off the tongue so much better than anywhere else. It was often rumored that there were sightings of Mary Claire's ghost. It was said it could plunge you into a life of unsettled emotions and turmoil, just like the town.

No one ever went to Middleton Lake again. The gates were locked and the keys held tight.

It was said the tragedy served as a disturbance for the more important things in Oak Grove. With the ominous lake's close proximity to the university, it would find divided tension in the community. And the dividing line started with fan support to both the local high school and college sports teams.

Middle Carolina University boasted an outstanding football program lead by their famous coach, Doc Winters. Oak Grove was at its best every fall when alums traveled from all over to attend the games. With all the visiting fans, it was a never-ending job to set a stunning scene. Anything unbecoming was unwelcome.

Every spring, magnolia trees' soft white blossoms put on a show as they lined the winding curvy Main Street. Canopy-lined streets and one large home after another dotted the idyllic way of Oak Grove. Tucked behind each house were neatly manicured gardens. Some held pools and tennis courts and most held pergolas for tea sipping on warm summer evenings under the verandas where the locals carried a deep familiarity that ran along Main Street. Most of the oldest wealthiest families on Main Street controlled the town but it was the outliers, the Sweetgum residents, farmers, and mill workers that were a complete necessity to provide the grease to keep the town moving. They knew their place. There was really no definition of who was local until you earned some nameless badge to become one.

Businesses buzzed with Monday morning gossip and tradition shaped everything. Visitors were always welcome. And though happy to see the weekend people, as they were so affectionately called, come for the ever-popular football games, the Monday people were always happy to see them leave with a little bit lighter pocket. There was an unspoken joy about leaving money in Oak Grove and taking their asses, even proud graduates, home to fill up their own towns and taking their problems with them.

Leaving was a way of life for the annoying outsiders. And it was an especially welcome relief when the Barnes family left. They just forgot something very important, the story of the tragic fate of their daughter and the continued reminder of her with the eyesore from the arch at the town's entrance.

Years went by, the teenagers all grew up, but even years later, Dr. JB Taylor often saw the young girl in his dreams. Her long blond curls fell gently around her wet shoulders and her face was permanently perfect in youth. Her slender body swam toward him, longing for his touch. He would lay in bed, eyes closed, plagued by that day. The birds and frogs attempted to sing him back to sleep. The melody spilled into his ears and drowned out her delicate voice as she begged him to stop. The last thing he saw before she plunged below the murky water was a dragonfly lighting on her head.

Chapter 2
Thirty Years Later May

Rita Faye Taylor's downtown shop, Dogwood Lane, was open early in anticipation of all the graduation parties this weekend. Families from one historically preserved home after another along Main Street hosted the grand festivities while well-wishers made their way from one shindig to the next, making it the highlight of spring in Oak Grove. And they counted on Rita Faye to have everything they needed to make their party perfect.

The elaborate affairs boasted one house out-decorating the other in their graduate's future university colors. So many stayed in town and attended Middle Carolina University to become proud Cottonmouths. And as soon as Rita Faye received her shipment of blue and gold supplies down at Dogwood Lane, there were lines out the door to strip the shelves of the popular colors.

Every fall when football kicked off, the first floor transformed into a collegiate colored filled stockpile. She had a section for the Cottonmouths to fill any tailgating needs, from colored coolers to car flags and decals. She carried an abundance of supplies for the two local high schools to accommodate Friday night tail gate essentials, as well. Parents raced to get the best selection.

It would only be one short year before she and JB would have to wait for their twins to graduate. Rita Faye dreamed about Carter and Caroline's college choices so she could stock up for their party next May. It would all come too quickly. For now, she would listen and help other parents to boast at their turn at the party turntable.

Rumors abound around her store for months about who would have the best party. The Hillcrests certainly could afford the most elaborate. Bennett Hillcrest had picked UNC Chapel Hill, but at the last minute decided to go to Virginia. The town loved to see prominent families have their share of struggle, even if was just a kid changing his college allegiance. So many people in Oak Grove didn't like Carolina. Sure, there were other state schools, like the reds of NC State and the black and golds of Wake Forest. But Rita Faye didn't know why people had such a contempt for the university. She had nothing against Chapel Hill or Carolina blue. The town would be on pins and needles to see if Beth Hillcrest, a close friend of her daughter's, would do the same thing next year.

This season, it was the University of Washington colors that challenged her. The purple and gold with their blinding tones were requested because Penni Lafoe picked the university. Giant Penni, a highly recruited defensive lineman, would be leaving shortly after graduation to report to school. His parents, west coast transplants, planned a traditional Samoan sendoff for the graduation party. His party was the talk of the town.

When Penni announced his school choice back in the fall, the chat boards lit up like firecrackers on the fourth of July when he didn't commit to Middle Carolina University. Doc Winters was the first one to catfish on the site. Whit Cain and JB Taylor followed suit. It all started with Penni's betrayal to Cottonmouth football and the community. It would only get worse until he left.

Signs were found hanging on the fence at one of the last fall football games, with his picture and the word traitor boldly written across his face. The parents were called in for a meeting to find a resolution. There was talk of getting behind the family, wearing some silly button in support of Penni, and even calling an assembly at school to talk about bullying. Nothing happened. The signs continued, with one dad being so bold as to hold one up the entire game every time Penni was on the field. The negative community environment became a constant for Penni and his family. Penni's dad, encouraged him and his mom, to ignore them. "They will soon settle down once football is over."

Rumors rose like steam off black asphalt on a hot summer day as to why Penni chose to go so far from what was now his home. And he had been dating a local girl, Melanie Birch, since he arrived his freshman year of high school. Why would he not play for the iconic Doc Winters? The weakness in the defensive line would have been filled nicely by his size alone. The Cottonmouth droppings chat site had become a hollow stand-in for truth. The community found great fun in speculating, because like most of the gossip on there, the intrigue meant more than the accuracy.

Penni was the most recruited player out of the high school since the high school head coach, Bobby Cottonwood. Schools like Tennessee and Florida State sent recruiting coordinators to watch Penni play. He listened respectfully and considered his options but, in the end, he wanted to go back to the west coast where he was from. Penni hoped to be playing in the NFL one day and all the local Oak Grove wannabes longed to hang their hat on his stand despite their criticism. It would have made a much better story if he had stayed in town and traveled the Doc Winters pipeline to the NFL, and the chat site never let up.

Penni was making a statement in his own quiet way. Not being from there, he was treated much the same way the weekend visitors were. Leave with your pockets empty and get the hell out. If it weren't for his football success, he may have been left alone. But he knew he made the right decision in the end with all the negativity that swirled during his final season. His parents supported his choice and were proud of him.

Like most visiting professors, the Lafoes were offered the Barnes' estate as housing. Though most visiting faculty would come and go for a semester at a time, the Lafoes would be taking up residence for five years. Despite the tragedy that befell the Barnes, the Lafoes were pleased to live in such a beautiful home.

It was party day for the Lafoe family, with traditional Samoan food like crayfish, snapper, and tuna all served that afternoon. Kids and parents lined the house, yard, and pool deck. Drinks were poured and the teenagers respectfully took notice of the no alcohol policy. Palusami, which consists of young taro leaves that have been baked in coconut cream and filled with onions and either meat or seafood, were Penni's favorite and the whole dish could be consumed. The whole party was an opportunity to enjoy an exotic buffet.

Teenagers splashed around in the pool playing volleyball. But the real game was on the side yard where several of Penni's football player friends were in a heated competition of corn hole.

Carter Taylor, a rising senior, and top football player, stood on one side of the corn hole board while his teammate and good friend Sam Evans stood on the other.

"Ok boys, who will be my next victim after me and Sam take you guys down?" Charming and disarming, he smiled over at Sam's girlfriend Harper without getting as so much of a glance back.

Jack and Tommy, two players from the team, stood defeated as their opponents showed no mercy.

Harper Davis, Sam's girlfriend, chatted while several girls stood cheering on the winning team. Carter tossed a sand bag and took a sip of his vodka spiked Sprite for good measure. He gazed at Harper again, hoping she would notice him while he tossed the next sand bag right into the hole.

"That one was for you, Harper. Let's see if your boyfriend can return the favor." He teased Sam.

Harper ignored Carter and smiled at Sam. He steadied his Coke in his hand, tossed a bag back right onto the board, just missing the target.

"Just what I thought, Sam, always missing the hole." Carter let out a cackle.

Sam shook his head. "You're such a dick, man." He tossed his bags on the ground and walked over to Harper.

"Don't quit, we're winning, dude. Come on, I was just giving you a hard time."

"I get so sick of you." Sam shoved him right into Melanie Birch while she stood close to Penni, twisting her blond hair.

Penni caught her.

"I can't stand that guy." They had been a couple since the first week he moved to town. "Dude you can be a real ass." Penni got in Carter's face.

"Come on guys, I'm kidding." Carter licked his full lips, ran his free hand through his dark brown curls and grazed Melanie with his cold cup. Now that Penni graduated, Carter was the all-star of the football team and one of the most handsome boys in the school. A group of swooning girls stood behind Melanie.

Sam grabbed Harper's hand. "It's time to eat."

Carter, always one to have the last word. "Hey Penni, if your girlfriend's Wal-Mart t-shirt won't rip, why don't you let her take a stab at corn hole?" Melanie felt her small frame tighten and her face flush.

"Carter, if this party wasn't full of people, I would kick your ass." Penni positioned Melanie behind him and moved closer to Carter. Melanie was looking forward to joining Penni out in Washington after she graduated next year. She just needed to make sure her grades were good enough to get scholarship money. But, being a shanty dweller brought bigger challenges than just being poor. It was the lowest place to be, not only in the high school but in the town.

Since Penni arrived, Carter made fun of him for dating her. But she dated Penni, was close friends with Harper Davis, Beth Hillcrest, and Carter's twin sister, Caroline. And she climbed the high school social ladder as a star runner on the track team. Between Melanie, Sam, Harper, and Caroline, it was anyone's spot to be valedictorian next spring.

Penni gave Carter a shove. "Stay away from her."

While Carter gained his footing, he laughed. "Yea, sure dude, whatever you say."

Penni led Melanie through the crowd. The BBQ pits were ripe and ready. Melanie whispered, "I think I'm going to head out after we eat." Penni turned, but when he started to say something, he was interrupted by one of his dad's colleagues.

She felt a large arm come sweeping around her tiny shoulder and when she turned, Carter had taken her under his large frame. "Hey girl, what's up?" He held her gaze as she felt her Sprite can slip a bit in her hand.

"Hey man back off." Penni gave him another shove.

"Don't get so worked up, big guy. I know she's your territory." Carter patted him on the back. "I just came to say I'm sorry."

Melanie wiggled out of his grip. "Leave me alone, Carter."

"I bet you could take any of us guys on." Carter's stare held her gaze.

"I'm heading out soon," she said.

Carter started to pull his arm back. "Don't forget to hydrate. You runners need to drink a lot as much as you move," Carter encouraged her.

She felt her Sprite can tip in her hand a second time as he released his large arm. She was relieved when he walked away. She moved over to the BBQ pit and fixed a plate. Melanie took a few bites and finished her drink. Within minutes she felt a wave of nausea. She stumbled her way through a sea of hundreds of faceless people. She was going to be sick and as she walked, plate in hand, she felt like she was losing her footing. Heat overtook her body, yet she was freezing.

Penni was standing at the glass doors and grabbed her. "You okay?"

"Yeah, I think maybe I'm a bit overheated." She leaned on him but continued to feel worse with each breath.

"Let me help you. You want to go to the bathroom? I can get you a cool washcloth."

"Sure," she whispered.

The two bathrooms downstairs were in use so Penni lead her up the steps but was interrupted by his mother calling him back to the front door to say goodbye to well-wishers. "Be right down mom." He left Melanie at the top of the steps. "I'll be right back."

Carter surveyed them as he stood at the bottom of the steps joking with a few friends. While Penni rushed past him, he easily slipped upstairs as soon as he had opportunity.

Melanie balanced herself against the wall the rest of the way up until she reached the bathroom. She steadied herself as her head drifted into a thick fog. She splashed water on her face and when she came out of the bathroom she fell onto the bed. "Get me a cold washcloth Penni, I'm burning up." She fought to keep her eyes open.

Chapter 3

A haze washed over her as she started the horrible descent into a fiendish nightmare fighting off an attacker. While her mind searched for clarity, her body felt like it was breaking under the pressure of his weight. She heard him whisper, "I know you want this baby," while she smelled his sour breath. His hand slipped down her shirt as the weight of his body immobilized her. She struggled to recognize his voice.

"Wow you are really hot for shanty trash." She twisted as she blacked in and out. Her body, momentarily stiff, felt the pressure of him forcing himself into her. She strained to scream but he held his hand firmly over her mouth.

"This is so good." She kicked her legs, but he was so strong.

"Stop!" she repeated through his pressing hand that concealed her mouth. She felt like she was falling down a tunnel, spinning and twisting while her voice grew weaker and weaker as he drove harder and harder.

Eerie sounds were haunted by nothingness in the room. She saw the form of a young girl, her blond hair and small frame shivering and naked. Melanie moved her head, begging, "no, stop, please stop, help me," as the spirit looked on, mouthing words she could not make out. It had to be part of the nightmare, as she was certain the young spirit was not real.

While her shorts dangled from one ankle, her body was ripping in two. Then she felt her body flip face down in the bed. She could smell Penni in the sheets and she quaked. She knew it wasn't Penni on top of her. She sobbed into his smell, fighting to get up, longing for it to stop. But something kept her in the fog.

She didn't want to remember anything after that.

She had never been with anyone and the pain that seared through her would make her never want to be. Ever. She fought nausea while he kept pushing harder and harder until he let out a grunt.

"Wasn't that awesome," he said.

Her chest and now her back were sore from his forearm holding her securely down. Her head pounded. She rolled her head to one side and stared at a sea of trophies. She noticed his neatly cut fingernails.

Melanie's face was full of snot smeared over her cheek. She lay face down in the bed, fighting retching. The boy got up and disappeared in the bathroom. She lay there, still, her head spinning. She turned to face the bathroom door. Fear paralyzed her. He would come back. Her face bruised, her arms sore, between her legs ripped in two and shame lay ripe in her body nestled right next to the pain. She moaned, fluttered her eyes away from the picture of herself and Penni that sat on his nightstand, feeling her soul follow down the same black hole that she drifted down.

*****

Carter ran his wet hands through his thick dark mane. He admired himself in the bathroom mirror, his dark eyes fixed on his reflection. *She liked it too.* He noticed a few bumps on his bicep. *Must be from the HGH,* he thought as he regarded his massive arm. He heard a little groan from the bedroom and grinned at his striking image. He shrugged his broad shoulders, tilted his head, and checked his fingernails. He walked out of the bathroom, paused, looked at Melanie passed out on the bed. Her panties and shorts dangled from her ankle and her now ripped t-shirt shifted on her back. *Oh well,* he thought. *I guess it got a little wild. No harm.*

Carter, with a grin on his face and his pronounced dimple fixed in his chin, shut the door behind him and walked to the top of the steps. No one noticed him slip down the stairs, purposefully rubbing his stomach as he waltzed his way into the crowd. Sam and Harper were standing at the bottom arm in arm chatting with a few friends when they looked up, noticing his wet hair.

"Hey man where'd you go? One minute we're playing bags and the next you disappear on us."

"Go easy, I got stopped by a few people, grabbed some food and the next thing I know I'm dashing up the stairs because all the bathrooms down here were occupied." He rubbed his stomach, "I didn't want to smell the place up after eating all this crappy foreign food." He smirked.

"Dude, are you sick?" Sam paused. "I didn't see you eat."

"It hit me hard. You know I didn't want to upset the party and use the downstairs bathroom." He lied so easily and guffawed. Carter gave a squeeze to Sam's shoulder and walked around him to purposely grace Harper's hand. She immediately pulled away and felt a darkness come over her. There was something that just didn't set well with her.

"Are you two love birds leaving?" Carter asked.

Harper moved behind Sam and whispered, "Yes," while Sam answered, "Yeah dude, we have a few more parties to go, like Bennett's. I want to stop by and see Harper's grandparents too. Her grandmother came home from the hospital late yesterday and I want to say hello."

"Aww, I'm sorry to hear that. You guys have fun at uptight Bennet's. Isn't Beth out in the pool?" Carter said.

"She left an hour ago. She was lucky to come for a little while."

"Tell your grandmother hello. I gotta grab a drink." He turned and melted into the crowd.

Sam and Harper watched him shifting his once somber mood to laughter. They made their way out, chatting to a few people. There were so many guests in the entry you could barely notice who was coming or leaving.

Caroline, hidden behind dark makeup with her slate blue, ethereal eyes rimmed in black coal liner, stood along the entry way. Thin enough to disappear, she was the total opposite of her brother. Carter took everything from her in the womb and continued to do so now. She showed up at the party late, despite Penni and Melanie being two of her best friends. These kinds of things were really not for her.

She watched the whole exchange between Sam, Harper, and Carter and wondered why Carter was rushing the conversation. She had caught her brother's descent down the staircase as well and questioned his wet hair. She heard bits and pieces, feeling disgust when she heard him laugh and when he touched Harper's hand. Harper made eye contact with her and they both raised their eyebrows while Caroline raised one side of her lip. She shifted back to her conversation with Helen, listening to her words and hearing nothing as she fixated on her wispy clothes, graying long hair, long necklaces and bracelet filled arms. Helen taught sculpting and art history at the university and brought adverse interest to the community with her Mala beads and yoga. Despite the distraction, Caroline regained focus and continued to chat about her sculpture that would be showcased in the September art show.

Chapter 4
May

Melanie fluttered her syrupy eyes, fighting to recognize her surroundings. Shock had stolen hours from her. There was still sun light so maybe she had not been there long. When she pushed herself up, pain shot through her body. Her twisted top fell off her shoulder while her bottom was bare. She reached down and felt for her shorts that dangled on one ankle.

In the movement, horrifying memories came flooding back. It was Carter Taylor, not Penni that came in the room. *Why would he do this?* She wanted to run.

She clung to her clothes and buried her head in the pillow. Fighting to get up, her fuzzy head made the room spin. So, she slivered off the bed, pulled her pants on and crawled to the bathroom. Every inch of her body ached. When she reached the bathroom, she pulled herself up by the sink and stared at the stranger in the mirror.

Life as she knew it was gone. She stared at the black mascara lines drawn down her appearance. Her long blond hair matted like a rat had taken up residence atop her swollen face. She grabbed a wash cloth, ran it under hot water and started vigorously rubbing every inch of her damaged body. She moaned as she felt for her cell phone still intact in her pocket.

"Mama come quickly. I'm at Penni's. I've been hurt. I need you." She whispered as the words quaked out from her shocked body. She was afraid if she was too loud, he would come back.

Tina Birch panicked, "What? What happened? I'm on my way." She dropped everything and would be there in seconds. The Piggly Wiggly was just around the corner.

Melanie pulled her torn clothes tightly around her. Pain without ceasing would be the grim reminder of her assault. But it was the image of the young girl watching them that haunted her. *How the hell? He drugged me.*

She walked back from the bathroom after she combed down her hair. She tried to wipe herself but the pain was too intense. Red welts emanated from her cheeks. The fog was clearing and her thoughts were now on her escape. Her heart rate quickened. *Who knew what happened?* She panicked, realizing what Penni would do when he found out. *Will he blame me?* Her mind was spinning irrational thoughts. *I just want to die.*

She slipped her hands around her clothes to make sure they were on properly and headed for the steps. It was late afternoon. The noise from the party walked up the steps while people lined the entry. No one would have heard her if she screamed, that would be impossible since Carter had his hand over her mouth. *I thought I screamed.*

Where was Penni? He was supposed to be getting her a cold wash cloth. She walked back in the bathroom and held the vanity, looking in the mirror, groggy and scared. She felt her face turn dark like granite and the life drain from her replaced with panic and fear. She tried again.

Melanie peeked around the corner of the staircase and saw classmates, parents, friends, so many people. This was not fun. She visited the thought again. She looked down at the cluster of people and stared at each step thinking if she didn't look up, no one would see her as she stumbled down the long staircase. Wasn't she invisible, after all? She was not one of them. Isn't that what brought her and Penni together to begin with? The differences they shared.

Her pulse quickened. She wanted to get out fast but didn't know how else to get out but to go through the congestion of well-wishers. She slipped on the second to the last step and in her slight fall buried her tiny self in the wave of bodies. The crowd was her adversary and her friend. She made eye contact with no one, as she raced to the backdoor and her mother's car waiting at the end of the drive.

Chapter 5

Caroline stopped Helen mid-sentence when she saw Melanie rush down the steps and make a right toward the kitchen. Without saying a word, she rudely pushed through the crowd and tried to catch up to her, but was swallowed by the mob. She noticed the faint smell of lavender follow her from Helen's outreached hand. Thinking she was right behind Melanie, she was caught off-guard by one of Carter's friends, Tommy.

"When you going out with me?" Never looking at Tommy, she watched Melanie make a beeline for the back door and out of sight. She cocked her head in curiosity.

"What the hell?" she whispered.

"Excuse me?" Tommy said.

"I wonder what made her leave so fast? Her hair was a mess."

"Who are you talking about?" Tommy said.

Caroline didn't imagine it. Melanie had been crying. She quickly turned from Tommy and raced to the huge beveled glass windows that spread across the dining room. Harper and Sam were walking out while Melanie darted past them. Caroline pushed to the front door and just as she reached it Melanie jumped into her mother's car, speeding away. Caroline turned around and took a few steps back when she heard Penni. "Was that Melanie running down the driveway?"

"Yes, did you guys get in a fight?"

"No, I've been here saying goodbye to people. I left her upstairs over an hour ago. She said she felt sick and needed to get a cool washcloth and lay down. She asked me to bring her a cold drink and, I was going to, but my mom had me saying goodbye." He stopped, feeling embarrassed that he forgot to check on her.

Tommy stood next to Penni. "Hey man, don't sweat it, it's a busy day." They headed out the door.

Sam and Harper stood at the end of the drive while they watched the dented blue Ford Fiesta screech away. "Melanie, Melanie, wait!" they yelled. She never did as she jumped in her mother's car.

"Was that Melanie's mom?" Sam turned.

Before Harper could answer, she saw Caroline, Penni, and Tommy heading toward them.

"What was that about?" Sam asked.

"I don't know. Where did she end up going when we all grabbed food? I saw her with a plate and then she was gone. I thought she left." Harper stopped.

"Yea I did too. Maybe she got sick too." Sam shrugged his shoulders.

"Who else was sick?" Penni asked.

"Carter," Sam said.

Caroline, pushing down panic and trying to be playful, punched his huge arm. "And the big guy forgot to take her a cold drink." She sighed, hoping her brother's entrance from the upstairs was not deceiving her.

"Well, I hope she's okay," Harper said.

Penni drew out his cell phone and called her. No answer. He tapped in a text, *Call me babe, you okay?*

Harper hugged Penni. "Great party. When I talk to her, I will let you know."

"Yea man, awesome food." Sam fist pumped him. "Let's stop by the Hillcrest party. I don't want your grandmother to wait on us for too long."

"Tell your grandmother hello." Penni said. "I'm sure going to miss her." He stared at the road.

Harper gave Penni a huge hug. "She's going to miss you. Who is she going to talk football with now?" Harper pulled back. They walked to their car and hopped in.

Caroline reached up and hugged Penni's neck. "I gotta go. You know me. I don't like to stay at anything too long. See you before you take off for sure."

"Hey Caroline, think about what I asked you?" Tommy grazed her hand.

Penni paused. "You know Caroline, you're alright. Maybe the six of us can go out before I leave." He looked at Tommy.

"Love you Penni." Caroline walked to her car. Between Melanie running out of the party and Tommy asking her out, her head was spinning like the swirl of cotton candy.

Chapter 6

Melanie clutched her torn shirt while she folded her arms over her body. "Go, mama." Tina impulsively pumped the gas and raced away.

"You okay, baby?" Tina's hands gripped the steering wheel.

"Carter Taylor," she whispered then stopped as if saying the dirty words would make it real. Melanie was 17 years old, "raped me, the most popular boy at school."

Tina slammed her foot on the brake so hard her wheels came to a screeching halt while the back of her car fish tailed slightly. She wanted to go in the party and take everyone out with the small gun she kept under her seat. Melanie's mom, with her leonine expression, braced the wheel then took her daughter in her arms. "Oh baby, no, no. Where the fuck is he?"

Her daughter begged her to take her home, her life now a sepia sheet of nothingness. "Just go." Messy signs of grief streamed down her face with remnants of black mascara. "I want to go home."

"We are going straight to the hospital and when we are done, Carter Taylor is going to pay for this."

*****

Melanie escaped into a world that so many women knew but never talked about. She wanted it all to end. Just a few short hours ago she was a beautiful blond, smart, athletic rising high school senior. *I'm really white trash now*, she thought.

Donna Hillcrest, the sexual assault nurse and Melanie's best friend's aunt, began the initial evaluation, while another nurse assisted. "At any time, you need a break let me know. And let me know if something hurts. This is important, right?" Donna took the time to explain each step. She did a once over on her and had her assistant document the marks and bruises as they measured each one. She drew diagrams and filled out forms as she went.

"I have to ask you some questions now, Melanie. Did you vomit?"

"No," a throaty sound, on the verge of tears floundered.

"Did you defecate?"

"No."

"Did you smoke cigarettes or anything else?"

"No," Her bottom lip quivered.

"Did you wash before your mom brought you here?"

"No" she paused, "My face." She reached up and touched her swollen eyes.

"Were you drinking and if so, about how many drinks do you think you had?"

"Just a Sprite." She locked eyes with her mom. "I felt sick so I went upstairs to use the bathroom." A tear slid from her eye. "I don't remember seeing anyone upstairs."

"Were there any boys hanging around you at the party?"

"Penni," she pressed her lips, "And Sam and Jack and Carter." She gathered the stiff sheets around her.

"Did you notice any unusual behavior from any of those boys?"

"No ma'am."

Donna made a note. "Was Beth there?"

"Yes, she was in the pool."

Donna felt slight relief as she reached over and patted Melanie's arm. "I know these are tough questions." She did not want to implicate Jack. He had been dating Beth for a long time.

Finally, Donna asked, "Do you know the person who did this to you?"

Melanie shook uncontrollably, so Donna's assistant quickly grabbed a heated blanket and laid it over her.

"I'm sorry." Melanie whispered. "I don't know. I don't know." The lie slid from her damaged lips while denial filled her with shame.

I'm unclean, the words crashed in her head like cymbals droning over everyone else in her pep band. Only now the music didn't make sense. *I'm nothing and now Penni won't ever want me*. She could not stop shaking. Carter took everything away from her and the dirty secret would forever niggle at her despite time and space.

Tina held Melanie's hand and gently rubbed her daughter's shoulder. "You're going to be okay honey. I'm right here with you." She felt rage rise as she watched her daughter suffer.

"I don't want to say, Mama."

"I know, baby, I know." Tina turned. "Can we get on with this? My daughter has been through enough."

Donna made a note in the chart. She would talk to Beth when she could and see if she suspected anything funny at Penni's party.

"Melanie, I'm not here to interrogate you but to help you. Let's move on. I want you take a deep breath. You've been through a very traumatic experience and are in shock. Let's get you comfortable."

Donna turned her back to the women and set out all the swabs and tools she would need to examine Melanie. She felt herself shudder at the thought of the young woman, a friend of her niece, going through such a horrific experience.

"Honey, I have to do the physical exam now. If at any time you feel uncomfortable, we can take a break." Donna pulled sterile wrapped swabs, vials, and collection bags from the kit. She carefully took her clothes and placed them in a bag. She took the swabs and began to collect possible semen, saliva, and a set of blood samples, explaining each step as she went.

"We're doing pubic hair pulls, we're doing swabs of the outside of the genitalia…and then we're doing a speculum exam, which is internal, and taking swabs that way, and if there was an anal assault, we're doing swabs there. We use a colposcope to take pictures of any genital injury." It was the hardest thing she had done in a long time. She could not erase the image of her niece, Beth, from her mind. She was at the party. Donna's thought's drifted, *it could have been her*.

She combed through Melanie's hair for any pubic hairs from the alleged assailant that may have been left behind and she began the process of photographing the injuries and trauma. She took her blood for the toxicological testing.

It was three grueling hours and by the time she was done it was 9 p.m. Donna was emotionally spent and despite doing this for many years, being so close to the victim exhausted her. She struggled with the fact that Melanie was not telling and wondered if she was threatened.

Donna left the room with all the samples and when she turned the corner, Whit Cain was waiting, a cup of coffee in hand, to question Melanie. She would choose her words carefully.

"I was called to come take a police report. Heard there was an incident at the Lafoe party." He towered over Donna.

"Go easy, she's been through a lot." Donna shuffled her feet. She would not let Whit question her patient alone. The site of him made her edgy. She knew he had, in the past, held up investigations when Doc's student athletes were involved. And with Melanie withholding the name, it put her on high alert.

"Come on now Donna, I'm a professional, I will." He held his notebook in his other hand. "I'm going in?"

Donna handed the evidence kit over to her assistant and led him in the room.

When Whit walked in and found Melanie Birch sitting on the edge of the bed and Tina standing beside her, he had to quickly compose himself. "Good evening, ladies." He watched Tina.

"Whit." Tina stopped.

"How ya doing, Melanie?"

"Fine," she whispered.

"Now tell me young lady," he moved his gum around in his mouth, "and start from the beginning, and tell me what happened?"

"I don't want to tell anyone," Melanie sighed.

"I need to file a report."

"It was horrible." She stopped.

"Now, I can't help you, young lady, if you don't tell me everything."

"I'm not pressing charges." She stiffened.

"Oh, well, we aren't there yet. I just need to know what happened. Let's just start there."

Donna stopped Whit's pressing. "Go easy on her," she said.

"The boy won't be in trouble." Melanie stopped.

"It's not about being in trouble. I just need to make a report." Whit held his notebook tight. "Did your boyfriend do this to you?" He chewed.

Melanie wrapped the blanket completely around her body. While Tina stopped him, "No Whit, it was not Penni. It was Car."

Melanie screeched. "Mama no."

Tina's slip of the tongue shook Whit. He clearly heard Carter, but that name would never come out. He would have to make Penni his pawn. Whit wrote Penni's name, like the report, would be misrepresented.

"Don't worry honey, your boyfriend won't be in trouble. We just need to have a little talking with him." Whit redirected.

Tina stopped. "That's enough, Whit."

"Call me later if she's up to it, she can talk then." Whit folded his notebook against his sizeable gut. He put his pencil in his front pocket and smoothed down his tight shirt, leaving his coffee cup on the table. He knew Melanie would never talk. The body language was enough to tell him that the girl was scared to death. Probably was even threatened. *Good for Carter.*

"I'm so sorry." He reached Melanie's shoulder as a reminder to keep quiet.

Just the mention of Penni's name that was floated down the rape river caused Tina to panic. She knew what Whit was capable of.

Melanie brought her back. "I want to go home."

Whit walked around the corner, leaned against the wall and texted Doc. *Assault at Lafoes could be a problem.*

The response: *BURY IT. We take care of our own.*

*****

It was nearly eleven before Melanie walked into their tiny clapboard Shanty house. The floor creaked below her unstable feet with worn gold and brown carpet to stabilize her gait. Purple bruises dotted her chest and her urinary tract was inflamed. Before she left, Donna watched her swallow a morning after pill and the first round of antibiotics. There would be no evidence nine months later.

She moved to the cold linoleum under her feet as she shivered, dropped her issued clothes to the bathroom floor and stepped into a hot shower. She prayed the water would soften her muscles. It failed miserably under the hot spray. She was afraid to be alone and felt as if there was someone watching her. She pulled back the curtain and stared at the steam while the form of a small girl melted into nothingness.

She shut off the water, quickly dried off, pulled on a hooded sweatshirt and old gray sweat pants, walked back to her small room, and crawled in bed. And she slept. She was up soon enough to pee. Pain shot through her body as the liquid drained from her crotch. She didn't want to wipe, so she gently dabbed her violated, dirty space. She looked in the mirror and gazed at her ghastly bruised face and felt sick from her soiled breath. The person staring back at her was no one she recognized. She decided she would not come out again.

She walked back to her bedroom and for a few minutes watched the rain drops race down the window as she stared into the darkness. A large oak tree spilled its branches against her window, scraping it's limbs like tiny fingers sliding down a chalk board. She pulled her yellow and pink covers over her head in a dark cave and finally fell asleep but did not rest. She could not stop hearing the tree limbs scratch against her window from the winds that blew in the late evening storm. The scraping reminded her of Carter's hands against her body.

What were once dreams of love and a future turned into toxic secret parts in her mind that traveled through a nightmarish hell.

Melanie didn't know what time Tina came in and sat down on the bed. "Honey I'm so sorry I wasn't there to protect you." Her words kept coming over and over like her gentle hand that rubbed her back. "I will make this right. I promise you. Are you sure it was Carter?"

Melanie rolled toward her mother, painfully thirsty, dry tears in her eyes, "Make me one promise mom." She wiped her slimy nose. Her gritty eyes, swollen face and large swollen lip. She could still smell him. She looked like she had been in a car wreck only she was totaled.

"Anything my love."

"Don't breathe this to a soul. He's a football player, He's Carter Taylor, and no one will believe me. And yes, it was him, it was his clean fingernails." Now she was broken and damaged beyond repair.

Life had laid a pile of misfortune on her since she was born. Melanie thought she could outwork the bad luck. She was hopeful that it would have stopped with her mother. It now spilled over into her. They were nothing in town. Carter was everything. His dad, JB, was a doctor. His mother, Rita Faye owned a popular store. The only words that kept playing over in her head. "No one will believe me." The biggest complication, Caroline Taylor was one of her best friends.

Chapter 7

Carter woke up Sunday morning with a splitting headache. He rolled over and felt a huge cramp run through his stomach. It was his impulsive decisions that got him in trouble, and they had ripple effects. He took one Seroquel yesterday when he was feeling anxious and agitated. He had more than a few drinks at the grad parties.

"I gotta give this shit up before the season."

He sat up in his bed and steadied his feet to the floor. He held his head in his hands while he rubbed his soft dark curls. After Penni's party yesterday, he felt a little bit off, so he stopped by his house to pick up a few more Seroquel. The last of his Rohypnol he had he slipped in Melanie's Sprite. He needed to talk to his dad with all the anxiety he was feeling.

The only problem, he was taking so many things that now his stomach was upset all the time. He sat on his bed and looked at his spotted arms. *This HGH is really breaking me out.* He made his way into the bathroom and sat on the toilet. He felt terrible a lot lately. *Fucking weird food at the party*, he thought as he stared at the white tile floor while he waited for his stomach to clear.

He had a great time on Saturday. *Too bad I missed the Hillcrests' party, Beth's hot*, he thought. Even though it was Bennett's party.

He was off Sunday from summer workouts. He considered going down to the beach. Maybe he could get Sam, Jack, or Tommy to ride down. He knew, if he asked the right way, his dad would let him go. He would be up early Monday morning to start training.

He would never ask his mother. Carter felt his face flush and a new round of sweat covered his body. He shifted off the toilet and started the shower. He flushed and moved to the sink to wash his hands. He soaped them well over and over and let the hot water run until they were red. He inspected each fingernail to make sure there was no dirt under any of them. He stared up in the mirror. "Everyone likes me. Especially Melanie."

He could not believe how lucky he was to have scored with her. *Fuck Penni* he thought. *He's leaving, I don't care. When I see something, I want, I get it. She asked for it, and all wrapped in Penni's arms.* He let the water run hot and stepped in the shower thinking about his good time.

Cottonmouth droppings chat site-Saturday night posts.

Hometown boy: Heard it was a busy night at the clinic for Donna.

Farm Boy: None of our boys are in trouble. Some high school girl.

Hometown boy: The police showed up at the Lafoe party. Damn foreigners are always a problem. Heard it was Penni's girl. Shanty trash.

Farm Boy: Who?

Stonewall: Penni was questioned.

Foxy: Stop this, now. You boys have no right to talk about this.

Hometown boy: There was an assault at Penni's party. Looks like he did it.

Farm boy: West coast people. You know free love and all that shit. It's better he's leaving.

Tat Man: Yeah most of them are gay too.

Captain Kirk: I heard some chatter on the radio.

Football Lifer: Who was the girl?

Stonewall: His girlfriend. No wonder he's leaving so fast.

Captain Kirk: Love 'em and leave 'em. #good riddance

Farm Boy: Thank god he wasn't recruited here. WE want local talent. It just makes me so mad that these out of towners come in here and try to take over.

Stonewall: We have Carter Taylor who will be a home town hero. Such weird names. #recruit local. #nooutsiders

Hometown Boy: Carter Taylor would never do a thing like that. And to think all the pressure that kid is under and look how great he behaves. Good family.

Farm boy: And to think he was the golden boy from the Pacific Islands. #cryinginourbeer

Stonewall: The perfect family is snake bitten.

Captain Kirk: Why would he rape his girlfriend?

Tat Man: Kid needs to be held accountable. That's how we do it here. That house is haunted.

Stonewall: His house, his girlfriend. Entitled. He was taking what he could before he left.

Farm Boy: Nothing bad here until he came to town. This town is better than him. Damn Yankees, foreigners. #gohome

Stonewall: I don't take too kindly to these types of people.

Farm Boy: They aren't like us?

Captain Kirk: So many people were there no one saw a thing.

Stonewall: Traitor! Don't waste space on that boy and your blind support. Fly the banners! Get him out of here and his dark-skinned family. You would have thought all the signs in the fall would have run him and the family out. This should do the trick now.

Chapter 8

Caroline sat at her desk scrolling through Cottonmouth Droppings. She felt a chill run down her spine when she thought about her brother sashaying down the steps at Penni's. Then Melanie tearing out of the house. *What is going on here?* Caroline hated herself every time she jumped on the site. *Who in the hell is posting this shit?*

So much had happened over the last twenty-four hours. And her suspicions grew the longer she didn't hear from Melanie. She slammed her computer shut and rushed down the steps. She didn't want to be late for church.

When she hit the bottom stair, Carter was sidled up to the kitchen island moaning about the spoiled food at Penni's last night. "My stomach still hurts."

She replayed the posts while she listened to his complaints and watched a dragonfly dance around the bay window on a nearby bush. "I ate the food and feel great today." Caroline walked by him and grabbed a bagel.

"Your brother isn't feeling very well, Caroline." Rita Faye tousled his hair. "Maybe you should stay home from church."

"Yes, you wouldn't want to give anyone what you have." Caroline tore a small piece from the bagel.

JB interrupted, "I cannot believe there was an assault at that party yesterday. Do you guys know anything?"

"No." Carter took a bite of his toast.

JB looked over at Caroline. "Like I would know."

"You can stay home if you want," Rita Faye repeated.

"I'm sure it was the food. I'm used to your cooking not that weird foreign food. But I'm good. Maybe I will drive down to the beach after church."

"You guys ready for church?" JB asked.

The family filed out the door, walking the short distance past all the beautiful homes on Main Street to the Baptist church.

It was the honest relationships within the family that Caroline longed for. When she didn't see Harper at church that morning, she decided she would pay her a visit. Caroline stood on the front porch of Harper's home thinking about how lucky she was. While enjoying the colorful gardens she noticed a red wagon under the large oak tree.

Harper Davis lived with her parents, Anne and Dr. Davis and her grandparents, Henry and Patsy Middleton, right in the middle of Main Street. Her home, surrounded by gardens, in a beautiful Antebellum style with massive porches, conveyed warmth and love just like the feelings inside.

Miss Anne came to the door.

"Good afternoon, Caroline." She hugged her. "Is Harper expecting you?"

"No ma'am, I was walking home from church and decided to stop by and say hello. I didn't see your family there and I wanted to check on Miss Patsy."

"Mama is doing much better since Friday. She gave us a real scare." Anne opened the door wider, "Oh, no, Wade forgot to get that wagon when he cleaned up the tools."

"Excuse me?" Caroline asked.

"Mama was sitting on the wagon when she passed out Friday. Wade cleaned up after all the chaos at the hospital. He must have forgot the wagon." Anne glared at the child's toy as if to blame it for Patsy's cancer relapse.

"I'm so sorry she's been sick. Harper told me she was rushed to the hospital."

"Yes, your daddy stopped in her room to check on her. Please tell your mama thank you for the lovely gift basket. Patsy just loves her."

"I will. She loves her too. It's a shame you two don't see more of each other. I just wish Mr. Henry and my dad got along," Caroline said, not meaning one word.

"Honey, we don't need to talk about that. They are grown men and will figure it out. I'm happy that you and Harper are such good friends. She's in the yard with mama. I'll walk you out."

The warm entry floors held a beautiful old tapestry rug and on top of that held a long antique side table with two large lamps and a display of family pictures from bygone years. Every generation was represented, while Harper's portrait held proudly in the middle.

The dining room opened to one side with a long antique table, a huge vase of fresh flowers, and a large painting of a young Patsy sitting on a swing holding a small blue flower. A yellow lab sat proudly next to her. Caroline heard endless stories of Cammie. Patsy loved that dog as much as she did Henry. She spoke of her so often from her childhood it seemed like she never passed, she was just asleep somewhere in a quiet corner of the house.

Caroline was happy to be distracted by the tenderness of the home. Anything other than the Penni saga. But now with the pitchforks out, she knew all too well the town would run the Lafoe family out of town. Now that they had a focus of demise. A diversion with Miss Patsy was always good for that.

Caroline followed Anne to the back of the house. *If only I could live here.* "I only have one year left," she whispered.

Anne interrupted Caroline's longing. "Harper was outside with Patsy talking about the grad parties and her eighteenth birthday party. I declare she won't take no for an answer when it comes to that party. She was out in the yard on Friday working on the gardens when she had her episode. That party isn't until October." Anne shook her head. "Go on out, I will bring you a glass of tea." Anne slipped her hand over Caroline's shoulder.

Caroline pushed open the sticking back door. She made her way down the stone steps and turned to find Pasty sitting alone opposite a teak table. Two large glasses of iced tea with a small sprig of mint floated on top. Caroline paused and watched Patsy with her hand gently resting on her chest just inside her shirt and her eyes closed in the soothing spring sun, while she wondered what she could be thinking. She could see the tired etched across her face.

Patsy had just folded the paper and laid it on the table. She tipped her head back and was soothed by the sun She didn't need all the flurry in the hospital to tell her that she was tired and dehydrated on Friday morning.

She held her hand down her shirt and fingered the precious gold locket pressed against her damp, scarred skin. There was an emptiness there from the mastery of her breast cancer. She called the loss of her breast's scars of medical necessity. She sat motionless for a minute as she felt the skin around her neck sag and fold like wet rags, knowing just below sat emptiness. She knew age was not a diagnosis for her troubles. When she moved her hand further down her denim top, she felt the scarred sick flesh that once housed her ample breasts. The same ones that fed her infant daughter decades ago, filled many dresses nicely, and brought pleasure to her marital bed. *They had their purpose,* she thought when she reached back up to touch the locket with her still strong capable hands.

The locket saw many generations of Bowen women. She felt it gently rise and fall with the beat of her heart. As if each generation left a part of them behind after wearing the lovely piece. It was close to her heart where it belonged. There were generations buried beneath the current pictures of Harper and Anne.

"Hello, Miss Patsy." Caroline interrupted.

Patsy tipped her head. "Why hello young lady." She pulled her hand off her chest.

"Don't get up, Miss Patsy." Caroline reached down and gave her a big hug, noticing how close her bones surfaced her skin.

"Sit down and chat." Patsy patted the cushioned chair. "You need some tea."

"Miss Anne's bringing me some. Where's Harper? I thought she was here with you?"

"She was but had to take a call." Patsy patted Caroline's leg. "How's your mama?"

"She's working a ton. You know everyone booked her for their graduation parties. She'll take a break sometime this summer."

"You should be proud of her. She has really done something special at Henry's old store."

"I am," Caroline mumbled. "She's just gone a lot and—" Caroline stopped. "She said she would get over to see you soon."

"I would love that. You know I miss her so much. Things just aren't the same since well." She tripped over her jumbled words.

"Since my dad…" Caroline stopped again.

"Don't trouble yourself with all the adult problems. Two grown men not seeing eye to eye in this town. That's not a first." Patsy didn't have the energy to talk about the Middleton Taylor feud.

"I hear your sculpture is coming along well. Helen talked about you all weekend."

"I would go to the studio today, but Sundays are family day for Miss Helen and Mr. Charlie. They spend the day on the farm with their grandchildren." Caroline took in the smell of the blossoming lilacs.

"Well, aren't you a sight for sore eyes. What brings you over this afternoon?" Harper plopped down next to Patsy, interrupting any private chat the two women would have. "Me and Mimi were talking about the birthday party, but I had to take a call."

"Can you share party details?" Caroline leaned forward. She wished her mom was sitting there chatting with them. But Rita Faye was distracted with her own problems, so Caroline cherry-picked substitute moms like Patsy and Miss Helen.

"Sure, we can," Patsy said. "But not until you get a tea." As if on cue, Anne rounded the corner with a large sweet tea and a small plate of fruit and cheeses.

"I thought you girls may want a little something. I don't want to miss the conversation." Anne sat down and nudged the bowl in the middle of table along with a small stack of napkins. "Ok, mama, now you can talk."

"I see lots of fall flowers and white tables of six. Harper I was thinking about small tea cakes. Don't you just hate a big cake?"

"Anything will do." Harper smiled.

"What do you think, Caroline? Big cake or small cake?"

What a treat to be asked her opinion.

"I think it would be fun to have one of those spit cakes. You know like at a child's birthday, and small cakes. That way she can make sure she blows out all 18 candles, spit or no spit." She felt a stab of pain in her heart, longing for her mother.

"Aren't you so funny?" Harper kicked her loose leg toward Caroline.

"I think that is a wonderful idea. I have an entire menu in addition to the cakes. I want finger sandwiches. Of course, there will be scones and a light soup and quiches. I want nuts and assorted cheeses and crackers." Patsy tried to continue, but Anne interrupted.

"Mama, don't you think the ladies will get their fill with just a few things. We are not feeding football players."

"Oh Anne, you know I love variety," Patsy scolded. "Besides it's my party and I get to set the menu." She turned her head toward Caroline. "What do you think?"

Caroline was thrilled that Patsy asked a second time. "I like the idea of variety. I may not serve soup with everyone in their dress clothes, but those sandwiches sound delicious."

"See Anne, I like this girl. She can give me an opinion without a scolding." Patsy gave a generous grin.

"Oh mama." Anne looked but was distracted by Harper's phone lighting up. She watched her daughter stare blindly into the illuminated screen.

"Let's ask the birthday girl. Harper?" Anne watched her beautiful distracted daughter. "Hello, Harper, are you with us?"

"Oh, I'm sorry mama. I keep getting texts from Penni and I'm texting Melanie but she isn't answering."

Caroline felt her phone vibrate. She pulled it out and saw a string of texts from Penni but still no reply from Melanie. She had texted her late last night with no response. "She has not answered me either."

"I'm sure she's fine, girls. So, Harper what do you think?"

"Oh, mama, you know I will love anything you and Mimi do. I'm just so grateful we will be together." Harper smiled at Patsy, knowing how hard she was fighting.

"Caroline, let's go upstairs. I got a new dress on Friday at Dogwood Lane. I think you should see it."

"Sure. Thank you, Miss Anne, for the tea. And Miss Patsy you look great. I'm glad you're feeling better."

"You girls have fun." Anne smiled.

*****

The girls made their way up the back staircase. Harper's room was filled with white and soft yellow hues. She had a bulletin board lined with dried corsages from dances over the years and right in the middle was a picture of Sam. Her long white dresser housed makeup, perfumes, and a large lighted mirror. She walked over and opened her double closet as dresses, shoes, and all kinds of beautiful clothing spilled out. Harper reached in and pulled out a familiar long white bag. "So, what do you think?"

The creamy, silk dress hung long on the hanger with its elegant scooped neck.

"I'm thinking it would be perfect for the fall dance. I have a beautiful pashmina in a darker cream and look at these shoes." Harper reached down and picked up a pair of dark cream open toed sandals with just the right amount of dazzle across the straps.

"It's pretty. I can't believe my mom is good at buying all this crap?"

"Caroline, your mom has incredible taste."

Caroline raised her eyebrows. "Too bad I didn't get it."

"I can't wait to find something for you to wear miss artist, hello. You do have great taste."

"Oh no, believe me, we don't have to look far."

"Exactly, we can go to your mom's store. I saw a bunch of stuff that would look amazing on you with your petite rocking body."

"I'm not going to any dance, not in the fall, not ever." Caroline was adamant.

"Oh yes you are. It's months away but you have to go. It's our turn to be the belles of the ball. We're seniors. And Tommy can be your date. Sam says he really likes you."

Caroline stood in front of Harper's massive closet and imagined what it would be like to put aside all her insecurities and dress in something so beautiful. And for a boy to actually want to be seen with her. For just a moment she quietly let herself dream. "What about Melanie?" She caught herself.

"I haven't heard from her." Harper turned and hung the dress in the closet. "Have you?"

"No, I have messaged her a thousand times. Penni's a mess. He called me late last night and we chatted for a few hours. He's been messaging me a ton today. He said he drove over to her house late last night and it was pitch black." Caroline sat down on the end of Harper's bed. "Do you think it was her?"

"Caroline," Harper sidled up to her. "We all saw her run down the drive yesterday." She wiped her nose.

"I was afraid something happened." Caroline fingered the white lacy spread. "Have you read the chat site?"

"No." Harper leaned in.

"It sounds like someone knows something."

"But who?"

"The site makes it sound like Penni."

"What?" Harper covered her mouth as tears fell. "Why would Penni hurt anyone, especially Melanie? He loves her. He would never do that. It's not like they have not had an opportunity to…you know." Harper felt her face flush.

"Oh, we both know that, but someone really has it in for him. You should read the thing."

"No thank you, and I wish you wouldn't. My papaw hates that thing. Says it's the devil's work and there's nothing good to come out of it. He says the people who post on there are rotten."

"You're probably right." Caroline leaned over and rubbed her friend's leg. "It's going to be okay. We need to find out where Melanie is, though."

The door cracked open after a light tap.

"Girls." Mr. Henry slipped his head in.

"Hello, Papaw." Harper quickly wiped her eyes.

"Your mama said you were up here. I wanted to come up and say hello. You okay Harper?"

"Yes."

He frowned. "Are you talking about Penni's party? I heard and I don't like the sound of any of it."

"Yes sir."

Henry walked over to Harper and folded her in his strong arms, burying her nose in the smell of his butterscotch candies. "It's going to be okay, peanut. I will make it okay."

"Thanks Papaw." She nuzzled her head into his sweet-smelling shirt. "I love you."

"I love you too. Now you two come on downstairs and don't let your grandmother see you upset. I picked up some lunch from Charcoal Willie's for everyone. Caroline, you're eating too."

Chapter 9

It was not unusual for the southern sun to heat up in the high 90s by late May, but after a steady late afternoon rain it cooled down in Oak Grove. A light breeze blew away the hot humid air. Caroline's short walk home for Sunday evening family dinner was enjoyable.

She walked into the kitchen as Carter scooped piles of mashed potatoes on his plate and grabbed two pieces of fried chicken before everyone was seated.

"You must be feeling better." Caroline watched him with disgust.

"Maybe there's something going around." JB filled his plate.

"Yeah, it was that shitty food at Penni's."

"Watch your mouth." Rita Faye turned from the kitchen sink.

"I'm not hungry," Caroline said. "I'm just tired." Caroline pushed herself away from the kitchen island.

"I'm heading back to the store. I have a full week with another round of graduation parties. Caroline, I want to talk to you, but it will have to wait unless you want to come with me right now."

"No thanks, can we talk tomorrow?"

"Of course, get some rest." Rita Faye took a bite of chicken as she stood over the counter.

Caroline headed up the steps, but not before she stood at the top and eavesdropped, hoping to get some information. Minutes later, she heard her dad tell Carter he was going to his home office. She rushed to her room when she heard Carter say, "I'm going up to shower and heading out with some guys from the team."

Caroline waited in her room until she heard the car door slam, signaling that her mom was heading back to work. She heard Carter yell out "I'm leaving," to no reply. It was only JB and her in the house.

Caroline walked down the long hall to her dad's office. "It's been a long day. I'm going to bed."

He didn't even look up from his computer screen. He was surfing Cottonmouth droppings from the banner across the top of the page. The one-time Caroline questioned him about being on the site, he said, "What respectable doctor would do such a thing? I'm better than any website or face page or whatever they call all that nonsense."

She made her way back upstairs, making sure she closed her bedroom door. She knew when it opened, it was her sign that JB was going to bed and she could sneak out. When she was in middle school, she had spent many sleepless nights in her own home curled up in the bottom of her closet hiding. Free in her own thin space. Blankets covering her so no one would see her.

As if anyone would look. She wanted to be safe. She would tell no one. She shook her head from the ghastly memories of her brother from years ago. She would wait a little while and head out her window, down the side trellis through the spongy grass and over to Harper's house. Or she would brazenly leave right out the back door.

Caroline propped herself up in bed while she listened to music and read. She had her hooded sweatshirt on and yoga pants but covered herself with her spread. She tipped her book when she heard her dad come up the stairs. As soon as he started to crack her door, she feigned sleep.

"Goodnight," JB whispered and closed the door.

She would wait a while longer, lock her door, and sneak out. There was something about the tiptoeing around that gave her a sense of freedom.

Her mom would be gone most of the night, and when she did come in, she barely made it to the couch. Usually there were food wrappers from McDonald's or Burger King around her when she woke up. Caroline noticed of late that her mother was not eating like she used to. She would ask her about that tomorrow when they had their talk.

She slipped out the back door, cut across the back yards, hoping no dogs or security lights would alarm their owners of her mission as she navigated through Patsy Middleton's secret door covered by foliage. She knew every rock and bush as she tiptoed around the large fish pond along the stone steps and slipped onto Harper's back porch. Harper sat in the corner where a small light was emanating from her iPhone. "Hey girl, I'm just finishing a text to Sam."

Caroline gently let the screen door close and looked through the long line of windows, noticing many of them open across the back of the house. A small light from Mr. Henry's study shone. "Is your papaw still up?"

"Heavens no, he went to bed with Patsy hours ago. He won't let her out of his sight."

"Why do we feel like we are running some covert operation every time we do this?" Caroline giggled.

"Because we are. And yet we could just text or talk on the phone."

The screens on the airy veranda protected them from the mosquitos that could be terrible in the summer. But not tonight. The cooler temperatures kept them away.

"Yep, but this is so much more fun." Caroline curled up on the sofa. "How's Miss Patsy?"

"She had a good night. Ate all her supper and actually was getting after my Papaw about the gardens. She is so fixated on my birthday party," Harper said. "I'm glad to see her fighting with him. That's her spirit."

"October will be here before you know it. God bless your grandmother, she's awesome and all her planning."

"You would think it's next week. But you know Patsy, there is nothing more important to her than her gardens. Apparently, she is really upset that Papaw will not let her pull some of the azaleas and replace them with lavender. She said no compromise. And is wearing herself out."

"She needs to rest."

Harper was quiet for a minute. "I think Papaw should let her do anything she wants at this point. I know he's just trying to get her to see that she still has it in her. He even said, 'As long as you're feisty, I know you aren't going anywhere'."

Caroline's eyes watered. "I just wish I had grandparents like yours. My moms are gone and my dad's," she paused, "he only has his dad and he's weird and drinks too much." She sighed away her disappointment.

The girls were startled when Anne popped her head through the door. "Good night everyone. Not too loud Harper." She kept it brief. They needed to share secrets. "Are Melanie or Beth coming over?"

"Maybe Beth, we have not heard from Melanie."

"Ok good night. Just keep it quiet?"

"Yes ma'am. Good night." As much as they thought they were sneaking, Anne and Wade always thought, what harm could happen on the screen porch.

As soon as the large French doors were shut Harper started, "Did you hear from Melanie this evening? She has not answered any of my texts all day. Penni is in a total panic."

Caroline looked at her phone. "I have like a million texts from him."

"I'm worried," Harper interrupted. "You saw her leaving the party?"

"I saw her come down the steps." Caroline paused. "She looked like she had been crying. Maybe when he went up there, they got in a fight. But why would she leave and why would he be texting us that she is not answering?" Caroline pushed the truth away. "He did run outside to try to catch her."

"Is he covering something up?" Just saying the words made Harper sick.

Caroline was apprehensive as she worked to clear the clouded memories of Carter. She didn't want to say too much, for fear Harper would blame her if Carter was the one who hurt Melanie. "I don't know."

Harper felt a wave of regret. "I should have stopped her. I was right there. I'm supposed to be her best friend. We are her best friends. I cannot remember when the four of us weren't friends."

"Tonight, seems odd." Caroline stopped her. "I mean here we are continually texting and calling her and well, the porch is not the same without her."

"It was her. I know it was her. Why else would she be missing?" Harper pressed.

Caroline leaned back in her blanket. The four of them seemed an odd pairing. Harper was popular and smart. Caroline the brooding, dark artist, Melanie the athlete from the shanty and Beth the sheltered but fun friend always ready for an adventure. Somehow, they worked.

It was sixth grade that bonded their friendship. The four of them were assigned a science project. The girls collaborated and took their bee box project all the way to state finals. It propelled the four into a greater place in the high school food chain. Being in Harper's science group gave Caroline and Melanie momentary recognition in the school. Beth Hillcrest didn't need Harper's place at the top of the high school food chain. But the girls' friendship grew with fervor. They discovered through their differences they were stronger. And the screened porch became their place of refuge and secretes.

"Promise me you won't say anything to Penni. I don't want to upset him anymore," Caroline said.

"I feel so bad for him. I mean he's leaving. I would be crazy if Sam did this to me." Everyone knew Harper and Sam were heading to Duke when they graduated. They both wanted to study medicine. Melanie and Penni would be reunited at the University of Washington next year when Melanie graduated. Caroline wanted to go to art school at NYU or Rhode Island. She had been researching for years and with the help of Helen and the upcoming art show, if it was successful, she had hopes of being accepted.

Harper curled up in the corner chair and pulled the blanket over her feet. The ceiling fans circulated the cool air. "It's chilly out here." When she heard a soft tap at the back door.

"Hey hotties," Beth started. "I only have a few minutes so catch me up."

Caroline lowered herself. "You scared us."

"Sorry. It's been a busy weekend with Bennett's party. Keep me warm." She cozied up.

"Penni said he went to Melanie's house this afternoon and again no answer. There was no car in the drive. He went by the Piggly Wiggly to ask her mother and they told him she took a few days off for a family emergency. Apparently, he made a scene."

"Did you hear his dad had to drag him out of there?" Beth interrupted.

"Yes." Caroline felt a surge of anger as her suspicions grew. "Why would she have not contacted him? Or us. He leaves for Washington next Sunday." Caroline curled her legs and tucked a blanket under her feet.

Harper watched the lights bounce off the fish pond and took in the smell of gardenia. "When did you see her at the party, Beth?"

"I saw her outside when everyone was playing corn hole. I was in the pool for a while. But left when you all went to get food," Beth said.

"She disappeared," Harper mumbled.

Caroline whispered. "I saw her run out of the party."

"And I saw her running down the drive," Harper finished.

Caroline said, "I think we need to get to her as soon as we can. Have you tried her mom?"

"Maybe she's sick and can't use her phone. Or maybe her phone got cut off. Sometimes her mom can't make the bills." Beth's words trailed.

Harper felt embarrassed for her. "This is not the way I wanted our summer to start." Harper looked down at her phone. "Sam and Penni are not coming over. Sam said he's hanging with Penni alone. He needs time to himself." She wanted to change the direction.

"We will figure this thing out. We all agree this is not like Melanie. And we all agree that by tomorrow if no one has heard from her, we will take drastic measures. I gotta split, girls. My dad is being super protective since all of this happened. I just needed a hug from my girls."

"Whoa wait Beth, let's talk about Caroline dating Tommy." Harper quickly switched direction. She didn't want to tell Caroline, but after Carter had run his hand down her arm at the party on Saturday not once but twice, she had a sick, sinking feeling. She didn't want to think about it anymore. She would talk to Beth later.

"Oh, I can't leave with this now." Beth started to sit back down.

"We are not going to talk about any of that," Caroline said.

"Jack told me he is dying to ask you to the fall dance. And," Beth glared at Harper, "You're going."

"Girls I'm done here." Caroline started to get up.

"Okay, okay, I will start the boring conversation. So, Caroline, when is your sculpture going to be done?"

"By August. Helen is on me about it all the time. I need it to apply to Southern Cal, NYU, and Rhode Island."

"My vote is NYU," Beth said.

"Southern Cal is too far away from me. I'm banking on Rhode Island," Harper said.

"It's only the top school in the nation. I'm sure they will be beating down the door to get me to come there."

"Patsy thinks they will." Harper stopped. She knew she was not supposed to tell anyone. "I'm sorry, Caroline. I didn't mean to violate your trust. It's just that my Patsy loves your work. Did you know she goes down to Helen's all the time to see what you're up to? And she stopped in at your mom's store to tell her how awesome you are."

Caroline squinted trying to make out the sincerity in Harper's face, "What?" she tripped over her surprise.

"Don't worry, Patsy tells me everything."

"I know," Caroline whispered. "I just had no idea that she thought that much of me."

"Oh, you know she loves art. She wishes I had your talent. When I'm healing people, you will be creating wonderful things for them to look at."

"Oh, now you're funny."

"Yes, I am. Now let's talk about you and Tommy."

"I better go home." Beth was anxious that her parents would discover her absence.

"Don't change the subject. He's a really nice guy."

"He really is a great guy," Beth said.

"I'm going home. I have had enough dating drama tonight. And now that you dropped that bomb in front of Beth, she will never let it go." Caroline stood up and folded her blanket. "I love ya, girl."

"And I'm out." Beth opened the door. "Love you, dolls." She blew kisses.

"See you later Beth." Harper turned to Caroline.

"I love you too." Harper gave Caroline a big hug. "Everything is going to be okay."

Caroline made her way past the sweet-smelling gardenia, through the yards, unlocked the back door and tiptoed down the hall. She peeked around the corner and saw her mom fast asleep on the sofa. A diet coke sweated on the coffee table. Carter's car was not in the drive, so she darted up the steps and into her room. She quickly pulled on her pajamas, brushed her teeth, and hopped in bed. She texted Harper and Beth and Melanie. *Home safe and sound.*

Harper texted her back, *Goodnight. Love you.*

Beth texted back, *Love you.*

The girls watched as the three dots pulsed, longing from a text from Melanie.

Caroline texted back, *Goodnight. Love you too.*

Beth texted, *you are going out with Tommy!*

Caroline texted, *See!* She rolled over in bed, but before she put her earbuds in and went to sleep, she texted Melanie, *I love you please let us know you're okay. I love you.* She got up and locked her bedroom door.

Chapter 10
June

Oak Grove is like a bright copper penny. It's valueless without both sides. And just like the shanty dwellers, the part in the middle is forgotten most of the time. With the large enclave of poor white and black folk just alike, who had seen better days, before many a hurricane wreaked havoc on their properties, they lived right in the middle of Oak Grove between the two sides.

Some of the more fortunate had moved out near the mill and to the farms in Sweetgum and were able to get work. But many of the older families could not muster the courage to move away from everything they had ever known. So, they stayed in hopes of employment generosity.

The history of Oak Grove was not very appealing. For many years the rich people owned the mills and would hide behind good works like Christmas care packages for the poor, turkey meals at Thanksgiving and a school supply drive every August. But it was always the same. There was never enough money for raises, good health or dental care.

It seemed the presence of the thin, unattractive middle of town invented the term a day late and a dollar short. The mill children, like a big tossed salad, were mixed in the same schools as the rich kids, only the addition was not so palatable. The middle of town, affectionally called, "the shanty" was really just the ghetto, not because of the color of people's skin but because they were left unattended and soured from years of suppression. The shanty was flanked by the stately homes of Main Street and the university.

The imposing university hung its hat on higher education, award-winning programs, and its beloved football team. Middle Carolina was a constant unattainable reminder for so many of the hopeless shanty dwellers. Despite it being a part of their town, it was never a part of their lives. Many shanty dwellers never set foot on university grounds unless they worked in maintenance or housekeeping. The town could never fix "the problems." But Oak Grove claimed it was not for their lack of trying.

It was always in the struggle. The rich tobacco soil had dried up after so many farmers lost their wealth to things like potatoes and cotton. And the large pig farms that had invaded the lands brought excessive money to the owners and warranted their neighbors' land unlivable. Or at least it was unsaleable because the local hog farms, although they employed many, drained a section of the town from any livable land. It smelled like shit, all the time.

Blame it on the hurricanes that roared through Oak Grove every few years. The poor would see devastation with widespread flooding. And the rich would duct tape it back together, linking it like a barrel of monkeys waiting for the next game of chance. Blame it on any of those things, but pure old jealousy often crucified the town.

The wealthy Oak Grove people were always looking for someone to kick around but hid behind it with their endless streams of non-profits and churches. The poor people were beholden, but most of them with their wrinkled skin of despair and ability, held onto faith.

It was the *Southern Magpie Magazine* feature that came out last fall that slapped a not-so-pretty cover on Oak Grove with resurrected questions surrounding Mary Claire Barnes' death. The piece started with the quaintness of the community, like Cottonmouth's tailgating traditions and the storied football teams and their beloved coach, along with a mention of one of the most controversial yet entertaining chat sites in college sports, Cottonmouth Droppings.

It featured charming businesses like Rita Faye Taylor's store, Dogwood Lane, anchored opposite Mr. Charlie's popular pharmacy that housed one of the most unique southern soda shops in the South. Helen, a famous artist in her own right, and her art studio made the cut that took the place for the trifecta of businesses.

Three houses were featured in the article as well, The Middleton's, with its gracious gardens, The Hillcrests for its stately architecture, and Helen and Charlie's for its rich history.

As with most journalists who have a nose for news, the article's hook highlighted the thirtieth anniversary of the unsolved death of Mary Claire Barnes. The resurrecting of the case and the lack of investigation piqued the interest of *Southern Magpie* readers. The mystery around the little girl's death and the spoiled beautiful locked lake that mocked the town made for one of their top selling months.

The writer's final sentence, "The locals love three things in town. Football, winning the tailgate, and gossiping on Cottonmouth Droppings about good Southern unsolved mysteries like that around the death of Mary Claire Barnes."

Cottonmouth Droppings

Stonewall: Who does that writer think they are coming in here and stirring up trouble.

Swamprunner: I liked the article. Could help Cottonmouth recruiting.

Farm boy: Football is king here and don't let anyone forget it.

Foxy: Who did kill Mary Claire? It seems weird that she drowned swimming with so many kids around.

Stonewall: That is old news. Isn't it time to move on?

Football Lifer: I like the details about our town. We sound like the real nice place.

Stonewall: Should have left out the alleged ghost story. Let the parents have peace.

Farm boy: Go Cottonmouths! Great for recruiting. And plays to the locals.

Hometown Boy: Yes, let's hope it helps with recruiting. We missed it with Penni.

Farm boy: Coach does a great job here. He's an icon. And Penni is no loss. His family needs to go and let's hope the pressure will get them to leave. They are not welcome here.

Foxy: That poor little girl. I would like to know what happened. Penni is a big loss. Leave his family alone.

Stonewall: Would you quit bringing that up already. Talk about someone's garden.

Swamp runner: Aren't you sensitive today Stonewall.

Foxy: Hope the parents didn't see the article. RIP MCB.

Chapter 11

JB had not slept well since last fall when the *Southern Magpie* article came out. He hated the chatter on Cottonmouth Droppings and wanted to forget about the incident from so long ago. In order to cope, he was forced to create a strict morning routine, and when it was interrupted it set a negative tone for his day. He woke up at 5:30 a.m. sharp, put a pot of coffee over, went outside and picked up his newspaper, and spent the first hour reading.

He would return emails, shower, and head into the hospital or to his office by 8:30. He was in a sour mood after the weekend. It seemed that walking across the street to drop off a gift at the Hillcrest party late Saturday afternoon was the extent of his participation in all the graduation fuss, and he was angry that Rita Faye had not bothered to do it herself.

JB spent most of the weekend in his home office, catching up on paperwork and glued to Cottonmouth Droppings. With the local chatter focused on the Lafoe party, maybe the town would stop talking about the article. It had been months since it came out. Maybe the Lafoe story would pull the attention away from the convoluted article. *Some things never seemed to die here*, he thought.

He would focus on a different preoccupation. No kids, no wife, just peace and quiet. He was happy he could slip away for a few hours late Friday and visit Tina. And he had a nice visit with Doc. He was pleased with how well he was doing with his pain management. Overall, his weekend was peaceful. And he didn't have to spend any time with his wife.

JB headed into the house, summer sun on his shoulder, newspaper in hand. The combination of the smell of flowers and the mist of the sprinkler system going off was a welcome change to the antiseptic smell of the hospital.

He came in off the back porch, chased a dragonfly off the landing. He tossed his shoes in the bin, poured a cup of coffee, shook a fentanyl in his hand, and washed it down. He sat at the kitchen island to read the paper and wait for relief to come. He gazed at his fingernails. He slipped the carefully folded paper out of the plastic sleeve and opened up the *Daily Voice*. Right across the right fold the headline derided him. With the kids still asleep and Rita Faye snoring on the couch, he was free to read the article without interruption.

Grad party out of control

University officials as well as the local police are investigating a report filed by a 17-year-old female student that alleges she was raped at a high school grad party, according to documents obtained by the *Daily Voice*. The gathering inside a university-owned home on Main Street near the campus has all the hallmarks of a high school graduation party gone awry. Late Saturday night police showed up at the home of star defensive player Penni Lafoie, where he and his parents were questioned. There was no search warrant but the Lafoes cooperated. The young woman would not release a name after a full exam was performed at Middle Carolina Regional Hospital.

It was at this house party where the young woman was allegedly sexually assaulted, according to police records. Prosecutors allege the students snuck alcohol into the party. Several inebriated teenagers were found at the home, according to court documents filed by police investigator, Whit Cain. "We have enough evidence to continue the investigation. But if the young, high school female will not cooperate we cannot do anything. The parents have assured us that they did not supply any alcohol to any underage students at the party."

The parents of all-star football player Penni Lafoie have been questioned and any suspects' names are being withheld to protect the victim.

The victim, whose name has been withheld by authorities, is underage and a rising senior at the Oak Grove High school who runs track. There is no suspect at this time, but a full investigation is underway.

"The inquiries have nothing to do with the Lafoes' activities either as a student or an athlete at this time. Lafoe will leave for the University of Washington in a few days." Whit Cain said.

He found his new fixation. JB noticed they spelled Lafoe wrong in the first paragraph. Cottonmouth Droppings provided plenty of speculation that it was Penni. Whit and Doc had done a great job planting that seed after the lengthy phone call they had on Saturday night. The newspaper would pander to the popular story to sell the *Daily Voice*. The radio station in town would do the same thing, never searching for the truth like real journalists. They would do anything they could to drive the damage home so the family retreated, all behind the trolls of telling the truth.

It was some of the worst writing JB had seen. The power of the pen was known to take advantage of its position to sway the town. JB was proud of his part on Cottonmouth Droppings to incite his alias opinion and stir the pot even more when his phone chimed. His only challenge would be Tina.

Doc: Have you read the paper?

JB: Just reading. Great timing. We can use this to destroy PL.

Doc: Let's chat later I have a meeting. I need more "coffee" when can you bring some by? And let's strategize to update site.

JB: I will drop some "coffee" off later. Will call when I get to work.

Right in the middle of his text, Rita Faye rounded the corner and touched JB's back. "Good morning." He jumped from the stool.

JB dropped his phone. "I need more coffee." He jumped with his drained cup. "Don't sneak up on me."

"Looks like you've had enough." She ran her sausage swollen fingers over his shoulder.

He felt a wave of nausea roil over him. Despite her stunning face, according to JB's standards, she had let her body go since the twins were born over seventeen years ago.

Rita Faye looked around the beautifully appointed kitchen. She had a life she could have never dreamed of and yet it was empty.

"You got home late last night," he quibbled.

She clicked her acrylic fingernails on the cool granite countertop, pouring a cup of coffee. "Yep, you know Dogwood Lane is busy this time of year. This could be my best season. I had to finish a ton of gifts. And there are three parties this week." She kept her back to him. "I have huge orders for all of them." She stirred cream in her coffee, talking down to her mocha-colored cup. She turned around.

"Well, I have to get going. I have morning rounds." He looked down at his lighted buzzing phone.

"Do you need to take that?" She tapped her nails against her cup.

It was Tina Birch. "No, It's the office. I can call them back when I'm driving in."

"Do you have minute?" She stopped him before he walked up the steps and grazed the headline as she walked closer.

JB's palms grew sweaty. There had been a time when they had a good thing, but that had long passed when she decided to protect herself with a forty-pound layer of fat. And he decided since she had made an independent decision, he had the right to make his own decisions.

Despite looking elsewhere for his needs, he wasn't ready to call it quits with the marriage. It was for the kids, he had convinced himself, and despite her weight, she did contribute to the household with her successful business. It was good for him to appear stable. He had too much at stake to shake up his household. The kids would be leaving in less than a year and he could stomach it for a little while longer. For now, they coexisted. *Besides,* he thought, *I have the upper hand. My position gives her acceptance.*

Rita Faye pushed the paper on the table. "Can you believe this headline? The rag is at it again. I can't imagine the Lafoes letting anything like this go on."

JB slid the paper away before she could get too far into the article. "I don't think you ever really know anyone. What do you need?"

"Oh yes. I think we should keep a careful eye on the beach house this year. I'm not sure if Carter has been hinting around, but he thinks he's responsible enough to go there with his friends unsupervised." She took a sip of coffee. "I'm thinking we should not let that happen until after graduation next year. I just think we need to protect the kids. You never know what could happen."

JB pulled the newspaper under his arm. "I agree." He abruptly turned and walked up the stairs.

"Can we get the washer fixed, too?" She hollered. "I really don't have time to go to the Soap and Suds." She pleaded as JB dashed up the back steps. He slipped his phone to his ear and whispered, "Dr. Taylor."

Rita Faye bit her lip. *I'm so sick of him.* She thumbed through her phone and called the repairmen. They could be there next Monday. She set the appointment and walked to the laundry room, knowing she could not wait until next Monday. She would load the clothes in her car and when she had time she would stop and get them done. She waited for the shower to come on upstairs, wondering why he was taking so long.

"Did you see the damn paper this morning?" Tina Birch charged.

"No," he lied.

"There's an article about a possible rape at Penni's party. Did you see it says the victim is a runner? Who in the hell leaked this?"

"Of course, the press picked it up, but I didn't see any names except Penni's. What are you talking about?" JB knew Whit leaked information about her.

"I wonder who the hell went to them. Have you seen the chat page? It all but says it was my daughter." Whit Cain leaked that too. Doc asked him.

"I'm sorry I don't have any information in front of me."

"Oh, so you can't talk. You better find some time. Melanie is a mess and all because of your son."

"What does Carter have to do with this?" he lied. Whit told him exactly what Tina let slip.

Tina railed through his question. "It's bad enough she was assaulted. But this cannot go public. Do you understand me?" The phone went dead. "Hello, answer me."

JB spoke to the silence. "Yea, I did not sign off on that patient. You may want to call the other attending. If you look at the patient record you can see that he has been on a blood thinner since he was admitted." He paused. "Great I will be in soon." He continued to cover.

He turned the shower on and quickly called her back. Her voicemail picked up. "I'm sorry. I have no idea what you are talking about." He rounded the corner of his bathroom and stopped. He didn't want to say anything that may implicate his son. He was stopped by a text message.

"This is a golden opportunity for us to show the outsiders what happens when they don't follow our rules. We can now set an example. And make sure there is no heat on Carter," Doc wrote.

JB glared into space. He needed to play out all the possible scenarios. There were so many kids at the party, it would be hard to pin this on Carter. He spoke to his reflection in the mirror. "What the hell is wrong with her? He's a great looking kid. A star athlete and has a promising future. He could have anyone he wants. He didn't have to hurt someone to get it. I'm sure it was consensual." JB laid down his razor and hopped in the shower. He would have to contact Whit and make sure the rape kit was held up, even lost.

Whit was the master of burying evidence and slowing down investigations. He had been doing it since his first case with the Mary Claire Barnes drowning. He manipulated many cases for Doc's players. *The paper publicly reassured that she was not pressing charges.* He finished his shower.

JB would have access to the police file with Whit being the lead investigator. He would call him as soon as he left for work. *Damn women,* he thought. *Maybe Doc's right, if it ever came out that Carter was involved, Penni would be the perfect scapegoat. The kid should have gone to Middle Carolina. Doc did everything he could to get him to sign. Dinners out, a great recruiting weekend, and available attractive girls. Hell, even the parents were offered extras. But no, he sold out. And for what? Doc had a right to be mad at him. He betrayed us.* JB shut off the shower.

"Never seen anything like him. His Samoan size, he's good looking, smart, and would have been a great story. Penni sold us out." Those were the words Doc used that played over and over as JB finished getting dressed.

Chapter 12

Doc Winters, a wad of tobacco in his mouth and a slight limp from years of playing in the NFL, was loyal to everyone that displayed loyalty.

He was born and raised on rich tobacco farm land that was now raising cotton and soybeans. Tobacco was bygone, but not Doc. When he finished high school, he was recruited to play at Middle Carolina and he would realize a dream he didn't even know he had. After five years he would head to the NFL and become the untouchable small-town legend.

When his playing days were over and his body was riddled with injuries, he knew he wanted to be a coach. Working his way up the coaching ladder until his opportunity came, Middle Carolina University named Doc Winters head coach over fifteen years ago. Standing with him on that podium to announce his position, was his wife Dotty and daughter, May, along with the university president and athletic director. He could not be prouder to stand on that podium and tell Cottonmouth nation that he was the most "ethical man for the job. I'm back home."

After years of being a head coach, Doc noticed the young coaches coming up were more aggressive and would do or say anything to get young players to commit. They were fit and fresh out of the NFL and college ranks so Doc had to push his assistants to work harder on the recruiting trail. He kept everything in the silo of athletics and his football offices. If you were in, you better never betray him. His favorite saying, "Nothing, and I mean nothing, is rewarded like you football players. And I'm here to make sure of that."

He had a long line of players who came with a story. There were the behavior problems and single mothers who took their son's scholarship money for important things like getting their hair and nails done. There were the boys who came to school with babies at home and there were the ones who came with a troubled past. Doc thought he could coach it out of them. "My boys deserve a chance. If there is one thing those boys can do, they can take their aggression out on the field. It's my job to raise them up," he would often say to groups like the local rotary or Cottonmouth club.

But public criticism became more prevalent when his boys were taking their aggression out on their girlfriends or at the local bars. And Penni Lafoe posed the greatest problem for him. Something snapped inside Doc when Penni didn't sign with the Cottonmouths. He was out to destroy the kid. If you were his player, he protected you. But Penni didn't pick him and Doc made it personal. He now saw an opening to finish his attack with the assault at Penni's party. He could destroy the whole family and could easily manipulate the jock sniffers of the community to help him.

Oak Grove loved seeing their own come back. But it came with pressure. And that pressure was to recruit locally. Doc let a local all-star recruit slip through his hands. Now it was his turn to show the community that he made a good decision not bringing him on the team. And he could use it to reel in Carter Taylor. And JB would help him any way he could.

JB helped Doc with all his injuries. Bad ankles, knees, hips, and arms and his head may have had a smashing or two too many times to count. The pain pills that JB kept in a steady supply to him sealed the relationship. They needed each other. The only nemesis in town was Henry Middleton. They would have to be careful. He had been asking a lot of questions around the hospital since medicines had gone missing over the past several years.

Doc walked into his recruiting coordinator's office and threw the paper down. "We should have had this kid. We could have prevented this had he picked us."

"Who?" he looked confused as her searched for a name.

"Penni Lafoe. It looks like the kid may have assaulted some girl at his party."

"Wait where?" Coach Stevens scanned the article, "I don't see that in here. It says there was an assault. It doesn't say he did it."

"Come on coach. You can clearly read between the lines. We protect our kids. What was Officer Whit supposed to do? Lie about this? That's not how it works here." Doc lowered his large frame into the chair. He picked up the newspaper. "That boy was trouble and you know it. And if you read Cottonmouth Droppings, it clearly names him."

"You know best, coach."

Doc laid the foundation. "Come on Stevens let's get in the meeting. We have a long summer and I need to talk about our camp. I'm so damn mad at the kid." He picked up his cup and spit long from his tobacco-filled cheek while brown spittle laced his lips.

He walked in the conference room and threw the newspaper on the table.

"I knew this kid was trouble. Damn foreign family moves here from God knows where and then this kid goes and rapes some girl at his own party. Had to be his girlfriend. He was a big loss for our team, but I'm damn glad we didn't take him. And I will be even happier when the whole family leaves here."

The assistants gathered around the table and shared the paper scanning the headline.

"I don't see any names," Stephens said.

"I don't give a shit what it says. It happened at his house. Who else would have done that? I've heard the family is getting the hell out of town as soon as they can. What does that tell you?" He continued his lie.

"What? Why? I know his dad and mom. They're nice people," Stephens said.

"Where's the girl's name?" his coordinator asked.

Doc never answered. "I got a call from JB this morning saying Carter is torn up about it. Coach, I want you on the phone to him right away reassuring him that everything is good. We have to get this kid. You got it. Tell Carter if anything like this ever happens to him, we are here to protect him. We will use Penni as an example of just how bad it can get when you betray us."

Doc stood at the head of the table with a large white board filled with a list of players who had committed and their positions. "I need some of these holes filled. And I need Bobby Cottonwood to do his damn job and send us players from the high school. He's been failing miserably the last few years and I'm sure if it were up to him, Carter would not come here either." Doc sat down.

"I always feel like I have to babysit everyone around here." He slammed his cup. "Including that damn Bobby Cottonwood over there at the high school. The way I see it, this is all his fault. Damn coach should have made Lafoe come here. These kids don't have any idea what kind of problems can come knocking if they don't have people like us to take care of them. Now get your asses to work. And let's get ahead of this Penni thing before it hurts us with recruiting. Stephens, get over to the high school and pay Cottonwood a visit. Let him know he let us down, and we need him to do a better job."

The offensive specialists were lacking. And Carter Taylor's name was at the very top. They had just completed spring ball, and it was clear to Doc who they needed. Summer school would begin in a week, and, as with most college football teams, every player had to be back. They had summer camps to worry about. And he wanted to lock Carter down by early signing in December.

"You boys know that Carter is going to be looked at by every big school in the Southeast." Doc spit into his red cup.

"Coach, I think we have him locked. We keep getting assurances from his dad."

"I don't give a shit about his dad. I want to make sure Carter knows how important it is for you to get him here. I want to have a big spread in the paper by the end of the summer that he has verbally committed. Coach Grey, are you texting him most days? Hell, every day if that's what it takes."

Doc glared at Coach Grey, knowing he would probably leave after this season. He was an offensive mastermind. The coaching carousel spun quickly and Doc's staff only had two original assistants left from so many jumping off to go to bigger programs around the country.

His phone buzzed. Doc felt a sharp pain in his knee as he struggled to get up. "Damn legs." His body was riddled with agony this morning. He held too much weight for all the joints to handle the pressure. He would worry about that later.

"Okay, I want to see the camp schedule on my desk by the end of the day." He reached in his pocket and pulled out his pain pills, wishing JB could come by and give him an injection. He waddled out of the room. "What's going on Whit?"

"Coach we have to bury this. Tina just called JB and she's furious. She told him it was Carter." Whit loved being on the inside. "I read the paper. Thought my guy did a real good job with the article. I don't want to text anything to you." Whit whispered in the phone.

"Why the hell are you whispering?" Doc said.

"I'm in the hallway at work."

"Well, go outside and call me back."

Whit held the phone to his head and kept talking. He pushed his words right to the edge and said things to shake up Doc like a hive of bees.

"We have to get this boy now. After what he did to you, to us. I can get my guy to write more if you want me to. It's easy for him to write a retraction if he pushes it. Oh, damn, it's bright out here," Whit said.

"What's going on, Whit?" Doc grew impatient.

"Melanie Birch," he whispered. "That's who. Her mom is furious that the paper implies that it's her. She was pretty messed up."

"I know, so what? I was right."

"What?" Whit stammered, confused about what Doc was saying.

"So, was it her boyfriend? You know maybe she was a little drunk and they wanted to seal the deal before he left? Maybe she was confused."

"Can't say, Doc. It's consistent with an assault. Let's just say she wasn't begging for it."

The phone line was silent. Doc was spitting mad that there was nothing there to drag Penni down. "So, you can't give me anything else?"

Whit paused and looked around the parking lot "It happened in Penni's bedroom. There's something."

"Damn son, I wish I could get more than this, but we will have to work with what we have. At least you confirmed again who the young lady was and where it happened. You're telling me it didn't look like just some fun toss in the hay. A guy Penni's size could really hurt her though, right?"

"Yep. The medical report is graphic. And the kicker, there was no alcohol in her system. Only roofies."

"What the hell. Penni roofied her?"

"You could say that. Someone did."

"We have to make sure this never gets near Carter."

Whit thought a minute. "Let's push it on Cottonmouth Droppings. I'm sure we can put plenty out there to keep it away from him."

"Great work, detective. And find anything you can to hang the Lafoe family." Doc hung up the phone.

Chapter 13

Dr. JB Taylor walked down the long, white hospital corridor. It always had a lemony sick smell mixed with human feces and urine. *No wonder no one likes hospitals*, he thought as he reached his patient's room.

"Good morning, Mrs. Jones." He opened the door and extended his empty hand. "How ya feeling?"

"I've been better and I've been a lot worse," she whispered. Her elderly husband slouched asleep in the corner chair.

"Well, good news." JB opened his laptop. "It looks like you will be going home tomorrow if you behave yourself."

"Well, that is good news." Her heart warmed.

"It looks like your cardiologist thinks the coronary angioplasty and stent implantation is doing well and you have an all clear." He set his laptop down and reached over to feel her pulse.

"Thank you, Dr. Taylor. I don't like it here at all." She turned beet red. "I'm sure you work hard, but I have so many grandkids to look after. I really want to get home. You know there are so many graduation parties again this weekend, too."

"Mrs. Jones, you need to take it easy for a week or so. I think it's best you only go to one, maybe two. You're going to tire easily. Most heart patients do until they can build their stamina."

"You're right. I just miss home so much." Her eyes watered. "I'm sorry."

"Come on now, Mrs. Jones. Heart patients often feel very emotional after an attack. You're going to be fine." His voice calm and reassuring. "There is no need for me to come by tomorrow unless you get into mischief." He calmed her. "But I recommend that you go home."

She sheepishly smiled. "Thank you so much. I'm glad you stopped in."

He gave her a warm smile and walked out of her room. He headed down the hall. He was feeling a slight headache coming, so he slipped inside the doctor's private bathroom, pulled a bottle out of his pocket, put a fentanyl in his mouth and washed it down with a handful of water. He would have to fill a couple of syringes today if he got a chance. He was running low on meds and Doc needed some refills. Unfortunately, he could not get any from Mrs. Jones. He grew confident with how easy all of this was.

He stopped by the candy cart, chatted for a few minutes about summer plans with the Dragonfly Guild ladies and picked up a bag of M&Ms on his way to the ER. He needed to speak to one of the docs downstairs about a chart correction before he would move to the next patient.

In Internal medicine, JB saw patients daily. But, as a hospitalist, he was on call to address patients' immediate medical challenges, so if one of the doctors was seeing patients at their offices, he would be called to address the care of those in the hospital. Despite the new position at Middle Carolina Regional, it could position him nicely for being named chief of staff one day. And, it gave him the flexibility and access within the hospital that he needed. He was also the team doctor for the college football team. He had convinced the board to try it and here he was five years later making his rounds.

He walked down to the ER and chatted with a nurse. When he looked up, he saw Henry Middleton. Patsy had left her sweater in the ER on Friday.

Henry gave JB a conspiratorial smile from across the room. Any married man that carried on with another woman was never to be trusted in Henry's book. That and his ridiculous hospitalist position that he crafted to do God only knows what with to further his career.

JB walked over. "How's Patsy feeling?" He swallowed the last of his M&Ms.

"We are taking her to Chapel Hill." Henry watched him flinch. JB's dream to attend Chapel Hill Medical School was only that. He was never accepted. He went to Middle Carolina University instead and settled in Oak Grove when he married Rita Faye.

"So, does our oncologist not have what you need here?" JB turned his words as a knife of contention.

Henry postured. "Oh, I'm sure they could if they had a breast cancer specialist and up-to-date equipment. The hospital is too busy spending money on doctors that walk around popping their heads in patients' rooms just to say hello. Last I checked that was a social worker."

The breast cancer center was Henry's latest project and JB was trying his hardest to throw it out with the bathwater. Henry knew the community needed support. It was his home and he understood that everything that happened in the town was affected by the least in the town. Except for people like JB Taylor and Doc Winters, power was at stake here, and Henry's billfold wielded too much.

The men's tense conversation was interrupted by a page for JB.

"Excuse me. I need to answer that." He made his way down the hall while he called the front desk. He felt unsettled seeing Henry Middleton. "He's getting up in years," he whispered as he waited for the front desk to answer. He saw opportunity as he walked the corridors. Not having recurring patients was a positive.

"This is Dr. Taylor."

"Dr. Taylor there is someone here to see you."

"Who is it? I'm busy. Send them to emergency."

"Dr. Taylor, they insisted. She's standing right here. She said you would see her. You have important business to discuss."

"Who is it?"

"Tina Birch." The receptionist was annoyed.

Tina Birch came from a long line of country people. They were the color of dirt. Not black mind you, just dark. The dark hair missed her, but her skin was the color of sweet tea on a warm summer day.

And Tina was a fighter. It would seem that a deceased military husband would garner sympathy. But lack of support and the dark depression that followed him while he wrapped his car around a tree after a night of drinking cast rumors that he intended to kill himself. The police said he died instantly. His primary doctor, JB Taylor had put him on antidepressants and painkillers that didn't seem to make a difference. He suffered from intense pain and PTSD. The love of Tina and their young daughter Melanie were just not enough to keep him with the living.

Tim failed them since his death. What little bit of benefits Tina received sifted through her hands like sand. And rumors followed her around town like bees to honey. Her one redeeming quality was her beautiful and talented daughter. And Tina was raising her right. Melanie was as sweet as a Carolina morning and smart as a whip.

JB's heart stopped. *What in the hell is she doing here? We already talked this morning. And so public.* He looked at his phone to check his messages. "Shit," he saw four missed calls. With his rapid heart rate, he felt his stomach surge and flip while rage quickly rose in his belly. "Now what?"

They had a great Friday afternoon, but he could see the worry etched on her face from single parent living. *Maybe it's some money.* A slip of a hundred here and a bill paid there but he would never do anything to impugn himself. He felt a burden from a much deeper place. Now, he felt that worry himself. He held his phone. *This woman could be my Achilles heel.* "I would cut her off, if she didn't need me so much. Damn," he whispered.

"What Dr. Taylor. Are you still there?"

"Oh, nothing. Send her back to room 301. She must have a question about her sick friend. I'm sorry I forgot to look at my schedule. I had an appointment with her," he muddled.

He jammed his finger into the red icon on his phone, regretting his last words to the receptionist. As he walked up to the small conference room, he knew Carter's indiscretion complicated things. He was well aware of his son's behavior at the Lafoe party. And Tina solidified that with her accusation earlier that morning.

Carter and Melanie were together on Saturday. But it was just some fun. She was Penni's girlfriend. *Was Melanie crying rape now? Why am I so nervous?* But after the article on Monday, Carter and Whit's report did not align. Carter confessed late Sunday, before heading out with friends, but said it was consensual. JB excused him as he had longed for a high school experience like his son's and understood teenagers. But Tina posed a threat.

JB grabbed a Diet Coke out of the cafeteria as he glanced at the newspaper sitting next to an empty coffee cup with the headline about the grad parties. The whole place was a mess with papers and cups strewn across the tables. He would make a note to remind housekeeping to tidy the place up when he was in charge. He felt a slow drip of sweat slide down his chest as he walked to the elevator. He welcomed the cool condensation from the drink. It would be a challenge to explain Tina Birch's presence in the hospital, especially with him. But she was on his turf and he needed to think about his approach before he met with her.

"Come on in," he said, friendly, disarming her right away. "What can I do for you?"

"Your son raped my daughter." This was not Tina's initial plan.

JB slammed the door. "Hold on a minute. I don't know what you think you're doing, but that didn't happen."

"I picked Melanie up from Penni's party and she was hysterical. She told me Carter trapped her in Penni's room. He drugged and raped her. I brought her here and there was every sign that my daughter had been raped." She stopped herself.

JB flinched at the repeated use of the word rape. "So, why did she say it was Carter? Hell, he can get any girl he wants." JB believed Carter's version.

"She knows him."

"Are you sure they weren't just fooling around and things got out of hand and after she was just upset because, well isn't she seeing Penni? Maybe she felt guilty. Carter said he would never hurt her." JB slipped. "If Melanie is upset, it is only because Carter didn't want anything more and she risked losing Penni. She was caught with her pants down." JB jarred at his harsh words.

His relationship with Tina would complicate things, but he knew it was bad for her to show up at the hospital. "The sins of being good looking." He regretted saying that out loud.

"What?" Tina squelched. "You're a doctor, you know trauma to a woman's vagina when you see it. She now has a urinary tract infection from where he forced her," Tina swallowed, "where he forced himself inside of her."

JB looked at Tina. "I think we need to stay out of our kids' squabbles. I'm not sure what you want me to do, but I know one thing. Carter told me it was consensual. I don't agree with these kids sleeping around, but I do know that these girls think they want something, especially from someone like my son. You know popular, good looking an athlete. I think it was just a big misunderstanding and…"

Before JB could finish, Tina moved closer and held a picture of her daughter's chest to JB's face. "This is not a fun toss in the hay, asshole. See the bruises on my daughter's chest. That is from your son holding her down while he raped her. And when the rape kit comes back, if they find anything and I mean anything in her system, we are going to press charges. And let's see how much fun Carter has in jail. How dare you say that it was just a fun toss in the hay. My daughter is, was a virgin. She wanted none of that until…" She held the picture as tears smeared her face. "Her life is a mess. She's spent the last two days in her room. She won't shower, she won't go to work. All she tells me is she never wants to see anyone again. And to top it all off," Tina throws down *The Daily Voice,* "There is an article on the front page about an alleged assault at Penni's party on Saturday." She shoved the paper toward JB. "And that damn chat site. We have a real problem. Now what are you going to do?"

JB tipped away and took a sip of his soda. "What do you want?"

"I want you to make this right. To fix it. To make it go away. To pay for this."

"Are you blackmailing me?"

"I have more than enough to blackmail you, now don't I?" She leaned closer to him. "I need your help."

JB heard the words that snapped him to attention. "Let's regroup here. What can I do?"

"I want Carter to say he's sorry. To say he will never do anything like this again and to get some help." Tina's voice rose crescendo. "It was no fun toss in the hay for my daughter. She is ripped inside. So, I don't see where you can call this anything less than rape."

JB knew any accusations concerning Carter could be fatal. The kid was promised a scholarship to Middle Carolina. And there could be more offers coming. "Let me talk to Carter."

"I want him to come over tonight and apologize."

JB froze. "What, tonight, apologize?"

"Yes, I need you to help Melanie."

He softened, "We will come over tonight and make this right." Despite his never-ending need to be needed, his throat paralyzed with panic.

Tina's dark eyes reflected. "I'm done, JB. You make this right. Melanie is all I have."

He could not believe his son would ever hurt anyone. He was a good kid with good friends. *A typical teenage boy messing around.* He shook the thoughts. He would cancel his afternoon rounds, head home and talk to Carter.

Tina walked out of the hospital with her sunglasses covering her swollen face. She held her head high as she had given the performance of her life. She hoped things would take a turn in her favor. She would go home and lay the first of many plans out to Melanie. She knew her daughter was strong enough to withstand a visit from Carter Taylor, if only for a little while.

JB stayed in the small conference room and collected himself. His hands shook with anger. "Be home soon. We have to chat."

Carter responded. "Sure, everything ok?"

JB did not respond. This was not the way he wanted the summer to start.

He checked the chat boards, knowing the power they could carry. He would go on later and troll to guide anything away from his son. Carter was the star now and JB would use Cottonmouth Droppings to keep him there. The hate and divisiveness would work in his favor, especially when it came to outsiders like the Lafoes. His priority was to drive the entire family out of town, no matter the consequences.

Cottonmouth Droppings Chat Site

Football Lifer: Great spring game. Anyone banged up?

Hometown Boy: Nope. Doc has everyone in shape.

Firecracker Roger: Boys looked good. We have a complete team this year.

Farm Boy: Best place to start is with our own kids.

Stonewall: Carter looks awesome. Such a great kid and does the right thing.

Farm Boy: Hope Doc can get him. O coordinator is the best. Will make that kid a star.

Stonewall: Taylor is local and wants to stay local. Start shopping.

Weasel: Best damn player. Penni does not belong here. Never did. Big mistake.

Captain Kirk: LOYALTY. And, from the paper we can see he is now a rapist.

Frog Ginger: Wish our high school coach, Cottonwood could get the kids to stay!

Weasel: Carolina traitor. Not his job. He doesn't care about this town.

Swamp runner: Still a traitor but he has a hot wife.

Weasel: You folks are always looking for an enemy. Now it's Penni's turn.

Stonewall: Mind your business, Weasel. When we see something rotten, we throw it out of the barrel. No bad apples here.

Weasel: Hit a nerve, there did I?

Captain Kirk: Local is the foundation of this program. Keep Taylor here.

Stonewall: Taylor will always be loyal. His family is tried and true Cottonmouths.

Weasel: Easy recruit. His dad is the team doc. I hate outsiders!

Stonewall: Lafoe's party invited trouble with free booze. That poor girl. Penni should pay.

Hometown Boy: Great coaches don't let the local talent go elsewhere. Stonewall signed off.

Chapter 14

Helen pulled her long gray hair back in a high pony tail, her mala beads swinging from her neck and her colorful yoga pants and fitting top formed perfectly to her small sixty-year-old frame. She gripped the handle of her bike, noticing her fingers did not hurt today. Her hands, from years of working with oil-based clay, gave her some trouble from time to time. But that didn't stop her. It could take her weeks to build the armature for her next piece fitting pipes, plumbing fixtures, wires, foam, whatever worked to hold the massive weight of clay for her creation. Right now, she was working on a bernese mountain dog for a client. They wanted a replica of him sculpted and cast in bronze for their front yard.

She would work the clay on the form for hours on end.

"I don't see it, Helen, but I'm sure you do." Charlie, her husband, would often say. Days later he would come back to find the beginnings of recognition. She lined her studio with photos of her latest project. Angles of reference, the paws, babies, even as intricate as the claws on the dog were captured. She would take pictures of her subject standing, sitting, and running to make sure the muscle structure was exact.

"The sculpture will tell me what it wants when it needs it," Helen would often say to Charlie.

She drank dandelion tea for her liver cleanses and biked everywhere, keeping a large basket on the front to carry treasures she may pick up along the way. She had chickens that gave her an abundance of eggs and a garden to rival Patsy Middleton's. And she worked several days a week on the farm outside of town that she and Charlie owned.

Today, Helen stopped her bike in front of Patsy's house. She tipped it up and strode up the steps. She had eggs for her and her daughter-in-law had made a pound cake.

Helen tapped on the door and kindly let herself in. Just when she turned around Miss Clara was walking up the hall. "Good morning Miss Helen. You're up early."

"Had to stop by to drop off a few things for our patient." A strand of gray hair fell gracing her shoulder as she handed the bag over to Clara and gave her a strong hug.

"Thank you for this. Come on in. She's sitting in the sun porch having a cup of tea."

Helen followed Clara down the long hallway and onto the back sunroom.

"Miss Pasty, Miss Helen is here to see you, and she brought you some goodies."

Patsy leaned up in her chair as the white throw slipped from her lap.

"Don't get up, I just dropped off some eggs. And Maggie made you a pound cake." Helen bent over and gave Patsy a kiss on the cheek.

"Thank you."

"How you feeling? Your color is good."

"I'm much better. If I can get Henry to leave me alone for five minutes." Patsy adjusted the throw over her lap.

"That man won't give anyone a break." Clara started to leave the room.

"Clara, can you get Helen a cup of tea?"

"Of course."

Helen sat down in the corner chair right next to Patsy. "Now tell me, how are you really?"

"I do feel better. I had Harper and Caroline here yesterday chatting about the birthday party and that was such fun. And then Anne had to bring up my condition." Pasty gave a pause. "I'm really sick of talking about it. Now tell me, how's work?"

"Good. I'm really excited about working with Caroline. I have not seen this kind of talent in a very long time."

Clara interrupted. "Here's your tea. Oh, that Miss Caroline is something. Did you see the clay figure she made for my new grandbaby?"

"Thank you, Clara. You want to join us?"

"Oh no thank you. I'm going to visit her this morning."

"Have a good time. And kiss that baby for me." Patsy smiled. "Oh, and don't forget the gift on the counter."

Helen continued, "I can tell she's going to be good. She's very lucky to have you by her side. I was chatting with Rita Faye about her last week. I wish that she would realize just what she has with Caroline. I stopped in her store the other day and told her to come by anytime she wanted. She started to cry." Helen sipped her tea. "I told her I'm honored to work with someone like Caroline. She has real talent." Helen sat back. "We will be there for Rita Faye when she's ready."

"I'm here now." Patsy patted her hand. "So, tell me, will things slow down at the yoga studio with summer coming? I'm hoping to get up there this week."

"With all the college kids leaving it will. But I still have my private clients." Helen grinned. "Come down anytime you feel up to a nice slow class."

"I feel so much better after a practice."

"You either love it or hate it. Yet, I'm still here. A real beacon of peace." Helen smiled wide at her ailing friend.

"You are a beacon of peace. That is until the *Carolina Morning* magazine." Patsy sniggered. "I think you should go back to your maiden name."

"As eccentric and non-traditional as I am, I hate that name." Helen was conceived while her parents were camping up at Mt. St. Helen in Washington State. She was happy they didn't name her Saint Helen. They settled for Helen Olympia.

"Not Helen, Zappa." Patsy stopped her.

"Maybe if I was related to the famous Frank Zappa. The burden of explanation going from Helen Olympia Zappa Abernathy to just simply Helen Abernathy was really easy. Sometimes I do miss my name." She looked up at the ceiling fan as her thoughts spun. She longed for Patsy to be well. She had a pressing need to discuss the party with her but it would have to wait.

"That would have those crazy wives really talking." They hooted.

"I better get going. Charlie is at the pharmacy and I want to visit with him before I go to work. Thank you for the tea. Love you, dear friend." She reached down and gave Patsy a hard hug. "I will stop by later."

"I love you, and thank you." Patsy settled on her lavender smell as she left the room.

Helen rode though the quiet streets thinking about the newspaper article and the assault, *That poor girl.* She wondered if it was any of Caroline's friends. The kids came into the soda shop daily to see Melanie. And the girls were attending her yoga classes. She loved seeing young women discovering themselves through art and movement. She was so lost in her thoughts that she almost rode her bike right out in front of the trolley that ran to the university. She braked quickly and felt her pulse quicken. One anxiety yielded to another one.

She gathered herself and went straight to the pharmacy. She propped her bike by the side door. Charlie was not too keen on security. He worried more about his soda fountain than the thousands of dollars of prescription drugs that lined his shelves.

The bell rang above the door that she installed years ago. "Charlie…" She walked through the back office and into the pharmacy area. Charlie was sitting cross-legged on the floor inventorying medications that had come in late Friday.

"Well, good morning, sleepyhead. Did you see the eggs I collected from Henny Penny?" Charlie had named their chickens. He had two dogs too. The animals were his babies, and he would bring them to work if it was not a health violation.

"I saw that nice pound cake Maggie made." Charlie licked his lips. Maggie and Charlie, Jr. went to pharmacy school at Carolina too. It was the Abernathy tradition, and they both worked part time at the store. Mr. Charlie longed for his son to take over, but with two young daughters and the farm, they had more than enough.

"Yes, I just dropped some by the Middleton's. I wanted to see Patsy before the day got away from me." Helen bent over and kissed her husband on the head.

"What brings you in this morning? He looked at his watch."

"I only have art theory and one yoga class in the afternoon." Helen drifted down as she twisted her legs and sat opposite her husband.

Charlie reached over and kissed his wife long on her lips. "I sure love you, little lady."

"I love you too." She snatched a browning apple slice and a piece of cheese from his plate.

"I was wondering if we could walk over to the Middleton's this evening and take them a little dinner. I know Clara is probably cooking, but I thought your vegetable soup might do her some good."

"I will give her a call later. Better yet, I will call Anne. Patsy would never let us bring her soup. She keeps telling me she's not sick."

Helen settled herself. "What in the world are you doing back here?" Piles of boxes were tossed about on the floor along with pill bottles and a clipboard.

"Stocking medicines. I noticed a few were expired on Saturday and I thought I would get a jump before the pharmacy opens. The girls have the counter under control."

"Isn't Melanie coming in this morning?"

"Nope, I got a text from her mama earlier that said she's not feeling well."

Helen shifted her eyes to the crumbled newspaper next to Charlie. He leaned over and grabbed the mess, tossing it to Helen.

"And then I read this. There is trouble a-brewing here. I don't like the sounds of this article. Weren't you at the Lafoes on Saturday?"

Helen scanned the front page. She shuddered when she got to the part about the unnamed woman being assaulted at Penni's house and the insinuation that Penni was the offender. She shook her head in disgust.

"You know how disappointed I am when I waste my time reading this rag. It's stuff like this that makes me take pause."

Charlie ran his tongue over his top lip. "This could be very serious and even more scary is that it could be our Melanie. What with her not coming in today."

"For goodness sake, they are dating. Why would he pick his graduation party to assault his own girlfriend?" Helen gently jostled his arm. "Charlie, I saw something at that party that didn't look right," she whispered.

"What?" He turned from his pile of boxes.

"I saw Carter come down the stairs. His hair was wet. I don't know, it just seemed odd to me. I was in the hall talking to Caroline and when I looked up, there he was. I didn't think much of it at first but now with this article." She held her hand up to her face.

"What is it?" Charlie moved closer.

"About twenty minutes later, I saw Melanie sprint down the steps. Oh no, that poor girl." Helen stroked her long gray ponytail. "What if it was him?"

"You can't make assumptions. You don't know what happened. I'm thinking maybe that was coincidence. Don't you? And I'm thinking it's best we stay out of this."

"I don't want to think about it." Helen frowned.

Charlie got up on his knees and grabbed his wife's hands. "Let's keep this to ourselves, shall we? At least for now."

Cottonmouth Droppings Chat Site

Football Lifer: Can you believe the paper? What an article. Trouble in paradise.

Farm Boy: We don't need a rapist in our town. Run them out. Run them out!

Captain Kirk: Innocent until proven guilty. Let's hope Whit's not on the case.

Hometown Boy: Heard she's not pressing charges, just got out of hand.

Stonewall: That's good for Penni. He can leave and not have to come back.

Tat Man: Time for the Lafoes to go. Let's get the family out of here. I will fly a flag over their house. Or hire a plane! Time for some fun!

Swamp Runner: Not even out of school for a weekend and the kid can't keep it locked up.

Tat Man: Someone had to see or hear something.

Swamp Runner: Is it rape if it was his girlfriend?

Weasel: Penni sold out. Used us and left. Our defensive line could have used him. A real game changer.

Tat Man: Monday morning article was spot on. I wish the girl would press charges.

Farm Boy: Bad Family bad kid—The cottonmouths don't want him or his family.

Stonewall: Get the pitchforks and run him out of town. More room for players like Taylor.

Tat Man: We need them to leave. Hate the dad. Sucked up to coach until his kid signed elsewhere. Another jock sniffer in the bunch.

Swamp Runner: Girlfriend's a whore and her mamma too. Look what she did to her husband. Was probably her.

Confederate Fan: Shanty trash crying rape what a surprise. They're outsiders as far as I'm concerned.

Weasel: Don't you ole farts have anything better to do?

Farm Boy: Nope just answering to the greater good for our community.

Stonewall: Our community does not need this kind of trash from outsiders.

Farm Boy: We're happy he's not coming here.

Chapter 15

"WHATS WRONG? CALL ME!" Melanie held her blanket close to her aching chest as she stared at the capitalized words from Penni. "I wouldn't know where to begin." She wanted to tell him as she stared at her text message.

She rubbed her raw nose with a Kleenex and scrolled through Cottonmouth Droppings, hoping there was nothing to see. Mid-way down the chatter started about the assault at Penni's party. *Everyone knows it's me.* She read the posts that all pointed to her. *Someone must have seen me.* She thought about Harper and Sam. *They would never hurt me.* She rolled on her side.

Carter talked. Her body filled with disgust. Her thoughts plunged like a drop on a roller coaster. *I was sick and wanted to leave.* She clicked on the link to one of the comments and the newspaper article popped up.

Melanie scanned the article. Though her name was never mentioned, it was clear it was her. The word runner taunted her. *How could I let myself be with someone? If I tell Penni he will never love me like he did. Carter will always be between us.* Shame spread through her like a hot knife cutting butter. She tossed her phone on the floor, turned over and begged for sleep.

Melanie was made fully aware that her urinary tract was inflamed during the forced intercourse when she got up Monday to use the bathroom. It was only the second time she came out of her room since her mom brought her home late Saturday evening. She walked across the hall and squirmed on the toilet as the urine dripped into the bowl. When she stood up to flush there was blood mixed in the yellow water. She reached under the sink and grabbed a pad.

She walked back to her room to find her mom.

"How you feeling this morning, sweet pea?" It was the name her dad had always called her. Melanie thought about the chat boards and what people said about her dad and mom many years ago. Now it was her turn. Another shanty dweller stirring it up.

Melanie's sorrow seemed easy. Tina, in the gallows, raw hateful difficulties of her existence trapped, struggling to gain control. It would only make sense that Melanie would follow in Tina's footsteps. With this, she opened the door for a life just like her mother's.

"I'm going back to bed." Melanie never answered her question.

"I brought you some cranberry juice and a little something to take the edge off." Melanie picked up the juice and the pill and swallowed them both with her emotions. She would never let herself feel anything again. Her mom gave her a squeeze as she descended into her covers. Any act of love pushed tears to the surface.

"Can I lay with you a little while?"

Melanie moved while Tina pulled the sheet back and rubbed her in silence; torment trampled her mind. She kept questioning her role as she fixed the arrow of blame that pointed directly to herself. Had she sent Carter the wrong message? She was anxious for the Xanax to take so she could get lost in sleep.

"I'm not going back to work at Mr. Charlie's. Everyone knows." She whispered. "Everyone will think I'm lying. I mean it's Carter. What girl would not want him? He's rich and good-looking. I'm poor and..." She stopped and clung to her tattered blanket as tears slid against her hair. "I have nothing. We have nothing."

Tina rubbed her daughter's back. "We have each other, baby."

"I wish daddy was here. I miss him." She held her discolored stuffed bunny. "I want him to make this all go away." She thought about her father, larger than life protecting her. "He would know what to do. Why did he quit trying?"

"I don't know honey. He was just sad." Tina lay in the quiet and the unusual stillness of a Monday morning. They didn't have to be anywhere. Tim Birch was the man of her dreams. But he was a different man when he came home from his service. The man she married went missing in Afghanistan, along with his leg.

Tina thought about Melanie's first real birthday party. It was 2011 and a big year for the news. Occupy Wall Street was in full mode and Tim went on incessantly.

"Those damn rich bankers don't get it." He talked to the TV. "We military people, we work our asses off and get no support. I'm a decorated soldier and now, no leg." He took a tug of his beer and looked down at the empty space below his knee. "I can't even get a job at the local mill. Henry Middleton should be ashamed of himself. Hell, we even got our representatives being shot at." He started in about Gabby Gifford.

Tina fought for sweeter memories like Melanie's birthday party on July 22.

"Your tenth birthday party was wonderful with pink balloons and a Barbie cake. Harper and Caroline were there. Remember we had it at the park. It was a big deal to be in double digits." Tina stopped.

She could see Tim sitting in the corner sipping a beer like it was yesterday. He was cheated out of his military career. Cut short by a roadside bomb. He survived the bomb but not the carnage. The other two men that were with him were sent home in coffins. Tim, alone and alive with only his PTSD to cling to. Despite his ten years of service, he could never serve his country again.

Everything he did before his injury didn't matter to Tim. Flat, no expression, no smile, void, no soul behind the eyes, sat in the corner and watched all the screaming kids swat at the piñata.

Tina rubbed Melanie's back, remembering his handsome face.

"He was as blond as you. His grandmother called you tow head twins. I would say that's about right."

"When he first came home, he seemed good," Tina said. "But loud noises bothered him." Tina's heart hurt.

"You know he was obsessed with Amy Winehouse when she died. I held his hand while he cried. 'She was so young,' he kept saying. 'This young woman singing such beautiful music, found dead in her home in London. She's troubled like me'," he repeated.

Tina stopped for a minute. "It was right after your birthday."

"He died the next day," Melanie whispered.

"Yes, he did baby." Tina paused. "Government benefits could have saved him but didn't."

Suicide, many posted on the chat site. His problem wife should have known. Anti-depressants, anxiety and pain medications, along with alcohol ran amuck in his riddled body that he wrapped around a tree in his car. The chat sites didn't stop. He was a victim of what many speculated but no one knew.

Tina snuggled closer and wished the bad memories away. Just like she wished the weekend away. "We're going to be okay, honey. I promise you."

"I miss daddy," Melanie said.

"I know you do." Tina finally felt Melanie's body release. She got up and went into the kitchen. She picked up the medicine bottle and stared at the name. Dr. JB Taylor had prescribed her Xanax years ago when she was at her wits end. He prescribed anything she wanted or he thought that she needed.

"I'm here for you, your rock," he always told her. She threw the bottle against the wall.

"Why?" Exacting revenge was nothing. She was looking for a way out of her miserable life.

She sat at the small Formica table and held a photo of her late husband.

"I could sure use you right now."

She stared at the newspaper article from his horrific accident. A few of the spilled Xanax had landed on the table.

Chapter 16

Henry Middleton returned from the hospital with Patsy's sweater. He held it up to his nose and took in the scent of his wife.

"She loves gardenias," he said as he laid it on a kitchen chair. He wanted to read the paper and have a cup of coffee while the house was quiet. Patsy woke up earlier in a panic over her favorite sweater, so he ran over to the hospital to pick it up. Thankfully the ER still had it. It was not as if Wade could not have grabbed it. He had two surgeries that morning, but Patsy insisted Henry go get it.

"What if someone steals it?" She rattled.

He sat on the screened porch and opened the paper. The headline, **Graduation parties gone wild,** taunted him. Henry shuffled the pages and went to the third section to finish reading the article. A young woman was allegedly assaulted at the Lafoes' house.

"Oh, what this town will do?"

The article, after alleging who was guilty, was an indictment that these parties had been going on for years and the parents had very loose rules. Extending open invitations, alcohol, and even drugs were involved, and it was no wonder that something like this happened. Henry was so spellbound that he didn't hear Anne come on the porch.

"Who's writing that crap anyway?" Anne interrupted him.

After Cottonmouth Droppings, the newspaper served as grand marshal of ridicule parade. But this was different. The innuendo gave Henry great pause. Describing the young woman and withholding her name was as good as telling. He suspected Whit, Doc, and JB were behind this charade. It was bad enough that they were working hard to defame Penni for months, but not this, and not Melanie.

Henry learned long ago when someone is chasing power, there is always disaster around them. And eventually someone will get hurt. He was keen at observing people's behavior, then he would proceed. His whole purpose was to improve his community.

"Good morning, Anne." He folded the paper over.

"Can I warm up your coffee?"

"No, I'm good. Is mama up yet? What about Harper?"

"Mama was up earlier and visited with Miss Helen but is now asleep out on the back porch."

"I picked up her sweater. It's in the kitchen. When she wakes up will you tell her?" Henry paused. "When's Harper getting up?"

"You know Harper will sleep until noon if we let her. Of course, mama will too."

"I thought I heard some commotion upstairs," Henry said.

"Well maybe that was me."

"I guess so." Henry was short. "I saw Caroline and Beth come over last night."

"Don't you ever sleep, Daddy?"

"There will be plenty of time for that soon enough."

"Stop it. I hate when you talk like that." Anne smoothed the floral cushion and then her robe. "I just love the gardenias this time of year." She inhaled.

"What do you think the girls were chatting about last night?" Henry's sitting room was just a door away from the screened porch. A second screened porch jetted off the kitchen.

"I don't know daddy. What do young girls talk about, hair, makeup and boys." Anne smiled. "That's all I cared about."

He handed the paper to his daughter. "Do you think they were talking about this?" His brown spotted finger pointed to the front page. "They were at the party. Do you think Penni could have done anything like this?"

Anne took a minute to scan the article. "Daddy, this is just awful."

"Have you talked to Harper? Maybe she saw something."

Anne folded the paper. "No and I don't want to get her involved. This will upset her. This could have been our Harper."

When Henry turned in his chair, he noticed a car sitting in the drive. "Is that Penni?"

Anne leaned in. "Yes, do you think he's okay? His head is against the wheel. What's he doing here?"

"Let me speak with the young man. He's probably here to see Harper." Henry's heart sank. Why in the world would a young man, dating such a sweet young lady, be accused of assault? He heard the girls last night speculating about her whereabouts. Who would believe any of this nonsense?

"I have my suspicions." Henry said.

"Go check on Harper." He sat in the kitchen sunroom and waited for Penni.

Chapter 17

Penni drove by Melanie's earlier that morning and pounded on the door. He considered breaking in, but with the horrible article he knew it would be a mistake. Her mom's car was gone, so he walked around to her window but the shades were drawn. He slid down the clapboard just outside her bedroom and texted again in all capitals, *WHATS WRONG. CALL ME I'm right outside your window*. There was never an answer.

Penni fought back tears. "We had a plan." He cried into the steering wheel. The two of them were united with their school work and behavior. There was never a worry. Until now. He fought to douse out the idea that the assault could ever be her.

He tapped in his phone. "Are you trying to break up with me?" and watched the three bouncing dots mock him. He opened his car door and hoisted his large frame up the long front steps and knocked on the door. He was sweating, not from the June heat, but from the fear that gave rise to his uncertain future.

"Come on in young man." Henry gave him a hug. "It's early for any recent high school graduate to be up."

"Yes sir. It's just…" Penni struggled, "Harper wanted to have breakfast."

"Well, she's not down yet. Let's go to the sunroom and visit."

Penni walked into the sun-drenched porch struggling to collect himself. A long white table filled with fresh flowers and family pictures greeted them. His eyes immediately fixed on a photograph of Harper, Beth, Caroline, and Melanie, all clinging to each other in a candid beach shot. He chewed a dry piece of skin off his bottom quivering lip and chewed on the iron blood that leaked out. He was slowly coming unglued.

"How about a cup of coffee?" Henry asked.

"Yes. Thank you."

"So, what are your plans this morning?"

"We're going to breakfast. And then I need to get home and pack." He raised his brow.

"Well, there is plenty to eat here. What can I get you?"

But before Penni could answer, Patsy was at the door. "Oh, my. Good morning Penni. It's so good to see you?"

"Good morning, Miss Patsy." He gently hugged her frail body.

"You know we are really going to miss you around here." She patted his stubbled face with her cool hand.

"I'm going to miss you too." He shifted.

"You hungry? I'm sure there is plenty to eat. Let me go grab a tray of pastry. There's a delicious pound cake in there." Patsy walked down the hallway before he could answer.

Henry shut the door. He would start off slowly, but not before he was interrupted by Anne. "This is a wonderful surprise. Can I get you two some coffee?"

"Could you run tell Harper I need a few minutes with him before she whisks him away. And Anne," Henry paused as he looked over at Penni. "Can you help your mother. She's getting us some cake and coffee."

Penni looked up from his tired eyes. "Thank you. I appreciate it."

"Of course. Daddy, please don't wear him out with all your football talk. He only has a week at home and we want him to come back. You and mama could both worry him to death." Anne shifted with nerves. "Harper should be down in a few. See you before you leave."

"Yes ma'am."

Henry listened to the ticking clock. Dogs barked off in the distance, and he watched a few young mothers pushing strollers.

Penni waited, leaning into the quiet, appreciating the calming everyday noise.

Henry knew exactly who was behind all of this and hoped the conversation would start the long dismantling of the sickness that plagued his beloved town.

"So, Penni. It's been a tough few days hasn't it?"

"Yes sir. I have no idea what to do. And Melanie won't talk to me. Nothing happened. I told Officer Cain over and over again I was downstairs saying goodbye to guests."

Penni fought to compose himself. "I only have a week. I regret ever leaving her side. I'm hoping Harper can help. She insisted I come first thing this morning."

Henry studied the broken young man. "I read the paper this morning, and I don't think a damn bit of it's true. Well, maybe the alleged assault, but certainly not you being the one who did it. And I would guess the newspapers and that insidious chat site are trying to say it could be Melanie."

Penni tensed. "How did you know Mr. Henry? The newspaper never said it was her." Penni buried the possibility.

"Listen. I have my suspicions. I know Harper, Sam, they love you and know it's not been an easy road for you here. I bet it's hard to move across the country, to such a different place and start at a new school. You took the place of some of the best players on the team and then made a decision that is best for you and not for Doc Winters." He stopped.

Anne tapped on the door and set a tray of pastry and pot of coffee on the table. She poured two cups and gave Penni a wink. "Get some pastry." She quietly closed the door.

Penni dropped his shoulders. "Yes sir. You pretty much summed it up. But how do you know about all that?"

"It's my job to know. When you do as much for this community as I do, people tend to tell you things, and unfortunately, some of the things I'm told aren't always good, especially when it comes to Coach Winters." Henry took a sip of hot coffee. "I guess I could say part of me doesn't blame him. You're a damn good player. You're heading to a premiere football program. But let me just say, I would never condone anyone treating a young man the way he and his staff have treated you. It's a damn travesty. And now this."

"I can take it, but Cottonmouth Droppings is calling my family horrible names."

"There are people who are not happy that you didn't choose Middle Carolina. The community is looking for an assumed mantle. They don't like different. And you're a threat, especially when you didn't choose to stay and make their beloved college football team better." Henry paused. "Son, I love this town. But there are a few rotten apples here that make the whole barrel smell. I'm so sorry for you. In all honesty, I would worry if you did come here and well, for some reason you did not play as well as the fans think you should. I don't think either choice would have won the community over."

"I had to make the best decision for me."

"And you did." Henry set his coffee down. "So, you have not talked to Melanie." He remembered the girls' chatter on the porch last night. He knew young love. He suffered the same fate some seventy years ago when he fell in love with Patsy.

"No sir. I have not heard from her. I don't know what to do. I thought about asking my mom to look at hospital records. Maybe she could find out the girl's name." He leaned forward. "I would consider giving up my freshman year to stay and work things out." Oak Grove was taking him in head first and spilling him out like bile.

"You will do no such thing. Let me do some snooping and see what I can find. I will not let this thing get out of hand."

"Thank you, sir. I would never do anything to hurt her or anyone else."

"I know that. Do you think I would let my granddaughter hang out with you if I thought otherwise? And Penni, you're going. You worked hard for this opportunity."

"I want to, but I can't leave Melanie." He was tethered to her and the thought of leaving broke his heart. "Thank you."

"The minute this town has something to point a finger at, to blame, to hate, they don't stop. I saw it with the Barnes situation years ago. It's like no one wanted to have much to do with them after the death of their daughter."

"Such a generous gift but the house is haunted or something," Penni said.

"That house seems to unite tragedy. No one really knows what happened to her. Said she drowned. But I think there was more to it." Henry shook his head. "And since last fall's article, I have my suspicions."

With no warning, Harper pushed open the sunporch door. "Good morning Papaw. Good morning Penni. We were going to breakfast, but it looks like you already took care of that." Harper bent down and gave Henry a kiss.

"Oh, never you mind. You two go on. Better yet, sit out here. I'm going in to check on your grandmother."

Harper shook her head, "Yes, she's been out of your sight for what, five minutes?"

Chapter 18

JB had been stonewalled. He needed to think long and hard about his relationship with Tina. Carter was his primary concern, but he was not ready to give Tina up. Taking Carter over to Melanie's made him very uncomfortable, but he knew that may be the only way to keep her quiet. *Why would he mess around with some shanty town girl? He has a bright future.*

He opened the door and glanced down the hallway. After a few steps, he held his phone to his ear. "Hey there's a big mess around this assault. I want to talk with you about it. Tina just paid me a visit and we can't let any of this come near Carter."

"What about tonight?" Doc spat. "We know its Melanie. What does she want?" Doc answered.

"An apology from Carter." JB said. "In person."

"Come over in a few hours. I have some ideas," Doc replied. "And I have more HGH for Carter. Our strength coach will get him even stronger for the fall."

"I'm so pissed. After all I do for them, and she pulls this shit on me," JB complained. "She's been having a tough time."

"Well, we have an opportunity to do something about the Lafoe family. The more heat we put on them, the less anyone is going to go snooping around for Carter. This is going to be a first-class railing. Outsiders coming in trying to take what wasn't theirs and leaving all the garbage behind to be picked by the locals." Doc was ranting.

"She has some nerve. I think the girl is crying wolf. But she can make trouble for Carter if we're not careful."

"So, she wants an apology for what?" Doc stood in front of his desk. "Carter didn't do anything."

"I know that."

"And that's it. Are you sure?" He paused. "Do what you have to, but be careful. Hell, pay her off if that's what it takes, but I need your boy on my team next year. And in the meantime, pushing the family out will make your problem go away."

"Tina said her daughter was torn up pretty bad."

"I don't give a shit about her or anyone else." Doc's door cracked open.

"Hey coach you got a minute?" His Offensive Coordinator walked in.

"Sure, come on in." Doc put the phone on speaker. "It's Dr. Taylor."

"Oh hey Dr. Taylor, how ya doing?"

"I'm good."

"How's Carter?" he asked as he leaned toward Doc's desk, getting closer to the phone and handing him a slip of paper.

Doc interrupted. "Damn, I'm sorry this kid didn't get the grades. Any chance you can fix this?"

"I can try, coach. He's gonna have to go to summer school."

"Make sure he passes this first. No excuses." Doc spit in his cup. "We need his ass on the field this fall. I can't risk some arrogant professor not giving this kid the grade he needs to pass." He threw the paper back to his OC. "Is that all?"

"Yes sir."

"What's that about?" JB asked.

"Oh, these damn kids can't even pass a class. I have to personally make sure they pass."

"I get it."

"Yep, you sure do, even if it means paying these damn tutors to write these kids' papers." Doc made air quotes as if JB could see him. "But right now, let's talk about Melanie. Whit was here earlier and let me read over the report. Makes it easy that it happened at a house owned by the university, so Whit has access. That's one loyal boy."

"Any name I should be concerned about?" JB's palms sweated.

"Nope, none at all. She's not going to press charges. What does that tell you? No information can come out unless someone leaks it. And that's why Whit has been such a good source. He takes care of things before they get out of the hen house." Doc felt his confidence soar. "But before anything gets crazy, let's focus on your son."

"I'm just glad my son's name isn't in it. You know how desperate girls are. They will always target a good-looking athlete. Besides, it would be a disciplinary thing to me, not criminal. I'm sure it was consensual. She just feels bad now."

"His name will never be attached to any incident if I can help it. As long as he's coming here. Hell, half the time I think these young girls are asking for it and when they get it, they're upset." Doc said. "I know Carter's name is not in the report, but you don't want it mentioned around the assault. That's why we need to direct everything toward Penni. We can make it look like she changed her mind even with her own boyfriend."

Doc was the master at going to campus agencies and manipulating the system. Paying off anyone he needed to, from student affairs to campus housing, to protect his players. Even grades were manipulated to help Doc Winters win.

"Did she ever tell him to stop?" JB went back to the report.

"Nope didn't need that, then slam dunk no case, but hell, who wouldn't want to have sex with Carter?" Doc leaned back in his chair and laughed. "Boys will be boys. But we have a bigger problem, JB."

"What's that?"

"The Lafoes. If Penni is upset and his family is upset then they will demand answers. So, we both know what we need to do?"

"Get them all out. Who needs their son? He made his decision. Now it's time for them all to leave." JB felt a sense of relief.

"Can't trust the outsiders. I hate it when they don't know our ways. Like they are better than us or something. Let's get to work."

JB reached in his pocket and held the bottle of pills he would drop off later. "I have your stuff."

"You're a good man. And the chat boards are taking off like a match to gasoline. The town needs someone to blame, so let's make sure they jump on the Penni train and watch him and his family ride it right out of town."

Cottonmouth Droppings
Stonewall: Apparently the snake doctor's son is a snake. Can't trust outsiders.
Farm boy: It was him. Who else would it be? He used us to go to a big program.

Stonewall: They need to go. WE welcome people in and look what they do.

Farm Boy: Can't help but wonder who really hurt that young girl? Penni!

Stonewall: We know who did. Thank god he's leaving in a week.

Confederate Fan: Any way we can look at the police report. Whit is always reliable.

Farm Boy: We need to know the truth. I'm sure Whit will not let anyone take the blame for this except the person who did it.

Football Lifer: The truth will set you free.

Weasel: Ticket prices are high and I had my seats moved. Some bullshit renovation.

Hometown Boy: GET RID OF THE LAFOES. They need to go. I like the signs that were put up in their yard. Great idea from last fall. The ones at the games worked too. Heard the mom was really upset. Love the threats. Her behavior cries guilt.

Farm Boy: Was she really? Was it really a threat? Did they really mean anything?

Weasel: That boy hurt someone and he should pay.

Farm Boy: When coaches win they should be paid more.

Stonewall: WE need good players here. I heard that kid was trouble from the start.

Hometown Boy: It was him. We were all at the party. Heard the food made some kids sick.

Foxy: Leave the poor girl alone.

Hometown Boy: So, you know who it is?

Chapter 19

JB stoked the anger that drove him like a hot coal in his hand. He tossed it from one thought to the next so that the more rationalization run-off leached an ugly stain over everything he touched. The very hands that were supposed to heal, crippled from the toxic sludge that was drained from his ailing heart, spewed vitriol in his wake. His medical degree justified his every decision. He pushed himself with a seed that fostered his resentment. And that blurred reality fed the noxious fumes that he passed onto his family.

JB stood in the kitchen after a long day, shouting orders, knowing if he started a fight, it would be easy to leave the house with Carter that evening.

"I don't understand why the hell dinner always has to be such a production. I work hard all day. Carter was working out all day. Your mother is working and Caroline, you are at some damn useless voodoo yoga class until six o'clock. You're supposed to be helping around here." JB was locked and loaded as he pumped shells filled with toxic words.

Carter walked into the middle of battle. "What's going on? I'm starving." He filled a glass with water and dumped in a big scoop of creatine, creating a milky mixture.

"Your sister didn't get home to help with dinner so it's just getting on the table." JB shifted from Caroline to Rita Faye.

"Can't you hire some extra help down at your store? You have a family to take care of," JB fired at Rita Faye.

"It's almost on the table." Her mood sank. The new antidepressants kept her uneven and she was concerned her diet pills were interacting with them.

"Fat and happy," Caroline mumbled under her breath while she threw napkins on the table and watched her mother set an unidentifiable casserole down along with a bagged salad, some fried chicken, and mashed potatoes.

Caroline shifted from no feelings to disgust for her father. He had cast his ugly upon her mother like a sea worn net, but Caroline swam tirelessly to keep out of his tangle. *He even had Carter adrift*, she thought as he drank the cup of creatine.

Caroline scooped out a small portion of salad and chewed slowly. She passed on the casserole.

Rita Faye filled her plate with only salad.

"You okay? You have nothing on your plate?" JB started on her.

"I'm good," she said.

"Um," he mumbled and filled his plate.

Rita Faye chased her food around, watching the look of disgust on Caroline's face. *I'm going to make some changes.* She would make a doctor's appointment in Raleigh with a specialist that Helen recommended. Seeing the look just now made her feel the same way about herself.

"Caroline what do you have planned for the summer? Aren't you going to some art camp?" JB asked over the rustling of forks. Caroline ignored him.

"Would you guys want to take a trip, or is the beach enough? I'm thinking since this may be the last summer that you're home, we could take a vacation and you could invite a friend." No one answered him.

"Didn't both of you go to the Lafoe party? Did you see the article in the paper this morning?" Rita Faye asked.

JB glanced at Caroline then to Carter, who ate faster.

"Rita Faye, let's not talk about that poor girl. Hasn't she been through enough?"

"Oh, so you know who she is?" Caroline dragged the last three words like a hoe stuck in the mud. "I would love to take Melanie on our family vacation." Caroline waited for a reaction.

"No," JB stammered, ignoring Caroline's last comment. "It's all just a terrible situation. And I don't want to talk about it."

"So, does it concern any of us? Or do we just let it go, in hopes that the big bad rapist will be found?" Caroline eyeballed Carter.

"Just because we don't talk about it, doesn't mean we don't care about our community," JB said.

Caroline saw red rage rise in her father's face. "Yes sir," wanting to throw him off. "I'm sorry dinner was late. I got caught up working on a project with Harper." She lied, waiting for her brother's reaction.

"I thought I saw Harper in downtown." Carter perked up.

"Oh, you did. But as soon as she was done, she met me. We had coffee, and we worked on our summer English project. And we talked about Melanie." Caroline didn't think twice about lying to her family. But every time, she did she felt a small piece of her drift away like dust floating from furniture. *They forced me*, she rationalized. She watched Carter.

JB needed a diversion. "It's been decided. You need some responsibility. You have to let us know when you are going, but I'm giving you the freedom to go without us." He reached in his pocket. "Here are keys to the beach house."

Carter's eyes popped as Caroline dropped her fork.

Rita Faye stopped eating and glared at JB and when she started to open her mouth, Caroline beat her to it.

"Have you lost your mind, Dad?"

"No smart ass, I have not lost my mind. I just think you're ready for the responsibility. Carter will have to leave first thing after graduation next year because of football. And aren't you going to art camp this summer without supervision?"

"No, I'm going up to Penland with Helen for a week for a sculptor workshop. Don't you think letting us go to the beach house with no adults is a little irresponsible?"

Carter, confident his dad was not mad at him after their earlier conversation, said, "Dad, I'm really happy you trust me. I'm really excited about summer. Maybe Sam would want to go before he leaves for his internship if Harper would let him. Of course, her grandparents have a place a street over, and maybe she could just stay there while all the boys are having a great time. Or she could join us."

"I'm happy for you and all your boys to go but my one rule is, no girls."

"I get it, Dad."

"And Caroline, I don't care if you want to take a group of girls down there this summer too."

"She doesn't have any friends, Dad, and I don't think the beds are big enough for the ones she does have."

"You're such an asshole, Carter. I purposely try to keep my friends away from you." She stared at him while a line of perspiration surfaced on his upper lip. "Does it seem hot in here?"

"It's hot in here." Carter echoed her words. "Why did you guys turn off the air? It's summer and I hate this humidity." He got up and slammed the back door.

"Wow, Dad you weren't kidding?" Carter grabbed the key.

Rita Faye had had enough. "Caroline, I'm really proud of you to take such a responsible position. I agree with you. Your father has lost his mind."

Carter ran right over her words. "Dad this is awesome. I promise me and the boys will behave." Particles of food were wedged in his teeth when he grinned.

"Well, aren't you going to say anything?" JB turned toward Caroline.

"What's there to say? I'm not going down there this summer without mom."

"What the hell, Caroline? Don't ruin it for me."

"Ruin what, Carter? You can go all you want. And do God knows whatever it is you do at parties." She stopped. "I just don't want to go. And I don't want to be down there with the chance that you and all your friends will be there."

"Don't be disrespectful," JB said, but Rita Faye interrupted.

"Caroline, great decision. We will decide when we can go. And I agree, it would be more fun without you two. Oh, and JB, I will not be responsible for Carter's behavior, since you made this executive decision without me. Don't look to me for support when something goes wrong. And Carter, don't call me when something does. Call your father."

Rita Faye scooted out and got up from the table. "Clean the kitchen, Carter before you go out. I'm going back to work." She turned and walked down the hallway.

Caroline shouted, "thanks mom." She stood up and pushed out her chair. "I'll go to Harper's beach house. It's more fun to be with them anyway." She pushed her words right under her father's nose to smell the very people he hated.

"Fine, you don't get one." JB grabbed the second key and shoved it in his pocket, like a five-year-old. "Finish up, Carter we need to go to the sporting goods store."

Carter looked confused. "What?"

"Didn't you text me today that you needed some new cleats?"

"I can go on my own, Dad."

"No, that's okay. I wouldn't mind some time with you."

Chapter 20

Melanie scrubbed her body until it was raw. It would seem she could not get the water hot enough to take away what was now a wasteland. The thought of seeing Carter made her shudder, but her mom insisted that she needed to be brave to ensure her future.

Tina's small clapboard shanty sat at the end of a street that housed several other heavily worn homes. Tiny Smith, a deacon and his wife, lived next door but, Mondays were pot luck and bible study, so they would be gone until nine.

JB understood the risk, with all the controversy over the alleged attack, but why would a respectable doctor be at her house? There was no place for him and a soiled reputation on Cottonmouth Droppings. He gripped the steering wheel, glued his eyes on the small drive, and made his way to the back of her house, slipping his Mercedes between two rundown cars. He was second guessing his decision, but his excuses would fall easily like leaves off a tree. Tina had an accident and had Melanie call Caroline.

"Dad she's nuts," Carter said.

"If anyone sees us, I'm driving you over here to drop something for a project you and Melanie have to work on for the summer. You got it?" The lie slipped easily off his tongue. "I told to my receptionist that rounds were light today, and I was taking advantage of your first week off school for you to help me move some files. Make sure you get these stories straight, will you? And don't forget, we're shopping for football cleats." JB sighed.

Carter sulked. "I can't believe you're making me apologize. I told you, it was nothing. You should have seen the way she was looking at me."

"Carter, I don't care what you two did. It's not easy being in your position. You're good-looking and popular, but you have to make sure you make it right with this girl. If not, she will never leave it alone. Guys like you don't have the privilege of their word when it comes to these things. You have to make better choices. If you drink, make sure you're careful. This girl could make your life hell from this point, and she's not worth it."

He reached his hand and grasped his shoulder for reassurance. "You've got this. I'm right here with you and I believe you, Son."

JB darted his head from side to side and briskly walked to the front door of the Birch shanty. "Why in the hell would anyone live here?" JB had been there too many times to count.

Tina's house held grief as a sentry at the door of life and provided her with constant reminders of Tim. The gallows of tragedy kept her in the cellar and a difficult existence trapped her in this community. She wanted to leave, but on her terms and when she was ready.

And Melanie was a mystery to most of the kids. She was best friends with Harper Davis, Beth Hillcrest, and the most popular boy's twin sister, Caroline Taylor. But she picked up rumors like lint on a sweater. After years of trying to pick it off, she kept to her circle of friends and boyfriend. Tina taught her to live in the single lane of her life: school, close friends, part time job at Mr. Charlie's and Penni, nothing else.

Carter and JB stood on the tattered steps. "Pretty gross, huh dad?"

Tina opened the creaking chipped door and invited them in. But not before she offered some reassuring words to her daughter. "You can do this, you have to for yourself. I'm here with you. He won't try anything." She patted the supportive gun that was shuttered in her pocket.

Carter walked in behind his dad and thought, *so this is how the margins of society live.* The furniture was well used and the kitchen, dining and living were all one room. No one would call it an open concept by choice. But the place was tidy. A large picture of Tim hung over the couch right above Melanie. Fate twisted a knife in Melanie in unexpected ways. It was as if she was destined to go down the same drain hole as either of her parents. *Funny,* Carter thought, *how could all those rumors be true, she looks just like her dad.* It was haunting how much she looked like her father. Those rumors were one of many that kept Tina in the gallows. It was a nice place for many townspeople to keep her so they would not be reminded of their own outdated stories.

Melanie stayed in the corner of the small living room wrapped in a blanket with her feet snug under her broken body. As soon as Carter looked at her, she began to shake and secured her cover.

Carter felt a pang of anger run through him. He resented the fact that he had to be here. He was no different than any other young man in his class.

Melanie didn't acknowledge them but wiped her face. Clearly, she had been crying and looked like she was suffering from some chronic illness. Carter felt a recurring wave of anger and realized it would be even more difficult once school resumed when he had to continually see her. *She will pay for this and won't have Penni to protect her.*

"Come in and sit down. Would you like a glass of water?" Tina offered.

They both answered no thank you and JB led the charge. "How you doing, Melanie?"

"Okay." She fingered the soft blanket.

"Look, we are all friends here. I'm sorry that things got out of hand. I know the weekend has been tough for you, but I want you to know that Carter and I have come over here to talk this out and make sure you two kids are okay."

Melanie felt like someone punched her in the stomach. It was bad enough that Carter had raped her, but now they were displaying pity. As if someone died in a bad accident and they came bearing a casserole and condolences. Why would she care if Carter was okay? *His welfare is none of her concern, not after what he did,* she thought. She looked to her mother while Tina leaned against the bookshelf spindles that led up to the ceiling. She had her arms crossed over her small frame and low-cut shirt. Her jeans were a bit tight and her feet bare.

JB watched her bright pink toes. In his other life, she thrilled him. He wondered if things would change now that all this happened. He wasn't ready to give her up. *That's the way the poor did things,* he thought, *more from desperation.* He was wasting his time coming over here.

Tina moved close to Melanie, gently stroking her hand and went right after Carter. "Do you have anything you want to say, Carter?"

JB answered, "I think we need to figure out what is best for Melanie and Carter."

Tina stared. "What's best for Melanie is an apology first and foremost and second is a promise that Carter will never do this to another girl."

Carter looked at his dad, seeking permission to speak. After JB acknowledged him, he said, "I thought when you were, you know looking at me when we were playing games that you were flirting and that you wanted me. When you went upstairs, I thought that was an invitation." He looked down at the brown and yellow shag carpet, grossed out by its appearance.

"Flirting? You held your hand over my mouth when you pinned me to the bed. You held your forearm over my chest. I have bruises all over my body. That is not something you get when someone wants you. You're sorry for what?"

"Look we both had been drinking. It was all fun. You kept making eyes at me."

"I don't drink. Your breath was awful from the beer. You kept holding my mouth closed and…" She stopped, swallowed hard, vibrated her head, trying to shake the words out of her mouth. "I'm sure I blacked out." She felt a tear splash down on her hand. "And now how am I supposed to face Penni? My friends, anyone for that matter? You took advantage of me, while I was sick. Why?" Melanie held tight to her tears.

Tina wiped her free hand across her nose. "You hurt my daughter. You really tore her up bad. You don't deserve to even be here. You deserve to be in jail." Anger slivered up her throat.

JB cut everyone off. "Look, No one's going to jail." He bobbed his head like Gomer Pyle solving a case in an atta boy fashion. "I brought Carter here to apologize and put this whole unfortunate incident behind us."

"How could you, Carter? You have known me since first grade. I know we are not the best of friends, but I'm always around. We are in track together. I thought you were Penni's friend?" She struggled. "I know you think my family is trash. I hear what you and all your friends say. Well, we're not. We are people just like you with feelings. And I'm not that kind of girl who sleeps around. I have never done that before and now the horrible memory of my first is with you. And with someone who never loved me," she recoiled.

JB reached his hand onto his son's leg and gave him a nudge. "Umm, I'm sorry," Carter cleared his throat from the whisper of words as a few quiet minutes passed between them.

"Sorry for what?" Melanie begged.

"Look I fucked up. I was drinking. I fucked up, for having sex with you."

"It wasn't sex, it was rape. And it hurt." The words shot out like a cannon in the dark and hung in the air for anybody's guess as to where they would land.

"I want you to say it. I want you to promise me that you will never do anything like this again. Go get help. Go do what you have to, but I never want another girl to feel the way I do. If I ever hear that anything like this happens again, I will report you. I will tell," she threatened.

Carter continued, "I'm sorry. I have never done this before and I will never do it again. I'm sorry I raped you and I promise that I will never do anything like this again." He repeated as tears of anger burned his eyes. *How can my dad put me through this? She's such a bitch.*

"You did this to me, Carter and you walk away, but it will always be with me and I will never be the same. I want you to know just how much you hurt me."

Tina interrupted. "If I ever hear you do this again, I will see to it that you are put in fucking jail. Do you hear me?" She struggled for control.

"Yes ma'am," Carter whispered.

"So now what are you going to do to help us?" Tina shifted.

Stunned, JB burst, "Oh so it's this. You want money?"

"I need you to understand that Melanie cannot work this summer at Mr. Charlie's. She can't go into town and face everyone after this horrible incident. It's all over that damn chat site and before you know it, it will come out that it was her. What is she supposed to do, sit here all day?" She flicked her hand at her wilting daughter.

"What do you want, Tina? We don't want either kid to get in trouble. Think of his future." JB's blood boiled. The very hand that was helping her was now being nipped at. "I won't be blackmailed. Carter apologized, now it's over. This whole thing can have real consequences."

"I was thinking it may be a good idea for her to spend some time away this summer. Get some perspective and come back to finish her senior year. And now you can help us."

JB pulled out his wallet. "How much? I can pay until you're ready to go back to the soda shop?"

Carter looked stunned. "What?"

"Now who's blackmailing who?" Tina started. "I just need some help." She wilted.

"This is all a big misunderstanding, and I will help you out. I can talk to Mr. Charlie."

"No," Melanie cried. "Please don't say a word."

JB gazed down at his fingernails. He needed to come up quick with a plan. "Why don't I send you to some of those fancy running camps for a few weeks and we will pretend you got a scholarship and call it a day. It will give you some time. You know, time to collect yourself and when you get back you can go back to work for the rest of the summer." He shrugged his shoulders. "And Carter here will keep his mouth closed."

He was proud of his solution. If all this did was cost him a few dollars then he wasn't out much. "Well, it's solved. I will find a camp."

"She can't be here this summer. It's too much," Tina said.

"Oh, wait, I have a better idea. I have a friend of a friend whose brother runs a Christian camp in Tennessee. Not too far from home but far enough to give you a break." JB rambled. "Maybe go there. They always need help."

Tina fixed her eyes while he went on and on about how he was going to solve all of their problems. Her body tensed as he continued on about how easy it would be for Melanie to forget what happened. Something this awful, *you never forget*. She hated him for his callousness and the way he dismissed them. Treating them like everyone else did in town. Falling on hard times was not a crime, but the people who kept you there should be jailed. She didn't deserve this. And her daughter certainly didn't. Carter was spoiled and entitled. And JB was cheapening the relationship the two of them had. *What was I thinking ever getting involved with him?* Tina would not let another entitled, rich Oak Grove family get away with this. JB would pay anything to keep it all quiet but to treat her so poorly was inexcusable.

"We can't be bought," Tina said.

JB stared. *You women are all the same. You want sex and when you get it you cry that you didn't.* He turned to his son. "Let's settle this?"

Melanie started again. "You ruined me, Carter. I hope you can live with that for the rest of your life."

Carter was not remorseful, but as his dad coached him earlier he admitted, "I need some fucking help. I promise I'll never do this again. I didn't mean to hurt you, Melanie."

"I cannot face anyone after this. Not now and maybe not ever." She felt her mother's hand on her leg.

"So, I will call the friend. Is that reasonable? That will give everyone some time to cool down and put their lives in perspective."

"Thank you, JB. You understand, you have a daughter," Tina said.

"So, everything is good here right?" JB finished.

"There's one more thing. If any of this gets out, Carter, we will go straight to the police. You will not embarrass my daughter any more than you already have. And I want you to stay as far away from her as possible. Do you understand?"

"Yes." Carter wanted to tackle both of them.

"And another thing," Tina stood up, "If this ruins Melanie's chances for a scholarship, JB, you will be paying for her to go to school." She stopped. "That's all."

JB reached for the door. "Goodnight. I will be in touch with your mom, Melanie."

Tina locked the door and pressed her head into the cool aluminum. "Do you think it was all clear enough?"

Melanie fished her phone out from under her blanket. "Let's see." She pressed play on her cell phone.

"If they don't stick to the agreement, we at least have this." Tina sat beside her.

JB and Carter walked to the car without saying a word. When they got inside JB said, "I'm proud of you, you did a good job in there. I know that wasn't easy. If all I have to do is pay for a summer camp we are in the clear."

"Such bullshit, Dad."

"Just promise me you aren't using those pills I gave you to drug girls. She said she wasn't drinking but passed out. I was wondering what the hell that was about? I gave you Rohypnol and Xanax to help you sleep and with your anxiety."

Carter looked at him, "I would never do that."

"Good, because that could really hurt me."

JB and Carter drove in silence until Carter saw the phone call came through the Bluetooth. Tina's name and number flashed. "What's that about dad? Did she forget to blackmail you out of more money?"

"I don't know son, I'll call her later. I'm not in the mood for her shit anymore."

The dash went black.

Chapter 21

The money was inconsequential to JB, since Melanie would be out of sight. He knew the distraction, and thought it would be good for the girl anyway after the stunt she pulled. It was obvious to him that it was consensual.

Carter would never have to force himself on any girl let alone drug them. She cried wolf after she got exactly what she wanted, Carter. It was probably all catching up to her with the stress of Penni leaving and instability of her own family. *Melanie could really use some help*, JB thought. He would offer Tina some medicines to get her daughter through. He would hate to see her turn to alcohol, just like her father, as a coping mechanism. It all made sense to him.

JB needed to ensure that she would not come back on his son. Carter's future was riding on this next year. He was going to make a verbal commitment to Middle Carolina as soon as the fall, if not this summer. JB liked the leverage Carter carried right now with recruiting.

He especially liked Penni being the scapegoat for the assault. It could only help Carter if he and Doc continued their postings. Cottonmouth nation would never let up that it was a good decision to let Penni go to another program. All he wanted to do was drive the whole family out of town. They could make trouble for him if they started snooping around. *Especially when Melanie comes back from camp*, he thought.

They pulled into the canopy covered drive. The side lights twinkled off the small waterfall. JB looked over at the climbing roses that Rita Faye had planted years ago. A large camellia tree stood proud on the side, and a small cement bench sat close to the base. A statue of a small girl and boy holding hands playing ring around the rosy stood close. He noticed a dragonfly lighting on the statue and could not get the image of Mary Claire Barnes out of his head. His beautiful home was tainted by her memory. He felt a heaviness as his head started to throb.

Carter reached for the door handle. "Not just yet. I want to talk to you. We need to be on the same page with this Melanie thing." JB rubbed his temples.

Carter swallowed. He was sure his dad believed his version of the truth. It was Melanie's problem, not his. He was glad she would be gone for the summer so he wouldn't have to see her at the pool or around town. "Yeah dad, what's up?"

"Promise me you'll keep this quiet. Keep a low profile. Those two women are scorned, and I don't want to hear back from them." JB thought about how he would make this up to Tina. "In one short year you will be rid of Melanie, but for now, you need to lay low. With her being gone this summer it will help the chatter die down but if anyone asks, you don't know a thing. Did anyone see the two of you go in that room?"

"No dad. No one saw me."

"How did she know it was you?" JB was curious.

"When I got in there, she kept calling for Penni. But then I sat by her and she reached for me and well, you know, I thought she wanted to fool around. You know what high school was like dad? She was irritated and asked for something and that's when I gave her a Xanax. I thought it might calm her down." He didn't tell his father about the other pill he had slipped her earlier.

"Carter, you can't hand that stuff out like candy. I prescribe things for my patients. Don't play doctor, Son. You're lucky it was Melanie. This could have had far more serious ramifications if it was not a shanty girl. I know what they need, just like I know you have some anxiety issues and it helps you, but when you went in that room you should have thought. She may have been overheated or something may have not agreed with her," JB paused.

Carter opened the door to a blast of gardenia. "Close the door, I'm not done."

"Stay away from that girl. You need to work hard this summer. You have football, workouts, an advanced math class and now lots of beach time. Do your thing and when you see Melanie this fall, go the other way. Carter, I cannot say this enough. You have a target on your back. You're a good looking, popular athlete. Girls are going to throw themselves at you. You come from a nice home with privilege and money. Stay away from the girls that are desperate. They are looking for a meal ticket." JB paused. "What if she's pregnant? How do you explain that one? Did you use protection?"

Carter shifted his eyes to the tan dashboard. "We can blame Penni."

"That won't work." JB spoke with only love and concern for his son's welfare. "Paternity tests won't blame Penni." JB gave Carter's shoulder a firm grasp. "You don't have the privilege of being sloppy. You are a Taylor and I'm telling you, you have to watch yourself. Here, I filled another prescription of Adderall for you. Before we go in, remember we were at the sporting goods store."

"Thanks. I need these before summer workouts. Glad you reminded me. I was going to say ice cream?"

"Why would we have not invited them? Are you seven?" JB looked at the darkened back windows of the house.

Carter laughed at his dad's lightheartedness. "Okay, the sporting goods store. They both hate that place. I'm starving."

"We just had dinner."

"That was hours ago. I'm trying to bulk up for the fall. I worked out today."

"Okay son."

They walked up the sweet-smelling pathway and up the back steps. The screen door was open and a light gentle breeze blew the fragrant gardenia smell into the kitchen. JB switched on the light and pulled the container of biscuits and chicken out and the fresh green beans.

"Is this enough?"

"Yes sir." Carter felt justified after their meeting. There was no way that girl was coming near him again. It was a mistake.

He opened the cabinet and pulled out two plates while his father put the first container in the microwave. They put the plates on the large island along with their silverware and napkins. Carter grabbed a few sodas. Just when they sat down to eat the back door slammed.

"Hey Rita Faye is that you?" JB shouted.

"Nope, Caroline," she grumbled. She came around the corner and threw her backpack on the bench. "Eating again?"

"Yep." Carter swallowed a big bite of food. "Dad and I went to the sporting goods store for some summer gear," explaining their absence with obvious suspicion.

"Oh, nice." Caroline looked around the kitchen and walked by her father. JB's hand hovered over her shoulder as he gave her a gentle squeeze.

"Are you hungry? Grab a plate there's plenty," JB said.

"Where's your bag?" Caroline stopped.

Carter stopped chewing and pitched himself forward while Caroline moved quietly, waiting for an answer. It was middle school and hormones, it seemed, that made the twins grow apart. The small frail undersized Caroline watched Carter grow rapidly, with only her wit to shield her.

"I didn't say we bought anything. I said we went there for some summer gear. They didn't have what we were looking for." The lies, like crumbs of food, fell easily from his mouth.

"Oh, what were you looking for?" she pressed. "You seem to be in a better mood, Dad. I guess some guy time and sporting goods shopping was just what the doctor ordered." Caroline finished her part in the conversation, but not before casting one last reel.

"Why do you always have to be judge and jury, Caroline?" JB snapped, hoping to divert her inquisition, while Carter extricated himself from the complications of her challenge.

"You think you have your act together going into your senior year, Caroline. Hell, I'm going to be the first one to get a big tub of popcorn and sit back while I watch the train wreck of a show you call your life. Flitting around at Helen's art studio and brooding over your lack of popularity and friends. Have you even thought about what colleges you will apply to?" JB belittled his daughter, hoping his course words would stop her interrogation.

Caroline frowned. She could see the same look in his eye that he had for Rita Faye, disgust. She would never show her cards or her emotions. She was well aware of his relationship with Melanie's mom. She only kept quiet because Melanie was one of her best friends. But to stand there and listen to him took every ounce of strength not to lunge at him and scratch his eyes out.

"What do you mean train wreck?" She continued her feigned, sad look. "I was just hoping there might be something for me. You know how much I love shopping with mom, and I would rather have gone with you guys."

"No, you wouldn't. They don't sell those ugly beads you wear." Carter said as more crumbs fell.

"You're gross, Carter." She knew something was going on.

"Okay, that's enough you two. Come on Caroline, I filled a plate for you."

She sat down opposite her dad without taking a bite. She waited for just the right time to drop her bomb.

"I really wish they had the right cleats I was looking for." Carter continued chewing his falsehood.

"You'll find them," JB answered.

"Ever hear of Amazon?" Caroline was patient.

"Of course, dumb ass."

"Watch your mouth, Son. Don't talk to your sister like that."

Caroline saw her opening. "Speaking of mouths, you guys looked really comfortable in the car outside with the air on. I'm surprised you came in with no air."

Carter glared. "How long were you spying on us?" Carter started to reach his hand across the bar to slap his sister. He had had enough of women's bullshit tonight.

"I was walking up the street when you pulled in. I stopped to chat with Mr. Henry. He was sitting on the front porch enjoying a summer evening. I guess if checking on neighbors a few doors down is spying then, oh no, you caught me." She pushed her food around.

JB turned. "You know your sister is friends with the Middleton's." His tone echoed disappointment. But before he could finish, Carter stood up and threw his biscuit at Caroline's head. "You are such a bitch."

Caroline was unfazed. "No thanks. I don't eat them." She wiped the crumbs off the counter, making a mess all over the chair and floor.

She turned to JB. "So is Carter, Dad. He would do anything to date Harper if his best friend wasn't. Everyone knows that. Speaking of dating, it seems Melanie has disappeared since Penni's party? Harper was just asking me about her." Caroline took a big bite of the salty green beans, and left the plate exactly where JB had put it. She grabbed her backpack and was waiting for Carter to ambush her while she climbed the steps.

She needed to get to Harper's alone. They only had a week before Penni would be leaving and they had to figure out what was going on with Melanie.

Carter finished his food and went upstairs. He turned the corner and went to the other end of the hallway. It was the first week of summer break, and he was going to go over Jack's to hang out. Maybe Sam would be there.

"Finally, a night without Harper." Carter walked in his room and swiped his hand over all his trophies. "Wouldn't Harper love for Sam to have all these." Carter dropped his clothes on the floor and changed into some sweats. He felt dirty after being at Melanie's. *What a shit hole.* He walked in the bathroom, scrubbed his hands, and headed down the steps, but not before he tried Caroline's door again.

114

"Asshole," he whispered.

Caroline heard her door handle click. She knew Carter was trying to get in. No one knew she had a lock installed. "What a safe house?" she whispered, relieved when she heard him run down the steps.

Carter dropped down on the last step,

"Be home by curfew," JB asked. He pulled Carter aside. "This thing is sensitive enough to keep it to yourself. I understand the friendship with your boys and your need a place to confide, but Sam may share it with Harper or Jack may share it with Beth, so keep it quiet," JB cautioned. "In a just few short weeks everything will blow over. Especially with Melanie heading out of town for the summer."

"I know dad." He gave JB a hug and walked out the door.

Caroline stood behind her curtain and watched him pull out of the drive. She tiptoed down the back staircase and watched JB stand in the kitchen, typing away on his cell phone. She wanted things to cool down before she tried to get access to his phone. She would have to settle on his computer first.

JB picked his head up and turned it to the side as Caroline slipped back up a few steps. He headed toward his office. He would take the quiet time in the house to check the chat boards and see if his stirring had ripened the pot. Just before he left the kitchen, Caroline watched her mother walk in. "Hello is anyone home?"

JB rounded the corner. "You're home early."

"I needed to come home. I left some paperwork on the desk in the office." JB flinched. "Any chicken left?" a sliver of light shone when Rita Faye opened the refrigerator. Caroline pressed her slim body against the wall.

"I think Carter finished that."

Rita Faye turned, "Where are they?" She picked up an apple out of the fruit bowl.

"Carter is at Jack's and Caroline is upstairs."

"You want to have a cup of coffee and catch up?" Caroline noted her mom's desperate, tense voice.

"I have some work to do. And could you please ask me before you use my office. Sometimes I have confidential files in there. I wouldn't want you to be tempted to look." He turned.

Rita Faye could smell his strong cologne as it mocked her rejection. Another frayed thread in their relationship. "That's okay." Caroline knew her mom was on the move and may come up the steps. She quickly made her way to her room and sat at her desk.

"Hi," Rita Faye whispered as she opened her daughter's bedroom door.

"Hi mom." Caroline turned; a book propped on her computer.

"I got some new things in at the shop. You want to come down tomorrow and have a look? I ordered several things in your size. It might be fun. Harper was down there Friday and picked up a beautiful dress."

"Yeah, sure mom." Caroline began to feel sorry for her. Her eyes had a black cast and her shoulders hung in defeat.

"I'm tired, Mom. I'll see you tomorrow."

"You feeling, okay?"

"Yes."

"Goodnight." She leaned in and kissed Caroline on the forehead. "I love you and I'm really proud of you. I saw Patsy last week and she went on and on about your sculpture. I would love to come see it."

Caroline considered. "It's got a long way to go."

"Well, when you're ready. I'll see you in the morning."

Rita Faye walked down the long hallway, down the steps, and stood on the back porch while she stared at the trellis that housed her dark blue clematis before pulling her tired body into her car. "I'm done. It's got to be seeing Mr. Henry and Miss Patsy out for an evening walk. They were going so slow, holding hands and I could hardly tell where one finished and the other started they were so close." Her body braced and buckled while she gripped the steering wheel with tears streaming down her face, speaking to no one but herself. "What is the point of staying in this marriage? My family is a mess. I'm a mess." She stopped.

She needed something to hold onto. While tears slid easily, all the weight she carried began to slip from her body. Finally, she released her grip. Her willingness to hang on had come to an end. "It's over."

She wiped her face with an old Burger King napkin that was stuck in the cup holder. She picked up her phone and called Helen. It would surprise even Helen to hear from her, but she told Rita Faye months ago, "Call me anytime, I'm here for you."

"Come on over."

Rita Faye parked her car around the corner and walked her winded and weary body up to the Abernathy's house. She saw an outline on the porch. "I fixed us a cup of tea."

"I'm sorry. I just really needed a friend," Rita Faye said.

Helen grabbed her. "It's going to be okay."

When she was done venting, Helen handed her a few more tissue and guided her to a chair. "I want you to take some deep breaths."

Rita Faye listened carefully and leaned back in the rocking chair.

Helen whispered, "Inhale and hold for just a second and now exhale." She heard the long sigh from her exhalation.

"Now just sit quietly, eyes closed, and rock for few minutes to clear your mind. Don't think about anything. If you want to get a sip of tea, have one. If you want to cry more, go ahead, but no words." Helen stared at the cinnamon color of her tea while a slight light gave Rita Faye her space with the slow darkening sky.

The two women rocked. It had been a long time since Rita Faye sat quietly. She was frantic, always going, always doing everything fast, working, eating, talking. Her body fought the quiet.

Then in the quiet she noticed crickets chirping, and the distant barking of dogs while frogs croaked in unison. A gentle breeze swept across the porch and the harmony quieted her even more. She was safe in her own body.

Helen's soft words interrupted. "When you're ready open your eyes."

Rita Faye fluttered her crusty eyes open as they lightened from the fallen tears.

"Now, talk." Helen leaned in and handed her a cup of tea.

"Where do I begin?" Rita Faye started. "I feel so out of place. But I now know, I need this."

"You have all of that. I'm here. Patsy is too." Helen paused. "And your daughter is longing to talk to you."

"She hates me." Rita Faye felt a widening fissure in her heart.

"She's as confused as most seventeen-year-old young ladies." Helen gave her minute. "She needs you, but go slow with her. She doesn't trust, but she really wants you in her corner." Helen's advice was simple.

"My son hates me. My husband thinks I'm disgusting because of my weight."

"Oh, now let's stop there." Helen moved. "You can't control how others feel. But you can control how bad you feel about yourself."

Rita Faye leaned toward her. "I see the way he looks at me."

"Take care of you. I mean, take care of you. Like now, you called a friend." She paused. "Sure I want you to eat well, I want to see you in the studio. I always have time for you. Take time to spend with the kids. Keep trying. Listen to them even if it is for a quick update about their day. That's the beginning," Helen reflected. "And get off all the pills JB is giving you."

Rita Faye sipped her tea, "You're right. So, what about my marriage?"

"Start with one small thing. How about making a promise to yourself that every day you're going to do something good for you? Take a walk or eat one or two healthy meals a day. Have coffee with a friend." Helen sipped. "And your marriage, well you know exactly what you have to do. But I think once you start taking care of you, you will have clarity."

Rita Faye sat on Helen's words for a minute, "You're right. I have never really taken care of myself. First it was my daddy and my brothers then the frantic fight through college and working and now this business." Rita Faye stopped for a minute, "And my marriage, well it isn't."

"Hire more people to help around your shop and your house. I know you want control. I'm a business owner. But it seems like the harder we hold on, the more control takes us over, not the other way around. And all the women in town you're trying to live up to." Helen had hit a nerve. "Honey, they are more insecure than you. Why do you think they act the way they do? Quit giving them power."

"You're right," she whispered. She had never heard this from anyone before as she felt sadness and relief all at once. The places she was looking for friendships and love were not the places she would ever find them. They were literally in her own back yard.

"Start now." Helen whispered, "Start right now taking care of yourself."

"One last thing?" Rita Faye stopped.

"Yes."

"Thanks for being here for me. I have missed you and Patsy and Anne so much."

Helen smiled through the dark dishwater gray sky. "We never left. Now promise me you will see that doctor and get some help."

Rita Faye walked through the dewy grass, noticing for the first time how wonderful it felt between her sandaled toes. She would shed away the husk of her former self and never look back. She settled in her car and when she checked herself in the mirror, she saw the baskets of clothes in the back seat.

"Dammit, that will have to wait." She headed home.

Chapter 22

JB rustled through mounds of papers on his desk. If Rita Faye was snooping, there was nothing she could find that would cause problems. He opened his laptop and scanned a few entries of Cottonmouth Droppings and decided to post. He pulled his bottom desk drawer open and flipped the wood that hid the secret space. He carefully slipped it open and brought out a second computer. He opened the small laptop and logged on under his trolling name.

He scanned the chat site and found a place to start commenting. A lot had happened since the Lafoe party. There were all kinds of rumors twisting the truth out there and he wanted to make sure they were legitimized with his entries.

Despite the problem with the kids, he was feeling much better. And Penni would pay for Carter's wrongdoings, even if he had to sacrifice the whole family. Doc would make sure he destroyed the boy. He knew exactly how to spin this. And JB would happily help.

Cottonmouth Droppings
Stonewall: Why would we ever let anyone stay in our town who conducts themselves the way Penni has?
Tat Man: Boys will be boys let's not forget our college daze but happens too much.
Hometown Boy: He did it. Damn kid has nothing to lose. She's not pressing charges…He must have threatened her.
Farm Boy: A nice send off for him. I saw the police report. Guilty! He needs to be held accountable.
Stonewall: Doc made a great decision not to put him on the team. I hope his family is happy.

Confederate Fan: How did you see it? If the kid was loyal, he would have committed right away, holding out for something better, we don't like his kind. Taylor better not sign anywhere else.

Farm Boy: Lafoe did it. I was at the party and saw him come down the steps just before the young woman. It was her. Cute high school girl. But she was a real mess.

Stonewall: I was there too and saw the same thing. He took advantage of her. And now has something to hide. She should press charges. IF not get him out and his family.

JB could see Doc posting. He would banter back and forth as he continued to type.

Stonewall: I saw kids drinking too. Glad mine didn't go. The father was hammered. Anyone have pictures? They could be posted right here.

Farm Boy: Too much freedom in that house and that's why their son did what he did.

Tat Man: drugs there?

Farm Boy: There are always drugs. I know the mom works at the hospital. She has an unlimited supply.

Stonewall: Run them out! Get his parents to leave. I agree with you Farm Boy. The mother is a nut and so is the father. Fly the banners just like the signs last fall. That family has done nothing but bring trouble to this community. Look where they live? That house brings evil.

Farm Boy: What kind of people let their kid act that way. Scar on our community. If you get to the wife you get to the family. Let's show anger with our voice. No support. Put up a billboard if we have to.

Football Lifer: Just don't have our standards.

Stonewall: Hopefully they will follow their son. The dad probably encouraged the son to take what he wanted.

He would wait a few minutes until he could get someone to respond.

Farm Boy: Let's make sure they know they are not welcome here.

Stonewall: I'm in. Poison the dog. Run them out. Anyone work at the hospital? We can make it tough on her.

JB was satisfied and signed off. He finished his paperwork and headed up to bed, alone.

Chapter 23

Rita Faye was 12 when she tried makeup for the first time. She was excited that Anne asked her to go with a group of eighth grade girls to the spring dance and with no mother to help her, she would have to take a stab at it by herself. But before she could get out of the house, her brothers berated her. "Whore, color all over your face and look at your chubby body under that tent dress." The words haunted her all too often.

By the time she slipped into the back of Patsy Middleton's Pontiac with a tear-stained face and a veil of disgrace, her makeup was a mess. Anne quickly helped her recover. "Come on now, I can take care of this." She brushed a soft pink color over her cheeks while Patsy steered the car toward the middle school. Rita Faye never attended another dance. And she resented Patsy for loving Anne so much. Since her mother's premature death, her whole family spun like tornados, bearing utter destruction in their path.

Fear niggled at her constantly to work harder. *"But I'm still Rita Faye Jones, the fat girl from the revolting family who was kicked off Main Street."* She unloaded the clothes at the Soap and Suds. *"It's ironic, I'm at the place where all this started."* She dropped coins into the washers and settled her frame against the agitating machine. *"Anne has been a good friend."*

Buying back her grandparent's home on Main Street was her first step many years ago in recreating herself. *"But why did I stop there?"* Detoured feelings about her family kept her in a constant tunnel of embarrassment. She wanted to smash that outdated record. She would never talk to anyone, never speak up. And her marriage got too far down the road for her to turn around and stare down the devil in her home. JB was now at a place where his only responses were, get over it and move on already. He was exactly the same person that her dad and brothers were. He only hid behind it with a shiny education and a respectful title.

"I knew what I wanted my whole life, that should count for something." When she was a child, with her audience of dolls and stuffed animals, she played store for hours. She went shopping in the fields and gathered things to make artful creations out of grass, hay, and flowers. She would weave long strings of yarn left over from her mother's knitting to make necklaces. Her make-believe store offered her a world of ingenuity for what would become her life's work. "I was too blind to see the real support. But that is going to change." The washer shook on the rinse cycle.

Henry Middleton employed Rita Faye at his store when she was in high school. And had been her real support. *Why did I ever turn my back on that family?*

She rented a little apartment in Henry Middleton's student housing, worked hard in school and the store, and took a second job at the Soap and Suds for extra money.

"No man is ever going to want the fat girl, Rita Faye. Watch what you put in your mouth." She could still see a cigarette riding her dad's bottom lip, while he swirled the oily rag over his gun. He would pause to pick the skin on his thumb with his teeth.

She turned and watched the blinking lights caution her they were on the spin cycle. Her memories floated to JB like it was yesterday. There he was standing at the end of a bank of washers reading a book while his clothes agitated. She noticed him right away. He had a likable face but looked a bit drawn and tired as she watched him out of the corner of her eye while she loaded her whites.

JB watched the exchange unfold while he took a break from his medical book.

"Excuse me, ma'am, I need change." Rita Faye sought out the anorexic washing attendant. "Your change machine is not working and I'm almost out of quarters."

"The banks across the street. Sorry lady, I can't help you." Rita Faye watched the stringy, greasy hair sway away from her while she fingered the six quarters in her pocket.

"Ma'am I use to work here. I know you can open the office and give me change." The older lady ignored her.

Rita Faye leaned against the washer. The heat poured in the front door while the large commercial fans spun hot air around the loaded tables of laundry. Her baskets of laundry stood by her clammy hot legs. It was a redneck summer evening in the south. She felt her blood boil when she felt a tap. "Here you need some change?" A long-fingered hand handed her ten quarters.

"Thank you." She patted down her hair.

"You're welcome." JB grinned.

He was the boy of her dreams so many years ago.

Rita Faye leaned against the shaking washer and felt the jiggle of her stomach against the warm metal. "Was," she whispered to the machine, as she watched the memories dance before her. "Maybe it was just each passing year and not stopping to acknowledge the marriage." She felt the clothes finish in the washer and moved the last load to the dryer. As her mind wandered during the transfer, she had an epiphany. Marriage didn't happen, life did. It was work. As she tossed the last sock in the dryer and shut the door, she knew right there, where it all started, that neither one of them did the work. Rita Faye settled on the gulf that finished the divide between them.

All those years, she thought she was being true to the marriage when, in fact, she had been disloyal. Her lack of self-care, her never-ending fight with insecurity was her greatest form of betrayal. She was loyal to all the things that held her back from taking care of herself. She was blinded by her loyalty to people and things that really didn't matter. And the people that suffered the most were not her or JB. They were each other's willing pawns. *I abandoned my children.*

The very place she found the life she always wanted, at that moment, she realized she would lose it all because the most dangerous thing she did was lose herself. This life she created was over. But she had to do something to help her kids. She would start with Caroline since she knew exactly how Caroline felt. JB treated her with the same disgust and disdain.

"How could I have been so blind? Never seeing it." *I didn't want to see it.*

Rita Faye watched the clothes toss in the dryer as she wiped the sweat from her face while the minutes ticked down. *We were perfect for each other. But why in the world do I have to stand here doing laundry at the Soap and Suds when I have a washer and dryer at home?* Abhorrence coursed through her body. *There has to be someone else in his life.* Her mind listed all the women she could think of and finally landed on Tina Birch.

She stopped the dryer and caught a glimpse of herself in the large glass windows. *I have failed everyone around me.* Standing over the folding table, stacking clothes in piles, she realized she chose to turn a blind eye to everything. He was guiding Carter into reckless entitlement.

"He throws darts of advice to me and Caroline all the time." *No more*, she thought as she picked at the warm clothes. "I make excuses for everything. My weight, the kids, my husband's attitude, the house, my position in the community."

Rita Faye loaded the laundry. *Why doesn't he like Henry?* She had her suspicions, but what she didn't know is that the hospital had an ongoing investigation concerning missing medications. Henry Middleton knew exactly what would be exposed when the cotton was all picked and JB was sitting right in the middle of it.

The headline mocked her from the newspaper that sat on her passenger seat. "Grad parties gone Wild." She scanned the article. *It was Penni's house. And the mystery high school runner has to be Melanie. No more excuses.*

It was not up to JB to call her out on what she carried around with her. She knew the weight was hers to control. It was time to face all the demons that haunted their home, and the unrepairable disaster. *My marriage has ended right where it started.* She pulled out of the parking lot.

Chapter 24

"It's only temporary until I can figure this thing out," she kept telling Melanie as they drove the winding mountain roads.

Just when she thought she could get Melanie safely out of town, Penni had come in the Piggly Wiggly and rattled her cage earlier yesterday. Her manager told him she wasn't there. She ducked behind the counter before he saw her. Penni had threatened to break down a door if someone didn't give him an answer. Minutes later Fetu came to recover his son.

"I know you can't talk to Penni, but you need to," Tina told Melanie. "Just tell him you're confused right now. He needs something, anything." Tina stopped.

By the time they hit Tennessee, Melanie admitted, "I'm not sure being with Penni is good for me now."

"Melanie, you need time." Tina could see Penni being pulled out of the store, Fetu towing his large son out like a worn wet dishrag, distraught after begging the manager to forgive him. *More behavior to put on the chat boards and discredit the family.* Tina was exhausted. *The family is playing right into JB's hands.* She knew exactly what it was like to an outsider. But it didn't make it right. Her laser focus now was to help her daughter.

Tina took it upon herself to text Penni late last night and tell him that Melanie had been sick since the party but had great news. She was asked to work a summer camp in Tennessee, last minute, and the money was so good she couldn't pass it up. She would be leaving early in the morning.

"You will see, Melanie, this is all going to work out. You won't be there long, trust me." *Where did I go wrong?* Her mind raced as her car darted down the highway.

*****

126

Melanie stood motionless late Tuesday morning. "I won't contact anyone from Oak Grove, I promise," she repeated, as Tina held her in her arms.

"If my plan is going to work, I need you to trust me and let the whole thing play out." Tina swallowed her indignity and pressed onward. "You will be happy again. I promise." She studied her daughter's eyes, "I will make this right. You need time, Melanie. You can't let this thing beat you. And we will get through this, I promise," she repeated. "You know it's best that we have little contact. In case JB looks at my phone. If you need anything, only a short text. Remember our codes? You will have everything you need soon enough." She gave Melanie a long hug. "I'm going to make it all okay. I promise you." She watched her emotionless daughter in the middle of the cabin.

*****

Tina made the six-hour trek back to Oak Grove. She grabbed her bag and made her way up her crumbling steps. She tossed her keys on the kitchen table, lit a cigarette, and collapsed on the sofa. The house was void of noise. Leaving Melanie was the worst thing she did. She felt every empty place that her daughter once occupied. They had never been apart.

"What am I going to do?" She spoke to no one. "I really could have used your help, Tim." Her eyes were full while a slow steady stream of smoke ran from her nose. "I hate you JB. Look what you did to my beautiful daughter, to me."

Her worst offense after leaving Melanie was lying to Penni. She knew how much he loved Melanie. "I'm ruining this for all of them."

Tina held onto the image of her daughter standing in the dark cabin gripping her small bag, shaking in fear as she longed to catch one last glimpse in the rearview mirror. That image would push her to a place of courage she didn't know she had. Surrounded by tall pines, Mother Nature would not give her any reprieve. That pill she swallowed a few days ago would never pass through her if she didn't get real help.

"You be strong, honey. Don't you break. I've got this. I need you to get up every day. Go for a run. It's such a beautiful lake. You have two weeks, tops." Tina promised. "It's all going to be okay. I will make this okay." She ignored the darkness that clouded Melanie's eyes. She looked past her daughter's face all broken and wounded. It would only be two weeks before her real plan would be set in motion. She just needed Melanie to hold on.

"Just give me some time." She flicked her cigarette in the ash tray and got up. She needed to take a shower before she had to work the late shift.

Chapter 25

Talia stood at the nurse's station reading Becky Jones' chart. The baby was four weeks early but a good size and was thriving. What made Becky so special was the fact that not only did she have her baby early but she survived a horrible car accident which forced the early delivery. She would carry a couple of physical scars on her injured leg, but she would be back to normal in no time. Thank goodness she was wearing a seat belt or she could have sustained horrible head injuries. Instead she would go home with a cast on her arm, a bruised kidney, and a brand-new bundle of joy. A pediatric nurse practitioner, Talia would check in on the baby once they went home.

Becky Jones was a second-grade teacher until now. She was going to stay home. Her husband was part of the football staff at the university and with the travel and long hours he kept, she could not manage. It was their first and the thought of putting him in daycare was not an option, especially with her family a million miles away. Talia completed the notes in her chart as she thought about every young mother she helped. Having a baby was the most exciting and scary time in your life, and Talia wanted every one of her patients to feel good about being a mom.

She was just finishing when she heard a low conversation from the opposite corner of the nurse's station. With her back to the young nurses, they did not see her when they stood around the desk. "Of course, he did it," the young nurse said. "He's leaving, what the hell does he care? They are Muslim, right?"

"They think they can do what they want to do."

"Well if he did, shame on him. I really don't like the family anyway. Kind of weird. Have you read the chat site? Whoa, are there some accusations on there."

The weekend had been long with the incident at the party and the police showing up late in the night to question Penni and the family. But Talia never expected to come to the hospital for rounds and hear such double talk about her son. Her pulse quickened as she felt her heart sink. She never expected to hear this from the women she worked with.

Talia was paralyzed with sadness as she stood and listened to the train wreck that had become her life. She interrupted their dark conversation "Good morning girls." She felt the words quiver from her shaking lips.

Shock filled the Southern politeness slipping from the nurses' faces. "Good morning, Talia. How's our young girl in 423B?" The full figured, blond nurse jumbled.

"Bless her heart she sure took a big hit," the other nurse said. "And to think she was pregnant too."

Talia paused in her isolation fighting indignation that was crawling up her from the bellows of her stomach and feared she had nowhere to hide her disgust. She was deliberate with her words. "She's just fine, girls. She's grateful to be alive. I know she is certainly not finding enjoyment in other people's misfortune." Talia set the chart down on the counter, looked over at the paper, and walked away. The pain was so deep she knew she could never turn back. Her heart ruptured with unforgiveness. Not in Oak Grove. Her life would never be the same here. She wanted to turn around and ask them how they would feel. She could hear faint voices from the three of them as she walked down the long antiseptic hallway.

She refused to meet eyes with anyone and made her way to Dr. Hillcrest's office. She slipped her key in the door after giving it a tap, opened it and kept the light off. She called Fetu. No one else would understand.

"I see their stares, the chatter behind my back. The nurses are saying horrible things about our son. It's bad enough they are all ignoring me but the whispers and the quiet is so loud it's deafening." She complained. "Our son didn't do anything wrong."

"Of course, he didn't. I'm getting it too." She heard fragility in his otherwise confident voice.

"I'm paranoid right? But even the stares."

"Can we talk tonight," Fetu said. "I have a meeting with my dean in a few minutes."

Talia hung up the phone. She sat at Dr. Hillcrest's desk for a minute to collect herself. She had to think of her patients and what was really important. She headed back to stop at the grocery store and then headed home. When she pulled in the drive there was a sign in the yard with a huge pile of dog shit underneath that said, "Go home, rapist. We don't want your kind." She pulled in the garage, closed the door, and pounded her steering wheel in anger. It had been a horrible day, and now this. She rushed out front and pulled up the sign, fearing Penni had already seen it. *He only has less than a week.*

Fetu walked in a few minutes after she had the groceries in the house, and when she saw him, she exploded. "I can't do this." The words oozed like festered wounds. "Who would do such a thing? Who is making this so awful?" She ranted. Talia kept repeating herself. "He's a good boy, Fetu he's a good boy."

"He's a good boy, Talia." Fetu held her for a long time.

"I'm leaving with him. I can't stay here, Fetu. I won't stay."

He pulled her away. "Let me think. You can't leave me."

"Yes, I can," she whispered.

Fetu knew if she read the chat board, she would pack up tonight and go. He could not let his family endure this.

"I only have one year left on my contract." He settled her down.

"I won't stay here. I'm scared," she whispered. "There was a sign on the front yard and a big pile of dog shit right next to it. Who is so horrible to do a thing like this?"

"What? What did the sign say?"

"Go home rap...." She could not finish uttering the ugly word; it made her mouth dirty.

Fetu shook his head trying to stay calm. He could not have his wife and son both upset. He already had pulled Penni out of the Piggly Wiggly yesterday after he made a scene.

"I promise, Talia. I will talk to my dean. But I will not let you go away with regrets." He felt Talia's body press against his large frame.

"Anything we had here has been tarnished now." She felt like she was looking in dirty dish water for her sponge. The water was all brown and gray and muddled as she cried into her hands, seeing the black from her mascara press onto her husband's white starched shirt. She smeared the light lipstick form from her bottom lip. "I have never been treated so horribly in all my life."

"You are my beautiful wife and I love you. We will get through this."

"I'm leaving." She was already packing in her mind. "And you won't change my mind."

Chapter 26

With his bags packed, Penni would be leaving for Seattle on Sunday. Summer school started that week, along with workouts.

Fetu would not leave his side after the grocery store incident. He was embarrassed for his son. *A young man in love,* he thought. He would have done the same thing back in his day. Fetu was relieved that Tina texted him to come quickly to aid Penni. He could have been arrested. And when he arrived, Tina was nowhere to be found. Her last text: *We will talk soon.* Fetu did not share that with Penni.

He could not understand any of this. Tomorrow was not soon enough to get him out of town. Penni would learn of his parents' departure long after they themselves were gone. Fetu had met with the dean of his department along with the chancellor and after much deliberation decided it was for the best. Fetu called his old department head at Stanford, and they were thrilled to have him back.

But the pain they both felt in one short week was unbearable. The chat boards flowed toxic bile against the family, adding to an already raging condition. And with Melanie's name circulating as the victim, it only made it that much worse. With all the confusion, Fetu took it upon himself to invite a few of Penni's friends over for a goodbye cookout. But at this moment he was second guessing his surprise.

Fetu sat at the table listening to his son go on and on while distracted chatter ran in his head. Nothing was lining up. Melanie's disappearance, the rancor from the community and the perpetuating chatter on Cottonmouth Droppings where two names seemed to post the most.

"I don't understand why the police have not done anything else?" Penni complained.

"If it was such a horrible crime, they should not stop trying to figure out who did it. I will give them a vile of blood to test."

"I know the accusations are just terrible." Fetu wanted him to stop but slipped with the indictment. His unassuming family had been pulled through the mud. He had to stay calm.

"I'm not giving up on this." He held his large hand up to his head. "No one seems to know what really happened to Melanie. Her mom texted me telling me she wanted to make a clean break and decided to go off to a camp for the summer. Can you believe that?" he questioned.

Talia walked over. "I don't understand any of this. At one point we are having a great time celebrating and now," she motioned over to all his things, "now we are sending you off to what should be the most exciting time of your life and here you are so upset. I'm so sorry." She rubbed her son's large shoulder.

Penni grabbed his mom's hand and looked out the long bank of windows. "I think I should stay here."

"Wanting to stay and take responsibility for what is not yours to take is not an option." Talia shook her head at the oddity. "You must go and make your life." They both watched a dragonfly light on the rocky waterfall in the pool.

There was no mistaking that the tragedy that had befallen their family was one that seemed so disturbing and unfair that they were locked in confusion. If they fought back, they would draw more attention to an already muddying situation.

"How could something so horrible happen in our home and how in the world could a community accuse you of such an awful act? And who in the world would do such a thing to her in the first place?" Talia continued.

"It would be so out of character for you both. You are two hard working young people who care about each other."

"This is a witch hunt." Talia slammed her hand against the glass.

"I'm not sure I can leave like this, Mom. With all the chat board stuff. And Melanie leaving me. Do you think Coach Winters would take me? That way, when Melanie comes home, I will be here for her," he rambled.

"Calm down," Fetu said.

"This community is nothing but rotten. Look what they have done to your son. Look what they have done to Melanie. Look what they did to Tina when Tim died so many years ago. They are like rabid animals when they see a weakness," Talia said.

Fetu stopped her. "We cannot let them win."

"Face it, Mom, we have been targeted since we got here. I can only think of one person who hates me enough, Doc Winters." He looked at both of them.

"I cannot fathom any college coach doing this to any young man. There has to be more."

Talia held her tongue while all the thoughts of sabotage ran through her head. She knew her son had a difficult time and the recruiting process was not easy. It should have been exciting but took a very ugly turn with Doc Winters. He made it crystal clear that he was none too happy that Penni would be leaving the area to play college football. Doc shot straight for Penni's back the minute he did not sign with Middle Carolina University.

Fetu thought about the chat site and the two repeated names, Stonewall and Farm Boy. *I will figure it out.* But first he had to get Penni out of town.

Talia was relieved she had taken the rest of the week off to help Penni get organized. After long late-night conversations, she and Fetu decided that they would go as well.

Fetu knew things did not work in the equation. "Penni," he paused. "This has been a terrible time for our family. It feels like an eternity. But I will not let you give up on your dream. I will not let you quit something that you have worked for. I know you feel betrayed. But you need to know two things. Melanie will be okay. And you will too. You can't stay here. This town, these people they have hurt you and Melanie. I will never question your feelings for her."

Talia reached over and grabbed Fetu's hand.

"I met your mother when I was younger than you and we have loved each other well for many years, but Penni," Fetu struggled to finish. "You have to go. You have to move on and fight hard for what will help you and Melanie for your future. One day you will know but for now," he stopped to contain himself, "For now, you must go and work hard." He watched his son sit up a little taller with a renewed promise.

"You're right, Dad. I can't go on like this. I have to fight. But how can I fight for her when I won't be here?"

"There is always a way," Fetu whispered.

Talia's face was flushed with anger. She had watched her son in one short week go from an excited young man to a broken downtrodden rubble. "We will be there to help you," she whispered.

Penni looked up at his mom as she let the words fall from her mouth. "What?"

Talia started. "We are leaving."

Fetu stopped her. "As soon as you get settled, your mother and I will come see you."

Talia's thoughts tangled around her rational thinking. *This place is soiled. My husband has set up the facility and finished his work here. He understands that family is far more important than career.*

"Dad, are you losing everything because of me?" Penni folded his large hands inside each other and gripped hard. Both parents could see the anger pulse through his arms as they stood on either side of him.

Talia let go of her son and reached up and pulled a strand of her gray hair away.

"We are not giving up any of our dreams. You are our dream. Your dad came here and did a great job at getting the facility started that will be here for a long time to help with research and save lives. You don't worry about us. All this mess will soon pass and the community will find something else to talk about." She kissed her son's head.

"Your mother and I are going to make a trip across the country to the Grand Canyon and come see you. We are excited to see you play ball. And watch you make something of yourself. You will see son, it will all work out." Fetu was relieved when the doorbell rang.

Penni's friends gathered on the large front porch. Harper was holding a box of her grandmother's famous fudge. "She put mint in it from her garden just for you."

Caroline was holding a small clay statue. "You know you love it."

Beth had several huge bags of chips and some sodas. Sam and Jack gave their friend a huge hug.

"Hope we aren't interrupting anything?" Tommy walked in behind the rest of the kids.

"Come on in." Penni led them to the kitchen. "Look who's here."

Fetu was pulling out snacks. "I know how all you kids eat. I have potato chips." He winked at Sam. "This is a celebration."

"Let's get some food out," Talia said. The kids headed outside by the pool while Talia and Fetu prepared to grill. "This is so good for our son to have his friends come by." Fetu smiled.

It was hours before they came out of the pool area, eating and chatting.

The kids sat out back when Fetu walked out front to put a few more things in the car. When he turned around, he noticed a shadow in the front yard. There in black and white stood several signs: "Go home rapist" and "A scar on the community." Exactly what Farm Boy had said on the chat site.

"Who in the hell are you Farm Boy?" Fetu pulled up the signs and stuffed them in the trash can, folding them under a bag of garbage.

He walked into the back yard. "Thank you all so much for making this a great day." The kids were in the pool splashing around. The surprise was perfect. He was hoping it would be memories like these that Talia would hold onto. Now that his family was distracted, he knew calling on Henry was the smartest thing he could do. Leaving Oak Grove would ensure his family's safety and that was the best decision he had made.

Chapter 27

"I hate to see you go." Dr. Hillcrest finished and gave Talia a hug, "I know this is terribly hard for all of you, but I also know that wherever you guys are going you will be a great asset to the community, just like you were here. Who can I rely on to go the extra mile for our patients and their families? You have given tirelessly to the Ronald McDonald house and made sure every child in the hospital at Christmas receives a toy. What am I going to do without you?"

"Thank you, Dr. Hillcrest. I'm so sorry."

"I'm embarrassed by the behavior of the people in this community. In all my years of living in Oak Grove, I never thought people were capable of this."

An overwhelming sadness swept over him.

"Beth is going to miss Penni so much and now I will be sad to have both you and Fetu leaving. You keep in touch. And let me know how your boy is doing. I expect great things out of him." He stopped to collect himself. "I will send your things when and where you tell me to. Remember, call in sick." He rubbed her arm and gave her a slight smile.

Talia had grown close to the lovable pediatrician. *There are some good people here.* She only wished they had a louder voice than the bad ones. She turned the corner and walked back to her office and found a note lying on her desk. There's a package for you to pick up at the Piggly Wiggly by 7 p.m. tonight.

Talia looked at the scribble. "Amy, do you know who left this on my desk?"

"Yes, I did."

"Who called?"

"It was someone at the store. They said you had a package delivered there. Probably some Amazon delivery mistake."

Talia looked at the note, afraid of what she may find in the mysterious package despite the store being an Amazon pick up center. "Did you recognize the voice?"

"No, sounded like some kid."

"Thanks, Amy. See you later." Talia gazed at the young sweet receptionist, knowing she would never see her again.

"You okay?" Amy asked.

"Yea, I'm good. Just tired." She walked back to her office, picked up her bag and purse, and walked to her car, bracing herself for any nasty notes on her windshield.

She was so paranoid she was hoping that this was not some prank or mean-spirited joke from yet another community member reminding them to get out of town.

She pulled up to the curb and sighed. "I hope this is nothing." She opened the car door and as soon as she walked in, she saw Tina Birch standing at the customer service desk. "I got this note today that said I have a package here." Talia was polite.

"Oh yes," Tina reached under the counter and pulled out a medium sized box.

"Do you know what this is?"

Tina looked around. There was a line at aisle three because the bag boy was slow, but other than that there were no real emergencies. She leaned close to Talia, "Yes I do."

"What?" She whispered, mimicking Tina.

"It's nothing. I needed you to come in here and I could not think of any other way to get you here. I was afraid to text you."

Talia started but Tina interrupted, "Of course I can grab a quick cup of coffee."

Talia was confused. "Coffee what?"

"I haven't seen you in a while. I know it's been tough. When does Penni leave?" She didn't give her time to answer. "Melanie misses him so much but had such a great opportunity. I can go get a cup of coffee now."

Tina grabbed her purse and walked out the door, hoping Talia would follow.

Talia followed Tina down the strip mall to a small sandwich shop. Tina thought it would look bad if they were sitting in a car, so she felt like the best place to see her would be out in the open. Just two women whose kids had been dating for years, having a cup of coffee. If JB questioned her, she would tell him Talia reached out to her.

It was 4 p.m. and no one was in the shop for lunch or dinner, only a few teenagers working the counter and a couple in the far corner with their eyes glued to their phones.

Tina ordered and the women walked over to a corner away from the working young people.

"I have a lot to cover in a short amount of time. I needed a reason to get you in the store, and, well I couldn't think of anything else." She took a sip of her coffee. "First of all, my daughter was hurt at your house and I know it was not your son. I know he would never do anything like that." She sat on her words, trying to read Talia's face as her eyes softened and grew milky.

Talia gasped, "Oh my." She felt her bottom lip ride her teeth. "He would never hurt her. My son loves your daughter very much. I just wish the community could know this."

"They can never know." Tina felt her blood boil. "They will destroy my daughter if they know who did it."

Talia looked at Tina and realized the situation was far more serious than she could ever imagine. "What do you mean, destroy her?"

Tina said, "I know Penni cares about Melanie. But listen, we need to work fast. Melanie is at a camp for now. But, she's a real mess. I know Penni is, too. I'm afraid I have not advised her well but," Tina stopped. "I don't know exactly how to help our kids, but I'm hoping we can figure this thing out together."

"I'm listening." Talia waited to hear her out. *How could a woman send her daughter away so easily*, she thought, *And in her state?*

"Melanie can't stay at that camp," she paused, "and the person who sent her there cannot know she left. She is about as equipped to be a counselor this summer as I am. Especially with the…" Tina stopped. "I just need to get her out of there." Her words trailed. "Please tell Penni she is not angry. She's so ashamed."

Talia felt a darkness come over her and leaned forward. "She has nothing to be ashamed of. She was raped." Talia rushed the ugly word off her tongue.

"I'm so worried about her. I just don't know what to do, but I can't do too much because…" She stopped.

The warm, stale air sat heavy between the two women, despite the soothing smells of fresh baked goods and welcoming coffee.

Talia was anxious. She wanted to run out and rescue both Melanie and Penni. She leaned in, "Because I know who has something on you and he is holding your feet to the fire."

Tina gulped. "How do you know?"

"I have known about the someone you have been involved with for a long time. I didn't want to believe it. He is supposed to be an upstanding person in this community. And now, after everything he and his friends have put us through, not just this week but this past year, well, it is all making sense to me. I can only imagine how trapped you must feel. I suspected it was Melanie. Only I could not figure out who. But I can guess." Talia stopped.

"I can't tell you. But please promise me you will tell Penni everything will be okay," Tina pleaded.

Talia fingered the handle on her coffee cup. She needed a minute. She looked over Tina's head at the graying sky, expecting it to open up any minute with a late afternoon storm. She lowered her gaze.

"For now, I won't think about the monster who did this to our sweet Melanie but promise me one thing?"

"What's that?"

"Promise me you will let Fetu and me help her. We will get Melanie on our way out west. And promise me you won't interfere with the intense counseling she needs to get her through this horrible situation. I know it's been a tough go for you both, and I don't fault you. You have raised an amazing young woman. But the relationship you're carrying on with has clouded your judgment and made it more difficult for your daughter."

"You're leaving?"

"Yes and no one can know just yet," Talia implored.

Tina held her cup and watched the mocha brown coffee, "I promise to keep it to myself. And I intend to take care of the mess I made."

"No, you haven't. You have been taken advantage of," Talia said. "You have let the wrong people help you. People who truly care about you don't expect," she swallowed, "don't expect what that man does in return."

Tina grabbed Talia's hand, "I don't know what to do? I can't sleep, I can't talk to her and…" Tina stopped when she felt Talia's hand slide over hers.

"We will make a plan."

"Melanie won't press charges. She's afraid. I'm afraid," Tina whispered. "And she's convinced that Penni hates her and never wants to see her again."

"You let me worry about my son. It's nothing Fetu and I can't handle. But first, we have to get Melanie. She needs professional help now. Not some camp job that will only bury the trauma she endured. Let's get a plan together to get her out of there and somewhere that is good for her."

Tina said, "I do have some ideas." She looked around the shop. "But I will have to be very careful."

The two women leaned in and whispered. "So, limited texts." Talia promised. "The codes we came up with will work when we need to talk."

Tina pulled out her phone. "I will change your contact's name so if someone is snooping, they will think it's…Do you have any ideas?"

"Yes, change it to Piggly Wiggly. That way he will think it's your work. I will share all of this with Fetu. I know he will do everything to help Melanie."

Tina gave Talia a big hug. "You are a trusted friend. I just regret that I never gave you a chance." Tina felt a huge burden of guilt. "But now, I know I was wrong, I trust you implicitly."

Chapter 28

Fetu strolled around the old Barnes estate. "Such a beautiful home."

The gardens, the pool with its rock waterfall, were perfect. Except for the stain left on the house by the continued dark cloud that held steady from the death of Mary Claire Barnes. Fetu knew the tragedy that struck the family had now struck his. *It has to be this house.* He thought about the young girl that once lived here. *It must have been magical for her.* He watched the waterfall. *Until she died.* He could not help but think how ironic it was that the family had a beautiful pool in the back yard and the young girl died of drowning.

"What an incredible gift for the university to come from such tragedy. Such a shame." He longed to dismiss the gnawing in his mind.

Fetu ran his hand along the iron chair. "I wonder what really happened to her? And now with the heartbreak of my own family. How could a community be so cruel?" He had read about her death and the toll the community put on the family. "Blame is laid all around like a mighty fortress and impossible to break, but it must be this house."

He looked over at the rock wall and watched a dragonfly dance across the sparkling water. "We have had some good times here. I will remember those."

He fought for happy memories but was reminded once again of Mary Claire when he turned to walk in the house and saw the small handprints cast in the cement when the family built the house. Her initials were scratched just below.

It was the lies, the shunning, the painful thoughts that seemed to take over. Fetu knew the hurt was temporary, but the damage permanent. He knew his son would never have hurt Melanie. He knew the love those two had for each other and he could not understand how things got so bad so fast. Fetu and Talia loved Melanie like she was their own daughter. Tina had some challenges but she was strict with Melanie and parented her well. It was her other life that Fetu questioned. "Why would she have anything to do with JB Taylor? With

Caroline and Melanie being good friends, wouldn't that be enough to make her stay away? There had to be more."

He walked into the house, and ran his hand along the gallery of photographs that stood on the hall table. Penni's senior football picture, and the one from his senior portraits were off to the side. But it was the one Fetu picked up that gave him pause, Penni and Melanie locked in an embrace at senior prom. It was not your standard prom picture. Caroline had taken a picture of the two of them outside at Patsy's in her garden. They were not posing like the rest of the kids but off to the side, holding hands. Penni was smiling at Melanie and she had her head slightly tilted up at him. Fetu knew exactly how they felt about each other from the picture. There was no one else in their world at that moment, even though they were surrounded by five other couples.

Sadness drained down onto the frame. The whole town hurt him his wife and son.

"Why are you not speaking to my son? I know it had to be you that was hurt in this house."

It's the secret that Fetu held that convinced him that Tina was just a victim of her circumstances. Fetu was picking Talia up from work one late night and watched Dr. Taylor and Tina locked in an embrace and a long kiss behind his car parked off in a distant hospital parking lot. They were not hugging as friends, and it was then that he realized Melanie's home life was as compromising to her as it was for her mother. He would caution Penni to handle Melanie with real care. By the time Melanie entered her junior year and Penni his senior year, Fetu realized Melanie was so much more than her mother.

If you are destined to be together it will work. Fetu set the picture down while he remembered that he would never speak a word of Tina's affair to anyone, including Talia. He felt his chest heave. He knew he had made a mistake.

"Hello Fetu." Talia threw her keys on the table.

"You might want to put those in your purse. The movers will pack them with everything else and we may never find them." He tried to make light of their current circumstances. "They will be here day after tomorrow," Fetu said. "And I may not get to this table then. I'm happy no one knows we're leaving.

But I'm sad we will be leaving this way." They held each other with the picture of the two kids between them.

"It's unfinished business, Fetu and I know I will have to deal with this sometime," she whispered into the soft hairs on his neck. "But right now, I have to talk to you."

He held her away and gazed into her eyes, "What's going on?" Fetu was hopeful that Talia was softening despite the chatter continuing to grow in Penni's absence.

"It's a sad day for the university to have a facility of this caliber and so promising to the region. But to lose someone as renowned as you are is a huge scar on the university," Talia said.

"I think you're partial, my darling."

"I don't. When I met with Dr. Hillcrest today, he was genuinely upset about the loss the community would have from the both of us leaving. In some way I felt vindicated." Fetu knew how only a few people spoiled it for her. He led Talia into the kitchen.

"Do you want a drink?"

"Coffee, please." She settled herself on a stool. "Tina Birch and I met today."

Fetu stopped. "What? Why?"

"Melanie was the one that was hurt at the party, but she will not give up the boy's name. Tina is devastated." Talia slammed the bomb to the floor without any warning of detonation.

"So, where is she? What is going to happen?"

"She will not press charges. She said she's afraid."

"Oh, that poor girl." Fetu sat down across from his wife.

"We are going to get her." Talia stirred her coffee.

"Where is she?"

"She's at a camp in Tennessee. She cannot be off at some damn camp and not get the proper help she needs. We have to get her," she repeated.

"Summer camp?" Fetu was stunned.

"Tina has assured me that she will do whatever it takes to make her daughter better. But her hands are tied."

"What do you mean, her hands are tied?" Fetu's mind raced with questions.

Talia stirred. "We are going to pick Melanie up on our way out west. Oh, Fetu we cannot tell anyone. We must help her. I know Penni will support her.

But we have to wait to tell him. Tina will take care of things on this end. Do whatever it takes to not let…" Talia stopped.

"To not let JB know." Fetu finished her sentence.

"How do you know?" Talia screeched.

"I saw them, long ago, in let's just say a place that they should not have been. But my question is, why would JB care?"

"Tina would not say anything else. She's upset, Fetu. I really think that woman has been a victim too." Talia put her head on Fetu's shoulder. "We have to help our Melanie."

Fetu held his wife close. "I will take care of everything."

"And I think I know who did this to Melanie," Talia whispered.

"I do too, and that is why she will not talk. Should we stay here?"

"No, I want to go home. But I will not leave that young woman behind. JB Taylor is behind all of this and I wouldn't be surprised if Coach Winters is, too. We can get her help in Washington, not here. I don't trust anyone," Talia said.

"I trust Henry. I wasn't going to tell you because you have been so upset, but I'm meeting with him." Fetu held her hand. "It's all about this."

"Tina asked that I contact him. This is bigger than we can imagine. I'm just so sad for Melanie," Talia said. "I think you should be the only contact to Henry."

"It's going to be okay." Fetu pulled her back in.

While they embraced, a bright light shone by the back door and an image of a young girl. "Fetu turn around, did you see that?"

"Do I see what?" he turned.

The back door was dark.

Chapter 29

Fetu parked under the carport at the Middleton's house away from any roaming eyes. He unclicked his seat belt and stared at the deep blue and white clematis crawling up the side lattice. A dragonfly lighted on the soft green leaves. "*I will miss you my friend.*" He felt such comfort when he came and visited with Henry and Patsy while he spoke the soft words.

But today was about business. They were trying to be as discreet as possible, and with all the chatter on Cottonmouth Droppings, he refused to give anyone anything to say. He wanted to leave no stone unturned when it came to Melanie's whereabouts and the challenges that lay ahead for him and his family.

Fetu gave the door a light tap. Miss Clara was there in an instant and gave him a strong hug. "My goodness your family has been through it."

"They have, Clara. How are you doing? How's that new grand baby?"

Clara lit up. "She is fat and sassy. She only cries when she's hungry. I like a fat baby. Don't you?"

Fetu was reminded of Penni. "Yes, I do. They are most fun."

"Mr. Henry is back in his office. I hope you can get past Miss Patsy. You know how she is. She loves your family and will talk you to death about Penni. Oh, that woman loves him. Do you know he stopped by here the other night just to see her?" She chatted while Fetu followed her through the grand old home. Before he reached Henry's office, Patsy saw him. "Fetu, is that you?"

"Yes ma'am." He rounded the corner and watched Clara's face smirk and shoulder lift, signaling "I told you so."

"Come on in here. How's Penni doing? How's Talia? I sure miss seeing that fine young man." She beamed.

"We miss him too. He's well. The first few days are behind him, and he says it's hard but good."

"I bet it is. I want to hear everything about him once the season starts. I would like to think I can get well enough to make a trip out there." She sniffled.

"Well, I certainly will let you know. How are you feeling these days?"

"I'm much better. Henry is keeping tabs on me so I can't get away with too much, but at least I can get outside in the gardens in the early morning. You know Harper will be 18 in October and the big celebration is just a few months away."

"Yes, I've heard. It will be a wonderful time for all of you." He felt an overwhelming sadness leaving them. He hoped Talia could appreciate their friendship someday. It was as if her capacity to love anything about their life here had been turned off like a water spigot. She lost any of the feelings toward people like the Middletons that poured their soul in the community.

"How's Talia?" Patsy asked again as if reading his mind. "I know this has been a terrible time for her."

"She's been better." Fetu could not finish.

"I have called but have not heard back from her. I'm worried. Please tell her I'm here for her."

Fetu gave Patsy a gentle hug. "I needed to hear that. You and Henry are very special people."

"Come on Mr. Lafoe, Mr. Henry is waiting for you. You don't want to keep him." Miss Clara gently stopped Patsy.

"See you later." He waved his hand. He followed Clara to the office. "Good evening, Henry."

"Good evening, Fetu." Henry turned around in his chair to greet his friend. "Thank you, Clara. Can you bring us some coffee?"

"Yes sir." She winked. "Mr. Fetu got to see Miss Patsy."

"Thank you, Clara."

Henry gestured for him to sit down. But before he got comfortable, he handed him a piece of paper. "I have friends in powerful places."

Fetu looked at the address. "She's at a camp in Tennessee. It's called Ridgeview. I'm not sure why she is there other than I heard it was a last-minute summer job that pays well. I know for a fact it does not. Those camps are strictly donation based and are supported by the churches that send the kids to them." Henry cleared his throat while Miss Clara put down the coffee and a plate of warm cookies. "Thank you, Clara."

He watched as she closed the door. "And here's how I know. Patsy and I sponsor several kids from here to attend those camps." Henry picked up a cup of coffee and handed it to Fetu. "I'm not sure what's going on, but I have my suspicions. I've heard she's having a tough time. Heard the counselors are concerned she will not be able to lead anyone when the kids come next week."

"Talia met with Tina today. She gave her the same information. You know it was Melanie that was hurt at our house. Henry, this thing is bigger than we can imagine. I cannot thank you enough for getting this for me. I'm especially worried about Tina. And what about Melanie when she comes back here?"

"Tina left a message this evening too. She sounded really upset. Said we needed to talk. It's JB, I'm sure." Henry did not hold back. "I will keep an eye on Melanie when she comes back. She's here all the time with Harper."

"I'm afraid Tina is in way too deep with JB, and he is holding something over her head."

"I will see what I can find out from Tina and see what I can do."

"I cannot let that young girl sit there and suffer. Talia said it was a hasty decision and Tina did not know what else to do. It was JB who offered."

"Why?" Henry looked stunned. "Which means there is a reason he wanted her to leave. Which can only mean that the young man that hurt her is..." Henry stopped. "That damn man has to be stopped. I can't wait until this hospital investigation is wrapped up. I know it's him that's stealing medicines. At what cost?" Henry sipped his coffee.

"So, if she was forced to send her away by JB that can only mean one thing." Henry repeated.

"I'm thinking exactly the same thing. Carter Taylor assaulted our Melanie." Fetu gnawed his lip.

"And JB wants to take any attention away from his son and is willing to sacrifice both those women to cover it up."

"And Doc Winters will do anything to help because he wants Carter on his team." Fetu stopped.

"And what better person to destroy than Penni? The kid who betrayed Doc." Henry sat back. "When are you getting her?"

"We're picking her up tomorrow. Talia was on the phone all afternoon scheduling a rape crisis counselor. I just don't know what to expect when we see her." Fetu grasped the paper. "Tina said it was the only option she could think of. Melanie is so afraid. And she needed insurance," Fetu said.

"I think the most important thing is to help Melanie right now. Tina said she can handle JB," Fetu whispered his name, "on this end. But I'm worried about her. And how in the world is he not going to find out that we picked up Melanie?" Fetu said. "Will you just keep an eye on Tina? She and Talia have a plan. And, so do I regarding Doc. But this is all too much for her."

"Robyn, the camp leader, will help me with a story. And I can take care of Tina. That girl means something to me. You know she worked for me down at Middletons? She left when she had Melanie. She had a lot on her plate when Tim died." Henry felt a surge of anger. "Thanks for filing the report to the NCAA. The investigation at the hospital should be wrapping up by the end of the summer. Both of these men will soon realize that they can no longer take advantage of this community."

"I feel so bad leaving you with all of this mess. It seems that taking care of Melanie will be the easy part."

"I will take great pleasure in making sure JB and Doc get their due."

Fetu leaned in. "Henry we are forgetting one thing."

"What's that?"

"Caroline is in the middle of all of this. She's good friends with these girls, and if this is her brother it could destroy her."

Henry watched his old grandfather clock tick feeling settled by the rhythm. "I will make sure Caroline and her mother are not in the middle of this. It will be hard enough on them if it is Carter."

"Thank you for overseeing our things. With Wade looking after us, we know there will be very little attention."

"Fetu, can I change your mind? You know I would change all of this if I could. Penni is going to be okay, and I know Melanie will be better once she sees you and Talia. I will call Robyn tonight and let her know you will be coming and will make sure that the three of you can have all the privacy you need. She will keep all this to herself. I have done a lot for that camp."

"Thank you, dear friend. My wife, I'm afraid is not willing to stay. The signs in the yard, her work. She will never feel the same way about this place. She," he stammered, "she is not a person who can forget."

"I don't know who would," Henry boiled.

"You have been a good friend to me and my family. I thank you." He stood up and extended his hand.

Henry grabbed Fetu. "You are a dear friend. You take care of your family and we will talk soon." Henry felt a tear slide down his weathered face. Goodbyes seemed to get harder and harder.

*****

Fetu and Talia sat in the driveway of the Barnes estate early the next morning with a full car and empty hearts. "The flowers and gardens are certainly beautiful," Talia said.

"It will be a long trip to Tennessee." Fetu reached for her hand. "We had some good times here, Talia. You will see. We will have many more."

Talia was silent. She had grown quiet since her meeting with Tina. Nothing had hurt her quite like the deafening silence from the town. "I'm afraid to feel. Afraid to see Melanie. Afraid of what the future holds for our son." She leaned into Fetu. "But we will have good times again." She noticed a small shadow fill the front door.

Cottonmouth Droppings

Stonewall: Rumors have it that we have been successful. The Lafoes are out of here.

Hometown Boy: Saw a moving truck at their house. Bye Bye rapist. Good riddance.

Confederate Fan: Leaving in the middle of the night. And no goodbyes. They have something to hide. Snake doctor was fired. Should have been. Where do they find these people?

Turncoat: They should only hire local too. No one wants fresh and innovative ideas in this shit hole.

Foxy: I like the family. They were good people.

Stonewall: Guilty! His wife probably under investigation at the hospital too.

Turncoat: Oh yes, I'm sure she was taking meds illegally and giving them to all the little kids she was taking care of. It would seem it would be easier for a doctor to do that that has access like the hospitalist job.

Stonewall: Who are you, Turncoat? I have not seen you on this site before.

Turncoat: I'm a good friend. Go Cottonmouths!

Tat man: Any news on Howard and the O Line. That kid is awesome.

Farm Boy: GUILTY. No one like them should be a part of this community.
OUTSIDERS

Stonewall: Were the charges dropped against our two linemen?

Beach Blanket Bobby: Fetu and his wife did a lot for this community. Leave them alone.

Tat Man: Trumped up charges. Let's hope whoever did this to the young lady doesn't hurt anyone else here. If it happens again, I don't think it was Penni.

Stonewall: Should have been looking at Penni, not two college players who did nothing. And it won't happen again. The problem is gone!

Hometown boy: They will take care of them, heard it from a good source charges dropped.

Tat Man: I hope we can get Taylor to stay in town. We need some speed on this team. That boy can run.

Stonewall: He's the real deal. A good kid, unlike Penni.

Tat Man: University needs to give back the haunted Barnes house. Too much money and too much bad luck are in that house. It's costing us a ton just to maintain the thing and now with all the trouble in that house.

Chapter 30

Melanie laced up her shoes, stretched her calves and took off for an early morning run. *I need to eat more.* She ran through the grove of trees and onto the wooded path. She replayed the text message from Penni over and over in her thoughts as her small frame moved swiftly. "I miss you, Mel." The words held her steady as she dodged tree limbs and stumps. "How in the world am I going to get through this?"

The nightmares never stopped and the vision of the little girl she saw in Penni's bedroom haunted her day in and day out. She would startle awake, only to find herself thinking about the assault all day. She needed to sleep. The dreadful visions started the same way. Her body pinned to the bed, only she could never be sure who was holding her, she could only smell a sour odor and see his fingernails. As she fought to get up, pushing and screaming to get away while Carter's weight held her, pushing her down harder and harder. And the little girl standing and staring. Blond curls soft on her shoulders and a soft pink dress clinging to her frame.

As each foot rhythmically hit the ground, crunching sticks with each stride, she could hear Robyn saying, "Have fun with them, hiking, boating, swimming, crafts, camp stories, all the things that every kid wants to do in the summer." Melanie ran faster to stop the noise. "I will never have fun again."

Today was not a good day. The nightmares mocked her last night. She stopped, leaned over, grabbed her knees and threw up. As a yellow mixture competed with her saliva, she said, "I can't do this." She cried. "I hate you Carter." Her eyes fixed on a mound of ants marching on the generous earth's mossy floor.

She panted and snapped up. She walked back to her cabin only to stop to watch a dragonfly dance between the sun rays. "Penni will never speak to me again when he knows the truth."

She headed for the showers, pretending it was another normal day. She was on point with her routine, get up, run, shower, eat a little something, sit through training, run again, and have dinner. All alone while her thoughts tortured her.

It was late morning and the humidity was on the rise. Her cabin was sticky, even with her window fan. She lay on her bed listening to music. When she heard a knock, she jolted up, tensed and grabbed her blanket. "Who is it?"

"Melanie it's Robyn," her camp director. "Can I come in?"

Melanie slipped off her bunk and opened her door.

"You have visitors. They are in the dining area." In only a few short days into her training, Melanie confessed that she had been assaulted but quickly shut down. Robyn knew not to push and hoped she would talk when she was ready. It was a much-welcomed phone call from Henry Middleton earlier that gave Robyn the clarity she needed to ensure Melanie would be taken care of.

"They?" she asked.

"Come on, I'll walk with you."

"Who's here? I wasn't expecting anyone."

"I have no idea," She lied. "They said they were good friends of your family and were driving through and wanted to stop in and say hello."

Robyn threw her arm around her tiny shoulders. "You're going to be okay, you know that." She gave her a tight squeeze.

The dining hall was quiet. "This time next week it will be full of screaming boys and girls rushing around to get as much food as they can put on their plates." Robyn laughed. They walked across the lonely room and down a long corridor. Robyn slowly opened the door and when Melanie saw Fetu and Talia standing near a table she collapsed. "How did you know I was here?"

Talia cradled her while they made the descent to the floor. Robyn's eyes filled with tears as she gently pulled the door closed, knowing this was the beginning of Melanie's healing. Robyn would keep her secret all summer to protect the wounded little bird she had lovingly called her.

Fetu sat on the other side of Melanie and they held each other for a long time while the tears flowed. "We are here for you," he repeated.

Talia wiped Melanie's face. "It's okay, it's all going to be okay. We are here." She would not let her go. Fetu gently stroked Melanie's back, intuitively knowing when it was his time to give the girls some space. "I'm going to find some drinks," he offered.

"Thank you." Talia whispered. "Take your time."

Melanie clung harder than she had held anyone for a long time. "I'm afraid to let go." She whispered into the echo of stillness.

Through the tears and Talia's thick hair, Melanie muttered, "How did you know I was here? Is Penni okay?"

Talia pulled back, wiped Melanie's eyes, and pushed a few strands of her soft blond hair away from her flushed face. "Penni is at school."

"Is he okay?" She was afraid to hear the answer.

"Tired, but he's okay."

Melanie felt her body release. She could not believe she had anymore tears left after the past few weeks. "I'm sorry. I'm so sorry."

"You have nothing to be sorry for. You have good reasons." Talia took it slow.

"I, I "Melanie stuttered, "I'm so ashamed. I didn't want to hurt Penni. I didn't want to hurt you."

Talia held back. She and Fetu knew the truth. The horrible chat site had done so much damage, but the town had done even more. To think that the community was capable of such malice was one thing, but to mar such a fragile young woman was unforgivable.

"There is nothing to be sorry about." Talia held Melanie's face as she met her watery blue eyes, "You are the victim."

Melanie let out a big sigh, "I should have told. I didn't mean for it to happen."

"You didn't mean it. Of course, you didn't honey. You didn't do a thing wrong."

"I didn't mean…" She swallowed. "I was raped." As soon as the words fell from her lips, Melanie's body shook as if she were freezing.

Talia cradled her. "Let it out. Let it go. You didn't do a thing wrong. You're not to blame. We are here to take care of you."

Melanie buried her head in Talia's chest, gripping her. "Am I in trouble? How did you know I was here?"

"Of course, not dear, we are here to get you." She licked her lips. "Your mother has told me a great deal. She orchestrated this. She wants you to get in counseling this summer and get well."

"She did this. This is her plan?" Melanie's watery eyes met Talia's.

"Yes, and as far as anyone is concerned, you are going home with another young woman who is terribly homesick and spending the summer with her." Talia leaned her cheek against Melanie's.

"What, I'm confused."

"That's your story. You will be going with Fetu and me to the west coast. We have already set you up with a rape counselor and we will be spending the summer with Penni."

Melanie buried her head further. "He won't want that now. I'm dirty." She whispered into her soft bosom.

Fetu returned with sodas, three packs of cheese crackers and some apples. He found the two of them sitting in the exact same place he left them, Talia holding Melanie while he helped them both up to the table.

Talia repeated, "You cannot stay here. JB cannot know that you left and if he does, the story is homesickness and traveling to, what's her names home to spend the summer with her. Let's call her, Susan."

"I can't leave. My mom and JB had a plan."

"Your mom has a plan. We all have our roles in this charade concerning JB. And at the end of the summer, you will be ready to finish your senior year," Fetu said.

"You certainly can leave. We will take care of you and when you graduate, you can go on to Washington with Penni."

"He won't have me," she whispered at the black dots all over the Formica table.

"Oh, if he was here right now that would be the last thing he would think. He's so worried about you."

Fetu interrupted, "Here, eat something."

Melanie felt a calm wash over her for the first time when she realized exactly what was happening. She popped open a soda. "Thank you for saving me. I cannot believe my mother is helping with this."

"Oh, your mother is good and mad at everyone right now. The whole thing is complicated, but we will work it all out. Trust us, Melanie." Talia opened her soda.

"So, did she tell you everything?" Fetu chewed on his crackers.

"What do you mean?" Melanie asked.

"We are moving to the west coast. The chat boards, the community, so many things have blown up in Oak Grove. We are certain there are a few people in town who are happy to see us leave. I'm going back to Stanford, and, well, Talia can easily get a job in nursing. Penni does not know yet. We got him off last week and we left early this morning," Fetu said.

"Why didn't you tell him?" She shook her head.

Fetu, wiped crumbs from his lips and said, "We didn't want to give him another thing to worry about."

"I can't believe you're here." She reached over and rubbed Fetu's arm.

"Okay then, we need to get you packed up and on the road. We have a few stops to make."

"We have to think about this," Talia said.

"Think about what?" Fetu stood, anxious to get going.

"We need to make sure we get all our stories straight. So, you have it down, right Melanie? You are going home with a homesick counselor, from," Talia paused, "from Nashville."

"Sounds good to me."

The three of them walked to her cabin. "I don't understand why Dr. Taylor is so involved in this?" Fetu fished for the truth.

The walk grew eerily quiet while Melanie felt her skin start prick. "Because Carter Taylor raped me."

Fetu turned. "I was so afraid that is what you would say." He and Henry had come to that conclusion just last night, and Melanie spoke it into reality.

"I will see to it that that young man pays for this." Fetu quaked after hearing the confession.

"No," Talia commanded. "We cannot just jump into this without thinking it through. Clearly JB is protecting his son, and that's why he is blaming Penni." The regretted words escaped Talia.

"What?" Melanie shirked. "Blaming Penni? He would never do anything like that," she cried. "What have they said?"

Fetu could hardly contain himself. He could see that it was not the time for him to lose his composure. Despite the town winning, he knew one day Penni's name would be cleared. They were leaving, but Melanie had to go back. So, Fetu would choose his words carefully.

"What am I going to do?" Melanie cried.

Fetu walked closer. "We have all summer to figure that out."

Melanie felt her heart soften with a little twinge of mending.

"It is good that you are spending the summer with us. You and Penni can make things right. You will be stronger and prepared for what you have to face." Fetu rambled on.

"Thank you," Melanie said.

Talia repeated, "JB cannot know that you are with us."

"I don't ever want to see him or Carter again."

"We have to go over this with Tina," Talia assured her. "We will have a solid plan in place by the time you head back to Oak Grove. For now, we have you."

The three walked up the cabin steps and were met by Robyn. "I'm here to help you pack," Robyn said.

Melanie looked around the cabin and could see that Robyn had already started gathering her things. "I'm here for you, Melanie, if you ever need anything. Your secret is safe." She handed her one of her bags.

*****

Fetu, Talia, and Melanie sat at a small quiet café on the Oklahoma line. "Thank you for letting me sleep in the car. I have not felt this good since…" She stopped.

"Of course," Fetu said as he wrestled with his choices on the menu.

"I have decided to share something that could help." She pulled out her cell phone and asked each one of them to put an ear bud in and listen. They heard the exchange between Carter, Tina, JB and her. "This makes me sick," Talia pushed her menu away and sipped her water.

"This has to be kept for safe keeping. When we figure this out, we will make sure we have this for your protection," Fetu said.

"I'm so sorry this all happened to you." Talia stroked her hand. "I think we found an insurance policy to get you through your senior year."

"Now your mom needs one of her own. JB Taylor is a very dangerous man," Talia said.

"I'm not going to sacrifice my friendship with Caroline," Melanie added.

"Your mom had made a deal with the devil and all she wants is to get through the next nine months," Talia said. "I can assure you that she is done with JB."

"Helen is the best person to help with Caroline," Melanie said. "If we send the recording to her, well it's complicated with Caroline, but maybe she can include Harper and Caroline will…" Melanie stopped. "I just don't know how I would take it if I heard my dad and brother involved in something like this."

"With Caroline, you never know," Talia said. "Let's talk to Helen. But you need your friends when you go back."

"What if Caroline doesn't want to be my friend?"

"I wouldn't worry about that."

"I will talk to Helen," Fetu said as he sent her a text: *Can you talk tonight?* Fetu explained the whole thing to Helen late that night.

She was devastated. "She's like a daughter. You know she's worked for Charlie since ninth grade?"

"I know it's hard, but please just keep it to yourself. I know it's not right to ask but if you tell Charlie he may react much like I have wanted to if he knows. In time we will have a plan laid out and we will all have to be on board."

"I will." Helen hung up the phone feeling uneasy about keeping anything from her husband.

"We may need your help with getting information to Tina. JB is keeping a close eye on her. Will you let her know that Melanie is doing fine now that she's with us."

Helen typed in the last of her texts: *Of course.* She would hop on her bike and ride by the Taylor's to see if JB's car was there. Then she would head to the Piggly Wiggly to assure Tina that her daughter was safe. As she rode by the Taylors' she felt an overwhelming darkness come over her. *How can this all be so complicated for Melanie, Caroline, Rita Faye, and Tina.* She thought. *And I can't even share this with Charlie.*

She relayed the information to Tina as she put the few unwanted things in her bag from the store. Tina would pick Melanie up in Raleigh right before school started. She was relieved to hear the softening in her voice.

"I've got this end covered." Helen paused. "She's going to be okay."

She walked out into the night air hoping no one suspected her connection to the continued web of impediment.

Chapter 31

For the first time since the attack, Melanie felt safe. While her mind cleared with the fresh air, the three hiked the steep sided canyon to the Havasupai falls. Their guide, an old colleague of Fetu's named Violet, warmed up to Melanie immediately, chatting about her running and school.

"It was destiny," Fetu said as if his life depended on the Grand Canyon stop. Violet had the permit, a GPS file and a map. She was an expert and would guide them on their hike.

"It's a ten-mile hike that not only has beautiful crystal blue waters but may be the cleansing you all needed. Hard physical movement lets your mind focus on something more important than your problems," Violet said.

It was Fetu that interrupted. "I hope we see a snake."

"Enough already." Talia stopped to catch her breath.

Melanie laughed when he and Talia argued over his obsession.

As they walked, Violet went on about the Native American reservation. "It was named for…"

Fetu interrupted. "I never even knew this should be on my bucket list."

"The reservation is the most remote in the US. The tribe has been here for years. They have to be a hardy people. They have been shoved around for years with the reduction of their land. Through it all their land had been given back and they are very prosperous due to people like us coming to visit."

"It's good to see that people can come back from such horrible treatment," Fetu commented. Talia looked at her husband, knowing exactly what he was saying. Everything between them had become about Oak Grove and the way they were so unfairly treated.

"This is amazing." Melanie continued to hike, never realizing what Fetu meant.

They were going to stay at the Super Village one night, explore Beaver Falls, and head out to Washington the next day.

They stood in front of the cascading blue water while it continued to pour into the crystal-clear pool. The three of them felt close to God as they watched the water spill. Talia fought tears. "We left such a rotten place and to experience this, this beauty, this clean wonderful place. There is so much more to life than Oak Grove."

Fetu watched Melanie for any reaction. She would have to return there in a few short months. They sat atop the large red rock and listened as the water ran over the rocks.

"I feel so much better here," Melanie said. "I'm feeling cleaner."

They all needed this time. The steep switchbacks pushed their bodies to get stronger physically, and they enjoyed the fresh air. It was hot then cold from the shade and no breeze walking along the river and seeing the falls about 3 1/2 hours, walking uphill as mules carried their packs. They viewed beautiful plunge pools that they could hear before they got to them. It was refreshing and ironic to be in such an isolated area yet feel so purified after a horrible few weeks.

They sat for a while with the evergreens around the falls and gazed over the cliffs. The water trusted the falls to catch it every time. Melanie looked down on her arm. "Look, a dragonfly." She ran her hand across while the dragonfly rested softly on her jacket. She reached down to let the small insect light but in a small stream of light it flew up and over the bushes nearby. The clear view of a beautiful place made them all watch in wonder and awe of one of God's best kept secrets. None of them wanted to leave.

*****

"I'm happy to see you eat all three of your pancakes," Fetu commented as he watched Melanie inhale her breakfast.

"All that hiking gave me a huge appetite." She smiled.

"I'm hungry too." He reached for a stack and generously drowned them in maple syrup.

"Did you guys have any dragonflies in your room last night?"

"No, just snoring." Talia rolled her eyes at Fetu.

"I had one sleeping on my blanket. I found it when I woke up this morning."

"You know what that means?" Fetu said.

"No." Melanie scooped up the last bite of her pancake.

"It means you have good luck."

"I need some." She wiped her mouth.

It would be a hard twenty-four hours before they would reach Penni. Fetu stretched his sore arms and legs after the long two-day drive.

It was mid-afternoon the next day when they arrived at the University of Washington.

"It's a beautiful sunny day. I told you it doesn't rain here." Fetu reached in the back for their bags. "The skies are blue with streaks of white fluffy clouds." He inhaled and felt relief that he was near his son again. He could see Mt Rainier in the distance. "The mountain's out."

Penni would be finishing up his morning weights and head to class. They were meeting him at 2 at the hotel. They checked in and Melanie took a shower. *Would he even want to make things work?* She certainly didn't want his parents pressuring him.

As soon as he walked in the lobby and saw her, he ran, picked her up and held her. "I don't ever want to be away from you again. Don't ever shut me out."

"I'm so sorry." She didn't want to let go.

Chapter 32

JB strummed his pencil while Henry and Wade walked in the hospital board meeting. JB was certain Henry was going to make trouble for him tonight. *At least the Lafoes are gone and I can relax.* He tapped away, anxious to hear his name called for the next board head.

Everyone convened in the stuffy conference room at the hospital. After the invocation and the Pledge of Allegiance, Larry Jacobs opened the meeting. He was the head of the hospital board and would be coming off in the fall. The three candidates sat in the room. Henry skimmed the names. June Smith, a tenured professor in the nursing school and a lifelong supporter of the university; Bo Waylon, a supporter of the university who lived in Raleigh. And JB Taylor.

"All in favor for the reading of last month's minutes," Larry continued. Everyone in the room answered except Henry. "Henry are you in favor of passing the minutes?"

"Oh, yes, sorry I was just reading through the agenda." He glanced down to see where his beloved breast cancer center fell.

Larry went over some incidental items. There was a brief discussion concerning some medical equipment that needed to be updated in the surgical unit.

Finally, Larry revealed the last board vote for chair. "Well, JB it looks like you will have more on your plate this next year, congratulations." The members that sat on either side of him, shook hands.

Larry requested that everyone pull out the updated breast cancer center packet as this had been a standing agenda item for months. Henry was always the willing participant to take the lead and pay for any costs.

Henry held the detailed plans that had been sent earlier for review prior to the meeting. Larry presented on the evolution of cancer care. "Local breast cancer screening rates are below the state average." Larry took a sip of water.

June interrupted, "Our county is grossly behind when it comes to women's health care needs. I'm impressed."

"Women in rural communities tend to have lower screening rates, in large part because of anxiety about results and the lack of privacy during the screening process," Larry continued.

"I think this is important to update and at the very least we should approve and get started on this right away." June interjected again.

JB asked, "And what about the cost of priorities? Our budget is stretched pretty tight. I think we need to consider just basic care for our patients. We are failing at so many things."

Larry ignored JB's questions. "The other side of the center will house the infusion bays and a separate registration desk. Our hope is the center will serve the greater part of not only our county but all the surrounding, rural poor counties and will increase the low breast cancer screening rate."

"Of course, we have low screening rates. We have old equipment and the area feels like you are out in the middle of the hospital," Linda chimed. "I go to Raleigh."

JB stopped the conversations. "I agree that we have a need in this community for better screening, but I think this plan is far too aggressive. I think we invest in a 3D mammographer and revisit this in six months after we see our finances improve. I think…" JB was interrupted.

"I don't care what you think." Henry stopped him. "I have spent countless dollars, time, and energy on this, and I'm willing to cover the whole bill if that is what it takes. We owe this to the women of our community. I owe this to my wife." The room was stunned to silence.

"I understand your personal involvement. I'm sure this never would have been an issue for you if she had not gotten breast cancer, but can't you see Henry, this is not a priority."

"Then what the hell is, JB?" Henry leaned closer.

JB was tired of being ordered around the conversation. And of Henry throwing his money around town like leaves blowing off trees.

"I can afford Chapel Hill. But most of you know there are so many that cannot," Henry continued. "Aren't you going to say anything? This involves your family too," Henry spoke to Wade.

"I think this clinic is a fine idea. And I think as part of the medical community we have an obligation to look for ways to help our patients. If you are willing to fund the whole clinic, we only need to get state approval."

The ongoing investigation concerning missing narcotics was close to being wrapped up and he was cautious with his words. Both Wade and Henry wanted the cancer center, but Wade knew biding their time was the best avenue right now. He wanted Henry to stay calm. They were weeks away from receiving the full report, and if his hunch was correct JB Taylor, would no longer be a player on the board.

Larry spoke. "Let's vote on this and if it passes, I will personally send all the paperwork into the state to start the approval process."

"Those in favor." Larry's voice quivered under the tension. Henry and Wade's hands along with the two women's immediately shot up. Phil Lawson and Larry shot their hands in the air. JB kept his hand on his lap. The other five held steady with their hands in their laps. The vote was tied 6 to 6 with only one in question, Bo. "Well Bo, what will it be?" Larry asked.

"Henry, can we table this for next time? I just think it may look like a board member is bullying us around here because they have their own agenda. Just because you can fund it does not mean it needs to happen."

Henry sighed. "So, what does JB have on you, Bo?" Silence sliced through the room louder than the sirens from the ER.

"What the hell? This is exactly what I mean. Just because you want something doesn't mean you get it. Do I think we need a center for every disease here? Yes, but we have other challenges too. We have to do what's best for the community."

Henry slapped his hand on the table. "I can afford to open a private fully funded breast cancer center without the blessing of this board. We are better than this. This town is better than this. Bo, I'm shocked at your lack of leadership. If someone is willing to do something, why in the hell would you turn them away?" He glared at JB. "We all know there are things going on in this hospital." He felt a tug at his arm as Wade encouraged him to sit down.

"Let's revisit this in the fall." Wade stopped him. Bo did not want to be under any controversy. He was a huge athletic supporter and JB could make it very difficult for him if he voted in favor of the center. Bo liked his place in the parking lot on Saturdays and cocktails at Doc's after the games.

"The board will revisit this item at our next meeting. Until then." Larry tapped his hammer on the table and nervously shuffled his papers.

Short of breath, Henry stormed out. The board members walked down the hall with the coward in their eyes when Henry reached out.

"We need to have a few words." He grabbed JB's arm. "Look me in the eye and tell me what you know about the Lafoe thing."

Shock spread across JB's face, saying more words than the few that came out of his mouth. "I don't know what you're talking about."

"Oh, I think you do. I know about you and Tina. And I know you are behind the Melanie thing." He studied his face while JB licked his lips, showing his teeth like a wild animal. Small beads of sweat surfaced on his top lip.

JB wished he had taken more Xanax before the meeting. He felt his heart rate quicken. Better, he thought, he had the opportunity to take a small syringe of oxycodone this morning and replace it with saline, but Doc needed it more than he did. "Henry, I don't know what you're talking about."

Henry got in JB's face. "You stay away from me, you stay away from my family, and you keep your rotten son away from my granddaughter, you hear me. I'm on to you and when I get the chance, I will expose you for who and what you really are. You don't have me fooled for one second. I don't know what you have over all these people on this board, but I will good and find out and when I do"

Wade walked up behind Henry just in time.

"Come on daddy, he's not worth it. Are you, Dr. Taylor? Now only through the popularity of your son, are you the man of the hour."

JB glared at the two. "Don't bring my son into this."

Wade held Henry's arm close as they made their way to the car. "We need to talk about this." JB followed.

Henry felt a tightness and struggled to breathe. He collapsed to the ground, but not before he hit his head against one of the cars. Dark then light, heat then cold. Days ran together like his gray thick hair. He had a vague sense as his dusty old soul seemed to cave. A whole life in a dash.

In the far-off distance he heard his name called in the darkness from his adversary. As his vile enemy belched from hell, he felt a coldness run all around him. He had figured it out. He knew he was the man behind the chat boards, and he knew who was stealing medicines from the hospital.

JB dropped to the ground next to Henry, but not before Wade fell with him trying to catch his fall. He frantically worked securing his jacket on his wounded head.

"Get someone quick. We need a gurney." He glared at JB. "Get away from him. If you want to help, go get a gurney. NOW!" he screamed. Henry's heart beat faint and low. Before JB could answer, Wade said, "This is on your hands JB, you did this to him."

Cottonmouth Droppings

Farm Boy: How about Middleton falling out like he did.

Tat Man: hope he's okay. He gives a ton of money to the community. He's a good man. Heard Taylor shoved him.

Farm boy: Oh, we could be so lucky to shut him up. And Taylor did not push him.

Tat Man: Everyone knows JB hates the man. Heard Dr. Taylor got an earful from Wade.

Foxy: Dr. Taylor pushed him. Sounds like him. The man is a bully and so is his son.

Farm boy: Dr. Taylor is a good man. He's a community leader. This is another set up.

Stonewall: He'll be fine just a bump on the head and a few weeks in the hospital.

Farm Boy: Rich Assholes. We could be so lucky. Send him up to Moo U. They have a great vet school. It even smells like shit.

Turncoat: Nothing would surprise me when it comes to JB. He has had it in for Henry for years. Looks like he finally had the opportunity and he took it.

Stonewall: Toxic people. Penni now Middleton. They deserve it, both of them. Who are you Turncoat?

Farm Boy: Another traitor amongst the Cottonmouth flock. Get off our chat site.

Tat Man: Oh, come on now, He's a good man. And must be a Carolina guy for sure.

Turncoat: Go Heels! Go Pack! Go Deacons!

Stonewall: Go to hell, Turncoat.

Farm Boy: Hopefully he's leaving all that money to the athletic department.

Chapter 33

"Can you believe people are still talking about Penni?" Carter chatted with his dad while they stood at the counter making sandwiches. Caroline had just walked in the door and caught the tail end of the conversation.

"There's nothing innovative about rape." She glared. "Why do you two even care anymore? The Lafoe family is gone. Penni is gone. Even Melanie split. So why are you two so into the whole thing? Don't you realize all the pain this town caused them? In a few short days after the assault, people were leaving bags of shit on their lawn and signs saying go home foreigners and other horrible things. As if the chat site was not enough. Poor Mrs. Lafoe was even harassed at work. And don't you find it odd that this is the same town that judges Melanie and her mom for being poor. Yet they are given gift baskets at the holidays. Such bullshit." Caroline spat her words. "Ironic, isn't it? You do know what that means, Carter?"

Her father's lips moved like dried orange peels while the veins throbbed in his neck. When he spoke, his jaw carried his pockmarked skin from his acne troubled teen years up and down like runny cottage cheese. "Enough." The family had set a dangerous precedent. They were always bound by conflict.

Rita Faye walked down the back steps and right into the middle of the heated conversation. "You look tired JB."

Turning toward Caroline, "Are you hungry?"

Rita Faye ignored Carter.

"No thank you." Caroline climbed past her and up the stairs. She texted Harper. *It's like Carter and dad create scenarios to make people march around in their own misery. Be over later.*

Caroline would never share with them who she really was. It was Helen who taught her how to focus on what was really important. Her dad hated Helen. Caroline twisted the long beautiful pink stone necklace that Helen gave her.

"It's an amour of protection and confidence. Something you can grab to calm down." She spoke Helen's words as she held the precious stone close.

Many years ago, it was Mr. Charlie who suggested Caroline talk to Helen about sculpting.

Caroline mustered enough courage to ask and their relationship allowed Caroline to fill the emptiness inside of her from years of verbal abuse at the hands of her dad and brother. At the feet of Helen, she learned how to sculpt and how to express herself through clay. Yoga taught her to witness her family, not engage them. "I'm happy to step back and let my all-star brother be front and center. I will also be there to watch him spin out of control."

Caroline opened her laptop and clicked on Cottonmouth Droppings. She scanned the lines about Penni and Melanie and all seemed to be from Stonewall and Farm Boy. *Some great town with great people*, she thought. "I can't wait to leave."

In time, the Lafoe gossip would lose flavor like cheap gum. Everyone would look forward to the next incident to throw gas on the fire. It just seemed to be taking a long time. The lingering question was why Melanie would not press charges against the young man that did this to her? Caroline needed some answers. She sat in her thoughts when her phone chimed.

Can you and Harper come down to my studio tomorrow morning around 9? Please keep this to yourself, Helen asked.

Are you okay? Caroline texted her back.

I'm great. I have something important to discuss with you girls.
Did you text Harper?
No, can you please ask?

Caroline watched the three dots pulse while her mind did the same. *Should this be scaring me?*

Trust me.

Chapter 34

Helen cupped her hot tea while she listened to the birds chirping awake. It was four a.m. and panic seemed to be her only companion since she received the letter a few weeks ago. She could not bring herself to share just yet. How was she going to handle Caroline with the information? She sipped her tea, cast in the gray swept room of the early dark hour.

"Good morning honey. You're up awfully early." Charlie, always an early riser, interrupted Helen's burden of thoughts.

"Good morning. I couldn't sleep." She untucked her feet and stood to kiss her husband.

"I know. You were tossing and turning all night. So, tell me what's that all about?"

Charlie settled in next to her while she leaned against him.

She pulled the letter out of her nightgown pocket. In the silence of his reading she readied herself for his steadied reaction.

"Carter raped Melanie?" The dirty word fell from Charlie's mouth like he dropped a bar of lye soap. "How long have you had this?"

"A few weeks," she whispered. "It's worse, Charlie." Helen plugged her headphones into her device while Charlie listened to the conversation. "JB covered it up? Helen, this is stuff you should turn over to the police. And why didn't you tell me?" He held steady.

"I had to think about it." She paused. "And do you really think they would do anything?"

"I think we have a responsibility to hand this over. That's their job."

Helen steadied herself. "It's not your responsibility. And I won't do it. I'm not going to betray Melanie. You read the letter. She has asked me not to. I'm going to let Caroline and Harper know about this. She needs their help when she comes back here. And besides…" Helen paused.

Charlie felt her shiver, "What is it?"

"Whit Cain would never do anything about this. JB Taylor is so far deep with him and Doc that they would drive Melanie right over the edge. Those men would stop at nothing to protect Carter. Think of Caroline. I have to help her. This is going to be horrible for her."

"You're right, Helen. I never considered Caroline. My first thought was to let the authorities take care of this. But I think you should get as far away from this as possible. Nothing good comes from JB Taylor."

"I asked the girls to come down to the studio this morning to tell them."

"You're doing the right thing. If you need me for anything, I'm just around the corner. How are you going to tell Rita Faye? It's her son."

"I'm not. It's not for me to tell." Helen shook her head. "Charlie, these are wonderful young ladies. Melanie has been with us, working for you for years. And Caroline has such talent. How in the hell did this all get so complicated?"

"Take this as a compliment, my dear, they trust you to do what is right." Charlie held her close. "Just next time let me know sooner."

Helen leaned in and gave him a big kiss. "I'm sorry I didn't tell you. I could not do this life without you."

Helen rode her bike in the humid dark morning, passing the soft lights from the Middletons' front. She slowed as she went past the Taylors' veranda. *How in the world could such young lives already become so tangled?*

She moved swiftly down to her studio, propped her bike against the window, and unlocked her door. She pulled the bike in and switched on the light. She quickly closed the door and locked it, feeling uneasy. Helen was never afraid of the dark or shadows, but she felt a fear inside of her that she just could not shake. She needed some quiet time and would sit and meditate, hoping to calm herself.

Reading through some old mail, she noticed the sun was fully awake while the birds applauded its generous light up in front of the studio. She sent a text to Caroline. *Are we still on?*

Harper and I will be there soon.
The back door is open.

Helen walked to the back of her studio and unlocked the door. For just a minute she thought she should open the door and make sure no one was there. *Where is this coming from?* she thought.

She walked back to her office and waited for the girls.

Caroline was there first. She hopped off her bike set it against the back of the studio, slung her backpack over her shoulder and walked in the back door. She wiped her forehead and felt a small pool of sweat at the base of her back. It was horribly hot, even this early. The warm studio was dark.

"Miss Helen," she called out.

"Back here." A sheer white veil covered the door of Helen's office. A small desk sat in the corner as she sat on a medicine ball. Her dark glasses were perched on the end of her slender nose and her gray hair was braided, reaching long down her neck and past her shoulders. Helen's phone sat on a stack of papers. A yellow package sat on her desk with large black lettering and the words confidential across the side. It was hard not to notice. She had a silk wrap on her small frame and her favorite white shirt and colorful yoga pants clinging to her small legs.

Caroline bent down and gave her a hug.

"Is everything okay?" Her throaty rich voice now quiet.

"Yes." Helen fixed her a cup of tea while they waited for Harper.

Thank goodness it was summer and school would not be starting for a while. The girls needed to focus on more important things.

Caroline's mind raced with every scenario possible about what could be so wrong that they were summoned down in secret. Could it be the show? It was opening in two months. Maybe Helen didn't want her in it and asked that Harper come to comfort her. It was the opening weekend of football season and she was worried that her piece would not be ready.

Caroline and Helen heard the door unlatch and Harper holler out, "Hello."

"We're in here but first lock the door," Helen said.

Harper bounced in just like she always did. "Hey ladies. Wow, this is early. I thought this must be important to get me up before 9 a.m."

"Cup of tea?" Helen smiled.

"Yes, that sounds great." Harper settled herself right next to Caroline on the bean bag. Caroline pushed her backpack aside after Harper cozied up against her.

"I've been sad about Penni leaving," Harper said. "I'm sad about Melanie too." She nervously chatted.

"My dears," Helen started, "I received this from Melanie. I have struggled with telling you girls because I know what a burden this will be, especially for you, Caroline." Helen folded her lips. "But I also wanted to honor Melanie's wishes and let you know what she has sent."

Caroline sat up. "So, you heard from her. I know she texted Penni right before he left and said she was at some church summer camp and would be home right before school starts."

Helen stopped her. "Read this please."

Dear Helen,

Thank you for speaking with Fetu and Talia. I appreciate your willingness to help me. I know I can trust you. I have no one else. I could not send this to Caroline and I worry how she will be when she finds out that Carter was the one who assaulted me. It's been too much for me to handle. But please know I am so sorry to put you in the middle of this horrible situation, but I had no one else. I'm with Fetu and Talia and I'm going to be in Washington for the summer. Penni knows we are coming and we have spoken a few times since last week when they picked me up. I'm hoping, once he knows everything, things will be okay with us. I did not handle it well, and I only hope he will forgive me.

I must have your word that you will tell no one. Fetu said you assured him of this confidence but I just have to say it again. Please tell Caroline and Harper to keep this secret. My mom has been a great support. Fetu and Talia have rescued me and I will be getting help. I'm so grateful for them.

I'm not looking forward to coming back there. I'm afraid that I will not do well enough in school this year to get into Washington. I know you wonder why I'm telling you all this. I need insurance. I need to know that when I come back, I will be safe and that no one will hurt me. I need you to get in touch with Caroline, although this puts her in a bad position. Please tell her I am not mad at her. She is one of my best friends, and I know she would have never done anything to hurt me. I leave it up to you, Helen, to talk with her. After all, her brother and father are involved in all this. And Helen, I need you to help me. I know how much you love Caroline, and I know she trusts you more than anything. You and Mr. Charlie have been wonderful friends to me for many years. You gave me a job and Mr. Charlie has been like a dad to me. I am certain once I am better and get back to Oak Grove, I can get through this next year with the support of all of you. Thank you so much for your help.

Always, Melanie.

Caroline looked up at Helen with full eyes. "I'm going to kill him." Helen plugged the zip drive into her computer. "You need to listen to this."

"I'm afraid to." A tremor skated through her body and rippled into Harper's. "Have you listened to it?"

Helen stopped. "Yes. It's very difficult. I felt you girls needed to be together for this."

"Let's do this." The two girls snuggled together and Helen started it.

Caroline and Harper were stunned. Within seconds the voices were clear as if they were all sitting in the room with Melanie, Tina, JB, and Carter. There was something painfully familiar in the menace when Caroline heard Carter say. "I didn't mean to hurt you. I wasn't trying to get away with anything." It was an expression of hatred that had been kept out of polite company, but lived in the marrow of his soul, alive and accepted in his male dominated world.

"The false apology only let him get away with hurting Melanie," she said. "It was that Monday night." Caroline's mouth agape. "It was a tape from the night that the four of them met."

"Do you want me to play it again?" Helen asked. They listened.

"That is Carter. And he will haunt Melanie forever with this. And to think he has been elevated to such a height that even my father is defending him." Caroline stewed in shock and shame. "I feel so responsible. It's my brother, my father." Rage weaved in between her tears.

"Get it out." Helen dropped to the floor. "You cannot take this home with you."

"Anyone around him would do anything they could to make sure he gets exactly what he wants." Snot slid from her nose. "They needed him. My father has kept a confidence in his little citadel. It's like his skills are his undoing." Caroline stopped for a minute gulping for air.

"Who else is involved?" she screamed. "And look what they did to Penni?" Her voice grew rich with only sorrow as she babbled over and over again, "My family has ruined the Lafoes' lives."

Harper rubbed Caroline's back in silence.

"This has haunted Melanie for weeks. She was raped by my brother. What is she supposed to do with this?" Caroline fought to put it together. "I know that night. It was the Monday after the party. My dad and him went out to the sporting goods store. My ass. She's my friend." She couldn't stop. "He's been such an ass to me all my life, but now this. I always took what you said, Helen.

That scared people are hiding in scary people. I stopped letting Carter's insults get to me. Of course, I did for a time, but just like my father to my mother he did the same to me."

She wrapped up in Helen's lap and curled toward Harper, feeling an overwhelming sense of exhaustion.

"I'm so sorry, I'm so sorry." She saw a human blur, a pixelated version of her brother, a stranger. And to think her father took his side. "Who are these people?" She felt afraid. "Who the fuck are they?" she cried. "He wants to hurt me so bad he is hurting my friends." She sobbed into Helen's gray mane.

Helen stroked Caroline's back. She would not leave the girls. She made them both text their mothers and tell them they were together and grabbing a bite to eat at Mr. Charlie's. Not a total lie, since Helen owned the store as well.

"Caroline, tell your mom we are doing some extra work for the show." Helen's heart broke as the words spilled out of her mouth. She would deal with this aftermath in due time. She sat in the right now. They needed to be with each other. Helen was right, it was too much for the girls. And she could not fathom how Melanie held it together.

"I can't believe she mailed the zip drive here." Caroline sipped her herbal tea. "Play the drive again, please."

She heard Carter and Tina's voice. "I cannot believe my dad. Don't you wonder why exactly my dad was so anxious to ship her away? And now the chat site makes sense that there was so much trashing of Penni and his family. My dad is one of the people on that site." Caroline let the words hang in the air.

"Well now we know," Helen said.

"I just can't believe my dad. And my brother. What a piece of shit. I'm going to have it out with them."

"You can't say a thing. He can make it very difficult for her when she gets back. Caroline, you have to keep this for a while to yourself. Let the dust settle. You read what Melanie wrote, she doesn't want any trouble."

"I have to live with him, with them. And the way he hurt her. I'm worried he may mess with her when she comes back. Power, Helen, don't you see? He's the big star this year. Untouchable. And now he knows, as does Melanie, that my dad will cover for him, anything that he wants him to. I'm sure they think it was perfectly okay to rape her and let it go. I hate my dad." Her words tumbled.

"Melanie did it to ensure a good senior year. She knew it would be a warning. She was so paranoid that she would not even send it on her phone. She was scared, she said in her note. Scared to come back. Scared what people would think and scared what would happen to her. She said she knew she needed help."

Harper reminded them. "I'm glad the Lafoes are with her now."

"We need to stick together," Helen said. "Girls, promise me you won't tell a soul. No one," Helen reminded them. "Let me think on this for a while. We have nothing but time right now. Caroline, if you need anything, a break at home, you can come to my house."

"Yes, or you can come to my house. And you are always welcome at the beach," Harper said.

"School should bring back the normal. A schedule, things to do, accountability," Helen said, "Until then I need you two to call me and check in."

Caroline listened but could not contain her anger. "I want to hurt him. I want to make him pay for this. Break his leg or his arm so he can never hurt anyone again." She heaved an overwhelming wave of sadness as tears rose again.

"This is my fault." She was louder than she should have been. "No one will ever be my friend again."

"What? You have been a great friend to her. You could not have stopped this," Helen said.

"I knew," Caroline whispered.

"How did you know?" Harper turned.

"I saw him coming down the steps, and I just knew something wasn't right."

"You didn't know. No one knew except the four people on this zip drive. Let's leave it at that for now, Caroline, please," Helen said.

"The worst moment of Melanie's life has become her most devastating due to my dad and Carter." Caroline stared at the white washed walls as she felt her soul void of any possibility of any real friendships now.

"I want you to spend the day with me. Maybe do some work." Helen looked over at Harper. "What do you have going today?"

Harper rubbed Caroline's leg. "This." As she felt her body shudder with fear.

Chapter 35

Helen's studio was an eclectic mix of aged hardwood floors, clean lines, and soft blue colors. There were double glass doors across the back that lead to a garden with a fire pit. She would spend cool evenings there after a long day, sipping a glass of wine and discussing a good book with one of her students. That was her sanctuary.

Her office was tranquil, calm, and steady. The brown industrial low lighting set the mood for both relaxation and work. Her window was lined with small sculptures and a copy of August Rodin's *The Thinker*. She loved the sculpture because "it feels like everyone, unfinished, naked, and the vulnerability that everyone carries."

The airy paper Chinese lanterns were motionless while Helen settled over Caroline's shoulder and watched her layer clay.

"I can see what you are trying to do. Now think about what feeds you so you can make better decisions about your work. Where do you see the piece going?" She whispered in her ear. "Take a minute and visualize the piece before you continue."

Her process was a form of cleaning the mustiness out of her life.

"Where are the cobwebs? What is the lie? You are the true hero that endures the slings and arrows of everyday life and shows compassion to another person in the end."

She finished her train of thought out loud. After the morning Caroline had, she knew she was exactly where she needed to be.

Caroline's hands swiftly stroked the clay.

"Slow down. You have control. No one else does." Helen continued to coach her.

She could not wait to finish. Caroline pushed her anger down into the clay as if she was ferreting out the secret from her lemon-like soul. She was making room in the dark inner cracks, longing for a loving voice as she clung to

Helen's words. She felt tense, and all she could think about was the hollow eyes she was trying to create. Half open, half closed, "babies' eyes," She focused on the tick of the clock now and suddenly was overcome with exhaustion. She felt Helen's gentle hand glide down her arm and onto her own.

"Step back. Now take a deep breath and close your eyes. Imagine the figure you are creating," Helen guided her. "When you're ready, exhale all the feelings into the elements of your work. Let's go back to the clear visual image of what you originally sketched for me. Put that practice in your mind now. I don't care if it is anger, sadness, or love. Imagine all those feelings coming from your heart down into your fingertips and molding the clay over the sturdy armature that holds the piece. Let all those elements combine in the piece."

Caroline fondled the clay harder.

"Let all your disappointment, all your accomplishments blend into one and use that power, those images to create. Please take another minute." Helen knew she was pushing too hard.

She stopped her hands from gliding over the small faces. She could feel the tension. "Now take a moment to quiet your mind."

Helen stepped away and let Caroline stand in her quiet. Now that she knew the truth, the troubled young lady would have a greater challenge. And Helen would be careful with her counsel. *I have made a great mistake not sharing with Charlie, now I have to be careful not to guide Caroline in the wrong direction. I will not do that again.*

The conflict drove Caroline to create a piece that would represent far more than the many simple pieces that any young beginning sculptor would create. But Caroline's needs drove her, pushed her to a place that only radical artists go. Helen was the perfect teacher to let her go at exactly the pace she needed. Helen, as Caroline said many times, was given to her by God. What accomplished woman would live in a small college town and yet was so unappreciated by so many? A woman like Helen, authentic, who never fit in the narrow paths of Oak Grove.

While Caroline studied her work, she thought of Patsy. Caroline pinched a small pot and flower together in her art class years ago. What made the piece so unique was in the middle of the flower was a beautiful carving of Harper that Caroline had completed with a toothpick. Patsy was in tears when Caroline wrapped it in a beautiful piece of gauze cloth and tied with a lovely silk ribbon, and presented it to her. She wrote a simple note, "Get well." And left it on the doorstep for Patsy's birthday. It was the start of a very special relationship Patsy had with her granddaughter's wounded friend.

"What does an old woman like her want with a young impressionable girl like you? I don't understand your friendship with Harper but I really don't understand your obsession with Patsy," JB had said as he noshed on some coffee cake. Those words echoed in Caroline's ear as she started to push the clay over and over.

She held her head in deference for Helen. She and Patsy were the only two adult women she trusted right now.

Caroline got on her knees and slowed down as she gently buffed the clay. Helen wanted her to see the shattered thing inside her and piece it together in her sculpture.

Caroline worked tirelessly while Helen played ambient piano music. She needed some noise to calm her thoughts while she let her emotions flow into her piece. Helen moved to the window seat and watched the piece come alive. A stooped-over woman held one hand to her ample pregnant stomach. The pain etched on her face while one baby slipped out of the mother's womb, crying with a determined look on his face and the twin, half out of the womb, posterior, not correcting itself in the womb like most babies would, with one hand reaching down and grasping toward the hand of the boy.

There was no excuse for any of this. Helen knew the depth of pain Caroline felt from her twin. Her piece would make her greatest statement. The mother's only concern was holding her own painful womb. *Selfish*, Helen thought. The boy on the ground, strong, even mocking the much smaller girl, coming out the wrong way. *Brilliant*. Helen was honored to be a witness to such an amazing creation.

Everything in Caroline's life was in conflict. And the adults were throwing up sand in the wind to blind her even more. It was confusing in Caroline's sand box of the world. She was fighting to be herself as she was measured against her brother, who beat her at everything. Helen leaned against the soft cushions. "Are you ready to stop?"

Caroline looked up. "I can't."

Helen steadied herself off the seat. "You finish and if you are up to it, come to class if you want."

Helen stretched her five-foot body as long as she could. "Great work today." She gently rubbed Caroline's shoulder. "This is going to be the finest piece in the show."

Caroline regarded. "I need to be done." She swallowed, "But I don't want my name on it. By unknown."

"It's been a shitty day." Helen said as she felt a release while she dropped the forceful words and grasped her shoulder and gave it a long squeeze.

Chapter 36

The coaching staff at Middle Carolina had a late summer tradition, a two-night retreat down at JB's river house. It was the much-needed break JB needed.

Just that morning he accidentally walked into Henry Middleton's hospital room and Patsy, usually a woman of grace, admonished him. Since Henry's accident, JB's life had been riddled with controversy as he continued to distance himself from the accident. Caroline's insistence to spend the entire summer with Harper in town or at the Middletons' beach house did not help. *What in the hell was I thinking going in that hospital room? I can't make mistakes*, he admonished himself.

JB checked the chat boards constantly after Henry's accident and they were unmerciful. "Was it really an accident or did JB push him?" *Thank goodness no one decided to pull their cell phone out and video the whole thing,* JB thought. *Wade made me look terrible. I was only trying to help.*

And soon Melanie would be back in Oak Grove. The only bright light was his recent meeting with Whit. The rape kit was still buried, and Whit assured him he would keep it that way. "*A few days at the river is just what I need,*" he thought. He patted the duffel bag in his passenger seat that housed various pills he had for the coaching staff.

And with the latest storm brewing, he knew Doc could use some extra help. The NCAA had contacted the university the first of July about reported allegations of cheating, grade fixing, and doping. The impact, if any of them were substantiated, could prove to be damaging to many people associated with Cottonmouth athletics. JB could easily become entangled in the whole mess as well if he didn't play it right.

We all need to get away. He steered his car down the long path and up to his river house. Tina had agreed to meet him tonight before the coaches came in tomorrow. After the fight he had with Rita Faye this morning, he needed a distraction.

Little River, a quaint town about thirty miles from Oak Grove, could be rough, just like the people. Whenever a hurricane blew through it flooded. But it was the one place the Middletons didn't have a home. They kept their house at Wrightsville Beach, refusing to let any hurricane wash away any family memories. Many summers playing on the beach and going out to the Bridge Tender at night kept the family away from Oak Grove.

JB loved his river house that separated him from the rest of Main street. JB had a place at Wrightsville but the river house was all his. And it was the river house that started the fight with Rita Faye early this morning.

"I need a place I can call my own and get away from the Middletons. You know they hate the river. They say it's dirty and full of sandhillers." It was quiet and dotted with very few homes. "I told you, it's my retreat."

Rita Faye played her one last hand. "If you want to go to the river, let's go. I can get away tonight."

"You know I keep that thing rented. But it's the coaches retreat and, well no women allowed." He hedged. "I'm the team doctor. And they need my support now with this NCAA thing."

"NCAA thing?" Her brow furrowed.

"Oh, it's no big deal." JB bit his tongue.

"It's always about what you need. It's always about your problems, your challenges, who needs you." Rita Faye felt her body tense as the words sliced through the air. Then she stopped.

"What the hell do you want? You have what you need. You have your career, the kids, you are plenty busy. What do you want?"

"How about honesty? Why do you have so many bags? What's in all of them?" She nosed to the floor.

Words cut JB, but he never bled. "Honesty, you want honesty. What about you? You think your weight makes me happy? Are you really trying?"

Rita Faye held her mouth slightly open as she fought for her confidence to stay intact. "Have a good weekend." She walked briskly down the hall as she felt the fabric from her too big dress sway against her melting body.

She palmed the loose material from her oversized dress. JB used his words like weapons, but she would not fire back anymore. She watched him pull out of the driveway, now grateful he would be gone a few days. She pulled off the oversized dress and slipped into a form fitting shift. She smoothed her hands over her now slight hips, turned in her full-length mirror and slipped on her soft cream pumps. "It's my turn."

*****

JB sipped a beer and rocked on the back porch as he thought about his wife. "This is my place. I deserve a reprieve from my hectic life and draining marriage." He looked over and saw a Dragonfly light on a bush. "Get out of my yard." He threw his beer can, taking aim at the constant reminder of Mary Claire. "Quit following me."

Tina would be there soon. *I should have told Rita Faye about Tina this morning. She would come unglued. Like mud on a pig, it would stick right to her.* He took pleasure in the fragility of both women. But he was worried about Tina. She had not been around very much this summer, and it was making him crazy.

Tina could be gooey as taffy, but cross her and she would shred you. Only JB was so busy saving her, he neglected to see the dismantling. Her desperation, so JB thought, kept her at the trough. Despite breaking class lines, he was not prepared to let her go just yet. JB watched the ripples of water toss back and forth off the shore when he felt smooth long fingers reach around his face and cover his eyes.

"This better be the woman of my dreams, because if it's anyone else I will have to shoot and ask questions later."

Tina fought nausea. It was the last place she wanted to be but needed to continue the charade to ensure her daughter's safety and future. She reached around and settled her small frame on a nearby rocking chair. "It's me you're referring to. I know your lovely wife won't have a thing to do with this place." She resisted a kiss on the lips, feeling bile rise when he leaned in with his pursed lips and shuttered eyes.

"How was the drive?" He tipped his head back, looked into her green eyes and watched her long blond hair float in the breeze.

"It was easy." Ever the chameleon, petite and attractive, she could be loud and combative but now she withheld as much as she could. She left high school with dreams and aspirations, only to find adulting didn't look so good on the other side of twelfth grade.

"You want a beer?"

The vulnerability that any young, lonely widow held played perfectly into JB's hands. Little did JB know that since his son hurt the only thing that Tina really loved. She was calculating her revenge. "Sounds good. I can get it."

"Grab one for me too." Without giving him a chance, she jumped up and headed into the house. She would have time to crush the first pill into his drink.

"I had a really tough week. My supervisor at the Piggly Wiggly called me out for taking a long break and when I went over to the apartments to clean, I had one young football player sass me about being a hot little woman and would I like to spend some time with him. It just sucks to be a woman. No man would have ever been treated like that." She handed him the beer, trying to say anything to keep him reeled in.

"Oh, come on Tina, you know you can be totally intimidating. You have more power with that cute body than most men do with any degrees behind their name." He started to reach for her, but she quickly sat down. "Most people are scared of that. I know I am."

"Well, honey, you should be." She pretended to take a long drink.

"Is that a threat?" JB got his back up.

"No, no threat," She twirled her hair, "It's a promise."

"Did you get some food?" JB dismissed her menace.

"Yep, picked up some barbecue from Charcoal Willies."

"Great. I'm starving. They have the best BBQ. Thanks for stopping there."

"Anything for you." She turned away. "Oh, By the way, how's your wife?"

"What's that supposed to mean?"

"I saw her the other day at the store. Looks like she is getting into shape."

"I haven't noticed." JB perjured himself.

"I'm sure you haven't."

"Look Tina, we don't do that anymore. We don't do anything."

"Oh, looks like you won't be fucking Miss Piggy anymore." She felt her body tense as she spoke such hateful words about Rita Faye. She had to hold her emotions. She really wanted to shoot JB and run and confess everything to Rita Faye, begging for forgiveness.

She knew she could not afford a slip now. She had to see this through. For the first time in her life she felt cheap. What she was doing to Rita Faye and Caroline was unforgivable. Rita Faye deserved better than this. And so did she. She earned her reputation. How could anyone defend her? She was done pouring sugar over shit and getting everyone to eat it.

"Well, I'm hungry. I'll fix our plates."

With her hands shaking, she crushed two oxycodone into JB's beans and quickly stirred. Along with the drinking, he should be passed out within the hour. Vigilance was her comfort for the wrongs. She poured him a shot of vodka and made herself a shot of water.

JB walked in the house and she handed him a shot. "To us and a fun evening."

"To us." He tossed it back.

"Let's eat." She pursed her lips. She was careful to take small bites while she watched him inhale his food.

"You okay?" JB noticed.

"Oh, my stomach has been a little upset the last few days." Tina rubbed her middle. "Excuse me." Tina rushed to the bathroom and sat on the edge of the tub making hurling sounds.

"You okay in there?" JB asked as he started to feel the room spin.

She sat on the edge of the tub, groaning and flushing while she texted Talia. "I'm good." She flushed again. She splashed water on her face, dragging her fingers across her eyes to soil her makeup. Black lines shaded her bags. She choked again, making the same disgusting sound. She opened a bottle of lotion and rubbed just enough on one side of her head to make it look like she got vomit in her hair.

"Good job being the overserved girlfriend." She snapped a selfie and sent it to Talia captioned, "This should keep him away."

Tina flushed the toilet a final time and stumbled out of the bathroom. "I'm sorry. I just need to lay down." She found herself on the couch.

JB stumbled over and felt her head. "You don't feel sick."

"Just let me rest a minute." She closed her eyes.

"That's a good idea. If you have something, I don't want to catch it." His slurred words stumbled out. JB went in the bedroom and never came out.

Tina laid still for what seemed like hours. When she raised herself off the couch she peeked into the bedroom. He was out cold.

She quickly looked for his cell phone. JB's phone sat on the edge of the bathroom sink. She sat down and relieved herself and tapped in his code and started the hour-long job of reading and copying texts.

Doc, "I'm heading down there early. Make sure your love bird has flown the nest?"

JB, "She's out cold on the couch. Threw up. Grosses me out!"

Doc, "Oh, that's sexy."

JB, "I don't want that in my bed."

Doc, "We have some real problems. Did you get the meds we need?"

JB, "You're all set."

Doc "Got any extras?"

JB, "Does a player need something? I can work that out. Get your ass down here. I will get rid of her ASAP in the morning."

Doc, "Seems like you get rid of one problem and now you have another. Like mother like daughter."

JB, "Yep, she needs me. I took care of your running back's girlfriend, by the way. No baby."

Doc, "That has to be the third girl he's gotten in trouble."

JB, "I get it. No worries. BTW I have three syringes with me. Was hard to get more. I only had access to one med room the last few days."

Tina quickly screen shot the conversation. She moved on to a string from Whit.

Whit, "Looking forward to the retreat, JB. Rape kit is still MIA."

JB "Me too. I gotta get rid of Tina. Wish you were here to help me."

Whit "Like I did with Mary Claire Barnes. Your lady will be trouble when her precious daughter gets back."

JB, "She's too dumb for that. And thanks, MCB will always have a special place."

Whit, "Clean her up, get her out. The boys will be there early."

Tina felt her body go cold. She was shaking so bad she could hardly screen shot the words from Whit. "He killed Mary Claire. He's buried Melanie's rape kit," she whispered. She was about to put the phone back, grab her things and get out when she saw her daughter's name in one last string.

Ron, "The bird has flown the nest."

JB, "WTF?"

Ron, "My camp administrator said she went home with one of the counselors to spend the rest of the summer. No word of who she went with or where she was going. The counselor said she woke up and all her stuff was gone." Henry had asked Ron to text JB. It never occurred to him that Ron was setting him up.

JB, "As long as she doesn't come back home, I don't care. Did you keep this from her mother?"

Ron, "No reason to let her know. Need anything else?"

JB, "No, thanks for your help. She's a damn mess. Let's hope she shows up here before school starts. Let me know if you hear anything from her."

Ron, "Will do."

Tina read the text over again and whispered, "That son of a bitch knew and didn't tell me. He's been playing me." She quickly screen-shot the messages, sent them to her phone then deleted the pictures. She would get to Henry as soon as she got back to Oak Grove. He would know exactly what to do. She stared at the three blinking dots on his phone. *How could I have been involved with this monster?*

Tina had to leave. She splashed water on her face but something was niggling her to open the medicine cabinet. Tucked inside were prescription bottles of various medications with Caroline, Rita Faye, and Carter's names all over the prescriptions. She quickly took pictures, but not before she saw several buried in the back with Doc and Whit's name as well. The last bottle she picked up pushed her over the edge. The name Melanie Birch was stamped on the top and it was full of OxyContin. Tina slipped the bottle into her pocket.

*****

JB reached for the water next to his bed. His head was full of cobwebs. *What the hell did I drink?* He looked at his watch. It was only ten p.m. He shook out a few pills and downed them. First the NCAA thing and now Tina getting sick. He was exhausted. How could he and Doc take care of all this mess? He reached over for his phone but it was not in its usual place.

JB stumbled to the bathroom and tried the door. "You okay in there?"

Tina's heart dropped. She cleared her throat, "Yeah, Sorry. I'm pretty sure I have something. I'm having chills."

"Is my phone in there?"

She buried his phone under a towel. "I don't see it." She flushed the toilet, steadied herself, and opened the door. "I'm going home." She kept her eyes on the floor.

"That's a good idea, but it's late." JB slipped past her and found his phone under the towel.

Tina grabbed her bag, shoved her few rumpled things into the small tote, and headed to the door. "See you later."

"Not even a kiss?"

"I might be contagious." Tina rushed to the car and lowered herself into the driver's seat. Shaking, she could barely get her key in the ignition. She never realized how long the tail of JB's kite was until she read the texts. He legitimized everything he did. He created a service for the team, handing out pills for aches and pains and abortions for anyone who might need to get out of trouble.

I have been involved with a monster. What does that make me? How could I have ever let Melanie near him or his son? Tina raced down the long dark, tree-lined road.

And what am I going to do about Caroline?

Chapter 37

Bobby Cottonwood had one thing on his mind when it came to coaching high school football, discipline. He was the all-star quarterback of the Knights some twenty years ago and led them to three straight state titles. When he was done with high school, he traveled right up the road to his beloved Carolina Blue Tarheels and led them to two ACC championships and two New Year's Eve bowl games.

What most folks called confidence from his disciplined work effort, Doc Winters called self-centered. Bobby Cottonwood had plugged the player pipeline when Penni chose Washington. And that plug caused a sink full of dirty water in Doc's world. Now Doc would see to it that Cotton would eventually be dirty, too. It was just a matter of time.

Now in his early 40s, Coach Cotton never missed state playoffs. Bobby loved the rawness of the high school athlete. Felt like it was his calling. He could take a young man who was virtually afraid of taking the big hits and mold him into the kind of player he needed to compete for his high school team. He was tough and had an illustrious reputation, not only in the county but around the state. And the college coaches loved him.

It was rumored that the big house on Main Street came from the money that was slipped to him from college coaches who wanted his players. It was his wife's family that afforded them the position. He loved his wife, his community, and God, and he preached that to the kids. It was the envelopes of cash that Cotton would find in his mailbox or in his back-screen door that would cause him to break out in a cold sweat. He would immediately hand the money over to his principal.

He knew this sort of thing was going on around town and would never succumb to it. Even when there were threats when Penni Lafoie didn't pick Middle. Cotton would not stand for any of it and cautioned his assistants often about accountability and such nonsense. The man would lay a great foundation not only in football but in life.

Cotton championed for Penni, using his signing to a major west coast university as a tool to inspire his team over the coming months. "Look boys, there's a whole new world out there. I went away and came back with an experience to share."

Carter half listened. It was the beginning of his senior year, and he wanted to have fun. Carter leaned over to Jack. "Cottontop is on a roll."

Cotton paced the floor with a broomstick in his hand while he watched his players slouch in the filled auditorium. He took the broom and hit the stage hard, boom, boom, boom, slamming the pole against the wood.

"A dusty bible always leads to a dirty life," Coach Cottonwood preached.

Every player sat up. "To be an elite player," Cotton looked right at Carter, "You need exceptional athleticism, but you need diversity in competition and play. Under no circumstances am I going to allow any of you not be a two-sport athlete unless you have an incredibly great reason to quit another team." He licked his full lips when he felt the ooze of salvia come to the edge. "I want each one of you to name the second sport you will be playing this year. Sam, you're first."

"Of course, baseball, coach."

Cotton glared. "Carter?"

Carter was ready to jump out of his skin. He had popped an Adderall earlier and it was taking some time to take effect. "Coach, I think I'm going to take a pass this year. I don't want to get hurt." His leg twitched.

Cotton interrupted before he could give any more excuses. "Oh, I see. Well what if I decide to make each one of you try out for your position this year? What if I decide I will recruit around the school? Some of these big farm boys don't get to play because they have to work on their daddy's farms and can't make all the practices. Maybe I will make an exception this year and let them have excuses for oh I don't know things like work and helping their families pay the bills."

Carter looked at his fingernails. He was mad he didn't trim them.

"Carter," Cotton hollered. "I don't give a shit what you want. You're going to play a second sport. You're not going to be lazy, drink, and head into college the player I didn't produce. You will not sour my reputation. I care more about myself. So again, what second sport are you going to play this year?"

Carter grinned. "Golf."

"Oh, so you're giving up football, smart ass."

"Okay coach, I will hang with ole Sam here and play baseball. Besides the team needs some real players." He grabbed Sam on the shoulder.

"Good answer Carter. I expect leadership out of you. I know we lost some darn good players last year, but we have a great squad. I'm bringing up a few boys from the JV team to fill the holes."

Carter slid back down in his chair. He was feeling tired from last night. And the next few weeks would be tough with two a day. The heat made it especially difficult. He was looking at his hands when Cotton called him out again. "Carter, did you hear what I said?"

"Yes sir."

"Okay what is the first thing that football can teach you?"

Carter knew the speech by heart. "Team work, sir, and how to compete."

"That's right. How to compete as a team. Not with each other but as a unit. The competition with yourself is important too. And we plan for both. Improve your body, improve your playing, improve your life."

"Carter, What's the second one?"

"Discipline sir."

"Yes, sir, discipline. I expect each of you to behave. Eat clean, work out, make good grades, get good sleep, be respectful to your parents, your teammates and boys, I say this every year. Treat women with respect."

"Sam what's the next one?"

Sam sat up. "How to be a leader and a follower."

"I put these two together because one is just as important as the other. You know I expect you seniors to be leaders. You worked hard for three years to earn that role. And followers, look to your leaders. Stand up when you see something is wrong." Cotton looked around the room, "How about you Tommy? What's the last one?"

"Accountability and respect, sir."

"Yes sir. Each one of you is not only accountable for yourselves but for each other too. If you see something, say something. Stand up and do what's right. I'm going to bring up a sticky situation." Coach paused.

"The young woman that was hurt at one of the grad parties." He looked out at the boys. "I know for a fact that someone saw something and didn't say anything. As a team you have a responsibility." Cotton paused.

"I need every one of you to toe the line. I have high expectations. We have team meetings today, some walk-throughs, and running. Today is a warm-up for what's to come next week. Everyone will be off the next few days unless your position coach has specific plans for you. For the seniors who have paper work and pictures and other business to attend to, get it done. I expect everyone back here right after lunch. Make sure your paperwork is in order. If you didn't get your physical for the summer, Dr. Taylor will be available this weekend. See you on the field in twenty." Cotton marched out.

It was horribly hot and humid and the boys gathered around in a large circle, jerseys on, just shorts, helmets in hands and listening to every word.

"We have a big year coming up and I expect great things from all of you. I have high hopes for the team. Knights protect each other. I said before and I'll say it again. Players protect players. I know you all had a good summer because most of you checked in with me. And I saw many of you in the weight room. Great job to those of you who were committed." Cotton looked over at Sam, who spent his summer on a mission trip. He was proud of him but disappointed that the young man did not attend workouts.

Sam stayed out of trouble, and if he played his cards right would be going to Duke on a full ride. He worked hard and was accepted to a coveted position for a rising senior for a summer international medical mission trip. "Fully paid," were the key words when he received the acceptance letter. His parents, both teachers, earned what most do, and his family didn't have much for extras. Sam played football because he was a good kicker and he was friends with many of the guys on the team.

"Kicker, I know you spent the summer doing the Lord's work, and I'm proud of you for that, but I'm thinking we may need to get you back in shape. Sam, let's take the team on a mile run. Go."

Sam had given up his summer job working in tobacco to go to Guatemala. It was the worst and best two months of his life. He saw things he never could imagine and met people that he fell in love with. He wanted to return one day when he was a doctor. It was a combination of mentoring, observation, and tutoring alongside spiritual guidance and children's programs that helped him understand the global healthcare issues. He was able to shadow doctors and get a behind the scenes of what his future could hold. He was more committed than ever, and he spent his first few days back going over every detail with

Harper, only to be thrown back into the fiery pit of football in August in North Carolina.

Coach Cotton watched Sam take off.

Sam coached himself. "After seeing the shit I saw this summer, this is nothing." He flew past the struggling boys running behind him. He had run all summer long in the hot Guatemalan sun. He would not let his team down. Sam finished his last lap as a few boys were just rounding their third, "Let's finish together." He pushed them. When they finished, most of them fell on the warm grass gasping for air, while he headed to the water cooler.

"Thanks," Coach Cotton grabbed Sam's shoulder. "I knew I could count on you."

Sam and Tommy walked up to their position coach. "Boys, welcome to defense." We are going to play a fast style this year. "Let's do some drills."

Chapter 38

The morning practice was grueling. Carter, Sam, and Tommy all stood at Jack's car.

"So, you guys want to come over?" Carter promised the boy's lunch. "Or Sam, you gotta go to Harper's and let her tell you what to do." Carter shoved him.

"Fuck you, dude. Don't be jealous. I can't help it if I'm dating the prettiest girl in town."

"Yeah, wouldn't we all be so lucky. I bet you two have to make up a lot for lost time. So, are her parents' home right now, or are you going to head over there when they're gone?" Carter licked his lips.

"Don't be a dick, man."

Carter shoved his buddy's arm. "One day, man, one day you'll get lucky."

"I'm already lucky. I'm just hoping she follows me to Duke and does not make a foolish mistake and go here." He took a jab at Carter.

"Come on guys, let's head over to my house. My mom just bought a ton of food."

The boys piled into their cars and took off. Carter had a few other guys in his car. Sam rode over with Tommy and texted Harper to let her know his plan for the beach.

They reached the Taylors' house and piled into the kitchen. Carter opened the refrigerator and pulled out all the lunch meats, bread, and condiments. He went into the pantry and pulled out bags of potato chips, candy, and anything he could find. He pulled out an oversized container of creatine and offered shakes to everyone. Packages of meat, bags of chips, and Gatorades cluttered the counter when Caroline walked in. She tried to hurry up the back staircase before any of the guys saw her.

Sam caught her out of the corner of his eye and gave her a quick wink.

"Hey Caroline," he said between bites when all the boys turned their head.

"Hey Sam, welcome home." She smiled. "How was your summer?"

"Great." He paused trying to act normal. "How was your summer?"

"Great," she mumbled. "I can't wait to hear about your trip."

Sam paused. "Yeah."

"Can we talk later?" She started for the staircase, "I have some work to do."

"Carry your ass up the steps, your kind aren't welcome here." Carter hollered.

She never turned around. "You're a real asshole," she heard Tommy say as she walked to her room. Caroline closed the door and locked it. She didn't want anyone slipping up behind her. She reached up in her closet and grabbed her duffle bag, slipped a few things inside, and walked in her bathroom to grab her toiletries. She set her duffle down and started sifting through her clothes to pack for the beach. It had been a few weeks since Helen shared the letter, and she was doing the best she could to avoid her dad and Carter.

Caroline was confused about the newfound interest from her mother. It was starting to feel normal, but she was still suspicious. "At least she's trying. She's taking better care of herself." She could hear the laughter downstairs fade.

Her phone chirped. *I'm sorry your brother is such an asshole. Have a fun weekend at the beach.* Caroline smiled at the text from Tommy.

She held her bag over her shoulder and swiped her long blond hair out of her face. She looked in the mirror for a second and wondered if she had the same capacity her father and brother had to be such awful people. She whispered, "Maybe I do. Or I can be whoever I want to be." Her eyes watered. "I don't want to be them." What surprised her the most was she thought about Rita Faye. "Why is my mom so stupid to stay in this horrible marriage?" She shook her long blond hair out and gazed at her hazel eyes. The dark circles of black liner were gone. Caroline didn't need it anymore. "It's my senior year and it's my time." She told her reflection, "Just like mom said."

Rita Faye spent most of the morning fighting with a paper company, but not before arguing her way to victory. Since she was taking care of herself, she had more energy. She had kept to her eating and exercise schedule with precision and it was working. She headed home to enjoy a few quiet minutes at lunch.

When she rounded the corner into the kitchen she came into the silence of a loud mess. There were empty bread wrappers, packages of meat, and empty potato chip bags strewn across the counters. Soda and Gatorade cans littered the kitchen island and, in the sink sat a stack of dishes with remnants of food. Carter had obviously hosted his football friends and didn't bother to clean up. She felt her pulse quicken as she grabbed the trash can and swiped the entire top of the island into the garbage, dishes and all.

"I hate these wedding dishes."

She grabbed the sponge and quickly wiped the counter. She stacked a few dishes in the sink, but in her anger tossed a few more in the trash.

Caroline hit the bottom step. "Mom, are you okay?" She watched her shove the broken plates into the garbage.

"Damn him." Rita Faye moved to the refrigerator to check for her garden salad. There it sat, safe in the refrigerator along with some mixed vegetables. However, the sandwich meat drawer was completely empty. She walked to the panty and all the bread and chips were gone. "Damn kid!"

"It's okay." Caroline dropped her bag on the floor and started toward her.

"I'm just so sick of it all." Rita Faye plunged to a stool. "I'm tired of getting angry. I'm tired of Carter. I have done such an injustice to him, as has his father. He can't even clean up after himself." It seemed her awareness was sharpened since her weight was dropping.

"I know, Mom." Caroline touched her shrinking arm.

Rita Faye turned, "I'm so sorry. I have been the worst mother. I'm just so sorry." She buried her head into Caroline's small frame while Caroline held her.

"You are fine." Caroline stroked her back.

"I won't replace the chips. If Carter wants chips, he can go out and get them himself," She recovered.

"Mom, he's a mess, I mean he made a mess," she corrected.

Rita Faye looked up, "Can we talk?"

Caroline felt her shoulders release. "Of course."

Rita Faye pulled a stool over. "Want to share my salad?"

"Sounds good." Caroline smiled.

Rita Faye handed her a fork.

"Caroline, I know things have been tough here, but I promise you I am going to make things better for you. You deserve a good home. And I have not given you one."

A tear slipped from the corner of her eye not knowing what to say. "Thank you."

"I will never not be available again. And you can count on me for anything."

"Mom, I have to be honest, but can we keep this between ourselves?" Caroline paused. "I'm going to the beach with Harper tomorrow to meet Melanie."

Rita Faye stopped chewing. "What? What's going on? I didn't know you were spending the weekend away."

"She's been getting help all summer." Caroline chose her words carefully. "And with school starting next week, we all felt like she needed some time with her good friends before she comes back here."

Rita Faye's heart broke. "I understand. Was she the one who was assaulted at the party?"

Caroline whispered, "Yes."

"I think you and Harper are wonderful friends to her, and I think if she was getting help that was the best thing she could do." Rita Faye searched her daughter's face. "You know I have been going to Raleigh all summer to meet with a counselor and a doctor."

"I'm so happy to see you taking better care of yourself, Mom."

"Thank you. I have done such a bad job at taking care of you though. But," She looked right in Caroline's eyes, "that is all changing and I promise you this. No matter what, I will stand by your side. Caroline, you can always trust me."

Caroline felt years of anger slip from her shoulders. "I love you, Mom."

Rita Faye reached over and held her daughter. "You go have a fun weekend at the beach with the girls. I'm so proud of you, Caroline. Despite me, you have turned out to be an amazing woman."

Chapter 39

The smell of freshly cut grass played off the heat that rested gently on the undisturbed football field. It was a sanctuary that only the brave would dare come to knowing Coach Cottonwood was in charge. Each player was handed a t-shirt. On the front was a picture of the school mascot, a golden knight, and the words emblazoned below, "Men of Valor."

"I want each one of you boys to put that shirt on and remember who we are. We represent honor, loyalty, and nobility."

After the last name was called Coach continued, "Remember we are one. And we are here standing on the shoulders of the great players that have come before you. There will be no excuses this year. We have some of the best linemen in the state. Don't let anyone get in your way of winning, boys. This is our sanctuary, our field, and we are going to protect our field. You know how important high school football is to this town. Let's give them a reason to come out on Friday nights and an even bigger reason to talk about us." Cotton looked around at his team. "You finished the first day strong."

The boys ran the plays effortlessly that afternoon, and Cottonwood was so impressed he let them go early. Sam was relieved because he needed to get on the road as soon as he could. He would stop by Mr. Charlie's with the boys and grab an ice cream soda. But he could not stay. He was trying to keep everything as normal as possible. His mom agreed to text him his marching orders.

Sam took the last sip of his soda. "Mr. Charlie, you make the best in the state."

"Thanks Sam." He wiped the counter and walked down to the end to chat with some of the kids.

"We going out tonight since it's our last open Friday for a while." Carter gave Sam a shove.

Sam said, "My mom is super pissed at me. I gotta head home." He showed him the text. *I need you home, NOW.*

"What's up?" Carter said.

"My mom wants all my clothes washed and ready for school next week. She said I'm grounded until I get it done."

"What the hell, you aren't a kid. Tell her to do it. You have football. My mom even had to go to the Soap and Sud this summer to do laundry." Carter laughed. "Get Harper to do it."

Sam was disgusted. "Yeah, my mom is not like that. You know she can be tough." Sam shuddered the harsh words against his mother. He knew the lies were continuing for the sake of protecting Melanie. He justified. "I gotta go man. I'm in enough trouble already."

Carter looked at Sam suspiciously. "So Harper can't do your laundry? Or why not get her maid to do it. Harper doesn't have to do a thing for herself." Carter wouldn't stop, "Yep, go run to your girl and leave your team. That's what you're good at, ole Sammy boy." Carter reached for his arm and held on a little longer than Sam was comfortable with.

Sam broke away. "I don't even know who you are anymore, dude."

"What the hell, man. I get that you're in love. Yeah, me too." Carter let out a cackle. "Oh, spoiled Harper can't help, she's probably with my loser sister somewhere anyway."

"You're such an asshole, Taylor." Carter had become so malleable Sam could easily walk away. He needed to get home, get his room cleaned up by tomorrow, pick up Tina, and head to the beach. Melanie would be there.

Chapter 40

The girls changed into shorts and big T-shirts right after dinner. They grabbed their drinks and headed out to the back porch.

"Are you nervous about seeing Melanie?" Harper asked.

"Kind of. I feel like it's my fault," Caroline said.

"Well don't. You and I have a great plan for her and I think this weekend will really help her."

"I'm glad she recorded the conversation." Caroline held. "That's a safety net for her. I just can't wait to get to the beach tomorrow and see her. We have so much to talk about. I just hope when school starts next week, we can be there for her. I know I had my classes arranged so I'm in most of them with her."

"Her mom checked with the principal and made sure she has none with Carter."

"I'm glad your grandpa is home and doing well," Caroline said.

"Yeah, me too. His arm and shoulder are healing nicely and the pin removal went very well. The doctors thought, after some rehab, he will have full use again."

"That's awesome. I know your grandmother was worried. They have had a tough summer."

"The best news is he never had a heart attack or stroke. He had lost his footing in the parking lot. It was the fall and the subsequent head injury that set him back. He hit the front of his head and had some temporary memory and personality changes from a brain bleed. Once the swelling cleared, he's been great."

The girls heard the TV blaring from Henry's office. "That damn Alabama is always number one." Patsy screamed. She sidled next to Henry, rubbing his hand after she startled him.

"Don't get yourself so worked up, mama." He was fighting sleep.

Her eyes searched his longing face. "It's almost time for cake."

Henry fluttered his eyes trying to stay wake.

"Are you thirsty?" Patsy reached over and picked up his water.

"I'm good, just a little sore." His broken clavicle was mending.

Caroline and Harper headed to the doorway of Henry's den. "What were you hollering at Mimi?" Harper scolded her.

"Your grandmother thinks if she hollers loud enough at the TV it will make a difference to her sports teams."

Patsy nudged Henry. "Oh, you know, the preseason college football rankings are out."

The girls laughed. "Okay girls, I have a cake. Then off to bed. This one here has had enough excitement for the day. Come on Henry, let's go."

They followed Patsy like little ducklings and enjoyed the sweet taste of Hummingbird Cake that Clara had made earlier.

"Mimi, the cake is delicious. We are going to stay up a little later than eight so I'm going to say goodnight to you and papaw." Harper gave her grandparents a kiss.

"Good night, thank you for the delicious cake." Caroline followed Harper up the steps.

Harper was tossing countless outfits in her bag. "Do you like this one?" She held up a long dress.

"Shit, I have to go home and get my phone." Caroline stopped her.

"I can't believe you forgot it."

"Well, me and my mom were talking and…" she stopped. "I will be back in a few minutes."

Caroline reached her house in record timing. She raced up the steps and rummaged through the piles of clothes on her floor. Her phone was safe right in the middle of her discarded shorts and t-shirts.

She slipped out, carefully locking her bedroom and walked down the back steps. When she turned the corner, Carter was in the kitchen. Caroline felt her entire body go stiff. It was the first time since the tape that she was in the house alone with him. She spent the majority of the summer at Harper's. She fought hard to hold her tongue. All that flooded her thoughts were killing him. What he did to Melanie was unforgivable. *He's a pig.*

"Where are you going, loser?" He gnawed on a chicken leg from KFC.

"None of your business." She turned her back. "Oh, wait, I'm going out to see if I can get myself raped. But you wouldn't know about that, would you?"

"What are you talking about, loser?" She turned and watched red rising rage climb up his face. *Got ya,* she thought.

"You know exactly what I'm talking about." She was going too far.

"Believe me no one wants to do anything with you."

"Yep." She swallowed her words. "And if they did, they wouldn't have to force themselves on me." She held steady.

"What's wrong with you?" Carter wiped his mouth with the back of his hand. "You look better with your freak makeup on."

"Have a good night." She walked out the back door, slamming it along with his words.

"You act like I know what you're fucking talking about, you bitch."

Caroline looked back at the house. Wrath burned in her as she thought about the pain the community and her brother caused the Lafoe family. The question was why did he do it? Every girl in Oak Grove loved Carter. They may not want to sleep with him, but they certainly loved him. As Caroline walked, she realized why. Melanie was her friend and her boyfriend was the center of attention.

Caroline quickly followed the path to the back of the yard and turned right by the garage. She had an eerie feeling that she was being followed. She walked along the back street and quickly slipped behind the second neighbor's yard. She crouched low by their heavily shaded fence and waited a few minutes. Just as she thought, Carter raced by.

Caroline watched him turn past the Middletons' house. When she was sure he was gone, she slipped around the fence and watched his head bob along the opposite side. She walked through the neighbor's yard and down a hidden path right into the Middletons' back yard. After carefully unlocking the vine covered gate, she quickly locked it back. *He may guess where I'm going but he would never find Patsy's secret entrance.*

She opened the back door and scaled the steps.

"Why did you take so long?" Harper had just finished.

"Carter was home," she panted. "He followed me."

"What?" Harper peered out her windows.

"Oh, don't worry. Patsy's gate saved me."

"Thank goodness. I'm sorry Caroline," she paused, "but he creeps me out."

Caroline's heart leapt. "He creeps me out too."

"What did you decide to take?"

"I have two dresses and several short outfits. And of course, there are things down at the house. If you forgot anything, I have plenty for you to wear."

"What would I do without you? Our styles are so similar." Caroline laughed.

"You could do worse." Harper started. "Sam's calling."

"Hey," she said.

"Hey, Carter showed up and wanted to know if Caroline was with you. He said she needed to come home." Sam sounded anxious.

Harper looked over at Caroline. "Nope she's not with me. I'm at home with my grandparents. We finally celebrated papaw's homecoming."

Sam switched into defensive gear to divert Carter as he stood in front of him on his front porch. "I just don't get you. Ever since I got home you have been really tough to get along with. Maybe we need a break." Sam hung up the phone in front of Carter.

"Women, they can be a big pain in our ass." Carter stopped, satisfied with Sam's attack at Harper.

"They sure can. Hey man I'm still reeling from jet lag. Sorry I couldn't help out, dude."

"Oh, yeah, just worried about my sister. My parents really need her to come home. She's not answering her cell phone."

"I'm sure she's okay. You know how weird she can be." Sam twisted his words.

"Sorry you can't hang tonight." Carter stepped off Sam's front porch.

Chapter 41

"This is not easy," Harper looked at her phone. "Sam just hung up on me."

"He's playing the game." Caroline stopped her.

"I know, he's just not like this." Harper stared at her phone.

As soon as she felt defeated Sam texted her. "Sorry about that. Carter is getting weirder by the minute. See you tomorrow evening. Love you."

Harper quickly texted him back. "Love you too. You're right. Carter was there and Sam was playing the game. I'm not very good at this. You want to head downstairs and sit on the porch for a while? Beth wants to come over. She just got back from the mountains."

"Sounds good. I wish she could come to the beach."

"Me too. Her dad won't let her do anything since the attack. He said he doesn't want her around all the chaos. He's a smart man."

"She's been really busy with cheer squad anyway," Caroline said.

The girls made their way downstairs and onto the back porch. The ceiling fans moved the warm air around just enough to make it comfortable.

Beth came bouncing in the back door and settled on the couches.

"Hey ladies, I'm so jealous you are going to the beach. My dad won't let me do anything. Ever since the Lafoes left he has been super weird."

"It's all good," Caroline said.

"The bigger question is what should we do about Melanie? Her mom says she has this end covered. Whatever that means."

"I don't get it?" Beth asked.

Harper leaned in. "Beth, Melanie sent us something." She looked over at Caroline.

"If we tell you, you have to promise you won't say a word."

"You guys are scaring me." Beth dug deeper into the couch cushion. "But I want to know."

"You can't even tell Jack. You got it?" Caroline cautioned her.

Harper clicked on her phone and the recording started.

Beth tipped her head. "This is some serious shit. How long have you girls known about this?"

"About three weeks," Harper answered.

"Holy shit. Caroline, how are you? I mean this is your dad, your brother. Are you fucking kidding me?"

"No, it's no joke," Caroline said, "but our priority is to protect Melanie when she comes home."

Beth felt her heart race. "This creeps me out. I don't know how in the hell you have lived with this, Caroline. I would want to kill my brother if he did this to one of my friends and your dad." Beth covered her mouth.

"We are putting together a plan," Harper stopped her. "Melanie is going to need our help when she comes back."

"What are you talking about? I thought she was working at some summer camp. That's what my dad told me," Beth said.

"She was. But she has been in Washington with Penni and his parents."

"What?" Beth said.

"And when she gets back, we have to take care of her and protect her," Harper said.

"Do you want to listen to it again?" Caroline asked.

"I don't want to hear that ever again. I just can't get over your dad in this whole thing. Why in the hell would he be so involved?"

"I don't know, but we have to stay strong for Melanie and for you, Caroline." Harper sat upright.

"Yes, we do, and hearing that tape drives me to want to protect her even more," Beth said.

"Girls we have a long ten months on our hands. Let's hope Melanie comes back strong and with us by her side."

"And let's hope my brother leaves everyone alone."

Beth felt uneasy. "I'm here for you guys. I just hate being late to the party. I'm so sorry, Caroline."

Harper stopped. "Beth, we are heading down to the beach to meet Melanie. If you could come that would be great."

"I can't." She was not going to ask her parents again. "But I'm here when you guys get back."

Harper said, "We can fill you in when we get back on Sunday."

"Can we talk about something else?" Beth continued to have a troubled feeling. "So, Caroline, Jack says you and Tommy are hot and heavy."

Caroline felt a geyser of red run up her face. "Nope, change the subject."

Harper started, "It feels so good to laugh again."

The girls yakked for hours, never realizing that Henry was in his office.

Chapter 42
August

JB blinked a few times, hoping to slow down his spinning head. *I didn't think I drank that much.* He rolled over and picked up the bottle of Vicodin, tossed a few pills in his mouth and swallowed. *That will take the edge off.* He looked at his watch. It was 6 in the morning. The other side of his bed was empty. He vaguely remembered what happened.

Why didn't she wake me? Tina was growing distant. He reached for his phone and saw that he had six text messages. He leaned over and picked up his pants. He stumbled into the bathroom. When he walked into the kitchen, he noticed Tina's pink jacket. It smelled of poverty and sadness.

Melanie would be gone a few more days. He sat down at the kitchen table with a cool glass of water and he fought to remember last night. Tina told him she was heading to Raleigh for the weekend to see an old friend. But not before she got sick. Or did she tell him then got sick? She had to pick up Melanie on Sunday at the airport. Something didn't seem right to him.

JB struggled to replay the clouded conversation yesterday. "Melanie seems so not like herself. I didn't think she would pull away from me. All her texts are about her new best friend, Robyn." JB played the complaining words over and over again from Tina. He knew Melanie left camp weeks ago and he was proud that she was never the wiser.

"You did the right thing. She needed an adventure this summer. After all, I'm a doctor, and I always know what's best. You can trust me," JB reassured her.

"The summer's been long and lonely," Tina complained.

"I think she's doing just fine," he answered through his sip of wine, thinking how grateful he was that she didn't come back early. He didn't need her in town this summer making trouble for Carter. He could deal with Tina. But he knew Melanie was far too vulnerable.

"You have to let go sometime. I think this is good for her. She is figuring out how to solve problems for herself."

"I don't have family to have BBQs with, and I wish the lake wasn't polluted from the drowning. This town could use a good place for recreation." Tina continued to complain.

JB cringed. "No one wants to go to that spoiled lake."

"I feel like everyone is looking at me." Tina was proud of how masterfully she was playing JB with all her complaining, knowing she would be at the beach with her daughter by Friday night.

He leaned toward her. "No one is looking at you, and if they are it's because you are so beautiful." He leaned in for a kiss as she moved away.

"No, I'm the widow whore in town who lives in shanty town and killed her husband. Isn't that what everyone thinks? I just wish Tim was here. He would know what to do with her."

JB felt anger rise after her comment. "I'm sorry I couldn't help more with him."

JB tried medications for his depression and anxiety. And the extra strength Vicodin seemed to help. But mixing medicines with alcohol proved to be a dangerous cocktail for Tim.

"You can't bring Tim back."

The words stood still in JB's head. *Why would she be talking about him?*

"I'm trying to help you two the best I can." That is the last thing he remembered. And then she left.

JB picked up his phone and scrolled through his texts. Most were from Doc. He moved over to his pictures and went through a few of the screen shots he took off Tina's phone. He didn't realize that Tina and Melanie had planted text messages on her phone knowing JB was snooping.

"Sorry too busy to talk, Mom. Robyn and I are going on a hike. Will call later." Tina responded, "Hope camp has been good for you?"

"Camp has been so fun." JB looked at the date of the screen shot. It was just sent last week. He took a sip of water. *We all have our games.*

JB tossed his phone on the table. *I need a shower before the boys get here.*

Chapter 43

Caroline felt a sense of relief with their new-found alliance. Rita Faye promised to keep her secret. But it never occurred to her that Caroline would know who did it.

Caroline felt a sense of solidarity with her mom and was overwhelmed with a sense of calm.

The group would be at Harper's beach house over the course of the next few hours. Anne was happy to be a part of their big plan and support the girls. They were all apprehensive with Melanie coming home.

Despite the heaviness, they would have a blast eating fresh seafood, laying out, and finishing off their summer tans. The girls were as excited as they were weary. They didn't know what to expect from Melanie. They arrived, quickly unpacked, and checked out the beach. Melanie would be there soon.

The trip was long for Melanie, but Talia was by her side. They would meet Helen at Wilmington's airport and head down to Wrightsville beach. After two days, Helen would take Melanie to Raleigh to meet her mom at the airport and drop Talia off for her return trip to Seattle.

Helen saw Melanie and Talia right away. Melanie's long blond hair swept across her small back while Talia rolled her large bag behind her. The two of them looked relaxed. Helen hopped out of the car and rushed to them, holding on for a long time as tears and hugs covered each of them. They separated when they heard the parking attendants blow their whistle and ask them to load the car and move on. The three lifted the heavy bags in the car and made their way out around the airport exit.

The chatter started as soon as Helen got her bearings and didn't stop until they reached the beach house. The sun was just starting to set as the large yellow ball dipped into the water from the orange and pink sky, softening a blue ripple against the back drop. Melanie could smell the water as soon as they came to the bridge that crossed over onto Wrightsville beach. The smell of the ocean brought her back to beach music and the waves lulled her in the back seat.

Helen pulled up to the summer cottage and turned off the car.

"Before we get out, wait just a minute." She cleared her throat. "You doing okay?"

"Yes ma'am. It's good to be back here. I missed the beach."

"I know honey." Helen looked at Talia. "You are here for the next few days and they will be fun, but we need to talk about the next several months too."

"I can't wait to lay out tomorrow. Really, I'm good. I can't wait to see the girls and hang out with them. Thank you so much for helping me through all of this," she started.

"Look, Melanie. That is what we are all here for. We know your story, and now we can all help you. It doesn't mean it will be easy. It just means you have us." Helen turned in her seat.

"Exactly, we are all here for you." Talia reached back and grabbed her knee. "I think the summer was really productive with all the counseling. But you have to remember these next ten or so months could prove to be very long for you."

"I know," she whispered. "That's why I'm happy I have you guys. I could not do this without all of you. I'm starting to feel better and in control and I'm not going to let what Carter did to me define me."

"Good girl. And if you ever need anything don't forget we have you."

"I'm going to be okay." Melanie sat with the door half opened. "I know it will be hard, but I can do this. I just hope my mom…" She stopped. "She has so many problems and I want to lean on her."

"And you can because we are here for you, including your mom, even if you can't escape from our small town and all the chatter." Helen regretted her last words but knew they would serve as a warning.

"Yes." her voice was strong and resilient and unstable all wrapped up in her acknowledgement.

"Okay, let's head into the house. I'm so glad you're back, honey."

As soon as she opened her car door, she could hear children's voices echoing from the beach.

The ladies grabbed their bags, but before they could make it up the long staircase at the front of the cottage, Caroline and Harper were dashing down the steps to reach Melanie. Tears, hugs, and screaming filled the salty beach air as they hung on the long staircase clinging to each other.

Helen watched Melanie fold into Caroline and Harper's arms and took note of the three girls clinging to each other. It was a relief to know that Melanie had found forgiveness. It was not that Caroline had done anything. It was that she was Carter's sister. Helen wished the moment could last forever. Stuck in time and space when three teenage girls could cling to each other and love each other and forget about the ugly world that had entered their innocence.

"Come on, girls, let's head in," Anne's voice interrupted the moment as she stood at the top of the steps, holding the doors open, her eyes darting from one end of the porch to the next, looking as if she were running a covert operation while she tapped her toes. "Hurry in ladies." She reached over and gave Helen and Talia a big hug right after she grabbed Melanie and held her. "I'm so happy you are here." She grabbed Helen's bags.

"Pull your car in the open bay in the garage. You never know who may be down at the beach watching."

The beach house was filled with white overstuffed couches, large navy chairs, and a sixteen-seat dining table. Large windows spread across the back of the house that looked out over the ocean. They all walked in the spacious cottage while the girls made their way down the long hall to Harper's room. Harper had double bunk beds in her room. There were many nights spent at the beach house with friends and family.

Helen made it up the back staircase from the garage and joined Anne and Talia in the kitchen while Anne fixed everyone some iced tea and a tray of snacks.

"How is she, really?" She handed Helen a cool glass as she whispered.

Helen swiped her long gray hair off her shoulder. "From the short ride over here, she seems good. I think now that she has put some distance between the situation, she's had time to heal."

Talia leaned against the counter. "The summer has given her a break. But honestly, I think the worst is yet to be. I'm terribly worried when she sees Carter, she may have a huge set back."

"Carter," Anne stopped. "Oh, my goodness." She gasped. "Do you think the counseling helped? I can't believe it was him. Why didn't she report him?" Anne babbled. "I just can't believe it was him." She could not stop.

"Yes," Talia whispered. "I do. It was Carter. Fetu and I both think she should continue, but of course who in the world can she go to in Oak Grove? We have made some calls to Raleigh counselors, but I think that will have to be dealt with when the time comes."

"Let me take care of her counseling. I can get her to Raleigh at least one day a week. Especially since daddy and mama are doing better," Anne said. "Does Caroline know it was her brother?"

Helen looked over at her dear friend. "Yes, she has known since the middle of the summer. And somehow, she has kept it together."

"How in the world did she find out?" Anne asked.

Helen felt the first sip of betrayal cross her lips. She never considered when she involved Harper that she would not tell her mother. Her mind quickly reached for the right words. "She found out from me."

"What? How?" Anne was stunned.

Helen peered at both women, "Melanie sent me a recording of a conversation with Carter, JB, and Tina and confessed the whole thing."

"What recording?" Anne pressed.

"Anne, please don't think I was withholding, but Melanie did not want anyone to know." She took a deep breath. "Harper, Caroline, and I met down at the studio in mid-June after Melanie sent it to me. I didn't want Caroline to listen to the recording and not have someone who she loved and trusted with her. Maybe I made a mistake not including you, but I was so shocked. She needed help. She needed cover and she needed to let Caroline know what happened. It was after she went to Seattle with Fetu and Talia."

"Fetu sent the tape for Melanie." Talia interjected. "He wanted cover for her."

Anne was stunned. "I cannot believe Harper knew all this and didn't say a word. I'm not sure if I should be proud of her or angry."

"Oh, I think you need to be proud of the kind of daughter you have. Please don't be angry. No one was trying to hide anything from you. We are all in a place that I'm sure none of us would have chosen. But here we are, and thank goodness we all have each other. Harper has been a wonderful friend. And the letter that Melanie sent, asked for complete confidence."

"I think we need to have a long talk with the girls so they are all prepared for the school year ahead," Anne said. "I'm sorry I made this about me. I'm just so damned shocked and mad. I need time to process this. It's probably better with all the distractions from mama and daddy."

"I'm glad we have them here for the next few days," Helen interjected. "I have some ideas."

"How are things with Penni?" Anne asked.

Talia felt her heart melt. "He has handled this amazingly well." Talia paused, "Only," she licked her lips, "We did not tell him it was Carter. He knows she was attacked, but she would not tell him who. In time he will know."

Anne and Helen both paused. "Do you think that was a good idea?" Anne broke the tension.

"Honestly, we were afraid of what Penni would do. He is already upset that it even happened, but the two of them had a great summer. Fetu and I did not want to spoil it. We also think that soon enough he will know, but he needs to concentrate on his work and school."

"I agree. I don't agree with lying, but I think it's best that for right now the two of them work on their relationship. The poor girl has been through enough," Anne said.

"Yes, and my son understands. He is fine as long as he knows that they are together."

"Let's go sit outside and enjoy the evening." Anne picked up the tray of snacks. "I'm going to order some food from Sasser's Seafood as soon as the girls give me their orders."

The three women walked outside and made themselves comfortable on the porch. Anne curled up on one sofa while Helen and Talia both took a chair beside each other. The ocean breeze and the sound of the waves calmed them.

"There is one other thing," Helen said. "We need to support Tina, too. I think now that Melanie and Penni are doing well," Helen held her head, "I think this could all come crashing down on Tina. JB has done a lot of damage to that woman."

Anne shook her head. "I feel like I have been out of the loop."

Talia whispered, "JB and Tina have been carrying on for several years."

"What?" Anne shook her head in disgust.

"Yes, he has been feeding her pills, helping her with her bills," Helen made air quotes, "and doing it all now to cover up the sins of his son."

"And him." Talia chimed in. "I'm just glad my son is away from all of this. He would kill Carter." Talia took a sip of her tea. "The minute my son saw her, he picked her up and would not let her go." Talia reached over and picked up some cheese and crackers. "I'm sure he will do whatever it takes. Fetu has him talking to someone too." She took a bite.

"They are both wonderful young people. I'm just glad we can all be here for them," Helen whispered.

Anne sipped her tea. "I'm honestly worried she may have a setback when she comes face to face with Carter. And how are we going to keep all of this a secret this next year?" Anne swallowed hard. "And Tina."

"I know, she has not handled this well at all."

"Well who would? She loses her poor husband then a creeper takes advantage of her."

It was Anne's' turn to share a secret.

"You know mama told me this summer she thought JB and Tina were involved. She heard daddy mumbling about it. I told her it was nonsense. Do you think Melanie knows?"

The look on both Talia's and Helen's face gave it away.

"How could she not?" Helen said. "Where does this leave all of them? And poor Caroline. What a damn mess." Helen could not stop.

"I think our job right now is to support both of the girls. I just hope their friendships can stay intact," Talia said. "But I can tell you, after Tina's visit, that woman is out for blood. She told me she had a plan, and I'm glad she will be coming here to work out the care of her daughter." Talia sat for a moment trying to control her emotions.

"What the hell is JB doing messing around with Tina? And to think my son's name was smeared all over that damn chat site." Talia felt her anger surge. "And why in the hell did the police not get involved with the assault?"

"Let me guess who the cop was on duty, Whit Cain. You know he is in knee deep with JB and Doc." Helen stopped them.

"JB has dirty hands, that's for sure," Anne whispered afraid the girls may walk up. "He's bad news. My daddy hates the man and so does Wade. I know something is going on at the hospital too but they won't talk about it. Don't you feel sorry for Rita Faye? Here she is trying so hard to run a respectable business."

Before they could continue, they heard a loud rumble, and around the corner came the three girls dressed in bathing suits and cover ups.

"Mom, we are going to take a walk on the beach," Harper said as she looked at Melanie and smiled.

"Go ahead but go in there and mark on the menu what you want for dinner, and Harper, please order something for Sam and Tina too."

Melanie looked shocked. "My mom is coming?"

"Yes, honey, with Sam." Helen said.

Melanie shook her head while Harper wrapped her arm around her shoulders. "It's all good. We're just missing Beth." The girls ran into the house, and, after a few short minutes bounded down the steps and onto the beach.

"Seeing those three makes me so happy," Helen said. "I love their joy. Just happy to be together, running down the beach, dipping their toes in the surf and laughing."

"It was the best thing we heard this summer too," Talia said.

The women chatted for a while, talking about the latest news in Oak Grove. Helen once again mentioned Rita Faye and how well she was doing.

"Do you think she suspects anything?" Talia asked.

"If she does, she has certainly taken her concerns where they should be. She's lost weight, she's in yoga all the time, and she and Caroline are doing better than ever," Helen said. "I just know we have to be there for her, too."

Talia was beaming. "I always liked Rita Faye. She just seemed so sad. It's no wonder with a no-good husband like JB." Her phone buzzed. "Oh, I forgot to call Fetu and let him know we were here." She stepped into the house to talk.

"I better order dinner. It could take a good hour." Anne ordered dinner and before long the three girls came bounding in, sandy feet and wet hair and made their way to the bathroom to clean up.

They had a lot to cover in two short days. But the sun, surf, and the support would do Melanie a lot of good before she had to go back to Oak Grove.

Anne called Patsy to check in on Henry, and Patsy assured her she would call if there was any problem.

Sam and Tina pulled up to the beach house around 8 p.m. with small bags and a big appetite. Sam stopped at Chic Fil A, but Tina was so nervous she could not eat a thing. He knew Miss Anne would have better food anyway. When he saw Melanie, he grabbed for her and held onto his good friend. It surprised him that he would get that emotional.

"I'm glad you're home," he whispered in her ear. "I'm here for you if you need anything." He pulled back and took a long look at her. "How's our big boy Penni doing?"

Tina rushed from the car. "I'm so sorry baby." Tina pressed her cheek. "I'm here for you."

Melanie felt a huge sense of relief. The shame that she once felt had subsided. They all loved her and didn't care that she was damaged goods. She quieted the voice in her head quickly telling herself that she was not spoiled. The counselor in Seattle had continued to work with her on that and assured her that was all normal.

"Penni is doing well." She clung to her mother like lint on a sweater as they moved up the steps. "He loves school and football. I hope my grades are good enough to go there next year."

Anne stopped her. "Oh, I'm sure they will be just fine." She rubbed her arm. "Okay kids, food is on the way." As soon as the words slipped from her mouth, the kids took off up the stairs to be greeted by Talia.

"Hello Sam." Talia reached up and gave him a hug.

Sam turned around. "Hello Mrs. Lafoe. I'm so happy to see you."

"Let's get the table set. Harper, help Sam with his stuff."

Sam pulled Harper aside. "I was worried Carter may come down here this weekend with some of the guys. So, I texted Tommy and all the guys agreed to say no to him. He was pissed, but said he was going to hang out with Jack."

"So, we don't have to worry about him coming down here."

"No." Sam gave her a quick hug.

Tina reached over and held Talia. "I can never repay you for everything you have done for Melanie."

"You don't have to. I'm just happy the kids are doing so well."

"Not without you and Fetu."

Dinner was filed with laughter, fresh shrimp and flounder, hush puppies and slaw, and piles of French fries. The sound of chatter and chewing brought peace to Helen. But it was time to move into the living room. Both the adults and kids sat around on the overstuffed chairs wrapped in soft blankets. They all knew what they needed to discuss, so Helen decided she would be the one to facilitate the talk.

"Okay Melanie, we need to know everything so we can help you this year." Helen started.

Caroline stopped her. "I'm so sorry about all of this."

Tina interrupted. "You didn't do anything."

And Melanie echoed, "You didn't do a thing. Your brother did."

"I'm so sorry. I was so afraid our friendship would be over."

"Not in a million years," Melanie said. "You're, here aren't you?"

"How are we all going to protect you?" Caroline asked.

Harper leaned back against Sam. She found herself full of nerves. She didn't want to see Carter again for fear she would say something and was afraid of him. Beth had confided to her earlier that she didn't want to come to the beach because of Carter.

Harper wanted to keep things light, but knew the conversation had to be with a plan in place. The idea was to be at school early to meet Melanie and help her though the first day. But that was just one day. They wanted to be on the same page with questions about her summer whereabouts. Questions about Penni and the article in the paper that preceded that it may have been her. Just when Helen finished chatting about the article, Melanie moved closer to her mom.

"I'm ready to talk." She looked at her mother. Harper pulled a blanket tight around she and Sam. After all, Carter was once his friend they were talking about. She wondered how Caroline could even be here. Her dad was on that tape too.

"Mom and I decided that we would record Carter and Dr. Taylor. Mom thought we would need some insurance in case Carter started bragging about it." Melanie paused. "If you could have seen me the first few weeks." She looked at Tina. "I think mom just wanted me to be okay, and so she thought Dr. Taylor could help me spend the summer away from Oak Grove."

She sifted her words. "My mom thought it was best that I take a break. And I was in no condition to make any good decisions. She just didn't know what to do. I know I put Penni through hell. But I knew he could never accept me after," she paused, "After the attack. It was mom's idea to go away. But it was Dr. Taylor's to go to a camp." She stopped.

"At least that is what we were telling everyone," Tina finished.

"As soon as I left, Mom was going to go to Talia. I just had to hold it together until they could come up with a plan. I had no idea that our community would run the Lafoes out of town in just a few weeks. When Talia and Fetu showed up," she set her cup on the large glass table, "they rescued me."

"How did they get you out of there?"

"We all lied." Melanie didn't flinch. "There were two counselors there that helped us." Melanie looked at Harper, "And your grandfather."

"What did he do?" Harper asked.

"He knows the executive director of the camps, and he was able to get me out of there without anyone knowing. But it was Talia and Fetu that got me into an amazing counselor and with a lot of work I'm realizing that it's not my fault," Melanie said.

Helen jumped in. "Of course, honey."

Tina sat close to Melanie, listening, feeling responsible for all the pain that her daughter went through. She hated herself for ever getting involved with JB.

"There's one more thing. I'm sorry, Caroline. I was with your dad last night. I was able to get some texts off his phone, and he knew Melanie left that camp mid-summer. He thinks I didn't know. The story is she was with a homesick friend and went to Nashville for the summer."

"It's okay," Caroline whispered.

"I didn't think I could ever face Penni, so I decided it was best if we just stopped this whole thing," Melanie interrupted.

"Oh Melanie." Harper rubbed her arm.

"We just need to know what we can do to help you."

"The first thing we can do is hang Carter." Caroline could not contain her anger.

Helen slipped beside Caroline. "I know this is very difficult for you. And I can speak for all of us, we are very sorry you are dealing with this. But as important as it is for Melanie to be supported, it is equally as important for you. And Caroline," Helen looked her right in the eye, "we are all here for you."

"I know I am," Melanie said.

"Well, Seattle did you some good, you look amazing." Caroline felt horrible for the pain Carter and her dad put her through.

"I just need to get into school next year. I need to go back to Seattle and be with my real family." Melanie squeezed her mother's hand.

Harper had been quiet most of the time. "I wouldn't worry about that. You know you will get a full ride just like Penni. You two are insane with your grades."

Caroline listened while a gnawing rage filled her. "I'm glad you didn't give up on Penni."

"I know you love him Caroline and I know he was terribly upset with me and trust me he's been a rock." She felt herself slip.

Caroline turned and held her friend's face in her hands.

"My brother is damaged goods. He may have hurt you physically, but you are as beautiful as ever. Penni will never give up."

"Don't for a minute think we are not going to get you through this." Caroline looked around the room. "You have an army of friends here." Caroline reached around her friend and held her tighter. "Yes, and we need to have a great senior year. You have a lot to look forward to. No looking back."

Harper chimed in, "Yes we have this."

Chapter 44

Rita Faye thumbed through the mail. She grabbed an apple and a Diet Coke and made her way to the overstuffed sofa in the sun room. She settled in the warm corner light. She was happy to have the house to herself. Caroline was at the beach; Carter was out for the night and JB was at the river.

It was just after six on Saturday. She sipped the Diet Coke and looked at the can.

"I'm done with you too." She walked back into the kitchen and watched the brown, chemically clad liquid spill down the drain. She filled her glass with water and went back to the sunroom. She looked forward to the end of the school year because as soon as the kids left, she would make JB leave, too.

It was the beautifully etched yellow envelope made out to Caroline that caught her eye. She flipped the envelope over and saw it was from Patsy Middleton. Her heart sank. She wanted to open the invitation right away. Maybe she could steam it open and seal it back. She made her way to the stove, turned on the kettle, and while she was handling the envelope, she completely missed the salutation that was addressed to Caroline and her mother.

She quickly sliced the envelope open and pulled out the beautiful invitation. The sides were embossed with winding roses with pink buds and a vintage tea cup sat in the middle. For just a moment, Rita Faye wondered why she didn't order them from her. In beautiful handwritten calligraphy, the invitation was personally addressed:

Dear Caroline and Rita Faye,

Tea cups are lovely and flowers are too.

And what would Harper's 18th party be without you.

A luncheon will be served promptly at one, but please come early for some social and fun.

A cup of tea with your Sunday best in the garden as per Patsy's request.

Please join us Sunday, October 15, at the home of Patsy Middleton to celebrate the 18th birthday of her granddaughter Margaret Harper Lee Davis. Wear a hat or fascinator, as we expect the sun to shine.

Please RSVP by Oct 1.

Garden tea: 1–4

Patsy pulled a fast one and slipped a sweet little note for Rita Faye.

"Don't worry I will be ordering all the paper goods from you. And I want to chat about the tables. I'm really looking forward to working with you. You are a guest and I want you to enjoy the day, but desperately need your help so sent your invitation early."

Always, Patsy

Rita Faye held the invitation as if she was holding the golden ticket. She felt a lightness in her heart.

"I'm one of them. I would not miss this for the world. Another new beginning," she said out loud.

Chapter 45

Caroline walked up the long driveway, summer-kissed and spent.

It was good to be reunited with her friend and even better knowing that Melanie didn't blame her for the assault. Caroline flipped off her shoes, thinking the only person she wished that could have been there, which felt weird, was her mother. She needed Rita Faye with all the plans they had. But she couldn't bear to tell her it was Carter. Carter was her child.

She dropped her phone and keys in her bag and went straight to her room. She had to unpack her bags and get her laundry done. The fight in the house in June over the washer and dryer was the most ridiculous thing she had seen. And she was proud of her mother for standing up to her dad and getting the appliances fixed without his permission. Rita Faye taking control made headway with Caroline. She decided she could at least do her own laundry in solidarity.

She laughed when her mom announced that she would no longer be doing anyone's laundry, including JB's. She wasn't grocery shopping either. Caroline popped down the last step with her basket full of clothes and was met by Rita Faye coming in the door from the back yard.

"I didn't hear you come in. Did you have fun at the beach?"

"Hi mom. We sure did."

"You look great." Rita Faye hugged her, basket and all. Caroline immediately noticed her mother's outfit. "You look good mom."

"Thanks, you okay honey?" Her mom asked.

"Yeah, I'm fine. Just a little anxious about school starting."

"It's going to be your year, Caroline. You have so much to look forward to. And the first thing is your big show. Helen was telling me all about it last week when she was in the store."

Caroline looked embarrassed. "I'm…I haven't talked about it."

"Oh, don't worry. It's not like I've been around."

Caroline looked right into her mother's eyes. "I missed you, Mom." And she dropped the basket.

Rita Faye squeezed her daughter, "I'm so sorry honey. From now on, I'm here for you. I know it's a little late, but I promise." She reassured her.

"It's never too late," were the only words she could get out. When she cleared her throat she said, "I'm spending the evening at Harper's house. Melanie and Beth are coming over there."

Rita Faye leaned in. "You're a great friend, and I love you honey. But are you ever coming home again?"

Caroline hugged her a little longer, "Yes mom, I'll be home tomorrow for the rest of the school year." When she pulled away, she felt a darkness come over her mother, "What's going on, Mom? Really?"

"I'm glad you're back and when the time is right, we will talk." Rita Faye was not yet ready to let Caroline in on her plans. "You know we are invited to Harper's birthday party?"

"Did the invitation come?"

"Yes, I'm so excited."

Rita Faye reached in again, not wanting to let go.

"I can't wait to dress shop with you." She pulled back, leaned over and picked up the clothes basket. "I have some laundry to do myself. Let me do this. You get packed up and go have fun with your girlfriends. You only have one senior year." The invite sat on the table.

*****

JB was locked away in his thoughts as he rapidly typed. He was so focused he didn't realize anyone else was at home. He knew he had a lot to post on Cottonmouth Droppings after meeting with the coaches all weekend.

Rita Faye walked down the long hallway and paused, carefully eyeing JB through his glass office door windows. She slowly backed away and dashed up the steps. She grabbed her laptop and logged on to Cottonmouth Droppings and read as the posts dropped one right after the other.

Cottonmouth Droppings
Firecracker Roger 76: How about the breaking and entering charges.
Sweet Home Southern Boy: How about his NCAA thing?

223

Stonewall: Don't know a damn thing about it. All rumors. People are always trying to start something. The team is clean.

Captain Kirk: You mean like the Penni rumors?

Stonewall: Those aren't rumors. That kid deserved what he got and so did his foreign ass parents. Outsiders, and look what they did sneaking out in the middle of the night.

Farm Boy: I'm sure it's some damn girlfriend trumping up charges because she's pissed.

Foxy: Always the women, right? Those boys need to be held accountable.

Stonewall: They are being dealt with. Stop the lies. Women are always making accusations to get what they want.

Farm Boy: Big days for that kid.

Sweet Home Southern Boy: Did you see Doc's statement in the Daily Rag? On one hand, he says he doesn't support young men that don't represent our university, and on the other he says they will start this Saturday. What is it? Remember the pot smoking incident?

Stonewall: You don't know the whole story it seems like we had an unusual number of players held out of practice. Wondering if coach is holding them out and having them practice in closed sessions so no one can steal plays. Spies around here.

Farm Boy: Simply a misinformation campaign to keep our opponents unsure of what's happening.

Stonewall: Teams scout one another to glean useful information. Come on, everyone knows that. Look at Moo U.

Farmboy: Feeding them injuries that really don't exist. He wants to be secretive. Keeping the administration out of it. And those boys should play. They have not been found guilty.

Stonewall: Wants a healthy team for big game opener. You can't blame him.

Tat Man: Could have used Penni. We need a defensive lineman his size. Loser kid. Should be tried for rape. And it was his own girlfriend.

Stonewall: Big plays at the high school level for Carter Taylor.

Farm Boy: Taylor better sign soon. We already have his dad's word.

Foxy: His dad is a cheater and a pill pusher. Don't trust Carter Taylor either.

JB paused when he saw the post.

Rita Faye watched the blinking curser while the words tossed in her head. "Who is Stonewall, and why are they talking about Carter?"

Confederate fan: Wait, what? Carter Taylor is a great kid.

Stonewall: Great guys! Dr. Taylor and his son are wonderful men. He's here to serve the community. It's his duty.

Rita Faye stared. Those were the exact words JB said to her over and over again. He was just here to serve the community. It was his duty. She felt sick as she watched the words collect on the screen.

Farmboy: Way to get Penni out of here. Let this send a message to anyone that thinks we can't take care of people we don't want here.

Stonewall: Exactly. Their kind are not welcome in this town.

Foxy: Who cares. Dr. Taylor is a drug pusher!

Rita Faye saw Foxy post again. JB had put her on so many drugs, she knew exactly what Foxy meant. A gray light raced across her screen from the darkening moon. She was certain JB was Stonewall. Which meant Farmboy had to be Doc. But who was Foxy?

Farmboy: Penni was a pot smoking west coast boy, that damn long hair of his when he first moved here. I for one am glad he's not part of the Cottonmouth family! And the kids on Doc's team are always falsely accused. Athletes have targets on their backs.

A small black flicker bounced on JB's and Doc's screen with those parting words.

Rita Faye closed her laptop and shoved it into her bag. She walked into the bathroom, opened the medicine cabinet and stared at all the pill bottles. Her husband was a drug pusher. She would call Henry Middleton first thing tomorrow. She closed the door. *He has to be stopped.*

Chapter 46
September

There was always nervous excitement around the first day of school. Parents dragging their children out to the front steps to click a picture. Kids complaining about getting up early after sleepy summer days and seniors excited to be at the top of the heap. No one could enter the high school until the seniors walked down a tunnel of under classmen to welcome the leaders of the school on the first day.

Rita Faye watched her sleepy son assemble his variety of bags. There was one for football, a backpack, and a workout bag. She decided to pack him a lunch.

"I know you'll devour this before 10 a.m. Have a great day Carter." She held her cup of coffee tight and gazed at him as tears welled in her eyes. She could remember the first day of the twins' kindergarten like it was yesterday. Life seemed to be so much simpler then. No tension, just excitement over paste and colored pencils. Barney backpacks and My little Pony blankets filled with hugs and kisses.

"Bye mom." he gave her a quick hug and walked out the door. Today was the beginning of the end. In ten short months the kids would leave for school and she would start the process of dismantling her life. JB would have to move out. *This is my grandparents' home.* She thought as she sipped her coffee.

JB had not joined her this morning. He needed to get to the university early before he went to the hospital. How could he not be there for the kids the last first day of high school. Doc needed him. *He always needed him.*

She sat down at the table to read the paper but decided to go out and water some of the container plants before Caroline raced out the door. She was just coming back in, her robe tied securely around her now small frame and her cold coffee cup in her hand when Caroline bounced down the stairs.

"Well good morning, honey."

"Morning mom." Caroline gave her a slight smile.

"How did you sleep the night before your last first day of high school?"

"Pretty good." She paused.

"You excited?"

"Just anxious. I'm scared for Melanie. And the art shows this weekend too. I have worked hard but I don't know what to expect. I don't feel good enough." Caroline stopped. In truth, Caroline feared her mother's behavior would somehow go back to what she used to be.

"Honey no matter what, I will be so proud of you."

"Thanks," Caroline said. She was speechless but wanted to say more. *Like, do you know that dad and Carter are shit heads. Dad's cheating on you and Carter is a psycho rapist. And why are you putting up with all this?* Caroline bit her lips as she tasted the rusty tinge on her tongue. She folded her bottom lip in and moved her jaw back and forth ridding the crimson stain. "I gotta go mom."

"I love you, Caroline." Rita Faye watched her dart out the door, her blond ponytail swaying down the drive. She hopped in Harper's car.

It only took seven minutes to get to the high school. The kids could walk, but what fun would that be when you had a car to drive. Harper pulled in first, parked and turned in her seat. "We can do this. We have to do this for Melanie. She said her mom is dropping her off in the senior lot. Not the front door. I offered to pick her up but she said no way. She needed the time alone in the car with her mom."

Melanie was back. Of course, the girls had seen her, but now she was in the school environment and the fear of the unknown made all of them anxious. Her hair was combed out and long. Caroline jumped out of her side and ran around and grabbed her friend. "Hey girl."

Beth came around the corner. "Well, look at you, look at you." She held her close. Harper was last to open her door and grab Melanie. "You've got this." They were all snot and tears and hugs and laughing and crying.

"Get in the car girls we need a coffee." Melanie settled in the back by Caroline and showed her her phone.

"Isn't Penni just the best?" Caroline said when she read the text.

"What's it say?" Beth asked.

"I'm with you all the way. You only have ten months. Love you. P," Melanie read.

"He's a keeper, Mel." Caroline graced her hand.

The gate guard stopped them and grilled them about their departure as Harper easily fibbed about a forgotten backpack. "You know the excitement of the first day."

Mr. Andrews laughed. "Be careful and hurry. You have the senior walk."

The four girls zoomed down the road, ordered their coffees and zipped back to the guard gate. "Forgotten backpack ugh?" Mr. Andrews smiled as Harper reached out the olive branch and handed him a coffee. "Of course, we thought of you."

"Thanks girls."

They pulled into the senior lot and watched the long line form.

"Let's go girls."

They gathered their backpacks, held their coffee while each girl flanked Melanie and Beth took the front. As soon as they walked toward the senior line Sam, Tommy, and Jack met them at the end and walked on one side of Melanie and Caroline held tight to the other.

Carter stood tall with three of his football friends. He was not going to budge. All the advice his father gave him was gone. *I didn't do anything wrong. If I did, I would have been in trouble. She wanted me*, he rationalized.

Harper whispered, "It's time to drive Carter mad."

Melanie felt her knees buckle. Caroline clutched her arm and marched her right past her brother. "Asshole," she whispered as they walked by.

Sam said, "Happy first day guys. It's going to be a great year," and walked with Harper. Tommy held Caroline's arm and Jack walked with Beth.

Carter watched them walk by like they were encased in bubble wrap. He glared at Melanie. *Liar*, he thought. The secret was forming a small cancer in his gut.

Chapter 47

Gentle clouds washed the blue sky with pink and dark blue ribbons suspending them above the college football field. There was no place for beauty on the gridiron. Unwashed males smelling of dirt and sweat and testosterone oozing from their pores ready to hit and run and pass. Whistles blew and the smell of dirt provided an unkind surface for the boys of fall to prove their manhood.

When the teams won, any distractions the town once held dissipated. Whispers of the Lafoe saga still peppered the chat site, but the spotlight was now on Carter Taylor. Where would he sign his letter of intent in December?

The NCAA received a report from an unnamed source that there were allegations of grade fixing for college eligibility and cover-ups on Doc Winter's team. The retreat down at JB's river house proved to be productive with discussions on how best to quell the problems.

It had also come to light that Doc Winters had been covering up some unbecoming behavior from players for years after a nosey reporter from Raleigh decided to do his own investigation for a preseason newspaper article in the *News and Observer*. The article read like a cheap novel.

Allegations of cheating and cover ups of extramarital affairs from his staff were circling. The article went on to report that offensive coordinator Smith had been cheating on his wife with a student trainer for months. There were pictures from last year's bowl game to prove the misdeeds. The paper was calling for head coach Doc Winters to discipline his staff.

And with the latest incident from last season with Ronnie Harris, the star receiver, head butting a player during the bowl game, the reporter decided to be judge and jury. Not only did the reporter post a huge picture on the front page of the athlete committing the wrongdoing. He also added the link to see the footage from the bowl game along with pictures of Smith and his inappropriate girlfriend. It was not the way Doc wanted the press to write about the start of his season.

"What in the hell are you boys doing out there? If you're going to run around on your wives, for god's sake be careful. We all know what goes on in this business but shit, we can't afford this." Doc threw the paper down on the field.

"The NCAA is investigating us and we have to play this cool," he spit. "I don't need any help from you jackasses with your extracurricular activities."

He knew the NCAA moved like maple syrup, slow and gooey. It would take a long time for them to get to him. Middle was a nothing in the big sea of Division I programs. But Doc Winters wanted public support. He took care of them. They were a family and had each other's back and that's what family did. He was never shy of the press.

It had been easy for Doc to sweep things under the rug, like players roughing up their girlfriends, getting into bar fights, and drinking too much and getting behind the wheel of a car. Whit Cain would not stand for anyone mucking around in the business of the football team and he made it his business to take care of the Cottonmouths. So, it came as a surprise when the NCAA came knocking on Doc's door. The recent newspaper article was bad enough, but this was out of Whit Cain's jurisdiction.

"I can't help you here," Whit told Doc in the summer when the dye was cast.

"They got nothing on us," Doc told his coaches in their recent meeting. "You had better pray boys, you know we know how to conduct ourselves. I know some of you have gotten yourselves into some trouble from time to time. But watch yourselves. I can't fix all your problems. We are all about winning. And we are only giving the community what they want. We stand for tradition, hard work, and no excuses, both on and off the field. You know you can come to me for anything, and I will take care of it." He told the team, "I know you boys are ready to get back on the field and kick some ass. You have worked hard all summer. Now strap on your gear, get your asses on the field, and go to work. We got a season opener to win."

Doc walked over JB. "I think there may be a storm a brewing. We can't let it ruin us." He spit long and hard and walked away.

The players strapped on their helmets and ran out onto the field. Football gave them unity, and they were ready to take out their aggressions on their opponents. It was the start of a new season. It meant everything to the town and Doc was the gatekeeper.

Chapter 48

The high school football score 48-7, stretched across the front page of the paper on Saturday morning along with the headline, "Taylor college bound but where?"

The air was crisp and clean for a fall morning in the south. Tents lined the downtown while vendors set up their wares. The festival would be under way within a few hours. The weather cooperated, just like the football team that handed the town a victory with the low 80s and little humidity.

"You're here early." Helen pushed the kickstand on her bike.

"I need to get ready." Caroline moved away from the brick wall toward Helen.

"All this scheduling is in the stars for you, my dear. We are going to have a huge crowd today and I'm excited to see what everyone thinks of this budding artist." Helen unlocked her studio door.

"I'm so afraid no one will like it."

Helen pointed to the door. "Study this, my dear. I know exactly where your mind is right now." A well place quote from Buddha read, "Nothing can harm you as much as your own thoughts unguarded." She unlocked her door and pulled it open while Caroline pushed her bike on through and into the back office. The lights flickered on as Caroline met Helen standing in front of her sculpture. Helen was examining the final product. "It's truly amazing, Caroline. I could not be prouder of a student than I am of you."

Caroline nervously set down her bag. Every doubt had come across her mind in the last few days. Helen was right. *I mistrust my every move.* But she had worked hard for this and no matter what, she would fight to be proud of her showcase piece.

"The foundry rushed this one. But no worries, it couldn't be more perfect." Helen reached over and gave Caroline a reassuring hug.

A few of Helen's college students would be trickling in around 9 a.m. to help. Helen started some coffee and asked Caroline to pull out a couple of tables. They offered a nice table of refreshments. Caroline was heading toward the front with her arms full when there was a tap at the back door. "It must be some of your students, Helen."

Helen opened the door to meet Rita Faye with her arms full of table linens and decorations. "Come on in, my dear."

"Good morning, Helen. Isn't this just an exciting day?" Rita Faye beamed.

"Hello dear. Let me help you." Helen grabbed the stack of linens.

"Let me run out to the car. I'll be right back."

Helen returned to hold the door while Rita Faye walked in with two large baskets of goods.

Caroline rounded the corner of the art studio and stared at her mother in shock while the words slipped out faster than she could stop. "Mom, what are you doing here?"

"Good to see you, too." She chuckled in deserved pain. "I texted Helen last week and asked if I could do some decorations and she was happy to let me. Let's see what we have here."

Rita Faye set two large baskets on the ground and worked her magic. There were soft cream table linens. She had designed signs that read Art and Women in Oak Grove and had four of them for each section of Helen's show. There was the sculptor's area, chalk painting, watercolors, and photography. Helen had already hung the pieces she would showcase.

Rita Faye carefully placed linen over the block and Caroline gently lifted her sculpture from the wheeled cart onto the soft fabric. "It's pretty heavy."

"Oh, I'm stronger that you think." she grasped the side of the sculpture. Caroline adjusted the piece and Rita Faye stood back with a sign in her hand. "I need to hang this right over your piece."

"What does it say?"

Rita Faye lifted the sign to steady the frame.

Caroline read out loud. "Advocate for Women: An Artist's Journey." There was a picture of Caroline and a small bio.

"Thanks mom." Caroline was embarrassed.

"Oh, my goodness honey, I'm just speechless." She walked around the piece, lightly skimming the cool bronze. She looked back at her daughter.

"That's us?" she asked, fighting her emotions.

Helen rubbed Rita Faye's back. "This is the reaction I hope everyone has from this piece. This came from the deepest part of Caroline."

The three women stood and gazed at the birthing mother holding her womb while one child, the boy slipped out, while the baby girl grasped her brother's foot, reaching for help.

Caroline tilted her head as her words stayed in as if they were dried up dust. Rita Faye leaned into her daughter. "I understand your piece."

Helen gave them time to take in the powerful figure and finally interrupted. "Okay, ladies, doors open in an hour."

The entrance area was set up in minutes. Beautiful flowers on either stand reached high in their urns to frame the door. Patrons were invited to enjoy a coffee station and an assortment of pastries.

Rita Faye was just tidying up when the front door was unlocked, and a stream of people walked in. She needed to get to her own shop and open, but she wanted to see the reaction from people when they viewed her daughter's work. She quickly tapped a text to her staff: *I will be there soon*. She stood in the back corner, holding a cup of coffee and watched as people lingered at the beautiful creation. An older woman held steady as she sobbed over the piece.

Rita Faye walked to Caroline and gave her a big hug. "I'm so proud of you. You did this, girlie. It's all you."

She walked out the door a different person and vowed no matter what, her metamorphosis would continue. It almost seemed that every time she needed validation in the past few months, she got it, whether it was good or bad. Today was one of the best days of her life. Who knew a young, insecure girl that Rita Faye had the privilege of giving birth to could have such a profound effect on her. She grinned as she walked down to her store.

Chapter 49

"Oak Grove is a cult." Caroline sipped her soda sitting at Mr. Charlie's counter Monday mid-morning. "It takes years to fit in if you are not from here."

Somehow Helen managed to turn Oak Grove on its head with her art exhibition.

"The latest talk of the town is my sculpture. Did you see on Cottonmouth Droppings, and I quote, 'She had created one of the most magical, interesting, sacrilegious, sexual, inappropriate pieces ever seen. It's rumored that a big art dealer has offered Helen millions for the piece.' Whatever the rumor mill offered was authority."

Caroline, in her long peasant skirt and a white blousy shirt, had pulled her blond hair up with a large head band around her forehead. She decided to go makeup free today, with only bright red lipstick. She sat on the red stool, turning when the large bells clanged above the door. He made her one of the best cherry cokes and served it up with an extra splash. She sipped the delicious shake of therapy, while he listened. Caroline needed an ear today and Mr. Charlie was the man for the job.

Mr. Charlie seemed to know all the comings and goings of the teens. And he really listened to them when they came in. It was often said he just plain old liked them. His store was a mainstay in the town and people of all ages came to enjoy an ice cream and to be heard. He even mastered the latest Grande, skinny, two shot whip coffee around. He loved his job as a pharmacist, but serving sodas and listening was his passion and the high school kids loved hanging out there after school.

"Miss Caroline, you need to be proud of your work. You can't expect anyone here to understand the complexity."

She slid her glass back to him. "Make it a double. It's already been a long day."

Mr. Charlie pulled his large silver canister up and flipped it over. He squirted five shots of cherry over the ice. He picked up the soda gun and shot refreshing Coke over the crystalized ice. Giving it a gentle stir, he poured it into a tall mug. He tossed a large cherry into the refreshing drink and set it in front of Caroline.

"Here you go, young lady. So, it's been quite a day? Don't you have school?"

"Yes." Her extra-large watch jingled with her large bangles against the malt glass. "There is senior planning today. I already finished my work so I left early. And I go to Miss Helen's studio right after school."

"Sounds like a plan. At least people can't seem to stop talking about the art show. I heard it went exceptionally well." Mr. Charlie, an avid art collector, was curious. "Did you get any offers?"

Caroline took a long sip. "Yes sir." It was such an intimate piece she didn't want him to judge her. She was shocked enough that her mom was into her work. Of course, she never saw JB or Carter over the weekend. Football kept them away.

"Miss Helen said several people asked about it but said it wasn't for sale."

"Well, it's impressive. There is so much in that piece." As if he was reading her mind, "And no one would guess it was yours until your name was on it. Everyone thinks it's my crazy wife's creation." He laughed. "God, I love that woman."

"Well my mom put my name up along with my picture. I don't care, but people here just don't understand."

"Good for you. They can't appreciate anything with such depth." Mr. Charlie leaned further against the counter, knowing exactly what the piece would fetch. A couple that came in for the festival wanted the piece and had been in talks with Helen about a price. He also knew that that piece was likely to win Caroline a scholarship to any art school of her choice.

"Miss Helen would love to tell people it was hers. But she would never take any credit away from you, my dear. I know talent when I see it, and you, my dear, have talent."

"Thank you." Caroline took a long sip.

"Don't make yourself sick." He smiled.

"I won't. I need this today. I'm mad at the people on the chat board for saying such cruel things. What do they know?"

"Nothing." Melanie walked in from the back. She was back at work.

Mr. Charlie turned and gave her a careful hug. "How are you today, missy?"

"I'm having a good day." She pulled her apron over her head. "I just sent my application off to Washington. Let's keep our fingers crossed. If I can't get noticed by the track coach, at least I can try and walk on." She tied her apron.

"Let me tell you something, If I have to pay your way out there in that rainy place, I will gladly do it. I don't want you to leave here but I understand, and I for one will help you." He nodded his head and walked down the long counter into the back room.

Melanie turned toward Caroline. "I'm so lucky to have them."

"Me too." Caroline slurped up the last of her drink.

"I saw your sculpture. Wow, is all I can say. And ignore the chat site. Look what it did to me and Penni. There are morons on that thing."

"Thanks. How are you really doing?"

"I'm really good. Carter is staying away from me, and," she leaned close to Caroline, "Penni is coming out for the fall dance."

"If I didn't already have two of these things, I would have another one."

Melanie turned, "Are you sure? It's on me."

Chapter 50

Rita Faye steadied herself at the counter. Wrapping paper was spread all around her, while bows, tissue, and tags took up residence on her right. In the past she was always antsy when any of the Junior Leaguers came in, and she knew today there would be several. But those days were gone. She was a new person and with the upcoming baby shower of one of the most popular members, she knew a few of the girls needed to make their purchases. She stood at the counter carefully wrapping a baby gift, inhaling for six and exhaling for six. She wasn't invited to the shower and for the first time, she didn't care.

The Women's Club in town made the rounds when it came to showers, and no one was neglected. Unless you were in Dotty Winter's storied group. Rita Faye had never made the cut, even being married to JB.

Rita Faye smiled down at the beautiful bow she created and glanced up at the two women who had just entered the store. The negative thoughts were rivaling, trying to push open the damn and let the flood gates of sour thoughts spill their rapids of unworthiness into her joy. She was not having any of it and reached back for words from her counselor. "*The worst person I have been listening to is myself. Oh, and JB.*" She laughed out loud.

The two young women from the Dragonfly Women's Club walked up to the counter. "Hello ladies." Rita Faye looked up from her masterpiece.

Emily, who clearly had some Botox treatments, interrupted, "Hello Rita Faye, what a beautiful box. Is that a gift for Lauren Grace's shower?"

"Why yes, it is. Are you ladies here to look at her baby registry?"

"Of course. Let's take a look, Jenn." Rita Faye handed them the iPad. "You girls take your time I have a few boxes to finish. When you need help let me know." She looked back down at her work. "That baby is going to be as pretty as she is."

Emily sneered, "Oh yes, beautiful mama, beautiful baby." She stared at Rita Faye noticing how beautiful she looked and how beautiful Caroline was. "You look so good. Tell me what you're doing?"

"Oh honey, decided it was time for a change." Rita Faye was short.

"You look good," Emily said.

The two girls looked through the registry.

"Take your time."

"Oh, we will." They sang their response in unison like pledging sorority sisters.

"Are you going to the shower, Rita Faye?" Emily was agitated now, letting the compliment sit too long.

"Oh goodness no, baby. I have high school kids." She sneered at the foul ask.

What Emily had pitched in the air Jenn took a swing at. "Well, it's only for the Dragonfly Junior League ladies anyway."

"Why in the world would you girls even ask?" Rita Faye smiled.

Jenn's hooded eyes snapped like a bird, while Emily gave a short chirp. "Oh," like a wounded, defeated fowl.

"Now you just let me know what you girls need. I think you'll find Lauren Grace's list filled with varying monetary options. Just give this little bell here a ring when you need help." She turned into her storage area.

Rita Faye's hateful thoughts crawled up her throat wanting to be heard but she swallowed them back down. She caught the tail end of a few comments from the girls chatting about the art show and how inappropriate Caroline's sculpture was.

"What the hell do they know about art?" she wanted to say. She heard the small bell ring and walked out into the infant area. "Are you ready?"

Emily stood with two outfits in her hand and wanted each bib monogrammed, while Jenn held a soft pink blanket. "Yes," They both sounded.

"Oh, ladies these are such nice gifts. Lauren Grace will love them. Don't you just love the gingham on the edge of the blanket?"

Jenn examined the blanket. "I really do." She turned to Emily.

"I just love these outfits. And did you see the snap closures on the bottom. So easy for a young mom to get the baby cleaned up. Did you two get a chance to come downtown for kickoff weekend?"

"Yes," they answered in unison.

"Oh, wonderful. I was so proud of my daughter's sculpture. You know she has been offered quite a bit of money for that piece and now universities all over are calling her and asking her to apply to their art schools." She put her head down and looked over the first receipt. "Who would have thought my girl could one day be a famous artist?"

"Oh, you must be so proud!" Jenn said.

"I am. She's a hard worker. And you know she is tied for valedictorian as well. I'm one proud mama." She stood in her size six fitted dress. Her hair was cut in a cute blond bob and her fingernails were just the right color red. She picked up her water and took a sip.

"Okay girls, baby pink lettering."

"Yes, ma'am."

"Would you like to add anything else in the package? I can wrap it after I'm done or I can hold it out for you to see."

"Oh no Rita Faye, you can wrap it. We want to look around before you ring us up. We are both looking for new outfits to wear to the shower this Sunday."

"You girls go right ahead upstairs. I just got a shipment in."

"Oh, that would be nice." Jenn paused. "I'm so hoping I don't wear the same thing as Anne Davis." She looked at Emily. "I would be so embarrassed."

Emily looked at Jenn then over to Rita Faye for a reaction. And without missing a beat Rita Faye was on her game. "Oh, you girls don't have to worry about Anne or her mama. they won't be attending the shower this Sunday. They politely declined. They sent a really nice gift though." Rita Faye scored. "Besides, Patsy and Anne are busy with Harper's birthday."

Emily asked, "Oh yeah, isn't that party coming soon?"

"In two weeks. Thank goodness Caroline and I have already picked up our dresses." She watched the girls. No junior league uppity woman was going to get to her ever again. "Caroline and I just got back from Raleigh to get our dresses, hats, and gloves." She turned and walked to the counter and pulled off some ribbon.

"Bless their hearts," the girls sang out in unison. "I know the party is going to be wonderful." The two girls walked toward the beautiful wooden stairs that lead up to the ladies' shop. "Have fun up there ladies, there are some beautiful things."

Rachel, her assistant manager, came in around noon and took over. Rita Faye walked back to the small kitchenette, heated up her morning coffee, and took a break.

"I saw your list. I will get right to ordering and then start on the front display. I can't believe how great the weekend sales were." Rachel popped her head in the room.

"It's the season. I'm going to go to the bank and run some errands. I won't be back today unless you need me."

"Great." Rachel seemed surprised she was leaving.

"This is a busy year with the kids, and I don't want to miss anything." She sighed.

Rita Faye stood at the UPS store, willing the middle-aged woman with the super ugly legs to hurry it up. She needed to get to Helen's. Now she was judging people. *Hell*, she thought. *I'm sure everyone used to think of me that way*. The ugly raised veins, thin lips, pallid skin straw hair color, thin bones, all made her feel sorry for the gaunt lady. She was fragile. She draped herself in sad memories of never seeing her mother like that. What she would give to have her mother around right now. "Can I help you with the door?" she politely asked the elderly woman. *Shame on me*, she thought. She looked up at the cement sky and turned toward Helen's. *It's time I start folding the bad in with the good and making that enough.*

She rang the bell to the yoga studio and Helen immediately answered. "Come on in my dear. Are you ready for your private?" She locked the door behind her. "Can I get you anything?"

Rita Faye dropped her bag, "I'm okay, just really tired."

"All this change is hard."

"It is but in the end it's worth the work." Helen reassured her.

Rita Faye shook her head, "I can't believe I stayed in this marriage and have nearly destroyed my children."

"You're going to be good. Trust me." Helen continued.

"My husband has some serious problems." She wiped her nose.

"Oh my," Helen watched her emotions flow downstream. She noticed she had her toe nails nicely shaped with bright red polish and a slight vein rising up from a body of veins while the skin moved with her hand.

"I'm just not myself." Rita Faye started to paddle in the rapids of her emotions.

"Oh, you have always been yourself, you just decided to cover it up for a little bit."

Rita Faye looked up. "I'm so tired of pretending. And for what?"

"What?" She looked shocked that Helen would go there as quickly as she did.

"My dear. We are all searching. But," there was a long pause, "along the way you lost yourself. You lost sight of what was important. I'm so happy to see you finally searching. And now you are ready to do even more because you see how important it is to care for yourself first."

Rita Faye reached over. "I'm glad you're helping me."

"Wipe the shit off your shoes and find a new patch of grass to stand in. You have friends. You are loved. The problems at home will find their way. Now sit on your mat, close your eyes, and visualize the life you want and breathe."

Chapter 51

JB peeked out of the hospital medicine closet late Sunday afternoon with several small vials of liquid oxycodone tucked in his pocket. He had been careful to slip a small needle into the bottle and replace it with saline without anyone seeing him. He usually only took a vial at a time, but not today. Today he filled six. Even if someone came in, he could excuse himself away with any number of his patients.

Doc was in incredible pain after several weekends of standing on the sidelines. He also sprinted onto the field at the end of the third quarter after a bad call, jarring his right foot and ankle. There was also a defensive lineman with a tweaked hip that needed some pain relief so he could be ready for next week's game.

"The team needs this more than some of the patients in here." JB was certain no one would ever know who received the tampered bottle. "Pain management therapy in the name of victory." He excused his behavior.

It had been another long week of Carter complaining about Melanie and her friends and how he felt like his football buddies were turning on him. He was especially angry at Caroline, because she was the ring leader. He slipped into his car and hurried home. Rita Faye had insisted that the family share a Sunday evening meal together.

The dinner conversation hit a crescendo high-pitched excited tone of football that filled the room, but it was only between JB and Carter talking. They were only four games in the season for the high school and college team and both won. The play makers, of course, were Carter and Jack. He was the big star for the high school game that week and despite one all-star guy from the college being hurt, the college team had an unquestionable victory.

Rita Faye was over the waste basket scraping the plates, "So, Caroline how was your weekend?"

Caroline looked over at her mother.

"Oh, what happened, did some loser boy ask you out?" Carter, irritated as he spoke between chews.

Caroline chased the last few pieces of her salad around and grinned at all the secrets. If only Carter knew that Tommy had indeed asked her to go to the fall dance. Caroline didn't answer.

"I need to read the mail," JB walked over to the counter. The party invitation slipped to the floor. He reached down and picked it up as he thumbed. "Oh, what's this?"

Rita Faye turned, furious she had left the invitation out after she and Caroline were looking at it just a few hours ago. "Oh, that's been sitting there for a while." She plucked the invitation out of JB's hand and slid it right past Carter over to Caroline. "Just for the girls."

"Old news we already discussed it." Caroline looked at her father, brooding.

Caroline, of course, knew Harper was going to ask her to her party. She was just not happy that her dad and brother now would look at the invitation and make fun of it for the next week.

JB leaned over Caroline and read the invitation. "Isn't this a fancy event." He looked at Rita Faye. "Are you going?"

Her red nails clicked the counter as she picked up a cup. "So, are we going Caroline?"

Caroline stretched her lips wide across her teeth. "We wouldn't miss it for the world, would we mama?"

Rita Faye sighed with relief. She knew right then that she and Caroline were cemented allies. She was working hard to fight to the bitter end for her daughter. Sure, she loved Carter, but Carter seemingly had luck on his side and, of course, JB. It was Caroline that was short changed.

JB glanced at Caroline. "That's wonderful." He seethed, feeling the hate bubble expand for the Middleton family.

"Hanging with the lower class of society." Carter chewed. "And how are you two ever going to find anything to wear?"

"Well, Carter I'm so happy you're concerned about what we might wear, but Caroline and I have that covered. So why don't you just worry about the football field, since that seems to be the only thing you care about, and let us girls worry about the things we really care about." Rita Faye, for the first time in years, was brazen toward her son.

Caroline was proud of her mother. With the newfound weight loss, pampering, and now standing up for herself Caroline chimed in, "Of course we have, Carter, unless something as frivolous as what girls wear is now a concern of yours, too."

Rita Faye experienced a wave of excitement. JB was upset because it was the Middletons. But more importantly she felt a renewed strength knowing Caroline knew she was on her side. She turned to Caroline once again.

"So, Caroline, how was your weekend?" Caroline knew exactly where her mother was going with the line of questioning.

"I had a great weekend. Miss Helen has been talking to several parties interested in buying my sculpture. And I finished my portfolio. She won't let anyone buy it until I'm accepted into the school of my choice."

JB treaded in the dark waters more and more as he was grasping for control. And the absence of Tina did not help. It threw him off that the two of them were actually happy, almost giddy about the tea party and Caroline's craft classes. It was unlike Rita Faye to be happy. He didn't stop to notice it had been months since she complained incessantly about her weight, her lack of friends and the fact that she was never invited anywhere. He was so busy mucking in his own life he lost the line of control.

JB had to derail them. "So what other young girls do you think will attend this blessed event? What about Melanie and her mother, will they be there?" He carefully played his cards and watched for any reaction.

Caroline glanced at her mother. She watched Carter out of the corner of her eye and decided she had a better hand. She knew she could not risk her friend right now and say too much, but she wanted to throw a few darts.

"Oh of course they will be invited. Melanie is one of Harper's best friends. Have you seen her, Carter? Wow, didn't she come back from summer camp looking amazing. I wish I could have gone too."

Without missing a beat Rita Faye jumped in. "Caroline you need to have her over."

Caroline watched Carter. "Oh, I should do that, Mom. I know she would love to see you."

"I'm done." Carter shoved his plate at Caroline, got up, and left the room.

JB's blood overheated. *What the hell are these two up to?* Guilt and wrong living did that, even if you didn't think you were doing anything wrong. He would turn and tarnish their reputation the only way he knew, just like he did to the Lafoes. With all his trolling, certainly there was something he could use that would never be traced back to him. He was the master at throwing one line to the other, pretending to be friends to get people talking. He would go after Melanie again. And would even drop a few crumbs about his wife. *Nothing like ruining a girl's reputation. I won't be undermined by anyone, including my own family. I'm in control.*

He was sick of his weird daughter and insane wife. He looked over at Rita Faye with her back now to them as she finished the dishes. Her body so different. Yet the sight of her made him sick. *I will ruin you both for being disloyal.* Just like the town, he lived from one game to the next, and next week was the big rival weekend. He would need to focus on that. He walked to his office without saying a word.

Cottonmouth Droppings

Weasel: Any word on the NCAA investigation?

Beach Blanket Bobby: I heard it was grade fixing. Writing papers for the kids. The stuff other schools do and get away with.

Turncoat: Oh, I think there was more than some help. I heard there was an intern writing papers for the kids and handing them over to turn in. The kids weren't even doing their work.

Stonewall: Come on, nothing like that would ever go on here. This program is clean as a whistle. I think it's someone wanting to start trouble.

Stonewall wondered who Turncoat was.

Captain Kirk: What the hell are you talking about, Stonewall? Those kids signed a contract just like the coaches. They sign their life away only they don't get paid like the coaches do but they are supposed to hold up the integrity of the university. And I'm sick of losing!

Tat Man: Me too. We may be losing games but at least we are winning the tailgates!

Turncoat: You mean like Doc and his coaches?

Farm boy: What's that supposed to mean? Doc is upstanding and does the right thing.

Tat Man: Doc won't remove anyone until the kids are proven guilty. That's his policy

Stonewall: Great policy. Why should you be punished until the facts are out?

Foxy: You mean like Penni and his family?

Turncoat: Exactly. It sure seems like they got treated bad here. Where was the leadership in this community?

Farm boy: Different situation. They were outsiders trying to change our community.

Stonewall: Exactly. Can't wait for Carter Taylor to play for the Cottonmouths.

Turncoat: Oh, so you mean trying to make things better in the community is bad. The wife was one of the best pediatric nurse practitioners we ever had. What a shame. Hell, she took care of one of the football coaches' wives and the girl couldn't say enough great things about her.

Farm Boy: Okay, that's old news. Carter better sign.

Stonewall: Someone convince his mom to let him stay home. Hopefully his weird sister will leave though.

Farm Boy: Did you see that statue she made? Totally sacrilegious. Who the hell does that crap?

Weasel: I agree. Boy does Rita Faye look good these days though. What a hottie.

Stonewall: Finally! She was a real porker at one time.

Farm Boy: Who cares? She's married and this is for football not women.

Turncoat: I wouldn't come here for anything. Horrible place. Just terrible. Full of violations.

Farm Boy: Who the hell are you?

Stonewall: Yes, he does. Anyone know if Melanie Birch is being recruited for track?

Weasel: Wait what? We have a track team? Do girls play sports? Isn't that the girl who was raped last spring?

Farm Boy: Oh, come on boys, we don't name names.

Stonewall: Funny how she went away for the summer.

JB had set the stage. He signed off.

Chapter 52

October, with cooler days, welcomed homecoming week at the high school. The Knights were 5-0 and the team sprit was palpable. Everyone wanted in on the ride, from the store owners downtown to every student at the high school. It was a special year for the team.

Unfortunately, the Cottonmouths had lost within a single touchdown their last two games and were 3-2. With the more challenging schedule came chatter about losing hope of becoming bowl eligible. Most of the town looked forward to traveling to places like Orlando or New York around Christmas. Doc Winters had never let anyone down. But this year everyone was holding their breath. The chat site was prattling on about his age, health, and the pending NCAA investigation. Postings like, "maybe he's beyond his prime for coaching" flooded Droppings.

"No one wants to be a loser," Doc said at his last radio show, signaling a weakness. And it didn't help that Bobby Cottonwood's high school team was winning games seemingly in a snap. It would seem that the high school and college teams were now competing. And they had one person at the vortex, Carter Taylor.

Middle Carolina needed three more wins to go to a bowl game. Losing to their cross-state rival did not make the town very happy. The rival game ended with the West winning for the first time in twenty years, something that never happened on Doc's watch.

Cottonwood sang the praises of Carter Taylor, making recruiting for Doc that much harder. Doc took the liberty to announce that Carter was going to be a part of the Cottonmouths next year come hell or high water, which brought further acrimony to his team with the focus on the future.

The offense blamed the defense for letting up too many points and the defense blamed the offense for keeping them on the field too long. The dissension on the team kept them off balance. And the looming NCAA investigation and all the rumors swirling didn't help recruiting. They were riddled with injuries and their all-star running back, D. J. Smith, was out for a week with a bum knee. Once they jumped the three-game hurdle, they could finish up with a promise of post-season play. But the college team had taken a back seat to the Knights and Coach Winters was gasping for air to bring the spotlight back on him. He would fill the chat sites to try and clear things up for himself and his players.

It was the rival game for Sweetgum and Oak Grove, one that had gone on for so long no one could remember when it started. Main Street hosted the big parade on Thursday night. It was something to see the black and gold on one side and brown and green of Sweet Gum on the other. Colorful banners that the kids made hung, and each one seemed to be better than the next. Many of the parents would host cocktail parties along the parade route. The town loved spirit week and every year it grew bigger and bigger.

The chat site buzzed with friendly banter of promises of victory for both teams, but the focus was on Carter Taylor and his leading his team to victory after victory.

Spirit week was a long-held tradition, and even Patsy and Henry could fondly recall their spirit weeks at the local high school. It was always the biggest game of the season and despite Penni's defensive line intimidation, the Knights lost last year to the Burrs by a last-minute field goal. It was their only loss and hardest to swallow because of the rivalry. The boys were devastated, so this year they were hungry for blood.

Coach Cotton had the boys in a calm frenzy leading up to the game, which was always played at the college stadium. And Friday was the big game. This year many of the hospital employees worked on two of the floats they had in the parade, and JB rode in a fancy sport car as the head of the board of the hospital. The football players rode on the back of Mr. Weaver's flatbed truck, which he piled high with hay bales. The cheerleaders marched in front. The school band was top notch, and Mr. Charlie always had the honor of driving the former homecoming queen in the parade. He had an adorable red Mercedes convertible that held the coveted spot.

It was as if the two communities ordered the weather because the beautiful fall week led right up to an amazing sunny weekend. Mums were everywhere in Patsy's yard, filling her large pots with every fall color imaginable. It helped that Harper's party would be that Sunday, so the Middletons' yard was especially manicured. The parade went right past the Middletons' grand home, and the sidewalk would be lined with little kids waiting for a handful of candy from the procession.

The big game Friday night did not disappoint. It was Carter's record three touchdowns and Coach Cotton's never letting up that held the seniors in the entire game and onto a crushing victory. He was sending a message. The team won a decided 49-14. It was the biggest spread they had ever seen in the rivalry.

But it was Jack Thompson that got all the attention. He set his own record with three touchdowns as well. The defense claimed one for themselves, and Sam had a record night for kicking. The local press went crazy after the game, and Jack spent an exceptional amount of time answering questions from the local newspaper and radio.

Carter, in the chaos was only asked one: "How did it feel to have your teammate pace your record?" Carter answered, "I knew if you got the ball to Jack, you were going to score." He walked into the locker room, rage coursing through his disappointment.

Jack offered up his house for an afterparty after his mother agreed to a small number. His parents had ample outdoor living space, a pool, and plenty of yard for the fifteen or so kids to congregate. Jack's dad, Dr. Thompson, was the ER doc on duty that night, and Jack had assured his mother that nothing would go wrong. The kids were going to light the outdoor firepit and celebrate their victory.

Sam and Harper arrived, knowing Caroline and Melanie refused to go anywhere near the football team, so they decided to spend the evening after the game eating at Sandy's Shake Shack and would meet Harper when Sam dropped her at home.

Carter and a few of his friends were there, along with many other seniors. The party was in full swing. Everyone was enjoying the warmth of the fall fire.

"Get away from me," Beth pushed Jack. "Have you been drinking?" Carter had slipped in a few bottles of vodka and was pushing everyone to take shots. Jack flung his large arm over her shoulder. "Get away from me."

Harper walked over. "Come on Beth, are you ready to go?"

Jack swayed side to side almost stumbling into Harper. "Come on baby. We won the game. I set records. Don't you want to celebrate?" He gave her a sloppy kiss, missing her mouth and slobbering all over her cheek. "I'm feeling a little dizzy."

Carter stood off to the side and watched the whole exchange. *Poor bastard can't hold a shot.*

"You're wasted. What the hell is wrong with you?" Her sweet southern words made a confusing jump off her tongue. "Jack, you never drink."

"You are acting like such an ass," Harper interjected. "We need to go."

Jack shouted, "Loosen up bitch," as he swayed. He was trying to hold onto Beth but felt her slip from his grasp. "You know you're my girl. Don't leave. Don't be mad. Come back." He fell into a chair.

"I don't think you're funny. What's wrong with you? Did you get hit in the head?" Beth walked away.

Jack threw his arm around Harper his mouth high next to her face. "Come on, ladies. I'm just having some fun." Little did he know, Carter had slipped a pill into his shot and Jack was entering a compromised state.

Carter walked over to Sam. "Hey man, great game." He watched Beth run off.

"Come on Jack stop drinking. This isn't like you." Sam turned to Jack.

"I've only had one drink." He stumbled and fell into another chair.

Beth weaved through the sea of kids. "I'm going home." She stopped just short of the gate and threw up in the bushes. She slid to her knees. Through her tears she called for Jack. She was dizzy as she lost her footing.

Carter continued to hold court with the boys. He signaled another player over to prolong the chat while he watched Jack stumble. *I don't know why anyone wants to take my spotlight.* He listened to the group chatting. "Sorry guys, I gotta go take a leak." He walked to the back of the house.

Beth turned the corner and walked past the kitchen and pulled herself up the steps. She knew she was going to throw up again and didn't want to embarrass herself in front of everyone. She laid her head against the cool porcelain, reached up, grabbed a towel, and pulled herself up. She needed a drink to wash her mouth.

Beth managed to hold herself long enough to get to Jack's bed. She was in and out when she felt an arm come across her and push her down. At first, she tried to fight back, but she blacked out with such a sudden, unexplained change in consciousness.

She laid there, incapable of moving but struggling. She was held down on her stomach. He entered from the back. "So, your boy was the hero tonight."

Her blouse torn, her jeans a pile on the floor and finally it was over. When she woke up, she vaguely remembered him getting off her.

"No one is going to take my thunder." Carter pulled up his pants as the deceiving words trampled out of his swampy mouth.

The voice was not Jack's. Wounded, blankness spread through her and then she heard the door slam. She didn't remember much else until she was at the hospital and a shaft of light resentfully fell into the dark room while a video camera traveled inside her, looking for signs of rape.

Chapter 53

Dr. Thompson hated Friday and Saturday nights in the ER. It never failed that one team would send in an injured player. He never failed to get a few of the college students in for over drinking, a car wreck, or an occasional sexual assault. It was a string of bad decisions from Friday night until early Sunday morning.

But tonight was different. It seemed unusually quiet and despite the break, he could not leave. He hated missing any football game, especially this season, because it was Jack's last.

Jack was happy to be part of the team. He was destined to play somewhere in college but the recruiting letters were not coming in like they were for Carter. He would settle for a Division II school if it was a good one.

Until tonight Carter was the star. But tonight was Jack's night and when he called excited to get the gang together at their house Dr. Thompson agreed. "Behave," were his parting words.

His first patients of the evening were two young men who had a bar fight downtown. One really had a nice head wound and the young man would have to be evaluated for a concussion. He earned himself several stitches. He wouldn't remember a thing until morning. The other young man broke his hand hitting the side of a door when the police were hauling him out of the bar. Black eyes, a broken nose, a normal bar fight badge.

He had a young Hispanic in his third room. She was in early labor at 32 weeks and scared. Her husband sat by her side. He caught glimpses of their discussion but his Spanish was just not good enough to understand everything. He would transfer her to OB and was certain mother and baby would be fine.

His next patient came in with a deep cut to their hand. Friday night was steak night at their house, the woman explained, and her knife must have slipped right off her steak into her hand.

Dr. Thompson looked up. It was already 11:30.

Becky, the lead nurse said, "Congratulations on the win and your son's record night, Dr. Thompson." She had no expression as she typed away on her computer. "We have an assault coming in. Should be here any minute." Dr. Thompson heard the siren. He walked out to the bay to catch some fresh air and watched the ambulance pull around.

"Hey Dr. Thompson." The ambulance driver walked around and opened the back doors. "Seventeen years old, intoxicated. Said she was raped. A friend found her in an upstairs bedroom and called 911. You should have seen all the kids scatter when we pulled up."

The cop eyed Dr. Thompson. He would never tell him she was found at his house. He would let Whit know everything as soon as he had a minute. *Never know when I may need him*, he thought.

The tech in the back held the top of the gurney and the other grabbed the back while they lifted her out. She had a bruised cheek and dark circles lining her eyes while makeup ran charcoal streaks down both sides of her face while her hair was a nest of tangles and what should have been holding it back, the clip, sat on top of one side of her head. A blanket covered her battered form.

"You're going to be okay." Dr. Thompson waited for the gurney to stabilize the young girl. "What the hell?" He hollered out, "Let's go." Realizing it was Jack's girlfriend, Beth, he went into full emergency mode as his heart raced. He was trained to keep his cool as an ER doctor but this was different. He knew the kids were at his house. Certainly, this didn't happen there.

"Beth, oh honey, what happened?" Donna, the assault nurse, sidled up beside her as both medical personnel were frantic.

Beth sobbed as she tried to form words. "Aunt Donna," Stumbled out of her mouth, "I don't remember. How did I get in this ambulance?" Her big blue eyes looked up at her sobering aunt as her head fell to the side.

Whit walked up. "Don't answer that young lady. You know you cannot ask her any questions until a nurse has checked her out." Beth was out cold again.

"I'm the sexual assault nurse examiner."

Donna came into the ER following the medics. Normally a hospital this size could only dream of having a nurse examiner on staff, but Henry Middleton saw a need for one. She had performed the same exam on Melanie just a few short months ago. Donna left Whit's side and walked beside the gurney.

"Let's get you taken care of Beth."

They hurried her into a trauma bay and Donna quickly called her sister, Gail, while she started the exam. She would not go too far until her sister could get there. "Who called this in?" Donna started.

"It was Jack's friend Carter that found her out cold in the bed. When he went upstairs, he said he found her in Jack's room, face down. The door was wide open and when he tried to wake her, he realized something had happened to her. He quickly called 911 and threw a blanket over her."

Donna examined her further as she started to come around. Her aunt suspected she had been drugged.

Dr. Hillcrest and his wife Gail came in with a fury. "Beth, where are you?" Dr. Thompson stood just outside the curtain. He did not want anything to go wrong. Now that Donna was on board, he was relieved she did them. He listened in.

"Tell me what happened. Slowly. I need to take the report," her aunt said, while her mom sat holding her hand.

"Daddy," she looked over at her father. "I don't want you to hear this." Her father spilled tears all over the floor as he choked. "I'm so sorry, my baby. I will wait right outside here."

He pulled the curtain and Dr. Thompson grabbed his arm. "Hey, I'm so sorry. Why don't you go grab some coffee and I will have you paged when they're done?"

Donna winced when there were clear signs of forced sexual intercourse. She asked her sister to stand outside after Beth started crying. "I'm so ashamed, mama. I didn't mean for this to happen."

Her mother bent over and gently kissed her daughter on the forehead.

"You didn't do anything wrong. Your daddy and I love you and we will be right here for you." She walked out of the room in tears.

Dr. Thompson walked in. "How's it going in here?"

"She's doing okay," Donna said.

"Let me know how she is. After you're done, I asked that she get a line of fluids and a counselor to come in and talk with her." He patted the Beth's arm. "You are safe and well taken care of here." He would read the report before anyone else.

Dr. Thompson headed to his office. His first call was to his wife.

"I told you, no one was drinking. There were soda cans everywhere, but I did not find one bottle of anything. I ordered pizzas, we had soda," she cried.

"Put Jack on the phone."

"I can't he is out of it. He's passed out cold."

"What? What happened? I want him in here right now for a blood test. None of this makes sense."

"Jack was swaying, and I told him to go to bed. He met Carter at the top of the steps and Carter told him not to go in there."

"What the hell was Carter doing up there?"

"I thought the same thing."

"Something doesn't sound right."

"I told him to go to bed."

"He's going to answer for this."

Lori whispered in the phone, "He took one shot of vodka. Okay, I was mad at that, but when I pressed him, he seemed confused. He said as soon as he did it his head was throbbing. He said Carter brought the vodka. It hit him hard. Everything happened so fast after the police and the ambulance came that all Jack wanted to do was be by Beth's side. I made him go to bed."

"You made the right call. It's pretty tense up here."

"Bill, I know the Hillcrests have kept Beth away from everything this summer. Gail told me when school started. And I'm not making an excuse for Jack, but I think the kids were drugged."

Dr. Thompson sat on the phone for a minute. "I do too. I will get a blood sample. Get him up and bring him in, but don't come in through the ER. I want to keep this to ourselves."

Donna left the room with the kit and stopped by Dr. Thompson's office.

"It's done. I'm going to hand this over to the police."

"Anything I need to see in the report?" Dr. Thompson asked.

"Standard assault. I'm certain it was one of the boys at the party. The good thing is," she shook her head as if there was any good thing from this, "that I'm certain there was only one boy involved. And I'm certain she was drugged. Who the hell would have done this?" Donna asked.

"I don't want any to this to be handled inappropriately. You know I want to get to the bottom of this. I'm an open book. I have nothing to hide."

Donna sighed and walked to the office. Whit was waiting for the kit. "I'll take good care of this."

Donna held it back. "I have this one, no thank you." She walked back to her niece.

She handed her an antibiotic and a day after pill. "Take these."

"What is it?" Beth asked.

Never one to be dishonest, Donna said, "A morning after pill. Just in case you may have been impregnated."

Beth gasped and swallowed the pills. Donna received a text from the psych nurse that she would be there in a few minutes.

"I have given your mom some information to help you with after care and I will be by tomorrow afternoon to check on you. The police want to talk to you." Donna reached down and hugged her niece. "I love you, little girl. You didn't do a thing wrong, and don't you ever let anyone tell you anything different."

A bag of clothes had mysteriously shown up on the chair by her bed. Dr. Hillcrest, in his pacing, drove home and collected something for her to wear, knowing her clothes would be kept for evidence. On the way out, the door at discharge, Beth's mom was handed a tracking number. She was now a number in the rape system in the state of North Carolina. Just what she never wanted for her daughter.

Chapter 54

"Good morning, son, good game last night." JB continued to look down at his newspaper while he stood over the counter gnawing on his bagel.

"Morning dad," Carter mumbled as he made his way down the back steps. Each one he took made his head feel that much worse. His head pounded like the vodka last night.

"Did you get in late last night?"

"Not too late. Went over to Jack's after the game. He had a few people over."

"Looks like you got in late." JB chewed while he waited for his son to respond.

"I gotta go to film dad." Carter rubbed his aching head while he sipped on his creatine shake.

"So, your head hurts? Did you take a big hit in the game last night?"

"Yea, I think I may have taken a few hits last night."

"It should by the looks of your car."

"What, what's wrong with my car?"

"You parked it up on the lawn." He looked directly at Carter. "We live on Main Street. There is a college game today and everyone has to pass our house to get to the stadium. If you are going out and having a few drinks, you better get someone to drive you home. You have scholarships on the line and you're a leader on your team. And how many times have I told you, you have a target on your back. You have to look out for yourself." JB's voice was stern.

"I didn't realize I parked that bad."

"Next time, get a ride home. Did you hear about Beth, apparently, she was assaulted at Jack's party? Was she drinking?"

"I was the one who called 911. I found her." Carter felt his palms break out in a sweat. "Do they know who did it?"

"I'm proud of you for taking care of her. You did the right thing. I know you were a big help."

Carter stood taller. "I found her, Dad. She was on Jack's bed." He quickly explained, "I went up there to go to the bathroom. She was pretty messed up."

Carter walked over to the refrigerator and grabbed a Gatorade. "I gotta go."

"You going to come to the game after film?"

"Yep, I'll see you there."

"Your mom should be back soon with your sister. They had some things to do at the store this morning."

"Yep." Carter hoped to make it through film his head hurt so bad.

"Great game last night. Way to take down my high school. You guys should get a nice spot in playoffs. I'm really proud of you."

"Thanks dad. See you."

JB walked down the hall and into his office relieved. Whit had called him with all the details. Donna withheld the rape kit, but as soon as Whit had access, he would take care to delay it for months.

JB watched through the Plantation Shudders as Carter walked out to his car. "I should have moved the damn thing."

Carter walked into the film room in a somber mood. He was the last one. As soon as he sat down, Coach Cotton flipped on the bright lights and started, "I'm fully aware of the mess that was created at Jack's house last night. I'm going to pass around this clip board and I want you to write down your name if you were there. No details on this paper please just your name."

Carter looked for Jack, who was not there.

"I will not have anyone on my team behaving like this. A young girl was hurt last night and someone in this room knows something. I plan to get to the bottom of this. When I find out who, they will no longer be a part of my team."

Carter sat up in his chair. *I'll be a hero in all this. I found Beth.*

Cottonmouth Droppings

Stonewall: Can you believe something so awful happened at Dr. Thompson's house last night. Was it Beth Hillcrest? Such a well-respected doctor. And Jack is such a great kid. Let's hope Penni didn't sneak into town.

Sweet Home Southern Boy: Jack is a great kid. It's all over the place. These kids are out of control.

Swamp Runner: Who did it? Seems fishy to me.

Turncoat: Well, Penni is in Washington. They have a game today. He's starting.

Foxy: Don't post this crap unless you know the truth. So, who was there? Let's see, Carter, Harris, Tommy, Sam, Jack and the list goes on.

Captain Kirk: Whoa listing names. I'm sure there were other boys there too.

Turncoat: I guess it's time to run the Thompsons out of town too. Wait, aren't they an old southern family, locals even? Maybe Jack did it? It seems the boyfriends are running crazy all over town.

Farm Boy: Who the hell are you? Big win for the kids. I think these parties get out of control.

Stonewall: Those are four good boys you just named, Foxy Troll!

Foxy: Asshole. I named five. Wonder who pushed drugs last night? Carter?

Confederate Fan: Whoa calling out Taylor, that's a pretty big call.

Foxy: The girl's name should be kept confidential. Give her some dignity.

Weasel: Seems weird to me that this happened before and everyone blamed Penni.

Turncoat: You think?

Foxy: You think? I think we have a rotten apple in this town. Or should I say Doctor drug pusher. I heard she was drugged just like the last girl.

Tina pushed hard with her last comment.

JB felt steam rise from his head as he considered his next move and who Foxy was.

Chapter 55

A Cottonmouth victory was not enough to keep the chat site from the rape chatter. Patsy and Henry were invited to the President's tent but were only going to the reception. Neither one of them felt up to spending all day at the stadium. Patsy was exhausted and was relying on Miss Clara to take care of all the last-minute details at the house on Saturday for the big event on Sunday, which everyone around the house was affectionately calling since it was the single most important thing in Patsy's life.

Having Harper's 18th birthday tea for twenty of her best girlfriends and their mothers was daunting, let alone the horrible event Friday night that put a dark cloud over the weekend. Patsy would not let her spirits be dampened and was content to know after talking with Beth's mom that the girls would find solidarity by being together. Beth and her mother would attend the party and Melanie would be by her side. Patsy knew the girls would rally around her just as they did for Melanie. What was most disturbing was two of Harper's closest friends had been attacked. Patsy could not help but think it was a boy the girls knew and she was beginning to have her suspicions of exactly who that boy was.

But now, for just for a few minutes she wanted to sit in the quiet of the gardens and enjoy the sounds, smells and colors of all her hard work. The gardenias were blooming at the just the right time to provide a beautiful scent around the path while pots of mums lined the gate by the back entrance. The lavender refused to take a back seat and put on a show along the garage paths.

The hues of orange, red, and yellow of the celosias were showing off their morning flames. Patsy was proud of how hard she worked for the patch of them. The flowers seemed to obey her. They looked like they belonged in a Dr. Seuss book, which was one of Harper's favorite authors. She knew Anne would understand why she planted them. It would be a fun secret between the two of them.

Patsy gazed at the long table. Rita Faye would be there soon to put the light-yellow table cloths down that would hold the perfect settings. The flowers from the garden stood in vases waiting in line. There was a stack of toys Patsy had carefully selected to represent each year of her life. And her grandmother's china all lay in wait to be useful. Pink roses and gardenias played around the garden. That's what her daddy planted for Anne when she was born.

And in the simple yellow box on top of Harper's plate would be the diamond earrings from Patsy's grandmother and the locket that now hung around Patsy's frail neck. She listened to the birds wake up the flowers while she struggled with everything being right in her corner of the world. Despite her strength climbing back into her body, she felt an unease she had not felt in a long time.

She gazed up at the tall steady tree to the side of the yard. Its boughs clung to the sturdy trunk season after season. That tree held great power and spent many mornings with Patsy while she worked in the garden or sat on the beloved teak bench Henry gave her one birthday many years ago.

She was going to skip church today. She found God in her own back yard. It had been a long six months since her cancer returned, Henry's fall, and all the chaos surrounding Melanie. And now this last past Friday night's heartbreak. She sipped her coffee in the cool quiet morning and wondered how in the world young people could get to such a place. Patsy was worried about her granddaughter.

"Good morning, mama," Anne interrupted the songs of the birds. She reached down to her mama's blanket clad shoulder. "The rock wall is stunning with masses of billowy creamy clematis climbing around the cracks and crevices while the winter Daphne, with its fragrant flowers of pink played well with the creamy flowers."

"Doesn't the garden look nice?"

"It's beautiful. And look at the dragonfly. You outdid yourself. Harper is going to love everything." Anne looked at the colorful show the trees were putting on just for today. "I love all this. It reminds me so much of my own 18th."

"I love you, Anne." Patsy reached her soft, brown spotted hand up to her daughter. "Sit with me for a few minutes."

"Love you too, mama." She nestled her head into her mother's shoulder and took a seat right next to her. "I hope the girls are going to be okay after Beth's assault?"

They were interrupted by Clara. "Miss Patsy, the men are here to finish setting up the tables." She slipped the paper onto Patsy's lap.

"Thank you, Clara. Will you have them start with the prep in the third bay of the garage. And let me know when Rita Faye gets here."

"Yes ma'am." Clara rounded the long walk and made her way back up the steps.

Anne reached over and pulled the paper from her mother's lap. She anticipated the *Daily Voice* being full of articles about the attack Friday night.

"Mama, let's put this away." She tucked the paper under her arm. "We should get in and let the men do what they need to do before Rita Faye gets here."

"I can't help but wonder who did this to poor Beth. I'm proud of her for coming today. I hate what happened, but her mother said she insisted on being here."

Anne helped Patsy into the house. She would not allow anything to ruin this day for her daughter, but more than that she would not let it ruin it for her mother.

Patsy and Anne had not been in the kitchen for more than a few minutes when Rita Faye walked in the door, followed by Caroline with armfuls of decorations. "Good morning ladies."

Patsy said, "Good morning, Rita Faye. You look so wonderful." She stood back for a moment. "I don't know what you are doing but you keep doing it."

She helped her set the first round of things on the counter. And before Rita Faye could turn around and head back for the next load, Patsy was in full swing with her nose in all the bags.

"Wait Rita Faye, let Clara and me help you." Anne followed her to leave Patsy in inspection mode.

The ladies made their way back into the kitchen and had all the materials Rita Faye would need to start the tables. Each table setting had different teacups, small spoons, and a place card set personally set by Patsy.

While Rita Faye decorated each table, she moved around to each setting listening to Patsy and Anne chat, "All these toys bring back lots of memories."

This was one of the most wonderful things Rita Faye had ever been involved in.

Caroline noticed her mother's pause and walked by her as she swiped her hand across her arm. "I remember that Barbie doll, don't you? I wanted one and you said no that's for Harper. Remember mama?"

Rita Faye smiled, "I sure do. As soon as I told you that you picked it up and said, 'I will get a different one' and you did." She laughed. "You two are so lucky to have each other."

"You girls sure are. But now more than ever you need to stick together. There's a cancer in this town and I'm going to get to the bottom of it," Patsy said as she carefully placed each toy in the middle of the tables.

Caroline held her tongue. She was here to help her mother, not get involved with the conversation. "If you're almost done, I'm going to head home and shower."

"Go ahead, honey. See you in a few."

"Mama, can we not start this," Anne stopped and moved her head side to side in disapproval.

"It's as if someone is purposefully driving this whole thing. Between the chat sites and the, the incidents." She started to get upset.

"Mama, stop."

Rita Faye didn't want to talk about the rapes. She had a horrible feeling about both of them. She had been sneaking on the chat sites since she figured out who two of the people were. She was now trying to figure out who Foxy and Turncoat were. So, she sneaked on the chat site again this morning, hoping to find more clues. It was not good, first Penni and now Dr. Thompson and his son Jack.

It hurt her to see all the negative talk about Penni starting again. "Your gardens certainly reflect all your hard work, Patsy. I can smell the basil and roses over here." Rita Faye took in a big inhale. "I just love it back here."

Anne looked up from her ribbon tying and was hopeful that with Rita Faye's interruption about the gardens the chatter would stop. It was almost impossible to get Patsy off heated subjects. The cruel cancer was disfiguring and might have robbed her of some of her youth and beauty, but not her mind. It was completely intact. She would fight for injustice until the bitter end.

"There, I'm finished," Rita Faye announced. "I'm going to head home and get cleaned up. I should be back in about an hour. Is there anything else I can do for you two?"

The three women stood back after all the chaos and beamed. "It's beautiful." Patsy's bottom lip quivered.

Rita Faye draped her arm around Patsy's shoulder. "It really is."

"I'm going to lay down for a few minutes," Patsy said.

"You go on in and get some rest. We have a big day." Anne gave her mother a tight squeeze.

Pasty laid on her bed and stared at the white everblooming Mystery and Ever Blooming gardenias that sat in her vase. She loved the smell. They reminded her of her mama and how much she loved them. She could hear her mother telling her how to take care of the delicate plants.

"Patsy, the blooms will go right through until warm weather ends if you make sure they get enough light and heat. Make sure the soil is well drained and do not, I repeat do not plant them too near other plants. They just don't like to share."

Patsy rubbed her eyes awake. She glanced over at her clock when she heard light tapping at the door. "Come in."

Miss Clara walked in in a beautiful gold dress. "The girls will be here soon. Can I help you get dressed?"

"Yes ma'am. The caterer is here and Rita Faye is downstairs barking orders. Lal that lady knows her stuff. Come on, I have your dress ready." Clara helped her out of her robe and into her soft green dress. Clara gently combed her silver-gray hair.

"Patsy, you look wonderful."

"Thank you for everything." Patsy uncapped her lipstick and held up the tube of berry fresh. She had been wearing that Revlon color for years. She roused every bit of strength to get herself ready. She felt great this morning but was not feeling herself this afternoon.

"I'm more tired after I laid down. But I must press on and get the party going." She swiped the pink color across her dry tender lips. "Is your daughter here?"

"Yes ma'am. Laurel is downstairs with Miss Rita Faye helping with last minute details."

"I'm so thrilled she came. Harper loves her and you."

"And we love her. Now come on. You look so pretty Miss Patsy." Clara helped her dear friend in front of the mirror for one final glance.

The two women made their way down the long hall and into the oversized kitchen, where it looked like bees buzzing around the nest waiting for their queen.

Clara, Patsy, and Anne had polished silver for days and the pieces sat proudly on the counters next to all the tea cakes.

"Pinkies up ladies," Patsy said as she watched all the wonderful chaos. She felt a renewed strength.

"Everything looks wonderful," Patsy announced to the staff. She walked over to Rita Faye. "Isn't it time you act like one of the guests. You've done enough. Come on, let's head out to the garden. Where's Harper?"

As if on cue Harper and Caroline came promenading down the steps in their garden dresses. They were proud of Beth for being strong. Rita Faye beamed at how beautiful her daughter looked. A slight pink cheek and lip accented her cream floral dress.

Patsy extended her arms and Harper fell into them. "You look beautiful." She pulled back. "Caroline, you look so pretty. Come on girls, it's time."

There was a fire going in the stacked rock fireplace as the crackling glow of embers shown red licking up orange streaks. When they made it down the path there was a young man in a tuxedo opening the door for the first guests. Melanie and her mom walked in dressed in their Sunday best. Tina even wore a beautiful hat tipped just slightly to the side as her blond hair sat at the base of her neck in a chignon.

"Good afternoon ladies." Patsy gave each of them a hug.

While chatting with Anne, Tina regarded Rita Faye's new-found lease. Her hair was set perfectly against her soft creamy skin. Her fitted soft garden dress laid perfectly against her pinched waist and the sleeves fell just off her shoulders. Tina felt immense remorse for ever hurting her.

"Don't you look wonderful." She said in a repentant tone.

"Thank you." Rita Faye ran her hands over the soft gauzy material.

"How did you do it?" Tina felt complete joy for her.

"I've decided it's my time," she paused, "and I'm never turning back."

"You're a smart woman. Keep it up," Tina said.

Rita Faye gave Melanie a big hug. "I miss seeing you."

With the final guests arriving Patsy said, "Pinkies up, ladies. Please find your seats."

Each table was set for conversation with low flowers. Her grandmother's china fit the menu with pink roses and gardenias from the garden.

"That's what her daddy gave to Anne when she was born," Patsy pointed to a small box at Harper's place setting, while Helen and May took a seat by Patsy and Anne.

"Girls everyone, drop your phones in the lovely basket," Rita Faye's assistant moved to each table. No one is allowed to be distracted. "We have a photographer moving around the garden snapping shots."

"Today is Harper's day and the most important thing is that she is surrounded by all the people that she loves and that love her." Patsy reached down and opened the silk box. "It's time you wear my locket." She slipped the beautiful gold chain around Harper's soft neck while a small dragonfly lighted on the table.

Tina and Melanie proudly held up their teacups along with Beth and her mother, Gail, Caroline, and Rita Faye. The six women sat comfortably at their table for six while they toasted a family and friend that meant so much to them.

Chapter 56

The enchantment of the fall dance was upon them and carried many of the traditions that were the culmination of spirit week. The girls scrambled for months with important decisions like how to wear their hair and what dress they should pick. With tradition, it was usually a long dress to the prom and a short dress to the fall dance, so Rita Faye's store was stocked with dress selections.

As with every event in Oak Grove, it was tradition that the boy invited the girl. But the ask came with a burden of creativity. For couples like Sam and Harper, it was understood that they would attend together. A few boys sent silly text messages to Melanie hoping she would say yes, but she politely declined.

The real surprise came when Tommy made it public that he asked Caroline. It was only Melanie, Harper, and Sam that knew Tommy had asked back in September. He didn't make any big ovation. He simply showed up at the art studio during her big show in September as if he were just there to enjoy the exhibit. Standing next to her he slipped her a linen envelope.

I'm not sure this is proper since this is your time
But come late October I will be asked to come up with a rhyme
To ask you to the fall dance, the pleasure would be mine
And when you say yes, you will make my sun shine

But for now, could you keep this just between us
We wouldn't want to make it all a big fuss
With you on my arm it would make me classy
So, it's you that I fancy to take to the fall dancey
If you would like to go just give me a glance
And maybe you might think about starting this romance

Caroline looked up at Tommy after she read the note. She batted her eyes in embarrassment, but felt like she was on a magic carpet. "Yes," she whispered. They had dating ever since. It was only her mother that she shared such important news.

The week was all about the seniors. Senior pictures were taken on Monday and Tuesday along with a special luncheon. There were assemblies with guest speakers addressing the kids about careers and college choices. They were excused from school on Thursday but were required to attend a dinner hosted by the staff on Thursday night. The big game on Friday called the North South clash was played with the high school several towns north of Oak Grove.

And the fall dance on Saturday finished the week in style. It had been enough that Caroline was now softening her makeup and wearing more than just yoga pants and t-shirts, but to choose a dress for the fall dance was more than she bargained for. She felt very little pressure with dressing for Harper's tea with only girls in attendance, but when Tommy asked her to the dance back in September, she had nothing but anxiety.

With Sam and Harper agreeing to go with them, Caroline was set. She anticipated getting a ton of grief from Carter, but Tommy had been reassuring her for months that he could handle anything Carter threw his way. Still, she was nervous. Tommy, like Sam, had been pulling away from Carter. But with Carter it didn't matter. He held a lot power in the economy of high school and behaved as if he were untouchable.

Harper was with Caroline every step of the way. If she didn't want to go to her mom's shop or head to Raleigh, Harper had a closet full of dresses. She told Harper the only way she would go to the dance is if she could get ready at her house.

"I will sneak over to Patsy's and take pictures." Rita Faye was in full agreement with Caroline.

"I hate this, Harper." Caroline squirmed while Harper pulled on her friend's hair. Melanie was in the bedroom putting last touches on her make-up while the other two fussed in the bathroom.

"Hurry up girls, our guys will be here in a few minutes. Beth and Jack are meeting us for pictures," Melanie reminded them.

"I'm not even dressed. They will have to wait," Harper hollered from the bathroom.

"Just sit still while I finish your hair." Small tendrils of blond curls were liberated from the high curly pony tail Harper teased at the back of Caroline's head.

"I love the dress you picked out." She smiled down as she busied herself in front of her. "Sit still and let me finish your makeup. I'm glad you moved away from the black liner, but tonight you need to wear a little. I have an idea."

She stroked soft colors of pink on her eye lids and lined each eye with a soft brown pencil. She finished with a pop of cherry lipstick.

"You don't need much makeup you're so pretty. Now look," Harper made her turn around to the mirror. "You look so beautiful." Harper beamed with pride.

The two came out of the bathroom and when Melanie turned around, she gasped, "Caroline, you look awesome."

"Now let's get dressed, girls." Harper helped Caroline slip into her dress. It was a mid-length navy silk dress with soft touches of gold on the sleeves.

Caroline walked in front of the full-length mirror. "I'm not sure who I'm looking at."

"Stop that, lady. You should be thanking me. Give yourself a break. You are so beautiful. At least everyone thinks that. Boys are just afraid of you," Harper said

"What?" Caroline turned around and faced her friend. "Well they will be now when they realize you and Tommy have been going out for a while. He's a real catch."

Melanie paused. "I just think you put up this tough side and with all your crazy stuff like yoga and your friendship with Miss Helen, I don't think they know you."

"They don't know what to do with you," Harper joined.

"I didn't know I was that weird." She started to wipe the thick gloss from her sticky lips.

"You're not weird. You're different. Almost like you skipped all the foolishness of high school and leap in living," Harper said.

"To living, like you know what you are going to do the rest of your life. And talk about weird. At least you don't have to worry about your mom being talked about all the time." Melanie sat on the bed, "And people knowing what horrible thing happened to me last spring."

"Look at Beth, she is holding her head up high," Caroline said.

"You're right. It's just so awful though," Melanie said. "At least she has Jack."

"Well, Penni is certainly your rock," Harper said.

"Stop, Melanie. It's going to be so much fun when you show up with Penni." Caroline rubbed her hand.

"It's just been a lot these past few months," Melanie said. "First me, now Beth."

"I know what you're thinking." Caroline said. "And I am too. But when the results come back," she paused, "we will know."

"Stop you two, you will ruin your makeup." Harper was in her dress and ready.

"I don't want to hear any more talk about that tonight. We are going to be the center of attention. I mean just look at us," she laughed.

"You're right. We're going to have so much fun tonight. I can't wait to see Penni. Mr. Charlie was picking him up and taking him to Sam's house." Melanie smiled. "What a surprise he will be when we walk in the door of the dance."

"Stop licking your lips, Caroline." Harper grabbed her. "Don't ruin your makeup. You have me and Melanie, Penni and Sam and Tommy and Jack and Beth and we all love you. We are your family." Harper gently swept make up over Caroline's face and softly creamed more blush into her high cheek bones.

Patsy stood in the doorway glowing. She relished the sweet memories that they were not only providing for themselves but for her.

"Ok Caroline, you're done." Her dress was buttoned, makeup complete, and her stunning shoes strapped. She stood up, and before she could take a few steps Patsy interrupted with applause.

"You look so wonderful. All of you." Patsy beamed.

Caroline took herself in again in the full-length mirror and stared at the stranger's reflection. She had gone for so long covering the scars of abuse with the foreigner she pretended to be that she didn't recognize the reflection that was fighting to come out. Someone hard on the outside but feeling ever so soft and vulnerable on the inside. She felt a crack of vulnerability start to fissure. Her eyes stung and a tightness in her chest crept into a place she didn't recognize. It was time for her to let that hard person go. Like her mother said, "It's your senior year and your time." She smiled back at herself. *I look really pretty*, she thought.

Harper caught a shadow of Patsy in the doorway. "Hello Mimi."

Melanie and Harper rushed to Caroline and stood in the mirror. "This is one fine looking group." Patsy smiled.

"I think Tommy is one lucky guy. Your hair looks so pretty all curly and soft and your makeup is perfect." Patsy held the young girl.

She wiped her face. "I'm not sure I can go like this. It scares me."

"What, girl you look amazing. You are by far one of the most beautiful girls in our school. You just cover it up." Harper convinced her.

Pasty grabbed the young woman's hand.

"I get you." She whispered. "Take a chance," she paused. "You will have a great time and when people see you just say thank you." Patsy gave her hand a tight squeeze. "Now let's get downstairs. Your dates will be here soon and you know your mama, Harper, she is down there taking pictures of anyone that will stand still. She's fully loaded and if the boys are here, well between she and Rita Faye they may take off before they see you girls."

Chapter 57

Carter made his grand entrance at the dance with Tiffany, a cute girl from a good family. She was a sophomore cheerleader and was thrilled when the all-star football player asked her. Carter looked especially handsome in his dark tuxedo and crazy multi colored shirt. Tiffany wore a short red dress that she picked up at Rita Faye's shop.

A rallying crowd cheered Carter as Tiffany followed behind him. He knew they wouldn't be there long and was anxious to make his appearance and get to the big party at Nick's.

Waving his hands in the air and chatting it up with his buddies, he quickly noticed that Sam and Harper were not there yet. He was miffed at Sam for coming with a different crowd but would deal with that later. Before he could take another swig from his hidden flask, he heard chanting. "Sammy, Penni, Jack," Carter turned around and right behind him, Harper and Sam hand-in-hand, followed by Penni and Melanie and Beth and Jack and Caroline and Tommy, making a bigger entrance than he could ever imagine.

"What the hell?" It took him a minute to let it register. "What the hell is this about? You know I don't hang out with her." He pointed to Caroline then grabbed her exposed arm.

"Where's your costume, little sister? I hardly recognize you dressed like a girl. Aren't you missing charcoal around your eyes?" Carter didn't stop until Penni came up behind him.

"Knock it off and stop being an asshole. I see some people never change." Penni was even bigger than before. "I don't answer to anyone here. Let her arm go or we will take this outside."

Tommy was coming in to finish and quickly grabbed Caroline.

"Doesn't she look awesome?" Tiffany looked over at Caroline. "I love your dress."

"I guess even without her raccoon eyes," Carter sneered.

"Is she coming to the party?" Tiffany asked.

"Of course, she is." Harper finished.

Caroline felt a pain run through her heart. She was out of character with nothing to block her from the slamming words. Tommy grabbed Caroline's hand and held it tight.

"You look amazing."

Carter started to lunge toward Tommy, but not before Sam got between them.

"Stop. Stop all this bullshit or we are all going to get in trouble. We don't want to ruin our season over this. Just shut you damn mouth, Carter." Sam glared at him. "Come on Tommy, don't waste it on this shit."

"Asshole," Caroline whispered, feeling an urge to rip his eyes out.

Caroline tilted her head against Tommy's arm. Yet another betrayal from her brother. She hated how she felt at that moment, small and insignificant. Yet at the same time she had never had anyone stand up for her. She was violated, again, for trying to be woman. At least now, at that moment and despite the pain, she felt a sense of relief. She could do this. She was walking out of her wasteland.

Penni put his large frame between Melanie and Carter and guided her to the other side of the room but not before giving Carter one last shove. "Stay away from us."

Music played in the background. Decorations swayed from the ceiling. And there was dancing. The couples headed over to the drink table and grabbed some soda and found a table.

Caroline walked away into the crowd, holding onto Tommy's arm, her lip quivering with anger as she grabbed a drink. She would take so many steps forward, then feel disarmed dressed like this. She had to work on being comfortable with her awakening self.

"Come on Caroline let's go dance." Tommy put his hand on her back and gently moved her to the dance floor. Sam led Harper behind them while Melanie and Penni and Beth and Jack sat in the corner chatting.

Carter and Tiffany danced over to Harper and Sam.

"You know I love my boy Sam, but you two really stooped low on this one, Harper. You should rethink your date tonight." Carter winked at her. He swiped his hand down Harper's sleeveless arm. "You know you could date a guy like me." He grinned.

"Have you been drinking Carter?"

"What do you think?" He reached in his pocket and pulled out his flask. "You want some?"

Sam pushed him. "Hell no. Put that away." If he knew he wouldn't get in trouble for hitting the golden boy, he would. Tonight was the end of their friendship. They started to dance away, but Carter kept pulling Tiffany after them. Harper pulled Sam over to the table where Penni sat, knowing Carter would not follow them.

A slow song came on and Tommy and Caroline stayed on the dance floor under the reflection of the lighted ball. Caroline was a stranger on the dance floor, but Tommy led her. She never felt prettier. She knew there were no expectations with Tommy. They already had spent enough time together to know exactly where she stood with him. *This is my night.* Her mind drifted from Tommy to Carter's revolting behavior.

My dad accuses me of drinking and doing drugs. She knew she had to protect herself. She cringed in Tommy's arms.

"You okay? Are you cold?" Tommy pulled her closer.

She was so afraid to say anything. When it happened, it shocked her. At the time, she knew her parents would never believe her. She covered herself, she locked her door, she dressed terribly, wore heavy makeup, and never let her guard down. She was 11. And here it was six years later. And she kept in control.

"I'm good. Just a little cold," she lied.

She had been fighting the voice that said, I'm not enough. Never good enough. High school is hell. Sum of every bad thing. Dirty hair, bad makeup, all at the hands of her failing family. Tommy swayed her to the music. "I'm so happy to be here with you." She gently brushed her lips against his.

She rested close on Tommy's chest. He pulled her back. "I would not want to be with anyone else. I hope you're having fun."

"Of course I am." She gave him a tight squeeze. He led her off the dance floor when the song finished and back to the table to pick up some food.

They spent the rest of the evening laughing and dancing. They would head to the party later. Caroline felt like a princess for the first time in her life. Tommy had goals like she and her friends did, and she now realized that she didn't give people a chance. She never took the time to get to know anyone. Life seemed to be turning the corner for her. Her mom was right, this was her year. And tonight, she was secretly hoping that she would have a prom date after all

Chapter 58

"Sophomores should not be here," Tommy whispered as they stepped inside Nick's party.

"Hey girls," Tiffany ran over and greeted Caroline and Harper. "Oh, I'm so glad you guys came. Caroline, if you have time, I want to talk to you about the floats you made a few weeks ago. With the theme of the fall festival parade being, Animals uncaged, your designs were unique."

She was able to take chicken wire, and sculpt a tiger, a lion, and a giraffe for the senior float.

"Oh thanks, Tiffany." Caroline stepped aside to let other people in the door.

"I would love you to show me how to do all that," She gushed.

"I can show you sometime." Caroline could not imagine why she would ever go out with her brother. Except for the obvious reasons.

"That would be great. Maybe we can talk at school sometime." She smiled at Caroline. "I'm so glad you will talk to me."

Caroline paused, "Why wouldn't I talk to you?"

"Carter was so mad on the way over here, I was afraid of you."

Caroline said, "I'm pretty harmless. Have a good time." She rubbed her arm hoping that she would not suffer the same fate as Melanie and Beth. "Don't drink too much, okay?"

She walked further into the party, following Tommy and just for a moment felt a fear from a deeper place than anywhere she could imagine. Rejection, a pain that she would be alone, misunderstood. A life sentence as long as her brother was around. As they moved further into the party, she felt an increased nausea.

Like scraping finger nails down a chalk board, a low conversation hummed through the room while the music blasted. The conversation hit a high pitch. Caroline had never seen anything like it. Jell-O shots lined the counter, beer, plugged watermelons with vodka and red punch filled to the brim of a trash can, her heart clattered. Some kid was blowing up hot dogs in the microwave just for fun. And the smell of pot wafted pungent through the crowd.

She twisted a bead between her fingers as she felt her nerves fray. She saw everyone at the party and spoke to no one. Loneliness filled her core and she wished she was back at the front door chatting with Tiffany. It seemed safer up there. She walked through the kitchen, holding Tommy's hand.

"You want a drink?" he shouted.

"I'll have a soda." She gave it a second thought. "Just bring me a can of Coke, not opened."

"Me too." He smiled.

Harper and Caroline chatted while Sam and Tommy grabbed some sodas.

"I'm glad Melanie didn't come to this."

"Me too. She and Penni were going to her house. He has to fly back early tomorrow," Harper screamed above the music.

Carter stood in the corner watching the four traitors walk in. He was seething. It was his sister's presence and her friendships that cleaved them apart. He held his beer in his hand, his arm around another girl. Clearly, he was done with Tiffany. He glared at them thinking, how could his buddy bring his sister to the fall dance and now the party? And how could Sam continue to betray him? And to think Penni was at the dance.

Carter felt heat rise to his face. He took a big swig of beer and felt himself let go as the liquid courage ran through his system. He gave the unidentified girl a big kiss and moved toward his betrayers.

"So, you guys are really slumming bringing your dates to this. It's not their kind of party." He looked right at Caroline. "Shouldn't you be at home, alone in your room doing god knows what to yourself?"

Tommy flinched. "Hey man, what's your problem? Why don't you go find Tiffany and leave us alone? We don't want to start anything."

"I can see you have reached an all-time low, Tom ole boy." Carter put his big hand on Tommy's shoulder and gave it a squeeze. "Harper I'm not sure why in the hell you hang out with my sister. Maybe you two have something going." Carter felt a tinge of relief as the indicting words spilled from his mouth.

"Why don't you shut the hell up, Carter. You are such a pain in all of our asses. You with all your athleticism and might and you can't even get a girl to sleep with you unless you force them." Caroline shut her mouth like a guppy.

And as soon as she regretted her words, she felt Carter's hand come across her face. Stunned for just a minute, as if the whole room grew quiet, and before Tommy could catch her, she ran up the stairs and locked herself in a bathroom.

Harper glared at Carter and when she turned to look at Sam, who was as stunned as she was Carter slipped a pill in her soda can. *She will be out quickly* he thought. *Serves her right.*

Tommy shoved Carter. "You're an asshole, dude. Stay the fuck away from me and stay the fuck away from your sister." He started to turn.

"Hey, I'm sorry. You know how kids fight. I'm not used to seeing her at parties." Carter walked away, waiting for Harper to go look for Caroline.

Tommy made a pass through the house and rushed back to Sam and Harper. "I can't find her anywhere. Do you think she left?"

"I hope not," Sam said.

Harper reached for her phone. "I'm not feeling so great." She leaned into Sam while she started to text.

Caroline, locked in the bathroom, rubbed her makeup off with a wet washcloth. The noise from the party blocked out the pounding in her head. She was going to make a getaway as soon as she could. She was so embarrassed. Her brother slapped her in front of everyone.

Harper fell into Sam. "I'm feeling really sick. I'm going to the bathroom."

Harper tried the first bathroom but the door was locked so she headed upstairs and pounded on the only bathroom just off the bedroom. "Are you in there, Caroline?"

Caroline settled on the bathroom floor ignoring the pounding. She was hoping she could slip out soon. She slipped off her shoes and sat but within minutes she heard moaning from the other room. She cracked open the door and when her eyes cleared in the shadowy darkness, she saw her brother struggling to get on top of Harper.

Harper's dress pulled up, her hair splayed all over the bed. She was crying and saying no, under the struggle.

Caroline dropped her shoes and leapt through air onto her brother's back, grabbing him around the neck and choking him. Carter would get his way. He had never been told no. He struggled to get up, but his pants were twisted around his ankles and served as a restraint to better help Caroline free Harper. Caroline pushed harder and felt a sudden shock to her body when Carter threw her to the floor.

She scrambled to gain her balance. And as she pushed what she thought was him, she heard a big crash and she once again fell to the floor in slow motion. A large body moved in front of her and she stumbled in the dark, falling back against the floor. When she regained composure, she saw the curtain sway. The bedroom window completely shattered. She leapt to her feet and looked out.

"I killed my brother."

She conjured up the devastation with barely an ounce of effort as her mind raced with options. She struggled to get Harper up as she fought another strong arm. Her screams blocked any voices.

"Harper get up, get up." Caroline pushed her, willing her to get up. "What the hell did he give you?" She kept falling against the bed.

"Where's Sam?" Harper mumbled but nothing came out. Her lips were swollen and chapped. She kept trying to reach down and feel for her dress. She loved her dress but she couldn't move her arms. There was something pinching her arm. Her hand.

"Mama." She whispered. She kept mouthing. "Where's Sam? He left me at the party."

"It's me Harper, it's me," Caroline said. "I'm here."

It wasn't her bedroom. The voice now the voices sounded like they were off across the ocean floating, drifting away but coming closer in with the tide. She felt hot, like the sand was too hot to let her walk on it without shoes. Her feet were raw. She fought to get up, her heart was pounding. She opened her eyes and could only make out a dark figure in the room.

"I know who you are."

*****

Caroline grabbed her shoes and ran down the steps. "Go get Harper. She's upstairs and she's hurt," she screamed at Sam.

Caroline took off out the front door in her bare feet. Her feet were soon raw from the gravel that dug into her heels. She stopped and fell to the ground, crying as her knees hit the ground and pain ran up her thighs. She saw a dead woodpecker, it's red colors still brilliant as it lay against the gray sidewalk. It could have been there for hours.

She was an actor tonight. She killed her brother. What does that make her? Who would know it was her? No one saw her. But whose arm lifted her from the floor? She cried. Up again, walking through back yards, she kept low so no one would see her. She heard sirens, peeked out and saw police cars racing down the street. She counted her breath. Where could she go? She told her mom she was at Harper's tonight. And what about Harper? She'd never seen her drink. Caroline's endless mind chatter pushed her away.

*****

A long wave of nausea had passed. She wanted to sleep. She felt a soft hand slip in hers and on the other side a more rugged one. She tipped her head from side to side. Something smelled like smoke. She fought to raise her head and recognize the faces. There was loud music. She thought she was saying all this, but she could not figure out how to get the words to leave her mind and come out of her mouth. She reached up and ran her tongue against her crusty lips. Did she even have mouth? There was loud music, a hand glided around her neck, noise darkness and now some color washed over a boy's face.

"Sam?" She asked, then fought the sin going on in her head. But she couldn't move. Her body would not listen to her. The sounds of the party felt like a huge push, like someone fell on her. Her dress was ripped. And her legs felt cold and exposed. All of a sudden it was quiet then sirens. She was paralyzed.

"There's a pulse. Is she okay?"

"Start a line." Harper felt a pinch. "She's asleep."

"Is she okay?" A stranger's voice. She let the pain have its way, but slowly it lessened and she could breathe. She was warm.

Dr. Thompson stood in the ER waiting for the ambulance. He received a call that two teens were hurt at a house party. Both 18, one fell from a second story window. Multiple wounds, unconscious. And the other had appeared to have had too much to drink, drugs, and a possible assault. His stomach turned and twisted. He knew. He was sick. The first ambulance arrived. As he suspected, it was Carter Taylor.

"What the hell?" They scrambled to get him inside and rushed him to a room. The waiting room was filling with kids. They would wait for hours to hear the outcome of Carter's fate. There was a second ER doctor who would evaluate Carter. Dr. Thompson waited for the second ambulance.

With her clothes torn and red marks along her neck and chest, Dr. Thompson would attend to Harper and call Donna in to perform a rape consultation. Dr. Thompson knew Carter was responsible for Melanie, Beth, and now Harper.

*****

There must have been a full moon or something, because just when Anne was getting settled in her bed with a cup of tea and a good book, she thought she heard a door open. She started to get up and figured it must be Henry or Patsy getting something to drink. She settled back down and listened to Wade snore. She would never finish her book. She stared at the writing on the page and was just about to continue when her cell phone rang. At first, she only heard loud sounds and sirens but then she recognized the voice:

"Mrs. Davis, Harper has been taken to the hospital. Sam says she's okay, but she needs you there." Melanie hung up.

"Sam, where are you?" Harper felt herself being lifted onto a warm bed and whisked away.

Her drug-induced state carried her to the forbidden lake and the plunk and plop of turtles dropping off a half-submerged tree. A thicket of grass canopies and Spanish moss blocked the sun from the lake. A sewage green film uprooted red from hurricanes past kept the large body of water dirty. She picked her way toward a small piece of land no one else knew to meet Sam. She could see a few houses in the distance. And right before her eyes stood Carter, hiding behind a grin. Her body began to shudder. Runnels of water oozed from the sides. The lake was a wasteland, an outhouse, a cesspool of degradation.

"No." She cried, her words reaching along with her arms while she fought to get up. "I hate the smell. Where's my mama?"

*****

The streets were deep with shadows and Caroline felt scared. They were coming for her. She knew, inside any of them, they could be out there and take her. Would seize her, handcuff her, and throw her into prison. She would rot there before anyone would defend her. Her parents lost both kids tonight. But what she did was right. Carter was a menace. He was the one who raped Melanie and Beth and now Harper. He had to be stopped.

Why was her dad so involved? Penni's family was destroyed. The town hated them. They ran them out. Who could she trust? Everyone was under destruction at her father's peril. There were lives lost in the middle of the party, including hers. Lives destroyed and she left Harper. *Did I pass out?* Caroline wondered. *What did he give her?* All she could hear were her brother's last words, his mouth over Harper's as his words guffawed "You know you want me, baby." He laughed in her face, making fun of her trapped body as he struggled to pull up her dress.

Was I there soon enough? Her mind scrambled. *My dad would blame me for everything. I'm so scared. What if he was dead?* She felt her phone vibrate. It seemed like seconds but how long had it been? Was it an accident? She sat in the small alley behind Harper's house tucked behind the secret fence, crying. She needed to change her clothes. She was exhausted from the fight. She was done. Her family hated her. Tommy hated her. She killed her brother.

She made her way through the yard as she watched a few lights twinkle in the Middleton house. She could slip in the back door, get her clothes, and slip in her own back door. She found the back door unlocked, gently opened it, and made her way up the steps. She slipped in Harper's room, grabbed her clothes, changed quickly and slipped back out. *I will never be invited back here.* She felt her body shudder as she wrestled with her thoughts, *but I was defending Harper.*

She looked at her mom's text. *Call me now. Where are you?*

Caroline walked out the door.

*****

Anne and Wade rushed to the ER to find a gaggle of kids scattered everywhere. Rita Faye sat on one side of the room while JB paced the floor. Whit stood nearby. There were a few dozen kids in one corner. Sam, Tommy, Jack, Beth Melanie and Penni sat on the other side of the room whispering.

"Are you her mother?" An unfamiliar face came to Anne.

"Yes," before Anne finished, Wade flashed his medical badge and they were back in the room with Harper.

"Harper wake up, honey. Harper."

"Mama." The words slipped out of her mouth.

Anne's soft lips grazed her daughter's forehead. "You're okay, we're all here. You're safe."

Harper fluttered her eyes and looked at her mom with complete clarity. "Carter Taylor tried to rape me." She reached up to touch her neck. "I lost the locket."

She remembered Caroline screaming, willing her to get up, her voice a beacon in the shadowed stairway of her mind that was trying to guide her somewhere safe.

"Where is Caroline? Is she okay? She tried to get me out of there." Harper rolled slightly to her side.

Anne held Harper's hand, gob smacked. She could not believe the story flowing from her daughter. "Carter Taylor tried to rape me." Harper repeated. "He held me down, ripped my dress, and he...I shoved him hard. I punched him. I fought him and then someone pushed him off me before. Then I heard a crash. It happened so fast. The next thing I knew he was gone."

Harper's words tangled in tears, anger, and fear.

"I didn't mean to hurt him. He hurt me," she cried. "He held me down, he held me down. I knew it was him. I kept screaming for someone to help me. He was so strong."

"Enough Harper. It's okay." Anne tried to quiet her.

Whit Cain walked in the door. "I need to talk to Harper. It seems there's been an accident."

"Yes, there has and we are going to press charges" Anne said.

"Were you drinking, young lady?" Whit ignored Anne.

"No sir, I don't drink."

"Why were you there? Did you start something with Carter?"

"I came with my boyfriend. It was a party. He plays on the football team."

Wade walked in the door. "Stop talking, Harper, right now. Whit get out, now. You will not talk to her, not now, not ever. Do you hear me? Now get out. I will not have her upset."

Whit gave Wade a disdainful look and walked. "I'm not done here."

"You can talk to our lawyer. Don't you ever show your face again." Wade slammed the door.

Harper turned. "I caught his hand in my mouth and I bit him. He wouldn't stop. He kept saying, 'I know you have always wanted this. I could tell by the way you looked at me. My dad has the pills.' He was laughing. I was so scared, mama. I'm so sorry I didn't mean it. I didn't mean it."

Anne held Harper. "You didn't do a thing honey. It's going to be okay."

Donna walked into the room and asked Wade if he would excuse himself. She was going to do an exam. "I want my mama here," Harper cried.

"What a mess. We gotta keep this out of the papers," Whit repeated to the cops as he flicked his cigarette on the ground. "I need to make sure Harper doesn't talk. Carter can't and well we need to find out who else was in that room and who saw something." Whit turned to the ER. "Oh shit."

JB was in Wade's face. "What did your daughter do to my son? Carter's arm and leg are a mangled mess and he's on a board. His face is full of scratches. What did she do?"

Whit pointed at his young underling. "Get him in a room now." He turned to Wade. "You wait." He pointed at JB. "Stop, this isn't doing Carter any good."

Whit shoved JB into a side room. "You can't go off like that. I know it's your son."

JB would not let him finish. "The moment I realized it was Carter, I never hesitated with any of the decisions I would make. I had to do everything I could to protect him. He's a star football player. He's the most popular kid in school. I had to protect him."

"JB, I need you to stop talking right now. Do not say another word and calm down. Where's Rita Faye?" Whit wrestled with what little conscience he had.

"She's trying to find Caroline," JB said.

"I'm going to look for her. Can I trust you to keep it together?"

"Yes." JB fell to the chair while he held his head.

*****

Wade had enough of the Taylor family. But he knew he needed to find Caroline before her father did. He started to walk out of the ER, but not before he saw Henry and Patsy sitting in the corner. Wade gave Patsy a hug.

"She's going to be fine. Did you happen to see Caroline tonight?"

Patsy stood up and held Wade's hand. "I saw her come in the house about an hour ago. She went upstairs, changed her clothes, and when she came back down, I was waiting for her. She told me Carter was dead and she needed to get out of there. I couldn't stop her, Wade. I'm sorry. I tried."

Wade reached around Patsy. "Everyone is okay. You and Henry go on home. I'm going to look for Caroline."

Pasty reached in her pocket for her phone. "I bet she's with Helen."

Chapter 59

Caroline pulled her t-shirt over her jeans. She stuffed some clothes in her duffle and headed to the back door. When she turned the corner, she had a moment of clarity. *Carter is getting drugs from dad.* There were always drugs in the cabinet. And now that her mom wasn't taking anything, there was even more.

Her stomach burning, she made her way to the back door. She could see her mom and dad at the hospital identifying the body. She slipped a sweatshirt over her head. Her feet were raw while she sat on the back bench and picked small stones from her heels. She pulled on clean socks and laced her tennis shoes. She stopped and looked in the mirror. Her makeup had stained her face. Her hair was in knots. She slipped into the back bathroom, scrubbed her face, and twisted her matted hair into a knot on her head. *I need to feel some pain after what I did.* She pulled the hood of her dark sweatshirt over her head and slipped out through the back yards. Her phone buzzed.

"Hello?" She pretended to be asleep.

"Where the hell are you? Your brother has been in a terrible accident."

"What?" she slurred.

"He's in the ER. So is half the school."

"What happened? How's Harper?" She slipped. It seemed like the right question, she thought.

"Who gives a shit. I'll tell you what happened. You are never around for us, Caroline. Get to the hospital now. Carter is badly hurt."

"What happened?" she asked again, relieved he was not dead. Caroline could hear beeping and voices in the background.

"Harper Middleton pushed him out of a second-floor window."

Caroline felt her body tense. "He's okay."

"He has a lot of broken bones. They're not sure about any head trauma or spinal damage. He is getting an MRI now. We don't know if he will ever be able to play football again. She was always after your brother." JB's phone went dead.

Tears took her somewhere words could not. She wished him dead but was relieved. If only she could take it back. If only he could.

The darkness was closer than the light as she made her way through the back yards. Could she go back to Harper's, sit and talk to Patsy, sip some tea, change her clothes again. She hated the dress Harper made her wear now mangled up in the closet.

Caroline walked down the back alleys, thinking. She stared at her phone. She tapped on Melanie's name and watched the three dots bounce. *I can't text her.*

She slipped behind a tree and slide down the trunk. Tommy had called her a million times and sent her tons of texts. "You didn't do it!"

She texted her mother. "I'm scared. I need to get out of here."

"Where are you?" Rita Faye frantically typed.

"I can't come to the hospital."

"Tell me where you are. I can come get you."

"Are you mad at me?"

"No, I want to make sure you are okay."

"Dad is so mad."

"Tell me where you are."

Rita Faye waited for Caroline to respond as she stared at the determined dots.

"I'm sitting in Harper's back yard behind a tree. I need you."

Rita Faye looked up from her phone and stared at JB. She knew he was responsible for all of this. And she knew Harper Middleton did not push her son. She was upset enough about the injuries that Carter sustained, but when she saw Harper, there was no way a girl that size and in that condition could have shoved her son out of the window.

"I'm on my way."

Tommy sat in the corner of the waiting room next to Sam. *There was no way anyone could have seen him push Carter out the window.* He fingered the locket in his pocket. He needed to get to Caroline. He watched Rita Faye rush out the door. "I better get home." Tommy gave Sam a nudge and raced out behind her.

Chapter 60

Whit Cain was always the first on the scene. He had spent countless hours at the Lafoe house. He investigated the assault at Dr. Thompson's house too. He was at the hospital. And he was on the scene when the ambulances picked up Carter and Harper. He saw nothing in the room that could implicate Carter.

Now he needed to review some questions with JB. But after his confession, he needed to be careful. His first obligation was to protect Doc. And JB's assertion could sink everyone around him.

"You're a good kid. I'm sure this is all a misunderstanding. Women tend to get their minds a little tangled when they have feelings for a young man." He regarded JB while he gave Carter's arm a rub. "Don't worry son, I'm sure she got confused when you acted on her advances."

Carter was unaware of the words as he lay in oblivion.

Whit's stomach was about to pop the middle button as he held the black coffee in his hand. "Hell, we're just happy you're not a fatality." His fat jowl jiggled as he tried to make light of the situation.

Carter was hooked up to multiple IVs, his leg and arm were in temporary casts while he lay unconscious on the bed. He was in immense pain from the damage under his fragile cracked ribs. The doctors had put him in twilight. He would have countless surgeries in the weeks to come. But right now, they were just trying to keep him stable and determine how much damage there was.

"He hit pretty hard when he fell off the roof." Carter's lifeless body suspended.

"That bitch will pay for this." JB was loud. He unglued himself from the hospital sofa in Carter's room.

Whit pulled JB away. "You need to be careful. I'm not sure who witnessed what. Let's just slow this down."

A small nip in JB's heart quieted his anger as Whit softened his sandpaper words around the rough edges.

"First and foremost, we need to protect Carter. Let me finish some questioning and see what I can find out."

"Thanks Whit." JB's voice creaked like an old door. "Carter is laying here hurt. And the Middleton family is to blame for all of this. Even my daughter has betrayed me. Can you believe Caroline never showed up? Hell, it's her damn friend." He licked his thin lips, "And Rita Faye running out of here." His words slurred. "Where could she have been going? I've been here the whole time."

Whit rubbed JB's arm. "It's going to be okay."

JB leaned against the wall in Carter's room. "This kid has done nothing wrong. And now I can't fix this. What should I do? Do I need to call our lawyer?"

"It's up to you." It would be a long night.

The hospital door yawned open and Rita Faye walked in.

"Morning Whit, How's my boy?"

She walked over and gave Carter a kiss on his forehead.

"Where the hell have you been all night. In case you didn't notice your son was in surgery."

"In case you didn't notice we have another child who needs a parent, too. I knew Carter was stable and in good hands. I called in every half hour to check on him."

"Where the hell is Caroline? Sitting by Harper and Melanie?"

Rita Faye turned on him. "You are such an asshole. And why did you ask about Melanie?" Rita Faye was just getting started. "Don't you think Caroline is concerned about Carter, too? Or are you the only one in the family that is allowed to have an opinion about him?"

Whit stopped them, "Okay, you two. It's been a long night and we're all upset. JB, let's go down and grab some coffee." He looked over at the sleeping boy.

The two men walked down to the cafeteria and settled in the corner.

"You gotta watch what you say and do here," Whit started.

"I'm exhausted and I don't understand what the hell Carter was doing. I have warned him. He just…" JB shook a few pills in his hand and washed them down with his coffee.

"Look I don't know what is going to happen. The first thing is to get Carter better, right?" Whit hesitated, "But he crossed a line with Harper. I have the reports from Beth. JB, it was Carter. And we know what he did to Melanie." Whit puffed. "This is a tough one. Henry Middleton is out for blood and he's going to get it. His granddaughter was assaulted and your son was caught red handed. Thank God he didn't rape her. He's out of control, JB. Harper Davis is one of the best kids in town. And you know she didn't push him."

"Then who did? Someone needs to pay for this."

"I don't know. I searched that bedroom. There was nothing there. No evidence." He reached in his pocket and pulled out Carter's keys. "Except these. I'm sure glad I found these right next to the bed." JB stared at the keys. "Damn Carter. What am I supposed to do with this?"

"You better make sure you keep them safe. And don't let anyone know that I gave them to you." JB slipped the keys into his pocket. "I wish Caroline was more help with this. Hell, she's friends with all these girls. She's been really tough since the Melanie thing. Never speaking to me and when she does it is only a short answer. She seems to take everyone else's side but her family's."

Whit sat back in his chair. "I'm telling you right now, lay low. They found drugs in Beth's system and Harper's, and those drugs can be directly traced right back to you."

JB gulped, "I don't understand what Carter is doing. But I know he is not the only one that is wrong here, and someone will pay for his injuries."

The two men chatted a few more minutes, never noticing Henry Middleton sitting in the corner, reading the paper, sipping a cup of coffee. It was the last piece of information he needed.

Chapter 61

Caroline leaned her head against Helen's shoulder. She had been staying with her since Carter's fall. The morning storm cracked the late fall sun. Helen thought, *could be a bad winter this year*, as she stroked Caroline's long blond locks. "Your brother is like a dragon that got bigger and bigger. You stared him down and slayed him."

Caroline could see her reflection in the mirror across from the couch. Her eyes were heavy with dark circles.

"I'm the dragon, not Carter."

She heard the front door click and buried herself in Helen's arms.

"You girls need anything?" Charlie asked.

Caroline could smell the old burned coffee from the kitchen.

"Yes, honey, make us a pot of tea, please."

Sounds returned with him to the kitchen.

The two sat in the window seat and finally the heat broke as the rain drops slid down and made time on the glass panes while a lone blue jay hogged the feeder.

"I get you." She whispered.

"It was him. It was him all along."

"I know, baby."

Charlie walked out to the living room with two soft boiled eggs and a pot of tea.

"I decided to make you two some comfort food. Helen has just gathered these from the hens this morning." Charlie looked lovingly at his wife as if she laid them herself.

"Well, eat up before the rest get here. You two are going to need your strength." Charlie set the tray on the coffee table and walked out.

Caroline picked at the soft egg and thought about how her words were going to change her life from this day forward.

"How in the world are we ever going to get back to us?" Caroline asked Helen.

"Do you want to get well?" Helen asked.

"Everyone is in terrible shape since Harper's attack. She refuses to leave her room and will only see her family," Caroline said.

"I think you will see that once we get this all out in the open, you guys will start to heal."

Caroline moved to the chair across from Helen. "When are the others getting here?" As soon as the words came out Harper, Anne, Melanie and Tina, Sam and Tommy were at the door. Charlie ushered them in with coffee and pastry spread on the table.

The young people looked around the room. It had been a week since Harper came home. No one was talking. Helen decided it was time for them to meet and today would start the healing they all needed.

"Girls this has been too much," Helen said. "It's time to lay all this to rest. Everyone in this room is safe here."

Melanie had worn her grief until she felt like her own life was taken from her. Helen knew it when she saw her. It was as if it was happening to her all over again. They had to play a cat and mouse game to bait JB. Tina was as brave as she had ever seen her. But Helen was beyond concerned. She knew the damage JB had done to both of them.

And more than that, she knew how lasting it would be. No one would ever believe that JB Taylor, a respected doctor in town, would take advantage of a poor uneducated woman from the shanty. That's not how the economy worked in Oak Grove. Helen would have to take extra care. She knew these girls since they were youngsters and she would help them get through. Now was the time to come clean.

"It's a ripple effect. Don't you see, if someone doesn't come forward and tell, this will continue. And I think it's bigger than you at this point. You have a bright future ahead of you. I don't think you understand how your fear has been paralyzing you. I have lived a long time, young lady, and believe me I have lost parents and good friends. I have been cast aside like many of you. Don't think Patsy's cancer is helping much either, and the fact that I was part of all these secrets well," Helen paused as she looked over at Harper and Anne. "But you have to want to get better. You know the truth. You know what happened and you know what is happening right now. It's up to you to tell the truth." Helen looked over at Caroline.

"As long as you remain in this place, you will stay in pain. I can't imagine how you feel after being so violated, but I know when you let go and tell the truth it's a beginning." Helen leaned forward in her chair. "I hope everyone is hungry. Are you girls hungry? I have some fresh banana bread." She sliced the loaf and laid the pieces on a plate.

Melanie started. "I was afraid to be alone when my mom was not there." She looked over at Tina for reassurance. "I usually called Caroline or Harper to come over and get me or I would go to Harper's house. I'm sorry, Caroline, but I hated going to your house. Carter was so creepy to me. I know that hurt our relationship." She held a pillow over her lap.

Caroline stopped her. "I already know. You won't hurt me. This has to stop. And besides what you did when you recorded Carter and my dad, well that was the bravest thing you and your mom did. I'm just so sorry you were hurt by my family."

"Helen is right I have to come clean. But I'm afraid," Melanie said. "I would wake most nights in a cold sweat. I would see Carter's eyes staring at me while I tried to make sense of what was happening. My mom would not let me tell. I knew what she was doing with Dr. Taylor. She said we needed him, and if I said anything I would mess things up for us. We just couldn't make ends meet. We had nothing. I could not wait to get out of here. I had to fight to keep my grades up. And those first weeks of my senior year were tough, seeing Carter and all his friends. It's like they knew, they talked and whispered every-time I went by them."

"Fall track was my respite. I ran all the time and I worked hard. I know you were worried about me. But Carter got what he deserved, and I hope he never walks again. If that is the least that happens to him then that is good. He took something from me that I can never get back. I wish I was the one who pushed him. I would have gladly been the first in line along with you other girls. And now Harper, you're being blamed for the whole thing. Helen, you're right, I need to stop being a victim. I won't let Carter win." Melanie slid closer to her mother.

Tina had been playing the game for so long, she was unsure of her next move. It was Patsy Middleton that would help her get through. She needed understanding, and Patsy was willing to help her over the next several months.

Tommy, solemn in his gray sweat pants and an old college sweatshirt, with Sam by his side said, "I need to talk."

Caroline felt her heart race.

Tommy blew out every bit of air from his lungs. "It all happened so fast. You were on his back, choking him. I knew you were going to go out the window with him if you kept holding on. I had to help you. And when I saw Harper laying on the bed…" He stopped. "I felt rage like I have never felt before. It's like I was someone else. Carter was by the window and when he turned around to go back to Harper," he folded his lips, "I think you thought you had already pushed him, but it was me. I shoved him." he paused. "I knew it was him from the start. He kept talking about all these girls every time we were in the locker room. He did it to Melanie because he wanted to hurt Penni. Then it was Beth to hurt Jack. It's like it didn't matter to him as long as he got what someone else had. He didn't want anyone else to have something he didn't."

He looked down and fumbled around with the long gray cord on his sweatpants. "He was so pissed at Jack for breaking a football record. It's a fucking game." He shook his head.

"It's okay man, take your time," Sam cautioned.

"It's so weird. I could have stopped him. He would become obsessed and not stop talking about them." Tommy stopped. "I only hope you can forgive me and we can be friends again." Tommy held onto his tears as he looked up at the group.

"I'm really sorry," Sam whispered. "But you couldn't have stopped him. Who would have believed you?"

Caroline found strength in his omission of protection as she stood. "You are to never to breathe this to anyone. This secret dies right here. My brother deserves everything he has coming to him, and so does my dad. You were defending all of us." She wrapped her arms around Tommy's neck. "Please, we are all going to be okay."

Tommy dug into his pants and pulled out the beautiful gold locket and the broken chain. "This belongs to you." He handed it to Caroline.

Caroline rubbed the locket between her fingers. No this belongs to Harper. "It's over."

Cottonmouth Droppings

Farm Boy: Can you believe poor Carter. I hope the kid can still play ball. Damn Harper Davis. She is spoiled rotten and I hope he presses charges.

Foxy: He's a bad kid just like his father.

Stonewall: His father is an upstanding citizen, a doctor who has sworn to heal and help others. You know how this town likes to hurt people. Carter is innocent and a victim.

Turncoat: You mean like Penni? And the way he was treated.

Farm Boy: What a mess Harper Davis has created. Doesn't she have a boyfriend?

Stonewall: Not anymore, I bet. Don't they all and they want to take down Carter. Jealous girls, that's it.

Weasel: How about our line on Saturday. We played one hell of a game. I think our team is getting better.

Tat Man: Another loss and did you see the paper? Four players smoking pot in the hotel on Friday. Doc started them Saturday. Who leaked that to the press? There's a mole somewhere.

Foxy: So, it's okay for the players to smoke pot now? What's wrong with you?

Stonewall: We are looking better. And let's wait for the drug tests to come back.

Turncoat: They found drugs in their room you idiot! And they admitted it!

Farm Boy: NCAA violations are a lie.

Turncoat: The NCAA is just getting started. It's over! Entitled rich white privileged!

Tat Man: Time for Doc to be put out to pasture.

Chapter 62

JB scrambled to hide as much as possible but was not given enough warning. Carter had been in rehab for months and the path of his defense lead straight to JB. The special investigators office had called him and Doc in for questioning but never let on that they would be issuing warrants to search their offices and homes.

Rita Faye knew who was at the door. The local sheriff was there to arrest JB. He had been stealing medications from the hospital, writing prescriptions at a rapid pace, and had been prescribing meds to people who were not documented patients.

"He's at his office."

Caroline walked down the steps. "Who's here?"

The sheriff and his squad searched the house. JB's office was filled with boxes, vials, and various controlled substances. Under the trap door in his desk they recovered a hidden laptop and other papers. The paper trail would lead to many prominent people in the community. When they were finished, Rita Faye thanked them and closed the door.

The special investigator's office had been hard at work since Melanie Birch was raped. Not only did they find mounting evidence from her crime scene, but from Beth's rape as well. The DNA led right to the same young man that was wheeled into the emergency room left for dead and somehow miraculously survived a brutal fall from a second story window. He would never walk again. His left arm was so twisted and broken it required multiple surgeries.

It was the rape of Melanie Birch that raised the red flags for Henry Middleton. Along with JB, Doc Winters, and Whit Cain, they were all being investigated for months. With the help of his son-in-law, Wade, they suspected Dr. Taylor was creating a web of prescription writing, stealing narcotics, and falsifying records during his illegal tactics. A quiet investigation had been ongoing for more than a year at the hospital. All operating bodies fully cooperated, including the university, the hospital and the police force.

With the screen shots from JB's phone that Tina Birch gave Henry, the investigation was accelerated. Henry Middleton ensured that the Mary Claire Barnes case would be reopened and JB Taylor would be tried.

"He should have been stopped back then." Henry was quoted in the *Daily Voice*.

It was Fetu Lafoe that contacted the NCAA concerning cheating allegations on the football team. Luck landed in his lap the week before they were cast out of Oak Grove. He had a graduate student that was working for the football team as a tutor and Doc Winters had asked the unnamed young man to write papers for his boys. He complained about it days after the rape of Melanie Birch. Fetu would not have his son discredited and was handed the perfect evidence to put a stop to Doc. With the help of Cottonmouth Droppings, the authorities were able to trace the pipeline Doc, JB, and Whit had created.

Dr. Taylor was hard at work sifting through records and was going to open his hidden pill case when special agent Frost and his group of investigators raided his offices.

"Dr. Taylor you're under arrest." While Federal agents, along with state and local municipalities, spent hours combing through boxes. They led JB out with his hands secured behind his back. They interrogated his staff and confiscated hundreds of patient records and countless boxes of opioids. It was a quick investigation.

JB Taylor had been writing prescriptions to his children and wife for years. They had no idea he was using them for his personal gain. It was his son Carter, when he suffered an injury in eighth grade, when JB lead him down his destructive path with opioid abuse. Caroline and Rita Faye would be forced to testify before a grand jury that they knew nothing about the prescriptions.

Doc, aggressive from the lack of access to pain killers, plea bargained his way out of the whole mess, selling Whit and JB in exchange for his freedom. He claimed he had no knowledge of "Dr. Taylor writing him prescriptions in his wife Dotty's name and taking liquid forms from the hospital, replacing it with saline solution. I was a victim. I thought he was helping me with pain management and was assured that everything he was giving me was under prescribed use." Doc saved face.

At one time JB had a stock pile in his offices dating back as far as the late 90s, where he would get Vicodin or free samples, as he called them, from his drug reps. He was writing prescriptions to Doc and several of his coaches and in turn they would give the filled pills back to him so he could share them with the likes of his golf pro at his club, high officials at the university, and major boosters at the university.

JB was walking out of his office in handcuffs. His first call was to Rita Faye.

"Call your lawyer or Doc." Rita Faye hung up the phone while she looked on at the papers strewn all over his office.

Doc Winters would not return phone calls nor would Whit Cain. Henry Middleton and Wade Davis sat in a car in the back of the parking lot and watched as JB held his head down, his chin resting on his chest while countless reporters circled his office trying to get the perfect snap to make the front page.

He had been arrested on multiple counts of distributing medications. Doc Winters had been arrested for aiding in the distribution of illegal narcotics, and Whit Cain was arrested for obstruction of justice concerning the assaults of Melanie Birch, Beth Hillcrest, and Harper Middleton. Carter Taylor was charged with three counts of rape, and as soon as he was well enough would stand trial. Splashed across the front page of the *Daily Voice* were several articles about Dr. Taylor.

Dr. JB Taylor, 47, of Oak Grove, NC, a physician at Middle Medical Regional hospital and team doctor for the Cottonmouths, was arrested at his office last Friday morning. He has been charged with three counts of possession of a controlled substance. Dr. Taylor was held and court notes indicate that he admitted to writing prescriptions in the names of several of his patients for Oxycodone and Adderall that not only did he give for their use but his own. He pleaded guilty today to five counts of possession of a controlled substance.

"It took some brave people to come forward to seal the case," Special assistant Frost said. "Dr. Taylor has been handing out drugs for a long time. We are in one of the most widespread drug epidemics in our country. And unfortunately, it has hit our small wonderful little town. Dr. Taylor profited from his overprescribing of narcotic painkillers. Dr. Taylor has maintained his innocence, but he was the region's leading prescriber of pain pills. Dr. Taylor seemed to be everyone's doctor and it will take countless hours to sort out what families he has provided medicine to," Frost continued.

Dr. Taylor claims it was the long hours, the high stress of being not only a hospital physician but also the university's athletic department physician, his children growing up and the pressure of having a son who was an all-star athlete and his wife having her own business in town.

"Oak Grove living seemed so easy. I think the stress of all my work took its toll," Taylor said.

Prosecutors say he blatantly prescribed and illegally distributed massive amounts of high addictive opioids, including to his own son. Taylor said he was collecting the countless prescriptions for his family and would deliver them to his home. To hide his arrangement, Taylor created false patient files and entries in medical files. During his illegal system he obtained more than 5,000 pills that he then distributed. Prosecutors charged Dr. Taylor with health-care fraud and fraudulent prescribing. He pleaded not guilty but quickly changed his mind when a plea deal came to light.

Because so many people revered him and his son Carter, the judge was merciful and the sentencing was at the judge's discretion after a 2005 Supreme Court decision making federal sentencing guidelines non-mandatory. He received ten years of supervised release and 3,000 hours of community service. He would be ordered to pay $500,000 in restitution. He will not serve any prison time. Taylor will voluntarily surrender his medical license. Any decision to allow Taylor to practice medicine will be made by the state medical board of which he can solicit in five years.

An investigation has been opened into the death of Mary Claire Barnes, of which he has been named a suspect. There were no entries on Cottonmouth Droppings again from Farm Boy, Stonewall, Foxy or Turncoat.

Chapter 63

Rita Faye sat at the kitchen table skimming the newspaper again, only to stop when she got to her soon to be ex-husband's name, but not before she saw the article about Whit Cain and Doc, who would never see prison time. She would cancel her subscription. She watched a ray of light dance on the kitchen counter and thought about her family's future. She picked up the acceptance letter from Rhode Island School of Design.

"We are proud to announce your acceptance into our school and are pleased to offer you a full scholarship." She read the words out loud. "Caroline did it." She sipped her coffee.

She thought about her life at the moment. So many things to be happy about and so much heartache. *Maybe that's the way it's supposed to be.* She was relieved that Melanie, Harper, and Beth were not going to press charges, *but it was out of their hands,* she thought.

Carter would be walled in a wheelchair for the rest of his life.

Rita Faye thought about how unfair it was. Here, Carter was a victim of his father and Doc Winters. Of course, he was responsible for his deplorable behavior, but she could not help but think, *If only I were a better parent, he would never have been this way.* And now, despite Doc being let off scot-free, the community rallied their support on Cottonmouth Droppings and was outraged, spending several months trashing the president and athletic director. *Where's the justice?*

Rita Faye fought to stop looking at the paper. She took one last look at the front page, where there was an article about Doc with his parting words: "I have been falsely accused and I accept the community's apology, but it is time I give the reigns to someone else. I have loved my players and raised them up well. I have served this community for the past twenty-five years, and I appreciate the love and support you have shown me." No one would ever know the money Doc Winters had been paying out to cover the multitude of his sins.

The university was forced to "borrow" from other departments to cover any stains from the mess. He and Dotty would live a quiet life out on their farm, cheering on the Cottonmouths from the athletic director's box.

*****

"Good morning, Mom." Caroline hit the bottom step.

"Good morning. How did you sleep?"

"Great. I'm really excited about prom this weekend. Tommy picked a red tie to go with my dress."

"You should be. I can't wait to take pictures."

"Come on, Mom. When do you think Carter will be home?"

"Sometime today."

"What are you reading?"

"*The Daily Voice*." She folded the paper over. "I think we have been through enough."

"I do too. You need to cancel that."

"I'm going to. And I'm happy to see everyone all dressed up this weekend."

"Penni will be here and the gang is all going together."

"I heard Melanie got into Washington."

"Yes, she's going to run track. And her mom is going to move out there too."

"Caroline, all your friends are going to have a wonderful college experience." Rita Faye leaned in, thinking about the loss she felt for her son.

"Mom, everyone got what they wanted."

Rita Faye put her arm around her daughter. They both looked up when they heard the knock at the door. It was what she had anticipated. The home healthcare nurse was there to finish Carter's first-floor bedroom. "Your son should be here soon."

Carter had spent a challenging six months in a rehab facility for not only recovery from his injuries but from his addictions. Carter, his sins forgiven, would go to Middle Carolina University, a paraplegic the rest of his life.

A van pulled up while Caroline and her mother stood at the front door and the healthcare workers carried medical support supplies into the house. The back door of the van opened and from around the side, Carter was lowered down onto the driveway in his fully functioning wheelchair. Rita Faye watched as her son was wheeled up the drive by a nurse. When she turned, she saw JB sitting behind the wheel of his car just down the street.

"Look, Mom," Caroline said, "do you see her?"

"Who?"

"Near the fountain is the image of a smiling little girl with dragonflies circling around her."